Two Sinful Secrets

AMANDA MCCABE

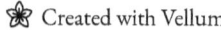 Created with Vellum

Acclaim for the Scandalous St. Claires

One Naughty Night

"In this intriguing first St. Claire Victorian romance, McKee introduces a delightfully down-to-earth heroine... Readers will cheer Lily in her quest for happiness, and look forward to the sequels."
-Publishers Weekly

"McKee sweeps readers into an enthralling story with memorable characters, a powerful plot and plenty of passion; it's the ideal evening's read that will leave readers dreaming of a love like Lily and Aidan's."
-RT Book Reviews

"A steamy, action-packed read... a vividly portrayed, sensual historical romance. Through Ms. McKee's beautiful prose, this story is brought to life, captivating the reader from the very first page. Brimming with emotion, a century-long grudge, complex characters, including an evil villain bent on revenge, witty banter, danger, suspense, sizzling hot passion and romance, this story is a winner. I look forward to reading the next story in this wonderful series."
-RomanceJunkiesReviews.com

Prologue

LONDON, 1844

LADY SOPHIA HUNTINGTON carefully studied the cards in her hand. Not a bad hand, but not as good as she would like either. Her usual good luck at the card table wasn't with her tonight.

Or maybe she was distracted.

Sophia peeked over the edge of the cards to study the man across from her through the beaded eyeholes of her mask. Dominic St. Claire. She knew it was him, even though he, too, wore a mask, a swath of stark black silk over his chiseled face. No one else she had ever seen had hair quite that shade of pure, molten gold, or such fine shoulders under his perfectly tailored coat. His eyes, the deep, pure green of summer leaves, gazed back at her steadily, making something flutter nervously deep inside her.

No wonder her parents didn't like her going to the theater, she thought wryly. One glimpse of such a godlike being onstage and she wouldn't be able to bear her pompous, pale, parentally approved suitors any longer.

And he was wrecking her concentration at cards as well. She definitely couldn't have that. Not when she had finally been able to escape her family's guard and sneak into the Devil's Fancy using her cousin Bill's invitation. It would be hard to come back again, so she would have to make the most of this evening.

But she might have tried harder to come here a little sooner if she had known Dominic was one of the owners. She had thought about him far too much ever since that glimpse in the park.

"Well, madame?" he asked, in his deep, smooth actor's voice. A small smile played over his lips, surprisingly full and sensual for a man.

Sophia, who was such a good card player in part because she had become adept at reading people's faces, couldn't fathom what that smile meant at all. Did he hold a good hand? Or was he flirting with her?

Sophia looked back down at her cards. "Two more, please."

Dominic took two cards from the deck and slid them across the small, red-draped table to her. He had beautiful hands, the skin smooth and faintly bronzed, dusted with pale blond hair, tapering fingers made for theatrical gestures on a stage or wielding a sword.

Or tracing a soft touch over a woman's skin, which she had heard he was quite adept at doing.

Sophia forced down an instinctive shiver at the vision of his hand on her body and forced herself to forget he was there, so close, watching her. She had just wagered the last of her quarterly allowance, and she couldn't afford to lose her focus now. She slowly turned over the new cards and almost sighed. Luck was really not with her tonight.

She laid out her cards on the table, hoping against hope his hand was worse. That faint hope died when he revealed his own cards, and he had her beat by several points.

"You win again, sir," she said with another sigh. "It seems Lady Luck favors a sinfully handsome scoundrel as much as the next woman."

Dominic laughed, and the emerald sparkle in his eyes almost made it worth losing. Almost. Sophia needed that money.

"Forgive me, madame," he said. He gathered the scattered

cards from across the table and lazily shuffled them back into the deck. "I take no pleasure in disobliging a lady. Shall we play again? Lady Luck is often fickle."

Sophia shook her head regretfully. She longed to play again and try to get back that money. It was what so often led her into trouble, the obsessive thought that with the next hand her luck would surely turn. Equally bitter was the thought that now she would lose Dominic's company. She had never enjoyed losing at cards so much as with him.

But she had nothing left to wager. She wore her grandmother's diamond and onyx earrings, necklace, and hair clips to go with her black satin gown, and her mother would definitely notice if they were gone.

"I'm done for the evening, sir," she said. "But I confess I've never enjoyed losing quite so much. It's no wonder your club is so successful."

His head tilted slightly as he studied her, his green eyes growing darker. "And how do you know I own this club?"

Sophia smiled and leaned closer to him, resting her arms on the table as she reached out to smooth one fingertip over a lost card. Oh, yes--he did bring out a spirit of the devil in her. "Oh, I know a great deal about you."

"That's hardly fair, is it?" he said, laughter lurking in his voice. Laughter and something darker, something she couldn't read. "I know nothing about you, except that you are a fierce opponent at the card table."

His fingers slid over her hand. It was a light touch, teasing, testing, his skin cool through her lace gloves. But Sophia felt as if fire had just licked along her arm, burning and shocking. She had to force herself to stay still and not jerk away and run screaming from the salon. She had never felt anything like it. It was almost-frightening.

She touched the tip of her tongue to her dry lips as his hand slid away. "Wh-what do you want to know?"

He suddenly frowned, as if a shadow passed over his face. "Everything."

Something seemed to sizzle in the air between them. Sophia couldn't look away from him. The game, which had started out so light and fun, such a dare, had become something much more. It had become something she didn't understand at all.

She had wanted to see Dominic St. Claire tonight. Something had driven her to seek him out after she saw him and felt so strangely drawn to him at the park. But now-now she felt afraid of what he awoke in her.

And Sophia was never afraid.

"Come with me," Dominic said. He rose to his feet, his gilded chair scraping back over the parquet floor, and took her hand in his. His smooth, polished, charming manners suddenly took on a raw edge, and it was as if she was glimpsing the feral power under his poetical beauty. And it made her even more afraid.

Yet she couldn't pull her hand away. She couldn't turn and run as she longed to. Something in her bound her to his touch. He was so very different from everything she had ever known, every convention her parents pushed onto her, every safe suitor and narrow expectation. Something in him called out to the secret darkness within her that always brought her to places like the Devil's Fancy, to card tables and deep play.

Something in him was the same as her. She had that terrible certainty as she looked up into his forest-green eyes. And she let him take her hand and lead her through the crowded salon.

The hour grew late, and champagne had been flowing freely, driving the laughter louder and louder. Ladies leaned on their escorts' shoulders as they watched the roulette wheel spin wildly, and she could hear music from the ballroom. But it was nothing to her, a mere echo. The only real thing was Dominic's hand on hers. What was she doing?

Where had he been all those long, dull months and years of her life?

He led her down the staircase, past couples who sat against the banisters whispering together. They went to the cold marble foyer where she had talked her way past the grim-faced butler earlier that evening. The man wasn't there now, and there was only the quiet of the night after the loud party.

Dominic opened a door half-hidden in the wall and tugged her in after him. When the door closed, they were closed off in darkness. The only light was a faint glow from a window high in the wall. Sophia leaned back against the door and saw they were in a tiny sitting room of sorts, crowded with the bulking shapes of furniture.

But then Dominic braced his palm flat to the door above her head, his warm, tall body close to hers, and she knew only him. He pulled off his mask and threw it to the floor. His face was lean and harsh in the light, his eyes brilliant as he stared down at her.

Sophia thought he must be a supremely intense Hamlet. It was no wonder ladies flocked to his theater. "Who are you?" he asked, his voice low and rough.

Sophia swallowed hard. "Just a woman who enjoys a good game of cards."

"And what else do you enjoy?" He reached up and gently traced the curve of her jaw with his fingertips. Sophia shivered, and his fingers skimmed lightly over her cheek. When she felt him touch the edge of her mask, she drew her head back. A little spark of reality came back to her. She was daring, true; something drove her to seek out places like this, to find somewhere beyond her small, restricted world. But she didn't want to be completely ruined, either.

And she also remembered the dark glare Dominic had given her cousin Aidan in the park. He did not like her family. He couldn't know who she was.

His hand slid away from the mask to toy with her earring and the curl of hair over the soft shell of her ear. His mouth followed, and Sophia gasped at the feeling of his hot kiss, the sound of his breath against her. Her knees went weak beneath her, and she pressed back harder to the door.

Dominic's lips moved along her neck, pressing light, caressing nips to her skin and then soothing them with the tip of his tongue. Sophia clutched at his shoulders to keep from falling, and she felt the ripple of his powerful muscles beneath the layers of fabric. She had never felt like this before. None of the kisses her suitors pressed on her in garden groves at Society balls could possibly compare. They always made her want to laugh at the ridiculousness of it all. But this...

This made her feel as if his touch had set her on fire and made her come completely, gloriously alive for the very first time. Not even the rush of a winning hand of cards made her feel this way.

Dominic groaned, and she felt his tall body press even closer against her. His arm came around her waist and pulled her up on her toes.

"Who are you? Where do I know you from?" he said hoarsely as he kissed the corner of her mouth. "Tell me."

Sophia frantically shook her head. Her thoughts went all hazy when he did that, so fractured and unfocused she couldn't put them together. She feared she would shout out her name for him.

"Tell me," he whispered again, and kissed the other corner of her parted lips. "I have to know."

"I'm no one at all," she answered.

The tip of his tongue traced her lower lip, and she opened to him with a gasp. His mouth covered hers in a hot, starving kiss, his tongue pressing deep to twine with hers.

Sophia's nails dug into his shoulders. This was definitely not like any other kiss she had ever had! Those fumbling caresses from boys who had groped at her in the dark, even as she sensed their fear of her, could never have prepared her for the force that was Dominic St. Claire. He would not be afraid of anything. He claimed what he wanted, and oh, but he was so *good* at kissing.

He drew back from her lips, his eyes a bright green in the shadows. "Tell me," he demanded.

And Sophia wanted so much to do just that, to give him her name and hear him say it in that wondrous voice of his. But then this precious moment would be shattered. She didn't know why he hated her cousin. She only knew she never wanted him to look at her that way. She never wanted his desire to become icy with hatred.

This moment was all she could have with him.

"No," she answered, finding strength in the sure knowledge that she had to keep him from finding out she was Lady Sophia Huntington. From finding out what his kiss meant to her. "I am no one. You have to let me go."

His arm tightened around her waist. "No," he said, his voice a low growl full of dark determination. "I've just found you."

Suddenly desperate to be gone, to not give in to the power he held over her, Sophia frantically shook her head. "Please, Dominic..."

"No! I need you to tell me who you are."

"Then I'm sorry," she whispered. "So very, very sorry."

His head tilted back from her. "Sorry?"

Taking a deep breath, Sophia brought her knee up hard between his legs. Her old nanny had once told her to do that if she needed to escape from a man, and she hadn't been sure it would work. But Dominic gave an agonized shout and fell to the floor, letting her go.

Absolutely appalled at what she had done, Sophia almost knelt beside him. Until he shouted a foul name at her, a string of the dirtiest curses she had ever heard, and she knew she had to get out of there while she still could.

"I'm so, so sorry!" she cried again and dragged open the door. She let it slam behind her and ran for the entrance as fast as her heeled shoes would carry her. With the one stroke of luck she had all evening, the foyer was deserted, and she found a hansom on the street outside.

Once safely in the carriage, Sophia yanked off her mask and covered her face with shaking hands.

"Oh, heavens above," she whispered, quite sure she was going to be sick. "What have I done?"

From the Diary of Mary St. Claire Huntington

March 1665...

I have always thought my sister to be the romantic soul in our family. She is constantly devouring volumes of French poetry, and wandering the woods sighing over their beautiful words of soul-deep love and flights of two hearts beating as one. She has always declared me a terrible bore, concerned only with prosaic, everyday reality! Concerned with running our father's house and trying to keep our family together amid the long war between king and Parliament and all the troubles that followed.

I only ever laughed at her teasing. I was quite sure it was far better to be dull and content with everyday matters than to long for romantic dreams that can never be. But I was very wrong. Horribly, wonderfully wrong. For I have met *him*.

One

BADEN-BADEN, 1848

WHEN IN DOUBT, Sophia Huntington Westman believed, give them a glimpse of stocking. That usually did the trick.

Especially when one is dealt an unfortunate hand of cards.

Sophia carefully studied the array of cards in her hand, but the colors on the faces didn't change. She sighed and tried to keep her own face calm and expressionless. She needed to win this game. Her stash of funds was growing astonishingly low, and she would be thrown out of her hotel if she couldn't pay soon. But luck had utterly deserted her tonight

Not for the first time, she cursed the memory of her husband, the poor, late, not much lamented Captain Jack Westman. He had been so very handsome, so exciting, so sure Sophia was meant to be with him. That charming confidence had been what convinced her to elope with him, despite her family's dire threats to cut her off without a penny if she married someone so unsuitable for a duke's niece.

But Jack's confidence turned out to come from the bottom of a brandy bottle. And when the alcohol killed him, sending him stumbling drunkenly in front of a milk wagon not far from where Sophia was taking the Baden-Baden waters, she was left here a penniless widow trying to make enough money to get home.

Though what she would do once she got back to England,
Sophia had no idea.

She peeked over the top of her cards at the man who sat across
from her. Lord Hammond had been her opponent in card games
before. He always seemed to be in the casino when she arrived,
and he always kissed her hand gallantly, fetched her wine, inquired
after her health. So very solicitous; so very watchful. Yet she had
hoped for an easier mark tonight of all nights. Tonight, when she
needed to win so badly. Lord Hammond was too shrewd a player.

But when he had taken her arm and invited her to a game of
piquet, she somehow couldn't say no. Lord Hammond, despite
his fine English-gentleman manners, was obviously a man who
expected to get what he wanted. That had been clear to Sophia
the first time she met him here at the casino, for she had encountered his type many times in her travels with Jack. Rich, powerful
lords, much like her uncle the Duke of Carston, who had every
whim indulged with a snap of their fingers.

But a card game was all he would get from Sophia, no matter
what else he might expect. She hoped never to be so desperate that
she had to give him anything else.

He was studying his own cards, a cool smile on his lips. He
was handsome, she would say that for him. Older than her own
twenty-three years by two decades, he was tall and well-built in his
expensively cut clothes. His dark hair, gray at the temples, was cut
short to frame his austere face and fathomless dark eyes. Women
flocked around him, as he was that singular rarity--a handsome,
rich lord. And he did seem to admire Sophia.

If she was really smart, Sophia thought as she looked at him,
she would take advantage of that admiration. She would cultivate
it and encourage it. Lord Hammond could make the financial
worries that had plagued her for so long vanish.

But she had never claimed to be especially smart. If she was,
she wouldn't have married Jack. And there was something in Lord
Hammond's eyes when he looked at her that she did not like.
Some icy gleam of speculation that sent a shiver down her spine.

She wanted to finish the game and be done with this wearisome night.

But first she had to win his money.

He raised his eyes from his cards and his smile widened as he looked at her. He was as good a card player as she was herself; she could read nothing about his hand on his face. Sophia remembered her thought about a glimpse of stocking, and returned his smile with a bright one of her own.

She turned slightly on her gilded chair, and her black satin skirts rustled as she moved. She glanced around the room. Everything in the bright casino was gilded or painted with lavish classical scenes, the floors covered in Aubusson carpets and the walls papered in patterned silks. The colors were rich and elegant, the perfect backdrop for the fashionably dressed and bejeweled patrons who strolled between the tables and gathered around the roulette wheel. Despite her woes, Sophia liked coming to this place--its opulence made her feel calmer, more sure that everything would work out in the end. That nothing could go completely wrong in such a beautiful place.

Only one other establishment had ever been so lovely, and that was the Devil's Fancy club in London. But she had not seen it in years, not since before she met Jack. Before she lost everything, when she was a spoiled, naive girl who thought there could be no consequences for sneaking out of her parents' house to go and gamble.

The thought of the Devil's Fancy made her freeze in her chair. She closed her eyes for an instant and it was as if she was there again. That long-ago night was so vivid in her memory. *He* was vivid in her memory. Dominic St. Claire.

She remembered his eyes, so intensely green as he looked at her across the card table. They would crinkle at the corners when he laughed, or grow dark when he touched her with those elegant, long-fingered hands. He had made her feel as if she was the only woman in the room, the only woman in the whole world, when he focused his intent on her.

And when he kissed her...

Sophia shivered when she remembered the way his lips felt on hers. She had never wanted a man before, never felt herself turn hot and melting under a touch, as if the whole world had vanished except for him. Not even with poor Jack, whom she had thought she loved.

But Dominic had too many women, and they all came so easily to him. Surely he made them all feel as he had her that night. He was like a dream to her now. A precious, lost dream she took out like a glittering little gem when life seemed too lonely and cold. It reminded her of the girl she had once been. And it reminded her of how gorgeous life could be, in another realm, another time.

But now was not the time for such memories. Now was the time for cold, hard reality. She couldn't afford to be distracted, not when faced with a man like Lord Hammond. She had to win tonight. Whatever it took.

Sophia opened her eyes and smiled at Lord Hammond. His own smile hardened, a flicker of some cold light flashing through his dark gaze. Sophia casually crossed her legs beneath her heavy skirts and let the ruffled hem fall back to reveal her black satin heeled shoe and a sliver of white silk stocking. She swung her foot a bit as she studied the cards in her hand.

Lord Hammond's attention went right where she hoped it would, to her slim ankle, and in the mirror behind him she had a quick glimpse of his cards in his careless moment. Not so good a hand as she had feared. She could still save this evening and come out ahead.

Her glance flickered over her own reflection. Her skin looked very pale against the stark black of her gown and the sleek, glossy coils of her dark hair. She had no jewels left to soften her austere attire and make her fit in with the rich crowd. There was only the narrow black ribbon around her throat, and a guilty pink blush on her cheeks.

Huntingtons never cheat! She remembered her father shouting that when her brother was caught once in a con artist's scheme and lost a great deal of money. The Huntingtons were an ancient ducal family, not cheaters. Not elopers. Yet here she was, driven to be both in her desperation.

I am doing what I must to survive, she told herself sternly. She had no room for honor or sentiment now, not if she didn't want to starve. Cards were the only thing she was good at. It was either gamble, or whore for the likes of Lord Hammond. And she was not that desperate--yet. Sophia turned away from her reflection, and from the memory of Dominic St. Claire's green eyes. She gently fanned herself with her cards and laughed. "My goodness, but it is warm in here tonight," she said. "I swear Baden-Baden grows more crowded by the day."

Lord Hammond's gaze slid from her ankle up over her décolletage in the low-cut gown, and his smile widened. Sophia knew that look in his eyes. It was the look of a man who believed his goal was clearly in sight now. But she had a goal, too. She would win his money without surrendering more than the merest glimpse of her person. They couldn't both win.

"Perhaps we should go for a stroll in the gardens," Lord Hammond said smoothly. "It is much cooler, and quieter, there. I have been wanting the chance for private conversation with you, Mrs. Westman."

"How very flattering of you, Lord Hammond," Sophia answered. Over his shoulder she saw a lady entering the casino, a tall, stunning redhead clad in dove gray silk with a truly stupendous collar of diamonds around her throat. It was Lady Gifford, who was rumored to be Lord Hammond's latest mistress. She gave him a stricken, wide-eyed look before she whirled away and vanished into the crowd.

Sophia looked back down at her cards. "There are so many who wish to-converse with you, Lord Hammond," she murmured.

"Ah, but I can see only you, Mrs. Westman." he answered.

"You look particularly lovely tonight. I am sure the gardens would be the perfect setting for your rare beauty."

"How sweet of you to say so," Sophia said with a smile. "But we should finish our game first, yes? It would be a shame to let the cards go to waste."

His gaze traced over her bodice again, slowly and with a clear intent. Sophia had to fight to keep her smile in place. "Of course, my dear Mrs. Westman. We certainly must finish the game."

As Lord Hammond ordered more champagne, Sophia requested two more cards and improved her hand. But beating her opponent was not quite as easy as she had hoped.

An hour had passed with neither of them pulling ahead enough to win when Lord Hammond's smile abruptly vanished. He folded his cards between his fingers and said with an exasperated note in his voice, "The night is wasting, Mrs. Westman."

Sophia peeked at him over her cards. "Is it indeed, Lord Hammond? It seems rather early to me." She really agreed with him, but not for the same reasons she was sure he had. She was tired and wanted to find her bed--alone.

If she went back to the hotel with enough money to pay for that bed, of course.

"It is too crowded here," Lord Hammond said. "So I propose we make this simple. We each draw a card, and high draw wins."

Intriguing. Sophia did like a high-stakes game usually. "And what are the stakes?"

"I will wager five hundred pounds," he said easily, as if that vast amount were mere pocket change. For him it probably was.

But it made Sophia catch her breath. Five hundred pounds. Surely enough to get her home to England and help her set up a new life, a new business. One where she wouldn't have to whore, or marry, again, or crawl back to her family and beg for forgiveness. One where she could be independent. All on the draw of one card.

But...

"I cannot wager such a sum in return," she said cautiously.

"I would not expect you to, my dear Mrs. Westman," Lord Hammond said with a smile Sophia did not like at all. "All I ask is that you walk with me in the garden, and perhaps accompany me to my suite. I have some paintings I recently acquired which might interest you."

Paintings her foot. Sophia took his meaning quite clearly, for he was not the first to propose such an arrangement. She let her skirts drop, concealing her shoes, and put on her sternest, most governessish expression. "Lord Hammond, how very shocking you are."

He laughed as he shuffled the cards. The gold signet ring on his finger gleamed. "And I fear missishness does not suit you, Mrs. Westman. I would never have thought you a lady to back down from a dare."

He was too right about that, Sophia thought wryly. She had always been too ready to run headlong into a dare. Anything her family didn't want her to do, she had always wanted to do all the more. It was what had led her here. She should probably get up and march out of the casino straight into homelessness. And it looked as if it might rain later, which would make being on the streets even more unpleasant.

Despite herself, she was very tempted by the wager Lord Hammond offered. With one turn of a card, her troubles would be over, or at least postponed. Or she could be in even more trouble than before. She shivered to think of Lord Hammond's hands on her, of those cold eyes looking at her naked body.

But there were no other promising games in the casino tonight, no other prospects. And she was down to her last farthing. That gnawing feeling of desperation deep inside had become all too familiar. It was time to leap before she looked.

"Very well, Lord Hammond," she said. She struggled to smile and keep her voice steady. "I accept your wager."

"Splendid, Mrs. Westman. You are ever intriguing. I knew you would not fail me." Lord Hammond raised his hand in an imperious gesture and a footman hurried over with a sealed pack of cards. As Sophia watched, Lord Hammond broke the seal and shuffled the cards. He laid the neat stack before her. "Ladies draw first."

Sophia stared down at the cards. They looked so innocent, mere printed pasteboard. She handled such things every night. Somehow she felt as if they would come to life and bite her when she touched them. She had truly fallen low.

She took a deep breath to steady herself and reached for the top card. Shockingly, her hand did not shake. She flipped over the card, her stomach in knots.

Queen of diamonds. Not bad. But it could be beat. Lord Hammond nodded and reached for the next card.

Sophia held her breath. It seemed as if time itself slowed down as he flipped it over. All the noise around her, the laughter, the chatter, the clatter of the roulette wheel, faded in her ears. She swallowed hard and looked down.

The six of clubs. She had won. She was five hundred pounds richer. A shocked laugh escaped her lips.

"Well," Lord Hammond said. "It appears luck favors you tonight, Mrs. Westman." His voice was low and tight, and filled with a barely leashed raw fury. She had never heard such a tone from the suave, cool man before.

She glanced up to find him staring at her with burning dark eyes. A dull red flush spread over his face and his hand clenched in a fist on the table. Another shiver slid down her spine, banishing the rush of victorious relief. Lord Hammond was not a man used to being thwarted.

"It would appear so," she answered slowly.

Lord Hammond nodded and waved the footman forward again. He spoke a curt word in the liveried man's ear and sent him scurrying away. "I have sent for the key to my safe. You will understand, Mrs. Westman, that I do not carry such a sum on me."

"Of course not," Sophia murmured, still half-stunned by what had happened.

"Will you have a glass of wine with me while we wait? I would consider it more than compensation for my sad loss."

Sophia did not want to have a drink with him, or sit here any longer than she had to. His smile had become too congenial, too charming, and those shivers along her spine had become even colder. She had the urge to leap to her feet and run from the casino. But she did have to wait for her money.

She swept a glance around the lavish room. It seemed even more crowded, and the laughter was even louder thanks to the freely flowing champagne. She surely couldn't get into too much trouble there.

"Thank you," she said. "A glass of champagne would be delightful."

Lord Hammond rose smoothly from the table and offered her his arm. Sophia had grown accustomed to acting in the last few months; the life of a gambler, traveling from one spa town to another, demanded constant deception. Yet it took everything she had to stand and slide her hand onto Lord Hammond's sleeve. She shook out her heavy skirts and gave him a smile as he led her from the main salon into the bar area.

It was no less crowded there. A throng of people, like a merry, fluttering horde of brightly clad butterflies, gathered around the gleaming white marble bar. The gold framed mirrors on the wall reflected them back in an endless sparkling vista. The black-clad barmaids scurried to serve them all.

Lord Hammond was immediately given glasses of the finest pale golden champagne. He handed one to Sophia and held up his own in salute.

"To your great good fortune, Mrs. Westman," he said. "What shall you do now?"

Sophia shrugged and sipped at her wine. "Try another town, I suppose. This one does not suit me so well as I had hoped."

"The sad memories of Captain Westman's demise, I would imagine," he said, all smooth, polite conversation. "But this place will be dull without you."

19

"Dull?" Sophia laughed and gestured with her glass at the crowded room. "I shall not be missed one jot."

"I will miss you very much." He studied her closely over the edge of his glass until she had to glance away. "I do wish you would reconsider my offer, Mrs. Westman. I could certainly give you far more than five hundred pounds."

Sophia fidgeted with her glass and studied the array of bottles behind the bar. Where on earth was that blasted safe key? She wanted to be far away from there as quickly as possible. "Your offer of a walk in the garden, Lord Hammond?" she said, trying to feign wide-eyed innocence.

"Oh, come, Mrs. Westman. I have made no secret of my admiration for you," he said, a note of impatience in his voice. "I am a wealthy man. I could give you whatever you wanted."

Sophia wondered what Lady Hammond, rumored to be an invalid back in England, thought of that. But the poor woman was probably quite used to it all. Sophia never wanted something like that for herself. She only wanted to be her own woman at long last. Free to make her own way, see the world on her own terms...

And perhaps find another man who made her feel like Dominic St. Claire once had. A man who, unlike Dominic, would think her the only woman he wanted.

"You are so kind to flatter me like that, Lord Hammond," she answered carefully. "But I am so recently widowed. I need time to mourn properly. I couldn't possibly think of a man other than Captain Westman just yet."

His eyes narrowed. "Quite understandable, my dear. But I hope when you are ready to cast off your widow's weeds you will think of me." Suddenly he reached out to lightly stroke a fingertip over the ribbon at her throat.

Sophia flinched and fell back a step before she could stop herself. Lord Hammond gave a humorless laugh.

"You deserve to wear diamonds and pearls," he said. "I could give you that. Just remember, my dear. One day you are going to need me even more than you do now, and I will always be waiting."

Sophia desperately hoped not. She turned to set her glass down on the bar, and to her relief she saw the footman returning at last with the safe key. Lord Hammond brushed away the man's apologies for the delay and took Sophia's elbow in his hand to lead her out of the bar.

"Come, Mrs. Westman, let us collect your winnings," Lord Hammond said as they made their way through the soaring domed foyer and down the marble steps to the lower level where the wealthier patrons kept their guarded safes. Lord Hammond was now all brisk efficiency, leading her along without another word or untoward touch, but Sophia couldn't shake away that urge to run. Especially as the noise of the casino faded behind them and there was only the whooshing echo of their footsteps on the cold stone floor.

He led her past the guards and along the row of iron safes until he found the one he sought. He turned the key in the lock and swung open the heavy door. Sophia glimpsed bags of coins, stacks of bank notes, and black velvet jewel cases. It was a veritable Aladdin's cave of riches, but she had only a glimpse before he hastily removed one of the stacks of notes, put them into a bag, and pressed it into her hands.

"There you are, Mrs. Westman, your fair winnings," he said. "Feel free to count it."

Sophia shook her head and held on to the bag tightly. It felt like such a slight thing in her hands, yet it was her salvation. "I trust you, Lord Hammond." As far as she could throw him. But yet she doubted he would cheat on a gambling debt, even one to a woman.

"Just remember my offer, my dear. I will be waiting." He reached for her free hand and raised it to his lips for a lingering kiss.

Sophia could bear his touch no longer. She snatched back her hand and spun around on her heel to hurry out of the casino. She pushed past the people in the foyer and rushed out of the doors and into the gardens to the public walkway. She didn't stop until she was in her hotel room with the door locked behind her.

She dropped the bag onto the end of her narrow bed and fell down onto the pillows with a sigh as her gown billowed around her like a black cloud. Only one more night here in this cursed place, and then she could catch the morning train somewhere else. One more night with the likes of Lord Hammond just beyond the door, waiting to snatch her up when she stumbled. One more night not knowing where her next meal was coming from.

She was free. Almost.

Sophia rolled over and reached beneath her pillow to draw out a book. It was quite old, bound in cracked brown leather with the pages yellowing at the edges. But that book had been one of her best companions since she left home with Jack all those long months ago. Every night she read a precious entry before she went to sleep, and she didn't feel so very alone.

She opened it where she had left off, carefully turning the brittle pages closely written in faded brown ink in a careful hand. But first she smoothed her fingertip over the inscription on the first page.

Mary Huntington, Her Book, Gifted in the Year 1665.

Mary Huntington, the first Duchess of Carston, and a woman completely unknown in Sophia's family. Unlike every other ancestor on the family tree, there were no portraits of her on the walls, no heirloom jewels that had once belonged to her. Sophia had never heard of her until she found this dusty book on a neglected shelf in her grandfather's Library one boring, rainy Christmas. When she began to read, it was as if Mary had come back to life and begun to speak to her. As if Mary were a long-lost friend, a woman just as impulsive and wild-hearted as Sophia was.

A long-lost friend with a sad tale to tell. Mary was terribly in love with her handsome husband, but miserably unhappy. He left her at their country house when he went off to Charles II's merry Court, and Mary wrote of her loneliness and longing, all the storms of her emotions, as well as the ways she kept herself busy in the country. Sophia felt as if Mary was reaching out to her over the decades. She took the diary with her wherever she went, and somehow she never felt alone.

She never wanted to be like Mary, with her whole life, all her emotions and everything she was, wrapped up in a man. Sophia had fallen prey to such fairy-tale dreams before, and she couldn't do it ever again.

Sophia traced a gentle touch over the worn leather cover. "Everything will be fine now, Mary," she whispered. "I can go home and start again. Things will be better in England."

If only she could make herself believe that. England had seemed such a distant dream ever since she made the romantic, foolish, impulsive decision to run off with Jack. Her sheltered, pampered life there hadn't seemed real. But the England she was going to now, and the life she would make for herself, would be very different.

Sophia slid the diary back under her pillow and sat up to reach for the bag of bank notes. They were all there, five hundred pounds worth. She fanned them out and looked down at them as she tried to make herself believe they were real.

As she started to take them from the bag to examine them more closely, there was a sudden noise at her door. Startled, Sophia dropped the bag and sat up straight, every fiber of her body tense and alert. The doorknob rattled as someone tried to turn it. When it held, there was a scraping noise against the old wood, as if that person attempted to pick the lock.

Hardly daring to breathe, Sophia slid off the bed and tiptoed to the door. She held her skirts tight against her to still their rustling with one hand and reached for a straight-backed chair with the other. She wedged it under the knob and stood back to listen, holding her breath.

"*Hier!*" she heard the hotel's stern owner cry in German, her voice muffled through the door. "I don't allow people who are not paying guests to wander the hallways at all hours. This is a respectable establishment. Who are you, anyway? What do you want with Frau Westman?"

"A thousand apologies," a man said, his voice deep and echoing, indistinguishable through the door. "I was merely returning something Frau Westman left at the casino."

"Then you can leave it with me. She already owes me enough for her stay."

Sophia listened as the stranger was bustled away from her door and their voices faded. She turned and hurried to the window to watch from the shadows as the hotel's front door opened. A tall figure clad in an elegant evening cape emerged, and Sophia felt that panic clutch at her deep inside again. It was Lord Hammond.

She had to get out of there. Quickly.

Sophia slid back from the window and pulled the valise out from under the bed. She could pack her meager belongings in fifteen minutes, and be on the first train out before it was light. It was past time for her to go home.

From the Diary of Mary St. Claire Huntington

He has asked me to marry him.

I hardly dare write those words for fear that putting them down in stark black ink will render them imaginary. It has been so long since we saw each other, since these wars between the king and Parliament have divided us, but now he has returned, and he immediately came to my father's house to see me. I thought my heart would burst when I saw him there in the lane, the sun on his golden hair, laughing as I came running to greet him. And when he kissed me--no woman could be happier than I am at this moment. My Love has returned to me.

The new king is making him a duke, the Duke of Carston. So I will be a duchess at the royal Court, by my husband's side. How can I bear such happiness?

Two

LONDON

SHE WAS DEFINITELY INTERESTED.

Dominic St. Claire watched the woman from across the crowded salon of his gambling club, the Devil's Fancy. She stood behind the chair of a gentleman considerably older than herself as he played a hand of loo, dutifully pretending to watch even as her gaze kept sliding to Dominic. She was tall and slender, with a generous expanse of white décolletage above a stylish, ruffled blue bodice, with blonde curls and the face of an angel. But the smile she gave him was full of pure deviltry.

Once he would have been there in an instant. He would have returned her inviting smile, raised her hand to his lips, given her a careless compliment, and stolen her away right under the nose of her portly companion. She was exactly the sort of woman he would share his bed with for a night or two.

But tonight--tonight he felt strangely unmoved by her beauty and the invitation in her smile. He didn't feel the leap of excitement at the hunt, the flare of hot lust he once would have. He only felt cold. Removed from the whole scene of laughter and bright lights. The Devil's Fancy, once something he had loved and taken pride in, had become merely a business and a duty. And that woman's beauty awakened no spark in him.

It had been that way ever since Jane died. Sweet, serene Jane, who was far too good for him but somehow had still considered marrying him. He had always loved his life, the rush of gambling and the lights of the theater, but Jane had made him start to imagine another way to be. She had made him imagine a home to come back to after his work.

And then, as swiftly as those new hopes rose, they were gone and Jane was dead. Six months ago now.

Dominic turned away, catching a quick glimpse of the disappointed pout on the blonde's face. He made his way through the crowd and automatically checked to make sure everything was running as it should and everyone was having a good time. In the time it had been open, the Devil's Fancy had become one of the most popular clubs in London, and it was full almost every night. All the noble and the wealthy clamored for memberships, and they were turning away people at the door every night because it had become too crowded.

They came for the high-stakes gaming, the luxurious surroundings, the people that could be seen there. And they came because it was owned by the St. Claires, and everyone always liked to gossip about them.

Dominic loved the Devil's Fancy and was proud of its success. But tonight he wished he was someplace else. Someplace quieter, darker, where he could lose himself in a good bottle of brandy and a woman. Not the blonde, though, and not any of his usual mistresses. Someone different, someone who could intrigue him, beguile him, and make him forget.

Dominic took a glass of wine from a footman's tray and drank it as he coolly studied the crowd. There were women everywhere, as there always were. Beautiful, readily available women who watched him and smiled at him. Dominic had been an actor, both on the stage and off, since he was a child, and he had learned to read human nature, to know how to persuade people to do what he wanted. His St. Claire looks, pale golden hair and green eyes in a sculpted face, didn't hurt either. Finding company was never a problem.

But tonight--tonight he felt strangely restless and removed. He wanted something, but he didn't know what it was. He tossed back the wine as he studied the crowd at the faro table. There was a lady with glossy black hair there, her back turned toward him, and suddenly something sparked to life in him.

An old memory came back, one he had not thought of in a while. A woman in a black gown with hair like that, her face concealed by a mask. A flashing smile, laughter--the taste of her kiss, so sweet and strangely innocent. She had intrigued him as no other woman had, with her beauty and her mystery. Until she kneed him the balls like a brawling street whore and fled.

He had looked for her for weeks after that, consumed with the need to find out who she was and to take some retribution for the way she had left him. He had wanted to kiss her again--and to take things much, much further.

Yet he never found her. It was as if she vanished in a puff of smoke, or was merely a dream. And there had been other women, beautiful, pliable women, and then

sweet Jane. But no one had quite gripped his imagination like the woman in black. He watched the woman at the faro table, wondering if maybe she had returned at last. That would certainly make the night far more exciting.

The woman turned and caught him watching her. She gave him a delighted smile, and he saw with a flash of disappointment that it was not her. This woman's face was the wrong shape, her skin not as pale, and she was a different height.

The woman in black remained a mystery then.

Dominic made his way past a cluster of card tables and stopped to greet some of the regular patrons. He automatically talked and laughed with them as he always did--it was good for business. But finally he found the slightly quieter surroundings of the dining room, where a lavish buffet was laid out. Once the suppers and dancing had been organized by his sister Lily, who had a flair for entertaining. But she was married now, and living in Edinburgh with her husband.

Her husband who was a Huntington. Aidan was the only tolerable member of that cursed clan. The St. Claires had hated the Huntingtons for centuries, ever since a Huntington abandoned and ruined his wife, Mary St. Claire. Hating them was second nature to Dominic now.

He reached for one of the hothouse grapes and ate it as he forced bitter thoughts of the Huntingtons out of his mind. He had better things to think about now.

"A fine evening," he heard his brother Brendan say behind him. "Especially for the Christmas season. The receipts should be most satisfactory."

Dominic turned and grinned at Brendan. "More work for you, then, since you've dared to take on the books after Lily left." As well as arranging the hospitality of the Devil's Fancy, Lily had kept the accounts. She was much missed.

Brendan shrugged. "Work of the best sort, making money." He studied Dominic closely, his expression as solemn as ever. Brendan had always been almost impossible to read, so intensely private and quiet was he.

"I saw Lady Rogers giving you the eye," Brendan said.

"Lady Rogers?"

"The blonde in the blue gown. She and her new husband are members as of last week." Brendan gave a rare, wry smile. "I suspect the gaming was not the only thing that drew her here."

Dominic shrugged. "If she is newly married, perhaps she should pay closer attention to her husband."

Brendan arched his brow. "Dominic! I have never heard you urge marital constancy before. Are you feeling ill tonight?"

"Not at all."

"But there is something not right with you. I can see that."

Dominic shrugged. Brendan might keep his own thoughts private, but he always watched everyone else far too closely.

"Perhaps I'm just distracted with everything we need to prepare for the theater engagement in Paris," Dominic said.

"We're all distracted by that," Brendan answered, his gaze sweeping again over the room. "Are you sure our mother's idea of taking James with us is the right one?"

"Surely he can't get into any more trouble there than he can here."

Brendan arched his brow. "Can he not?"

Dominic laughed, remembering all the follies his brother had committed in the name of romance. "All right, perhaps he can. Paris is full of temptations, after all. But at least we'll be there to watch after him."

"And perhaps Paris will offer you a share of distraction as well."

"Brendan..." Dominic said warningly. His family had been hovering ever since Jane died, giving him worried, secretive glances. He couldn't take it from Brendan, too.

"I won't say anything else. Just that Paris is full of beautiful women. There should be plenty to occupy us while we're there." And then Brendan turned and walked away, leaving Dominic to study the crowd alone.

Maybe his brother was right. Maybe distraction was in order now. Something to make him quit thinking about black hair and a pair of vivid blue eyes behind a satin mask...

Three

"VOITRE PARIS! VOITRE PARIS!"

Sophia smiled at the coachman's shouts and lowered the window of the large, lumbering diligence stagecoach to peer outside. She could only see a few scattered buildings, tucked back behind the thick trees that lined the broad lane, no grand bridges or turreted palaces yet, but those words told her they were near their destination at last.

Since fleeing Baden-Baden, Sophia had been making her way across the Continent, unsure of what she should do. Several times she had thought about going back to England and throwing herself on her family's mercy. She had been alone for so long; even when Jack was alive she had been alone, struggling to make decisions that would keep them from starving. Moving from place to place, never staying long in the same town or coming to truly know the people around her.

She had been lonely in her family, too, always surrounded by them yet never really seen, never understood. She was always their disappointment. But at least there she had almost belonged to something. Was it worth it to debase her pride and return to them? Sophia wasn't sure. Her pride was a fierce thing.

And that was what had brought her to Paris. She had

intended to stop in France only for a few days, to see some sights before she went on to England to decide what to do about her family, to see if somehow she could get back into their good graces. She had invested her winnings from Lord Hammond with a little judicious gaming on her journey, and was financially secure enough for the time being. She could indulge in something she hadn't in a long time--a bit of leisure.

In Rouen, she encountered a Frenchwoman who had befriended her in Monte Carlo many months ago, a woman she had much in common with and could laugh and talk with freely, have fun with. It had been a long time since she had a friend like that, and they had kept in touch intermittently after departing Monaco. Sophia smiled and sat back against the carriage seats as she remembered Camille Martine's joyous greeting in that Rouen cafe, their lively, laughing conversation over champagne.

When Camille heard of Sophia's rootlessness, her doubts about returning to her family, she shook her head sadly.

"Ma chère amie Sophie, you cannot return to such a grim life!" Camille cried. "You would wither away. I should know. If I had stayed with my mother-in-law after my dear Henri died, as she wanted me to, I would have become as dry and dull as her. Closed off from the world and life, shut off from all joy--bah! Not for me. And you are the same, I could see that from the moment we met."

Sophia had to laugh, Camille's words were so true. All her life she had felt as if she was suffocating under the weight of her family's expectations, the rigorous responsibilities of being a duke's niece. "Very true, I fear. It's why I ran off with poor Jack in the first place."

"See? You escaped once. Why would you go back?"

Sophia shrugged. "I haven't a great deal of choice. I don't have many talents to use in taking care of myself." She could have become Hammond's mistress, given in to the glow of lust in his eyes, his need to possess everything around him. But that would have been an even closer prison than her family, a drowning of her own soul.

Just thinking about it made her shudder, and she could say nothing of the whole bitter episode to Camille.

"You are an excellent card player," Camille said with a shrewd glint in her eyes. "And people like you. You draw them in wherever you go, you make them want to be around you. I saw that in Monte Carlo."

Sophia laughed wryly and thought again of Lord Hammond. "Sometimes the wrong people want to be near me, I fear."

"But it is a skill! A gift you can use to much success, especially in Paris where such things are valued. The French appreciate charm and style, and it is quite wasted on the English. You should come and work for me. I have no time to do everything I need to do, I need help."

"Work for you, Camille?" Sophia said. "I thought you were a widowed lady of leisure, traveling wherever the whim takes you. Do you need a secretary now?"

"I am no longer a lady of leisure. I grew so bored, you see. So I opened a small business near the Palais-Royal." Camille leaned across the table, her dark eyes sparkling with mischief. "A gambling club!"

"A gambling club?" Sophia said, intrigued. She had considered doing such a thing herself, until she realized her funds wouldn't allow her to open as elegant an establishment as she would want. A place such as the Devil's Fancy.

"La Reine d'Argent. It can't be called a gambling club, of course, not with such a fusty old stick as Louis Philippe on the throne. It is a salon, an exclusive little place for friends to gather and play a friendly hand of whist."

"Friends?"

Camille laughed. "Friends who pay a small membership fee, perhaps. I have just opened, and already it is so busy I cannot manage by myself. I could so use your help, Sophie."

Sophia had thought for a moment. A new life in Paris; a time to linger before she had to decide what to do with her future. Before she had to return to her parents.

"It would be so much fun," Camille coaxed. "You could make a great deal of money. And many of my guests are so charming, even the English ones! You might find one you like and marry again one day..."

Sophia firmly shook her head and finished off her champagne. "I am obviously terrible at marriage."

"Just as you wish. But it is good to keep one's options open, non? Come to Paris. It will be such fun..."

And that was how Sophia found herself on a coach, lumbering closer to Paris with every moment, rather than being sensible and returning home.

"It is just one more adventure," she told herself, but deep down inside she knew she would always crave yet one more adventure. Being sensible had never been her strong point.

She watched the trees swirl past in a blur as she curled her gloved fingers around the book in her lap. Mary Huntington's journal, which had been her companion ever since she left England, was going with her into Paris now, along with Mary's painful lessons never to count on anyone but herself.

"Almost there," Sophia whispered, the excitement inside her growing. This was her adventure now; she had only herself to think of here in Paris. It was an exciting thought indeed, but also rather frightening.

The carriage swung around in a turn in the road and careened down a steep, cobbled slope. Suddenly they were plunged into a darkened labyrinth of narrow streets, the broad country lanes left behind. Stone buildings, tall and packed close together, darkened with age, crowded in around her. The coach slowed amid a crowd of wagons, drays, fine carriages, and street vendors with their push-carts.

Sophia lowered the window even more and heard the cacophony of voices from outside, the rustle of wheels on cobbles, the laughter and French words. She could smell the mud and muck of the gutters, but also spiced cakes from the vendors, smoke curling up from the chimneys, and flowers creeping up from behind garden walls at the old aristocratic hotels. The smell of Paris.

The carriage slowly made its way out of the tangle of old streets and onto the avenues that ran along the river. The sunlight turned the whole city golden as the vista opened up before her. Sophia craned her neck for a view of the long vistas to bridges and turreted palaces, statues and tall gaslights. People hurried along on the walkways: fashionably dressed couples, ladies' maids in black carrying piles of packages, starched nannies with their little charges who scampered along laughing.

Sophia almost laughed with them, her spirits suddenly higher than they had been since before Jack died. She was in a new place, a place where almost no one knew her and she could start again. Where she could become anyone she wanted to be.

As they passed one of the grand bridges, Sophia glimpsed a man standing there leaning lazily against the stone balustrade. Something about him, something familiar, made her turn to look at him. He swept his hat off to bow at two giggling ladies walking by, and the sunlight glinted off pale blond hair, as radiant as the sun itself.

Sophia remembered Dominic St. Claire kissing her in that dark room, remembered running her fingers through his bright hair as a passion like none she had ever known exploded inside her, and she felt a pang for how long ago that magical night was. How many things had changed. For an instant her heart leaped to think that was him on that bridge, that she could be that innocent girl once more.

But then she fell back down onto the carriage seat, feeling ridiculously foolish. Dominic St. Claire was far away, and even if he was in Paris she wasn't likely to run into him. He had never even known that it was her he kissed, and he never would know. That memory was hers alone.

And she hated feeling like a silly, fluttery schoolgirl every time she thought of him! She had too much to do here in Paris to be daydreaming over a handsome man she would likely never even see again. Once the carriage arrived in Paris, she had to make her way to Camille's club on the rue Vivienne and learn her new duties. Paris was a fresh beginning for her. She wanted to make the most of it.

The coach jolted to a halt on the street outside a busy station, where passengers hurried in and out amid piles of luggage and harried porters. Sophia climbed down and took a deep breath of the Parisian air, glad to be out of the swaying vehicle at last. The city seemed to unfold in front of her, and she wanted to rush out and grab it all.

Just across the street was a row of shops. She glimpsed a sign in the bow window of an expensive-looking hat shop Aide Demande, "help wanted". It immediately caught her attention. She knew about hats. Surely a hat shop would be slightly more respectable to her family? And a bit more independent than taking advantage of Camille's friendship. She needed more money to get home properly, as well as more time to plan her approach. But she had hardly had time to contemplate the shop when she heard someone calling her name. She spun around to find Camille hurrying toward her through the crowds. The people seemed to part before her, as if she were a statuesque Parisian goddess in a fashionable green silk walking dress, her red hair shining in the sun.

"Sophie, chère! You are here at last." Camille cried.

She seized Sophia's hands and kissed her cheek as Sophia laughed. "And just in time for my new establishment to officially open."

Sophia had not known such a welcome in a long time, and it made her even happier to be in Paris. "I'm glad I made it in time."

"I will need your help in finishing the arrangements. I remember you had such lovely taste in Baden-Baden," Camille said, leading Sophia away from the station. Porters leaped to obey her when she gestured for them to gather the bags. "I need your help desperately."

"I am happy to help however I can," Sophia said. "But I do not want to take advantage of your friendship."

"Whatever do you mean?"

"I mean I must earn my own way! And not just by playing cards."

Camille laughed. "But you were so good at the cards."

Sophia sighed. "And that is just the trouble. Hopefully I can make my way back to my family soon, and they will definitely not approve of my livelihood. Also I can't take advantage of your kindness forever."

Camille shot her a puzzled glance as she ushered Sophia to a fine, shining dark blue carriage waiting by the walkway. "Your English ways are a puzzle to me, but you must do as you see best. You are welcome to stay at my club as long as you like. I am happy to have someone to keep an eye on the premises when I can't be there. Now, tell me--what happened in Baden-Baden after I left? I haven't had so much fun since then..."

Four

IT WAS ALL EVEN MORE beautiful than Camille had described.

Sophia stood on a small balcony high above the main salon of La Reine d'Argent and leaned her lace gloved hands on the gilded railing as she examined the crowd gathered below her. She had seen the rooms during the day, of course, and had admired their elegance. But at night, with the gaslight casting its ethereal glow, everything looked otherworldly and magical. A haven of fun and elegance that seemed to shut out the rest of the world.

After ill-fated attempts to find other employment, she had determined to do her best here for her friend's business and work hard until she found something else she could do. Working had kept her busy--and kept her from dreaming too much.

Sophia laughed at herself and turned her attention back to the salon below. It was the club's official opening night, and, despite the rain outside, people had shown up in droves. It seemed Camille's reputation for being a good hostess had spread far throughout Paris. It looked like an undulating sea of stylish, ruffled gowns in fashionable pastel blues, greens, and pinks, men's black evening coats, and flashing jewels, all blended together like the indistinct mosaic of a kaleidoscope. Footmen in gold satin livery and powdered wigs in the style of fifty years ago threaded their way through the throng, offering silver trays bearing crystal goblets of champagne and Bordeaux and plates of delicacies.

The tangle of conversation sounded happy and excited, light-hearted, and it made Sophia feel happy, too. When she first stepped out of her room and smiled, she hadn't been sure what that feeling was. It had been so long since she remembered anything like happiness. But here in Paris, she felt her sense of fun, so long buried under worries, breaking free again. She had to revel in it now, until she had to go back to her family and try to mend her fences there.

Despite the troubles the newspapers shrieked about, the unpopularity of King Louis Philippe and the ill-fated Spanish marriages, Paris seemed as eager to embrace fun and merriment as Sophia was herself. That desire for fun felt almost frantic in the air. Camille was smart to seize onto that desire for a good time, and Sophia was glad she was here to be a part of it, if only for a short time.

The door to the balcony opened behind her, and Camille cried, "Sophie, there you are! What do you think of our opening night?"

Sophia studied the crowd again. It already seemed to have grown as more and more people squeezed into the salon. "I think you will have a wonderful success."

Camille laughed, the diamond stars in her upswept red hair flashing. "Tonight, perhaps. They are curious to see what we have here--and to see my mysterious new English friend."

Sophia shook her head. "No one knows me here, and that is the way it should be. The way I want it" She would be leaving Paris soon enough, and the fewer scandals her family knew about the better.

"But you will not get your wish. Paris loves a beautiful woman, and one who is a mystery is irresistible to them. They wonder who you are."

Sophia laughed. "How can they even know I'm here?"

"Exactement! You have made them wonder. People have probably glimpsed you going to the shops, the beautiful lady in black who hides in Madame Martine's house, and they want to know your story." Camille tapped her fan on the railing. "I was at dinner at the Cafe Anglais last night and met a party of English people visiting Paris, theatrical sorts who are appearing at the Theatre Nationale. Even they had heard of you, and they asked me so many questions. But I told them nothing. I just invited them here tonight."

Sophia shook her head again, but secretly she was intrigued. English theatrical types? Could it be? But surely not. It seemed too unlikely that she would see him again, and it was probably better she didn't. She didn't need that sort of trouble, not now. "They will soon lose interest in me when they find out the dull truth."

"Then don't tell them anything! Just let them go on wondering." Camille studied the throng of guests below. "I do hope those Englishmen come tonight. The men were so very handsome, though one did have some rather fearsome-looking scars on his face. But one of them was very sweet, and seemed rather intrigued by you. And it wouldn't hurt you to meet more people. Then perhaps you will put aside these silly thoughts of finding another job. You are perfectly suited to this one."

"I will certainly do my best while I'm here. And I will meet anyone you like. It's the least I can do after your kindness to me."

Camille smiled happily. "C'est bon! That is all you need to do. And now, we should make our appearance before those ravenous hordes consume all our champagne. We want them happily tipsy, not falling down drunk."

Sophia laughed and followed Camille as they made their way down the narrow, winding staircase that led to a secret doorway. The building was an old one that had once belonged to a family awarded it by Louis XIV, and it had been used for all sorts of nefarious purposes in all the upheavals of France since then.

Camille had refurbished the palace rooms with polished

parquet floors, pale silk wallpaper, and new artwork and gilded furniture, but behind the scenes the old place was full of hidden stairs and corridors, and tiny rooms complete with peepholes for keeping an eye on everything that happened there. Sophia loved it; it was the perfect place for secrets.

But tonight wasn't one for subtlety and sneaking around. It was a time for having a bit of fun, before she went back to her old life again.

They stepped through a doorway hidden in the boiserie paneling of the foyer, where a stern-looking English butler checked names off the invitation list and maids took the guests' wraps. Everyone else had already moved into the main salon, and Sophia could hear the clamor of dozens of conversations through the closed double doors.

"Is everyone here, Makepeace?" Sophia asked the butler as Camille checked her hair in the mirror. Over the last few days, while Camille went out to find new patrons and put the finishing touches on the decor, Sophia had organized the servants. Her mother's calm, efficient example had served her well for once.

"Almost everyone, Madame Westman," Makepeace answered as he showed her the list. "And they all brought guests as well."

"I hope our supplies of champagne hold out!" Camille said.

"Me, too," Sophia said as she examined herself in the mirror behind Camille. Unlike Camille, who wore a fashionable creation of sea-green silk and tulle with diamonds at her throat and in her hair, Sophia had no choice but to wear one of her black gowns again, and she smoothed her hair back into a simple chignon. But even though the dress was unadorned, with none of the poufs and ruffles so stylish that year, the satin fabric was rich and glossy, and the low neckline showed off her white shoulders. In her ears, she wore her grandmother's pearl earrings, the one piece of jewelry she had managed to hold on to, and she had bought paste hair-combs with an advance on her salary.

Not too bad, she thought. If only she didn't look so pale, so anxious after the last few months. The patrons wouldn't have any fun if the hostess looked so desperate. Sophia pinched her cheeks to bring some pink to them and gave a bright smile. She had to enjoy all this while she could.

She spun around as Camille threw open the doors and swept into the salon to welcome her guests.

"Bon soir, mes amis! Welcome to La Reine d'Argent. A place where there is decidedly no gaming," Camille said as everyone laughed. "I hope that you will all find something to enjoy here. There is dancing, dining, conversation--anything you might fancy. Please, if there is anything you require, let me or Madame Westman know. And now go, go, have fun! The night is young."

Camille gestured to the small orchestra in the corner to begin playing a lively tune, and the crowd surged back into talk and laughter again as the footmen circulated with more wine. Camille disappeared into the crowd and Sophia followed. As she swept through the crowd, she could hear whispers about the "femme mystere" and they made her smile. That was what she wanted to be--the mysterious woman, the one nobody knew anything about. As Sophia turned to go through the salon, the doors opened again to admit yet more latecomers. Behind the laughing group, standing alone, was a tall man dressed in a fashionably tailored dark blue evening coat and cream colored satin waistcoat and cravat. The gaslight gleamed on his sun-golden hair, which was brushed back in sleek waves from a face too handsome to be real. It surely belonged on a fallen angel rather than a mere mortal man. It was a face she remembered very well. A face she had seen in her mind ever since that night she crept into the Devil's Fancy and challenged him to a card game--and more. And now he was standing right across the room from her.

For so long, Dominic St. Claire had been a fantasy figure, a perfectly handsome, perfectly charming dream she could think about when she needed an escape from real life. She had come to think no real person could possibly be as beautiful as her memories. Probably he was older than she remembered, or was clumsy and smelled bad.

But she saw now there were no flaws. In fact, he was even more handsome than in her memories. The real life was more vivid, more striking, than she could have remembered. And everyone else seemed to agree, as they all turned to stare at him as if they were not sophisticated Parisians at all.

Sophia felt her cheeks turn hot even as she shivered. Everything suddenly felt strange and unreal, as if the time had fallen away, and she was that headstrong girl again, swept away by her first taste of passion. She had the most powerful urge to run to him, to touch him to see if he was real. Yet she also wanted to run away, to vanish as she once had after he kissed her.

Instead she stood still, frozen, and watched him. He looked around the room, a half-smile on his lips, his expression unreadable as he studied the people around him. He was said to be one of the finest actors in England, and Sophia could see why. He was so good at hiding his thoughts as he stood there, as still and quiet as if he was making a stage entrance, but she fancied she could see a flash of some cynicism in his eyes. He seemed very remote from all that was going on around him.

Yet as she watched him she still couldn't help but remember that long-ago night when he had kissed her, touched her, in that dark room. She had never felt like that before or since. Did he remember, too? Surely he hadn't known who she was--at least she hoped he did not. But did he ever think of her, the woman in the mask?

Or was she merely one of dozens of women who blurred together in his memory?

She thought of poor Mary Huntington, of her helpless desire for a man who couldn't care for her the same way, who wounded and betrayed her. Mary had drowned in her unhappiness, and when Sophia read her words she vowed never to do that to herself. Never to depend on anyone for anything. She did desire Dominic St. Claire, of course he was so terribly handsome and, as she remembered, so very good at kissing. But that was all.

It was all it could be.

Dominic's brilliant green gaze suddenly turned--and landed on her. She could feel the heat of it even across the room. It felt as if he physically touched her skin, ran his hand over her bare body, and a chill ran up her spine.

Then his smile widened, but not with humor. It looked like the smile of a wolf spying a helpless rabbit just before he snatched it up. And she wanted desperately to be the prey he sought.

Oh, she thought with a flash of raw panic. *I am really in trouble now...*

* * *

It was her again. He had found her.

When Dominic first stepped into the crowded club and caught a glimpse of the woman's back, something that had felt long-frozen flickered to life within him. That glossy, black hair pinned in shining, heavy coils atop an elegant head, reminded him of the mystery woman he had once kissed, and who had run away from him. She had been the only woman he ever wanted who eluded him, and the thought that she was within his grasp again awakened the primitive hunter in him.

He had come to La Reine d'Argent as a respite from working at the theater, from getting the new play ready to open and playing go-between in quarrels between the other actors. He wanted to play some cards, have some fun, and maybe learn something he could take back to the Devil's Fancy when they returned to London. Camille Martine was a very fine hostess, as they had learned at her dinner at the Cafe Anglais, and he was sure her club would be a grand one.

He hadn't expected to find the woman in black as well. Dominic smiled and smoothed the velvet cuffs of his coat as he watched her. She was not very tall, but was slender and delicate-looking in her black satin gown. She talked to a group gathered around her, her lace-gloved hands fluttering in an exuberant gesture. Her head tilted back in laughter, and everyone around her watched her intently, as if caught in an enchanted spell.

Then she turned--and froze when their eyes met and she saw him watching her. The smile on her rosebud lips faded, and her already fair cheeks turned pale. And Dominic saw that it really was his mystery woman. Even though she had once worn a mask, he could see that the shape of her face, the delicate nose and slightly pointed chin, were the same.

"She is beautiful," he heard his brother James say. "They say she is a widowed Englishwoman who has fallen out with her family and came to work here with Madame Martine. That she wasn't married long and is heartbroken, looking for a new start. But I couldn't discover anything else."

"You seem to have discovered a great deal about her," Dominic said.

James grinned. "I was talking with Madame Martine just now. The woman is rather stingy with information about her friend, but I did find out a few tidbits to add to what we heard at dinner the other night."

"Who is she?" Dominic didn't take his gaze off the woman. She had turned away to talk to someone else, but he could see the way she held her shoulders rigid, the strain in her pretty smile. She glanced at him from the corner of her eye, but then her gaze quickly slid away. She was certainly not indifferent to him.

Dominic felt his blood heat as he looked at her, felt himself coming to life again. It had been so long since he felt that way.

"Her name is Mrs. Westman, an Englishwoman," James said. "Other than what I told you, I don't know much, but I intend to find out."

Mrs. Westman. Dominic studied her as he wondered what sort of man Mr. Westman had been to win such a prize. Had she been married when she was at the Devil's Fancy? Her kiss had tasted innocent, as if she hadn't been aware of such a spark of passion before. But now it seemed she was a widow, a woman of mystery in Paris. Like James, he intended to find out everything there was to know about the lovely Mrs. Westman.

"Believe me, James, you can't handle a woman like that," he muttered, and moved into the thick of the crowd, ignoring his brother's protests. He kept Mrs. Westman in his sight as he reached for a glass of wine from a footman's tray.

She had disappeared into the bright crowd. He moved through the twisting warren of elegantly cozy rooms, searching for a glimpse of her black gown amid the pastel crinolines of the other women. He finally saw the ebony gleam of her hair in the ballroom at the end of the winding hallways. An orchestra played a waltz as couples swirled around a polished parquet floor, looking like a brilliant summer bouquet under the muted glow of the gaslights behind their frosted glass screens.

Mrs. Westman stood near the wall, examining the gathering with a small smile on her face. She gestured to two footmen as if to send them on errands and straightened a painting in its frame. Dominic studied the graceful, elegant line of her white arm, her smooth, bare shoulders.

Yes, he did want her. Like he had never wanted anything before, and he was a man of stubborn single mindedness. He would have her this time.

Dominic stalked around the edge of the dance floor, keeping her in his sights. She had the strangest, most intriguing quality about her, a delicate, watchful air, as if she would take flight and vanish at any moment. She had done that before.

Dominic wouldn't let her go again.

From the Diary of Mary St. Claire Huntington

Our new home is not entirely what I expected.

I was so excited to leave the Court. The clothes and music there were wonderful, as were the theaters and balls after all the years of gray nothingness under Cromwell. But I want only my husband's love. I cannot take lovers, as everyone seems required to do around the king, nor could I bear seeing my John laugh with other women. I have never been a jealous woman before. What has become of me?

I thought all would be well once we came here to the country. We would be alone. We would find each other again. But still John sits by the fire and drinks so late at night, and I do not know what to say to him. Why can I not make him happy? Why can I not be happy, as I thought I would be?

Five

❦

SOPHIA WAS SO busy making certain everyone was having a good time that she didn't see Dominic St. Claire when he first entered the crowded ballroom. Which was most disconcerting, because she had been so acutely aware of him all evening.

Did he know it had been her that long-ago night at the Devil's Fancy? She was almost certain he did from the way he looked at her, so dark and intent, as if he was searching his memory for her. It made her feel as she never had before, nervous and acutely aware, almost afraid, but excited at the same time. As if she couldn't breathe wondering what might happen next, as if she was reading the story of someone else. Like Mary Huntington.

She had no time to desire a man right now, especially a man like Dominic St. Claire. He would never be easily dismissed, as Jack had been. The fact that their one kiss still haunted her showed her that all too well. She had work to do now. She had to figure out how to get back into her family's good graces. She couldn't be distracted by Dominic.

She pasted her brightest, most sociable smile on her lips again and stood on her tiptoes to study the ballroom.

That was when she saw him again. He stood just inside the doorway, studying the room. The dancers swirled between them, a cloud of silk and tulle, obscuring her view of him until they parted again and she saw that he had suddenly vanished. Startled, she spun around and tried to find where he had gone. She had that urge to run again, to hide from him and his intense green eyes, but she was caught between the wall and the dance floor.

And the potted palms lined up along the walls offered meager shelter. She suddenly wished Camille had decorated with chinoiserie screens instead. They might be a bit unfashionable, but they were always useful when one wanted to hide in plain sight.

Sophia spun around and took a step toward the orchestra, only to freeze when Dominic appeared in front of her. His smile widened, white teeth flashing like those of a pirate in a romantic novel just before he ravished the hapless heroine. To her surprise, she saw he had a dimple set in his smooth-shaven cheek, which would have made any other man seem younger, sweeter--harmless. But it just made him seem more like an alluring, seductive predator than ever.

Sophia had been the prey too many times in her life, at the mercy of men since the day she was born. She was done with being helpless, even if a part of her wanted very much to be caught by Dominic.

"Mrs. Westman, I presume," he said. He spoke quietly, politely, but the deep, slightly rough timbre of his actor's voice seemed to echo above the music and laughter of the party. "What a superb job you and Madame Martine have done with this establishment. You seem to have a great success on your hands."

Sophia made herself hold her smile in place, not turn and run. There had to be a reason he was here in Paris, here at La Reine d'Argent, and she wanted to know what that was. "I am afraid you have the advantage of me, monsieur," she said. "You know my name, but I have failed to find out yours."

One of his golden brows arched and there was flash deep in his extraordinary eyes. Sophia knew that he could see she was lying, that he had the instincts of a gambler, but she would fall to the floor in a faint before she would let him see all she was really thinking. And she never fainted.

She definitely wouldn't let him know how much she wanted to press her lips to that enticing dimple...

"How very rude of me," Dominic said. He swept her a low bow. "Allow me to introduce myself, since I have no friends here to do the honors at the moment. I am Dominic St. Claire. I met Madame Martine at the Cafe Anglais, and she kindly invited my brothers and me to her soiree tonight."

"Ah, yes. The actor from London."

"Acting is one of my professions, yes. We are embarking on a guest booking at the Theatre Nationale this week. Do you enjoy the theater?"

"I used to, but I haven't been to London in a long time and I rarely have the opportunity to indulge in the pastime."

"Then you must come to our opening night performance. You and Madame Martine, of course, if you can be spared from your duties here." Dominic's sharp gaze studied the crowded ballroom. "You and your friend have done an extraordinary job in a short time."

"You are a habitué of gambling clubs, monsieur?" Sophia said. She couldn't help teasing him a bit. Even when she knew better, her flirtatious nature insisted on surfacing. Especially when he looked down at her that way.

Dominic laughed, a wonderful, rich, dark sound that made Sophia's heart feel strangely lighter. "Another of my professions is part-owner of just such a place in London. Perhaps you know it, Mrs. Westman? The Devil's Fancy in Mayfair."

Sophia laughed. "I told you, monsieur, I have not been to London in a long time. I am sadly behind on all the gossip of what is au courant there."

"I would be happy to tell you all I know. At the Cafe Anglais after the theater, perhaps?"

Oh, Sophia was tempted. A quiet supper, laughter over champagne, a kiss in the shadows--she could envision it all, and she wanted to give in. To fall into those eyes and never escape. It would be far too easy. But she knew she could not, not with him. She knew that many, many unfortunate ladies must have felt just the same way she did now. "I have no time for fun anymore, I fear," she said. Those words were much too true. Life with Jack had been nothing *but* fun at first, and look where that had brought her. She had to be respectable now, or try to be anyway.

"Oh, come now, Mrs. Westman, everyone has time for fun," he said with another of those enticing grins. "Dance with me now and I will show you."

Sophia glanced at the dance floor. The last song had ended, and she hadn't even noticed because she'd been so occupied with Dominic. The orchestra was tuning up for the next set as the couples moved into place for a waltz.

"I can't dance tonight," she said wistfully as she watched them. She used to love to dance so much. "I have so much to do..."

"Too much to oversee. Believe me, I perfectly understand. But the proprietors of a club set the tone for a place. Patrons like to see them enjoying themselves. It makes them relax, as if they were at a party with trusted friends. And that in turn makes them play deeper and longer at the card tables." He gave her a roguish wink. "And that is always desirable, isn't it?"

Sophia had to laugh. She had no doubt that he charmed his patrons at the Devil's Fancy into losing a great deal of money indeed. They probably even enjoyed doing it, as she once had. "Yes, most desirable."

"Then one dance. Come, Mrs. Westman. What can it hurt?" His eyes narrowed as he looked down at her. "Unless there's something you fear? I would not have thought you a timid lady."

Oh, surely he could not be daring her. She had never dealt well with dares. They always brought out that wild, reckless side of her, a side that was never buried deep enough anyway.

She studied his broad shoulders beneath the cut of his fine coat, and she wondered how it would feel to touch them again. To feel his arms around her as they spun around the floor. She hadn't danced in so long, and she was quite sure Dominic would be a fine dancer.

Perhaps he was right. Perhaps she was being timid, which wasn't like her. What could one dance hurt?

"Very well," she said with a toss of her head. "One dance, that is all. Because I want to hear about your club." Dominic laughed again, and it made Sophia smile against her will. Oh, yes, she thought--this man could surely charm the moon from the sky. But she was done with charming men.

"Very well, Mrs. Westman, one dance only," he said as he offered her his arm. "For now. But I warn you, I am still holding out for that supper."

Sophia slid her arm into the crook of his elbow, the lace of her glove sliding over the fine wool of his sleeve. She kept her touch light and polite, but she couldn't help but feel his heat through the expensive cloth. His muscles were lean and hard, tense under her touch, and she thought whimsically that he surely didn't spend all his time sitting at a card table.

He led her onto the dance floor and into a place amid the other couples. Sophia smiled at them, looking to make sure they were all having a good time, but they all seemed to blur together and vanish when Dominic put his arm around her waist and pulled her closer to his tall, lean body. It felt as if a spark flashed through her when his hand curled around her.

She looked up at him as she took his hand and heard the music swell around them in a familiar rhythm. A half smile lingered on his lips and he watched her closely, but she couldn't read his expression.

And it just made him all the more intriguing, damn him.

They swung into the first steps of the dance, and Sophia found she instinctively remembered the patterns of the waltz she had once loved so much. Dominic led her smoothly into a swaying turn, and he was just as fine a dancer as she thought he would be. He knew just how to move, to lead her so lightly she scarcely knew where she was going until she was there. His hold on her was polite, but she felt very close to him, their bodies moving together in perfect, instinctive concert.

He spun her around a corner so fast her skirts wrapped around his legs and the other couples turned in a bright blur. She laughed with pleasure and heard him laugh with her. They settled back into the turns and patterns of the dance.

"I haven't waltzed in ages," Sophia said, breathless.

"Really? You dance as if you did it every day," Dominic answered with one of his half-smiles. His fingers caressed her waist as they turned, the merest brushing touch, yet she seemed to feel it to her very core.

"Only because you are a good partner," she murmured.

Dominic laughed. "A compliment, Mrs. Westman? I am astonished--and flattered."

"I am quite sure you hear such things from every lady you dance with."

"Not every lady." His smile slowly faded. "And none that are quite like you. I'm surprised our paths haven't crossed before."

Ah, but their paths had crossed before, and she had the sense he knew it, too, that he played with her in some way. But she just smiled and kept dancing. "I've been living abroad. I haven't been back to England in many months. But you did know my name."

"It's only polite to know one's hostess," Dominic said. "And only wise to know one's business rivals, even when they're in a different city."

"I'm not your rival, Mr. St. Claire; I am only an employee here. I'm a simple widow who has to make her way in the world now."

"One thing I am quite sure of, Mrs. Westman--you are *not* a simple anything. I'd like to know more about you. I wish you would let me take you to that supper, so I could hear your story."

And Sophia wished she could go to supper, more than she could ever let him see. But she had to be careful now. She remembered Mary's journal, her sad tale of what happened when a St.

Claire met a Huntington. "I have no story. At least nothing that would interest a man like you, Mr. St. Claire."

"Ah, but you have no idea what might interest me, Mrs. Westman. I want to let you know that as well." The music rose to a crescendo, and Dominic whirled her to a stop at the edge of the floor. But he didn't let her go. "I do enjoy a mystery."

Sophia shook her head. "I'm sorry to disappoint you, but I'm not at all mysterious."

He smiled but didn't answer, just offered her his arm again and led her from the floor. Sophia felt as if she should say something, some light, careless comment that showed him she really wasn't different, wasn't mysterious. Yet for once she couldn't find any words. She just wanted to be away from him and how he made her feel.

"Dominic, you devil! Of course you would be monopolizing the most beautiful woman in the room," a man said. Sophia turned, still holding on to Dominic's arm, to find a tall, lanky young man smiling at them. He looked a bit like Dominic might in a warped, wavery old mirror: taller, thinner, with an untidy sweep of lighter brown hair falling over his brow. He wore expensive, fashionable, black-and-white evening dress, but unlike Dominic's casual, careless elegance, the clothes hung on him somewhat awkwardly. But he had those same bright green eyes. He had to be related to Dominic in some way. And she didn't need another St. Claire in her life, no matter how open and friendly his smile was.

"James, you know our hostess, of course," Dominic said. "Mrs. Westman, may I present my younger brother, James St. Claire? He is also an admirer of yours."

A faint flush spread across James's high cheekbones as Sophia slid her hand from Dominic's arm and held it out to him. "I do hope you're enjoying your stay in Paris, Mr. St. Claire?"

"Enormously, Mrs. Westman! It's a beautiful city."

"I would love to hear more about what you've seen while

you've been here," Sophia said. "I've been so busy myself I've only had time for a bit of whirlwind sightseeing."

"Would you care to dance, then?" James said eagerly. "We could talk there on the dance floor."

Sophia laughed. "If we could hear each other above the music. But yes, I would love to dance with you, Mr. St. Claire."

James led her onto the dance floor just as the opening notes to a lively mazurka sounded. He was not as skillful a dancer as his brother, but in his arms she felt none of the heady confusion she had with Dominic. She could just enjoy the music and the easy, pleasant conversation. And he was a very pleasant young man, charming and open and light.

They chatted about the sights of Paris, the churches and museums, the people. As he twirled her around in a turn, a thought struck Sophia.

"You know, I think we might share an ancestor," she said, thinking this would be an amusing conversational tidbit..

"I don't see how we could," James said with a laugh. "I would surely have remembered you from a family gathering."

"Well, it's not a close connection. It was about two hundred years ago, and I don't think she had any children. But before I was Mrs. Westman, I was Lady Sophia Huntington, and a woman named Mary St. Claire married a Huntington in the Restoration era. It's quite a fascinating tale. I have her diary, though I haven't read it all yet."

James's face suddenly went white. His smile faded, and his hands tightened on her shoulder and her wrist. She sensed he would have dropped her if sheer politeness hadn't held him still.

Sophia was surprised. She certainly hadn't expected her trivial little conversational gambit to earn such a reaction.

"Perhaps you already know something of her," she said carefully.

"I--yes, I know something of her," James answered. He still looked down at her, but Sophia had the sense he saw something else entirely. "You say you are a Huntington?"

"I was once. But I haven't seen my family since I married. They don't exactly approve of me. What have you heard about Mary?" Sophia said.

"Just old family fairy-tales," he said. "I would like to read her diary one day."

"It's very old and fragile. I keep it locked away and only read a few pages at a time." Sophia found she didn't want to share Mary's diary. Somehow she felt protective of her. She had the distinct sense there was more to this than "family fairy-tales."

The music wound to a close, and James escorted her to Camille's group at the edge of the room before he bowed and left her. As Sophia watched him, he made his way to Dominic and spoke quietly in his brother's ear. Dominic glanced across the room at Sophia, his eyes narrowed.

And she wondered exactly what was going on with that far too intriguing man...

Six

"DAMN IT, Dominic! Are you trying to kill me?" Patrick Branson, one of the company's actors, cried as Dominic drove him back into the scenery as they practiced a stage duel. "I warn you, I have no understudy. And opening night is only two days away."

The haze of intense concentration that fell over Dominic when he was deeply immersed in a role suddenly lifted, and he realized he held the man pinned down onstage with the point of his rapier. He laughed ruefully, and swiped his shirtsleeve over his damp brow as he stepped back.

"Sorry, Branson," he said. "I just got carried away."

Branson leaped to his feet. "I suppose it's all in service to the play, so no harm done. I only hope I never *really* make you that angry with me."

"Just remember your lines and we'll have no problems," Dominic said jokingly. In truth, the anger inside him that drove him to practice the fight so fiercely over and over wasn't with anyone around him, but with himself. He hadn't been able to get Mrs. Westman out of his mind all day, and it was maddening.

He kept seeing her eyes, that strange violet-blue color, and her flashing smile. He kept remembering what it felt like to hold her in his arms as they danced, how she laughed and leaned into him as they turned and swayed, as if their bodies had been made to fit together just like that; the way she looked up at him, wide-eyed, breathless, almost startled, as if she felt that sudden, sharp pull between them as fiercely as he did.

His desire for Mrs. Westman had come over him like a lightning strike, hot and swift and just as unwanted. It had been a long time since he needed a woman like that, and he hated the feeling of being so out of control. That wildness that threatened to burst free just from the smell of her perfume.

And then James had said she used to be a Huntington, and that she had Mary Huntington's old diary, which was surely full of secrets she could wield over his family. The one woman he had wanted in so long, and she came from *that* family.

Dominic shook his head and turned away to toss down the rapier. He hadn't even thought of a woman since Jane died, not beyond a quick dalliance or a light flirtation. And his memories of Jane, so sweet and gentle, a haven of goodness in the world, were very different from the raw heat he felt when he touched Mrs. Westman.

A woman like that would never be a haven from the tumult of his life, a serene calm over his own turbulent nature. No, she would drag a man out into the very midst of the world, into violence and upheaval and noise, and glorious, messy life.

He had not known her long, but he did know that about her. When he looked into her bright, laughing eyes and saw the restlessness there, it was as if he looked at himself. At everything he had been trying so hard to tame, his anger, his wildness. He wanted to let go of the past, of his family's hatred toward the Huntingtons, and settle down into a peaceful life. A woman like Jane could help him become that man he wanted to be.

A woman like Mrs. Westman, no, Lady Sophia, would only push him to greater folly. And yet every instinct told him to go out and find her again. To discover all her secrets.

A towel was suddenly tossed over his head, and Dominic

swept it off and spun around in one quick motion, that anger roused in him again. He saw it was Brendan who stood there, a sardonic smile on his scarred face, as if he dared Dominic to fight him. Dominic balled the towel up in his fist and stepped back. His quarrel wasn't with his brother any more than it was with Branson.

It was only with himself.

"You are a bear today, Dom," Brendan said. "Surely the play isn't that bad."

"It's not bad, considering Lily's husband wrote it," Dominic answered as he wiped the sweat from his brow. "I think it will suit the French tastes very well. Romantic, funny, cynical."

"Not to mention it will give the ladies a chance to see you as a romantic hero, instead of the glowering Shakespearean villains you like so well."

"Glowering villains suit me."

"Lately they certainly do. Ever since..." Brendan suddenly broke off and shook his head.

"Since Jane died, you mean?" Dominic said. His family had been unsure of his match with her when she was alive, hinting that perhaps they were not entirely suited. They only seemed more unsure once she was gone.

"It's understandable that you would grieve," Brendan said quietly. "When you care about someone that way..."

"Based on your vast experience of caring?" Dominic snapped, then immediately felt a pang of remorse when something flashed in Brendan's eyes. As far as any of the St. Claires knew, Brendan had never been in love, but he was very private and quiet. An oddity in their drama prone family. "Forgive me," Dominic said, another rarity--a St. Claire apologizing. "It isn't you I'm angry with, Brendan."

Brendan shrugged. "Whatever it is, you need to get it out of your system without injuring our actors. We open here in two days, and there is still work to be done."

Dominic nodded. Work he understood. Work was safe.

"Speaking of that, where is James? He's meant to be overseeing the finishing touches on the new sets and I haven't seen him all morning."

"He said he had some errands. I think I heard him asking the concierge at the hotel about flower shops." Brendan laughed. "Maybe he has fallen for the charms of a French woman."

Dominic laughed with him. "That was quick work, even for James." Their younger brother always seemed to be falling in and out of love.

"Indeed. It seems as if he wouldn't have had time to meet anyone in Paris yet, it's been so busy here at the theater."

Dominic picked up the scattered rapiers and put them away in the open props trunk. He couldn't fight any more that day; he would hurt someone with all the emotions swirling inside him. "You know James. He could have become smitten by a girl he merely passed in the street."

Brendan leaned back lazily against a crate of scenery. "Too true. Our poor brother. He should have some sense knocked into him, so that he can see the world is actually not filled with romantic wonder and all that nonsense. It might save him from heartbreak later."

Dominic looked at his brother in surprise. Those were the most words he had heard Brendan say together in a long time. Usually he was just silently watchful, taking in the antics of the other exuberantly emotional St. Claires without saying a word or giving away his own thoughts.

But there was the bitter ring of conviction in those words.

"I think James likes the heartache," Dominic said slowly. "It seems to him to be all part of the glory of falling in love."

"It's too bad he's not much of an actor, then," Brendan answered. "He could get all that nonsense out on stage as you do."

Dominic laughed ruefully. He thought of Mrs. Westman and how he felt when he just looked at her. Not everything was given to the stage. "I think James was born too late. He would have been a great romantic poet in the Regency years, pouring out blood and anguish on the page and making the ladies swoon over how brooding and Byronic he is."

Much like Brendan himself, Dominic thought as he turned to look at his brother. Women always seemed to think they would be the one to touch his hidden heart, to coax out his rare smiles, but they never were in the end.

"I've read some of his love letters," Brendan said brusquely. "He could not have been a poet."

Dominic laughed again, and reached for his coat where it was draped over a crate. "Well, perhaps this new lady love can't read English very well."

"Did he meet someone at Madame Martine's establishment, do you think?" Brendan asked.

Madame Martine's? Dominic suddenly remembered James dancing with Sophia, that smitten smile on his face--until he found out who she really was. "Why would you think that was where he found her?"

"It could have been somewhere else, of course, but he was chattering on about the party at breakfast. How elegant it was, how Paris was so much finer than London..."

"There were many beautiful women last night," Dominic said abruptly. He didn't want to think about James being infatuated with Mrs. Westman--or his own reaction to her.

Brendan shrugged. "As you say. I'm sure it will all blow over soon, whatever it is. What are you doing the rest of the day?"

"I told Isabel I would take her to the Tuileries for a walk before she has to rehearse. Then we can try a new cafe tonight if you like."

"I may go to Madame Brancusi's later," Brendan said, mentioning the famous brothel. "Are you sure there is nothing else you want to talk about?"

Dominic shook his head. His family was the last place he wanted to talk about Mrs. Westman. He just had to forget about her, and make sure James did, too. "Nothing. What did you think about the rehearsal?"

* * *

It was much later by the time Dominic left the theater. There were script issues to resolve with some of the other actors and blocking to be done on the unfamiliar stage. He was alone when he left the stage door and stepped out onto the sidewalk.

But if the theater had become quieter as the hours went on, Paris was coming alive with the night. Well-dressed crowds hurried past him, their laughter ringing out like music. The cafes were opening their doors for dinner and dancing, and light spilled from their large windows onto the street.

Dominic studied them all as he turned toward the hotel, wondering wryly if he should have gone with Brendan after all. But he felt strangely removed from the merry scene around him, as if he watched a play he wasn't really a part of. His mind kept going back to Sophia Huntington, as it had far too often lately.

Suddenly a woman who was part of a large, rowdy group bumped into him, bringing him back to the busy street.

"Oh, pardon, monsieur!" she gasped, laughing as she caught his arm. "I did not see you there."

"Entirely my fault, madame," Dominic said, steadying her. When she looked up at him from under the feathers of her headdress, he saw it was Sophia's friend, the red-headed Madame Martine.

"Monsieur St. Claire!" she said with a smile. "How lovely to see you again."

"And you. We enjoyed our evening at your establishment very much," Dominic answered. He looked ahead to her group, wondering if Sophia was with them. He felt ridiculously disappointed that she wasn't there.

He looked back to Madame Martine to find that she was giving him a knowing smile, as if she could tell what he was thinking.

"I fear I am on my own tonight," she said. "My friend Madame Westman was tired and did not care to go out."

"I am sorry to hear that," he answered carefully.

"I told her she must enjoy Paris as much as she can while she is here! But all she talks of is venturing to England, to her family if they will take her back. So dull."

"Her family?" Dominic asked sharply. He had thought Sophia had left the Huntingtons to marry Westman. She was here, after all, living a life the Huntingtons surely could not approve of. "Is she not estranged from them?"

Madame Martine's smile widened. "Ah, so you know my friend's sad tale? I told her she does not need a family who treats her as they do, but she says she is tired of roaming. She wants stability, respectability, and she thinks to have that she must return to her family."

Dominic turned this information over in his mind. Sophia, who seemed so dashing, so scandalous, wanted to return to her staid family? It seemed absurd, and yet he remembered that flash of sad wistfulness in her eyes when she thought no one was looking. Maybe she did miss her old life of ducal privilege. But what would it take for the Huntingtons to accept her again?

Dominic thought of James's new infatuation for Sophia, and he knew that was one thing the Huntingtons would not accept--a St. Claire in their midst. Surely James's crush would fade, but the thought raised interesting possibilities in his mind.

"You see what I mean, monsieur," Madame Martine said. "Ah, well. I must catch up with my friends. But perhaps we will see you again soon at La Reine d'Argent?"

"Of course, madame. I wouldn't miss it."

"And Madame Westman will surely be happy to see you there as well."

She hurried off, leaving Dominic to head toward his hotel again. His thoughts were still filled with Sophia, James, and the Huntingtons. How they would hate it if Sophia was involved with a scandalous St. Claire...

From the Diary of Mary St. Claire Huntington

I think I am with child. Oh, God, please make it so! I cannot think what else can bring John back to me...

Seven

"SOPHIE, opening night was a triumph! And I must give a million thanks to you. You charmed everyone, and today they are all talking about the club. You will have to open your own establishment one day, though far away from mine, of course. Hopefully this has cured your talk of finding another job. You are suited to this one."

Sophia laughed at Camille's merry words and turned her face up to let the warm light of the sun peek under the edge of her black-and-green satin hat. She hadn't really wanted to take the time to walk in the Tuileries Gardens when Camille suggested it. But now she was glad to be out and about, letting the fresh air clear her head. She was plagued by doubts about what she should do next.

She hadn't been able to sleep well after the club closed last night. Every time she shut her eyes, her thoughts were full of unearthly green eyes and teasing smiles, of spinning around and around in a dance she never wanted to end.

Until it abruptly ended when she told James about her family name.

She shook away thoughts of Dominic St. Claire and studied the beautiful gardens around her. In London, she had gone riding in Hyde Park often, to see and be seen in the fashionable hours, but in her life with Jack there had been little time for wandering around parks. They stayed up late and slept late, living in casinos and ballrooms. She had never been much of a countrywoman and had thought she didn't miss the outdoors. But the Tuileries were more beautiful than anything she had seen in a long time.

A tall wrought-iron fence surrounded a pattern of winding paths, statues, bubbling fountains, and formal flowerbeds lined with straight rows of trees that cast lacy patterns of light and shadows over the grass and polished gravel. The vast hulk of the Tuileries Palace watched over the stylish parade, silent about all it had seen over the years. It was elegant and opulent, and seemed to belie the dark headlines Sophia saw screaming out at her from the papers that morning about how terrible King Louis Philippe was for the country. How France was on the brink of great change.

Here everything was serene and perfectly pretty. But was it merely the calm before the storm? Sophia felt a strange twinge of disquiet as she studied the laughing women in their plumed bonnets, silks, and pearls. And she was part of it all.

"Do you not think so, Sophie?" Camille said, startling Sophia from her daydreams.

She turned and gave her friend a smile. "I'm sorry, I must have been woolgathering."

Camille laughed. "Thinking of all your admirers from last night?"

"My admirers?"

"Mais oui! I cannot tell you how many handsome men asked me who you were. And both those English St. Claire brothers seemed quite taken with you."

Sophia felt her face grow warmer at Camille's words, and she feared she was blushing like a silly schoolgirl. Again. Dominic St. Claire had the worst effect on her. She knew she should avoid him and concentrate on organizing her life. But the thought of not seeing him...

She ducked her head to hide beneath her hat. "I danced with

them, yes. They were very charming. But that doesn't mean they were taken with me."

"Does it not?" Camille pursed her lips as if to hide a mischievous smile. It made Sophia laugh again, despite herself.

"You aren't trying to matchmake for me again?" Sophia said. "I told you, Camille, I can't marry again."

"Who said anything about marrying? I merely said they were both very handsome men who seemed to admire you," Camille said. "And I do hear that the St. Claires have quite extensive business concerns in England. Theaters, gaming clubs, all sorts of interesting things. You could do worse."

Oh, yes, Sophia knew about the St. Claires. Her cousin Aidan had married one of them, Dominic's sister Lily, and it had gotten him cast out of the family. Huntingtons simply did not marry into families that were on the stage, that owned gambling clubs, that harbored secrets.

Most Huntingtons did not, anyway.

"I thought you said I should open a club of my own," Sophia said. "Maybe I could move to London again and become a business rival to the St. Claires."

Camille smiled teasingly. "Ah, and I thought you were not listening! You certainly would have the ability to run such an establishment. But I think in the French way, and I see you are too young and pretty to have to scrape along for yourself."

"I doubt the St. Claires would want to help me out of my 'scraping.' Or possibly anything else. She had seen the raw shock in James St. Claire's eyes when she told him who she was and that she had Mary Huntington's diary.

"But did not Monsieur James send you flowers this morning?" Camille said, nodding and smiling to passing acquaintances.

Another thing that was odd. Sophia had been surprised to find that bouquet at the breakfast table--and dismayed at her pang of disappointment that the card was signed by James and not Dominic. She couldn't understand why either of them should send her flowers. Maybe it was James's way of apologizing for his strange behavior.

"That was a mere thank-you," Sophia said. "Plus perhaps a small apology. He reacted most oddly when I told him I thought we might have a bit of an old family connection."

"A connection? How very intriguing. You must tell me more!" But Camille was suddenly distracted by a woman calling her name, and she hurried across the path calling, "Ma chère madame la duchesse! So lovely to see you again..."

As Sophia started to follow her, her attention was caught by a flashing glimpse of sunlight on golden hair in the crowd. Her heart beat faster at the sight, and she knew, even without seeing the man's face, that it was Dominic. He stood at the edge of the tree-lined path, talking to a lady in a stylish pale blue walking dress. He held his tall-crowned silk hat in his hand so that his bright hair was bared, and Sophia could see he was laughing.

A *real* laugh, not the one of practiced charm she had seen him use at the club. He threw his head back with a flash of infectious humor more brilliant than a ray of the sun, and Sophia felt a wistful pang as she watched him. Who was making him laugh like that, so full of abandon? She studied the lady who stood beside him. She was young and petite and as exquisitely beautiful as a china doll, with fair, translucent skin and fine-spun, red-gold hair coiled beneath a feathered hat. Her small, gloved hand rested on his arm as she leaned forward to smile up at him from under her lashes. The two of them looked so happy together, so comfortable and easy.

So *right*. Sophia couldn't remember ever feeling that way with anyone, as if she just belonged right there. Even when she had lived with her family she had felt alone, different.

"Mon dieu, isn't that one of the St. Claires now?" Camille said. "How funny, after we were just talking about them. It must be fate. Too bad it is not your flower sending admirer, but Monsieur Dominic is certainly as handsome."

Sophia pretended a great interest in the handle of her furled parasol. It wouldn't do to encourage Camille when she was in a matchmaking mood. "Oh, yes, so it is." She wanted to stop herself from going on, but somehow she couldn't. "Who is that with him? She is very pretty."

"Oh, that is his sister! Mademoiselle Isabel St. Claire. I met her at the Cafe Anglais. I believe she is the twin of your Monsieur James. A friend of mine saw her as Juliet in London last year and said she was wonderful. We must go see their performance at the Theatre Nationale while they are here."

His sister. Sophia felt a ridiculous rush of relief at the thought and felt so foolish she had to laugh at herself. Dominic certainly seemed to bring out the worst in her! "Will we not be too busy at the club?"

"Nonsense, Sophie. You must know that meeting people and being seen at all the fashionable places is part of doing business. The theater will be...oh, sacre bleu!" Camille broke off with a gasp and a smile. "They are coming this way."

"Who?"

"The St. Claires, of course. And Monsieur Dominic is looking right at you. Smile, Sophie."

"What! He is not looking at me," Sophie said, feeling again like a silly schoolgirl wondering if the young man she fancied was watching her at a ball. She resisted the urge to peek over at him.

Or at least she tried to resist. She couldn't seem to stop herself and glanced in his direction from the corner of her eye. Yes--he really was looking at her, and so was his sister. Isabel St. Claire was smiling with a curious gleam in her green eyes, but Dominic was scowling, his laughter completely gone.

Disoriented by that angry frown, Sophia tried to spin away and find an escape route. But there was none.

"They are coming this way," Camille said. "Sophie, smile! You do look so fierce when you're all solemn like that."

Sophia automatically arranged her face in a smile, but it felt brittle as the St. Claires came closer, and Camille called out a greeting to them.

"Madame Martine, how lovely to see you again," Isabel said as they met under the arching shady branches of a tree. She was even prettier up close, as delicate and gold and white as a fairy princess. Dominic hovered behind her protectively, and Sophia wondered what it was like to have a brother like that. Someone who watched over his relatives, keeping them from harm. "And you must be Mrs. Westman! You must forgive my informality, but I feel I know you already. Paris is abuzz with the success of your friend's club."

"You must visit La Reine d'Argent and see for yourself, Mademoiselle St. Claire," Camille said. "Perhaps tea one afternoon?"

"I would adore that," Isabel answered. "If my jailer brothers would release me from rehearsal for a mere hour."

"You are here now," Camille pointed out.

"My first real outing since we arrived in Paris," Isabel said with a pretty pout. "I am longing to see so much more of the city. Tell me, where did you get that hat, Madame Martine? I must do some shopping while I'm here."

As Isabel and Camille chatted about modistes, Sophia surreptitiously watched Dominic from the corner of her eye. He seemed to be politely listening to his sister's conversation, but he also appeared to be watching Sophia. Expecting something from her.

What a puzzle the St. Claires were, Sophia thought. She had met so many people in her travels, learned so much about their emotions and their foibles, but she couldn't decipher this family at all.

They all turned to walk on through the park, and Isabel St. Claire fell into step beside Sophia. "You are certainly every bit as pretty as James said, Mrs. Westman."

Sophia laughed in surprise. She wouldn't have thought "pretty" would be the adjective James would use after the abrupt way they parted at the club. "I thank you and your brother for the compliment, Miss St. Claire. I was afraid he did not care for me after we parted."

"Of course not! He has spoken of nothing but you all day. He does tend to get a bit tongue-tied around women he admires, which I fear can give the wrong impression. But did he not send you flowers? He said he was going to."

"Yes, he did. They were beautiful."

"There! Then he has truly apologized."

"There was no need to apologize. Your brothers were charming," Sophia said. She slid a glance at Dominic, who was talking with Camille. "What did they tell you about me?"

Isabel shrugged. "Not a great deal. They do try to keep secrets from me, though, when they go places they think I should not. They haven't realized I have many methods of discovering information all my own." She leaned closer and whispered, "I heard some sort of dark muttering about a diary. Do you know anything about that?"

"I'm not at all sure. Your brothers seem rather dramatic," Sophia said cautiously.

Isabel laughed happily. "They are that. But tell me, Mrs. Westman, do you enjoy the theater? Will you come see our show when it opens?"

Sophia opened her mouth to answer, when she suddenly noticed a man standing near the wall. As she fell silent, everyone went on chattering and moved off to examine a nearby flowerbed. The man shouldn't have caught her eye at all, he was such a nondescript figure. A rather portly man in a brown tweed coat with his hat tugged low over his brow, a newspaper in his hand. But somehow his very stillness made him stand out in the pale swirl of the crowd.

And he was looking right at her.

"Mrs. Westman?" Isabel said.

Sophia turned to smile at her, and when she looked back the man was gone. But someone even worse was in his place. It seemed the man in the brown coat was merely a searcher, leading the hunter to its prey. For it was Lord Hammond who watched her now.

He smiled as he caught her eye and strolled leisurely toward her. Sophia watched him, frozen like a hare before the hunter. She had thought she left him behind in Baden-Baden. She should have known better.

"Mrs. Westman," he said as he stopped at her side. "How charming to see you here."

Sophia glanced toward the others, who still stood nearby but not close enough to hear the conversation. Dominic watched her carefully, as if he tried to figure out who this man was and what she was to him.

Sophia swallowed hard and forced herself to smile at Hammond, leading him a few steps further away from the others. What else could she do in such a public place? Hit him over the head with her parasol and run? As tempting as that was, she didn't want to cause a scene.

"Lord Hammond," she said. "What a surprise. I hadn't heard you were in Paris."

"I merely stopped on my way back to London, to perform an errand for my cousin the Duke of Pendrake." He stepped closer to her, too close. She could smell his expensive cologne, and the cloying scent of it seemed to wrap around her like tentacles.

Sophia made herself keep smiling. "You must be eager to reach England again."

"Not at all. I'm glad my errand brought me to Paris so I could see you again. We parted much too abruptly in Baden-Baden."

"I thought all business between us had been concluded, Lord Hammond," Sophia said coldly.

He laughed, as if her attempts to maintain distance amused him. "You took something from me I would very much like to win back. Mrs. Westman."

"If it's the money, I will happily play cards with you again any evening at La Reine d'Argent. You could attempt to win it back, but surely I was the victor fair and square in Baden-Baden."

He waved those words away with a quick flick of his elegantly gloved hand. "The money is nothing at all. I would happily gift you such a sum whenever you wish, and more. I told you before, my dear, I am a very generous man."

"But I have no need of such generosity. I am finding work here," Sophia said. "And I'm afraid I don't understand why you would wish to help me at all. You didn't seem at all happy when you lost our little game."

"I never take kindly to losing, Mrs. Westman. I am not accustomed to it." Lord Hammond suddenly frowned, his affable facade vanishing. "And I don't care to play games with you any longer. Farewell--for now."

Sophia held her breath as he walked away until she saw he was truly gone. How could he have come back into her life now, making veiled threats? She felt herself trembling with fear and anger.

Eight

IT HAD BEEN A LONG, profitable evening, but Sophia couldn't help worrying as she made her way up the back stairs of the club, stripping off her long silk gloves as she went. She kept thinking about Lord Hammond at the park and worrying about where he might appear next. About what he wanted from her.

She paused at the top of the stairs to peer down over the railings at the shadowed kitchen below. Everything was quiet now. All the servants had departed after tidying up the salons, Camille had gone home, and Sophia was alone in the dark stillness.

This was normally the time she liked the best, once the rush of the night had passed and she was alone with her thoughts. But tonight the silence made her think too much about things she would rather not, and not only Lord Hammond. Things like the loneliness that she could keep at bay while she worked, while she lost herself in the cards, but that came out to plague her at night. She and Jack had never gotten along after the first passionate rush of their elopement, especially once the drink got to him. But still she felt as if she wanted someone with whom to

talk, to go over what had happened at the club, to laugh at the patrons' silly antics, or to ask advice about what she should do concerning Hammond.

Things like the need to have someone touch her, hold her in the cold darkness.

Sophia shook her head. "You are being ridiculous," she whispered aloud. Perhaps she did need to go back to London and its foggy sensibleness, back to the shelter and limitations of her family. It seemed Paris was making her romantic and moody, two things she certainly did not want to be. Just as she shouldn't have been watching for Dominic St. Claire all evening, and yet she had been.

But for right now she would just put her feet up by her own fireside and have a nice brandy before she went to bed.

She turned at the small landing on the third floor and opened the door to her sitting room. The small apartment seemed like a cozy haven after the long evening. The fire was already burning in the grate, laid out by one of Camille's maids before she left, and a tray of bread, cheese, and brandy was left on the small table next to it. The fire was the only light in the room, its flickering, red-orange glow casting shifting shadows around the few pieces of furniture and the filmy curtains at the windows. Sophia leaned back against the door and smiled as she took in this little domestic scene, the books piled on the table and the cozy rug on the floor.

How could she be lonely when she had this? Her little home, after so long in one hotel after another. Her sanctuary after fending off men like Lord Hammond for too long. But it didn't feel like a sanctuary tonight.

She dropped her gloves onto the nearest chair and reached up to unfasten her pearl earrings and black ribbon choker. Suddenly there was a sound, a rustle of something like fine wool fabric, the creak of old sofa springs, and Sophia froze. She suddenly had the paralyzing feeling that she was not really alone. That a trap was closing.

Holding her breath, she reached behind her to grasp the door handle. If she could just get it open and run fast enough...

Then a man sat upon the sofa, and she saw the firelight gleam on pale blond hair. It was Dominic.

"What are you doing here?" she cried. She let go of the door-knob, but she didn't feel any safer. In fact, he was probably the very last man she should be alone with.

He smiled at her, that careless, unrepentant grin of his, as if he was found in a lady's private sitting room every day. And perhaps he was. Sophia saw the way women of all sorts were inexorably drawn to him, bright moths to a fatal flame. Just as she was drawn to him, against all her better judgment and all her experience. Even now her heart was pounding so hard she feared he could hear it.

"I was waiting for you, of course," he said. His tone was light, but Sophia could hear a thread of pure, unbreakable steel underneath. "Your sofa is quite comfortable."

"You should not be in here," Sophia said, feeling foolish as she stated the obvious. "If you wished to speak to me, you should have made an appointment. There is an office downstairs we use for club business."

"I do want to speak to you, but not about office sorts of things," Dominic said. "I won't take up much of your time."

"You already have." Sophia hated the tiny quiver in her voice. She stood up straighter and tilted back her chin. "What do you want to talk about, then? It's late and I'm tired."

He rose from the sofa, a slow, graceful unfolding like that of some powerful jungle cat. Sophia held her breath as she watched him move toward her, forcing herself not to run as he leaned his palm against the door near her head.

Sophia studied him warily. The firelight behind him seemed to cast a halo over his bright hair, but he looked far from angelic. His cravat was untied, hanging in loose, crumpled folds, and his shirt had fallen open at the throat to reveal a vee of smooth, bronzed skin. His hair was tousled, falling over his brow in waves that made Sophia long to brush them back. To feel their silkiness against her fingers.

She tucked her fists into the heavy folds of her skirt and watched as his smile turned teasing, as if he guessed what she was thinking. He leaned closer, and Sophia could smell the lemony crispness of his cologne. He didn't actually touch her, but it felt as if the warmth of his body wrapped around her and drew her close. She remembered her longings of earlier that night, that need to be touched and held in the darkness, and it rushed back onto her a hundredfold with him so close. She did want him to touch her, far too much.

"What did you want to talk to me about?" she whispered. All sorts of wild fantasies flashed in her mind, images of him kissing her, touching her, his skin warm against hers...

Dominic's smile faded, and his hand curled into a tight fist against the wall. "My brother."

"Your-what?" Sophia stuttered. All those heady fantasies fled like a cloud sliding from the sky. She hadn't been expecting *that*.

"My brother James. I am sure you remember him, since he sent you flowers. Or perhaps you don't, since you seem to have so many admirers."

"I-yes, of course I remember. He seems like a charming young man."

"He is quite infatuated with you," Dominic said calmly, tonelessly.

Sophia had to laugh. This conversation felt so strange. "Is he indeed? We have only met once. How impetuous of him."

She pushed herself away from the door and past him, but he suddenly caught her arm in his grasp. It wasn't painful, but she found she couldn't pull away from him. His hand was warm and strong on her bare arm, and his touch made her shiver.

She glanced up at him, and his eyes glowed in the flickering shadows as he stared back at her. All of his usual careless charm was gone, and he looked frighteningly intense.

"Don't encourage him, Sophia," he said in a low, hard voice. "He is much too romantic, he hasn't learned how the world works yet."

"You think I have encouraged him?" she cried. She tried to

twist her arm away but he held on to her. "I have barely even spoken to him."

"You've smiled at him, danced with him."

She had to laugh. This man, the one she thought about far more than she should, was here in her home telling her not to smile at his eager young cub of a brother? "I smile a great deal. Are you saying I should refrain from that? That I should go about being terribly stern in order not to encourage anyone?"

Dominic's hand suddenly slid from the wall to her shoulder, where her skin was bared by the black silk of her cap sleeve. His fingertips skimmed over her, the merest, lightest brush. It awoke something hot and alive inside her. "I don't think you realize the terrible power of your smile," he said roughly. His hand curled around her waist and drew her closer to the hard length of his body. "It's so bright yet so full of mystery, as if you tease us with secrets we will never know."

"I-I have no secrets," Sophia whispered. She reached out to grasp his shoulders because she was sure she was falling. The room was so dark and so warm, and it seemed to be growing even smaller. Narrowing in and in until there was only her and him. Only his fingers on her waist, her touch on his strong shoulders.

"We both know that's not true," Dominic whispered. He leaned closer until his lips brushed her ear. She felt his warm breath against the sensitive skin of her neck, and her eyes slid closed. "I don't want my brother mixed up in them. He's much too prone to leaping into trouble when it comes to a pretty woman."

"I've heard you're not immune to trouble yourself," Sophia said. She opened her eyes and found herself staring at the smooth skin of his chest where his shirt fell open. A tiny, crystalline bead of sweat gleamed at the hollow of his throat. As she watched, fascinated, it slid down his skin, and she had the most powerful urge to lean forward and trace it with her tongue, to taste him.

He seemed to sense her fantasy, because his hand tightened at her waist, and she heard him give a low, hoarse moan. "So you've heard gossip about me, have you? Even here in Paris?"

"Of course. The French are fascinated by beauty, you know. And I remember hearing about your family before I left London so long ago. The St. Claires are of endless interest there," she murmured. She traced her palm lightly over his shoulder and along the lean line of his back. Under the fine linen of his shirt and the soft wool of his coat, she could feel how hard his body was, and the graceful power of him as he shifted under her touch.

His lips traced the soft, vulnerable spot just below her ear, and Sophia's fingers clutched at a handful of his shirt. "And you listen to the gossip about me?" he said. "I would have thought you above such things--Lady Sophia."

His use of her title startled her, making a tiny touch of ice pierce the heat of her desire, but then he kissed her neck again and the cold skittered away. "Gossip is part of my business," she said, trying desperately to think clearly again. "I need to know as much as I can about everyone."

"Very shrewd of you," he whispered against her skin. "And what have you learned about me?"

"How women can't resist you," Sophia said. She flattened her hands on his chest and tried to push him away so she could think again. She could definitely see the truth of the gossip about him now. What woman could resist his skillful touch?

She could not afford to be another of their number. Not if she wanted to get back to her family somehow.

"That's not true." He drew back and looked down at her, his eyes narrowed. "You seem to resist me just fine."

Sophia laughed. Resist him? Oh, no. She wanted to resist him; she knew she should. She should just shove him away from her and order him from her home. "Is that why I'm letting you touch me now, because I can resist you? How absurd."

Dominic shook his head. He watched her closely, a frown on his sensual lips, as if she were a play script in some foreign language he couldn't quite decipher. "You won't let me in. I can't read your thoughts at all."

Did he want in? Sophia was startled by the thought. No man ever wanted to know her thoughts. It was enough to them that she was pretty, that she had once had family connections. That they wanted to sleep with her. It was all anyone ever saw or cared about, even Jack. She just hadn't seen that in the heady days of their elopement, when she had thought he was different.

She was sure Dominic was not different, either. He just wanted her to stay away from his brother. Perhaps he was attracted to her himself. That was all. But it was so hard to remember all those difficult lessons when he touched her, looked at her, the way he did now.

"My thoughts are very boring," she said.

His hand slid over the curve of her hip and pulled her even closer. Caught off balance, Sophia went up on tiptoe and wrapped her arms around his neck. His hair fell in silken waves over her hands, and she twined her fingers in them.

"I don't believe that at all," he said, and he sounded angry. Rough. "You are much too fascinating for a man's sanity."

And his mouth closed over hers. Sophia closed her eyes and tumbled down and down into that hot whirlpool of desire with him. He tasted so delicious, of brandy and lemons, and his lips moved over hers in soft caresses, first one corner of her mouth then the other before he moaned and pressed closer.

His hands were hard on her hips, and his tongue slid inside her as if he was just as hungry for the taste of her as she was of him. But Sophia didn't care anymore. His rough passion awakened that fire inside her and she felt that wondrous life sweep through her again. She wanted more of him, more of that feeling.

Her fingers tightened in his hair and he groaned against her mouth. As she twined her tongue with his, she felt his hands close over her bottom and lift her high against the wall. Her skirts fell back and she wrapped her legs around his waist to pull him deeper into the curve of her body.

Over the years, she had come to think the memory of her kiss with him at the Devil's Fancy had become more than it really was. A girl's first real kiss, magnified into something it really wasn't. But she saw now that the wild, passionate need had been real. And now that she was a woman with a woman's needs, it burned even hotter.

As she lost herself in his kiss, her mind was flooded with wild images. Dominic entwined with her on her bed, his mouth on her breast, her legs wrapped around him as the sheets tangled over their bodies. His hand in her hair as he stared down into her eyes and thrust inside her.

"Sophia," he whispered against her lips, and the dreams and reality merged. His mouth traced the line of her jaw, and her head fell back. She felt his hand brush away her skirts and slide under her thigh, lifting her higher against him. She rubbed against his body, and the feel of his erection between her thighs, hard and heavy even through her clothes, sent a shiver through her.

Still holding her against him with one hand, he moved his other into her hair and pushed the pins and combs out of the heavy waves. Her hair tumbled over her shoulders, and he buried his face in it. His breath was harsh and warm on her neck, and she just wanted to be nearer to him. She whimpered and buried her fingers tighter into his hair.

Suddenly a loud clattering noise broke through the blurry haze of her desire. Sophia jerked her hands away from him and bent her head back against the wall. It was only the sound of coal being delivered on the street below, but that everyday noise seemed to shake her harshly out of her dream-state of lust.

Dominic froze against her, as if he had also forgotten where they were and what they were doing. He slowly lowered her feet to the floor and stepped back. He raked his hand through his tousled hair, and his eyes seemed dark as a nighttime sea when he looked at her. It seemed as if he had never really seen her before.

Sophia pressed her hands back hard to the wall to hold herself up. She still couldn't quite catch her breath. "You want your brother to stay away from me," she said hoarsely. "But perhaps you should have warned me away from *you* instead."

Dominic laughed ruefully and ran his hand roughly over his jaw. "Perhaps I should have." He looked away from her with a frown, and the look in his eyes made it seem as if he suddenly was very far away, somewhere no one could follow him. Only a moment ago, Sophia had felt so very close to him, closer than she ever had to anyone before. Now it felt like miles were between then, and she couldn't figure out why. Or why it made her feel like crying.

But she would not cry. She had finished with tears long ago. She smoothed down her skirts and pushed her loose hair back over her shoulders as the silence stretched between them. It was broken only by the crackle of the fire and the rumble of the coal wagon on the street.

"You made me forget why I came here in the first place," he said, a strange, faraway tone in his voice.

"Did you not come here to warn me away from your brother?"

"James told me something else," he said, that note still in his voice. He looked at her, but he didn't seem to see her now.

"Oh?" she said, trying to sound careless and light, to not give away any of her own thoughts. "And what is that?"

"That we share a common ancestress. And that you have her diary."

James had seemed taken aback by her words when she told him about the diary, but now Dominic wanted to know about it as well? It seemed very strange. No one had ever been interested in Mary but her; no one else seemed to know anything about her.

"I do have her diary, yes," she answered slowly. "I found it in my uncle's library years ago, and I have kept it with me ever since. She lived in fascinating times."

"And she confided her secrets to those pages?" Dominic said, and Sophia didn't like something about the sound of his voice or the sudden, tense set of his shoulders. She sensed he was holding something back from her, that his interest in the diary was no mere idle curiosity. She had the feeling that she needed to protect Mary in some way, which was ridiculous. Mary had been dead for hundreds of years.

"She writes the usual sort of things women do in their diaries," she said cautiously. "Household management, local gossip. I merely thought James would find it amusing to know we had a shared family link, though a distant one. I can't imagine why you would be interested in reading such dull stuff."

"Dull stuff?" Dominic's stare suddenly shot up to her face, and she almost fell back a step at the harsh glow in his eyes. What was it about the diary that made him that way? "I would like to read it."

Sophia shook her head. "It's a delicate old book and I rarely take it out. But if I were to find something pertaining to your family in it, I would be happy to copy it out for you."

Dominic went very still. "Are you refusing to let me see that book? I would pay you for it. Whatever you like." Now Sophia was sure she did not want him to get Mary's diary, not if he was so desperate for it. "It is not for sale. And if those are the only reasons you came here, to warn me off your brother and get Mary's diary, you had best leave. It's late, and I am tired." And she wanted to start reading the diary again immediately.

Dominic shook his head. "I would do anything for my family, Sophia. Just remember that. I won't let a Huntington hurt them again." He gave her a stiff bow before he spun away toward the door. He vanished through it quickly and silently.

Sophia hurried over to the window and stared down at the street below until she saw him appear under a circle of gaslight. The light was blurry in the mist, and it made him look like a ghost, slipping away into the night and leaving her with far more questions than answers.

She slowly sank down onto the carpet, her skirts pooling around her as she buried her face in her hands. He knew who she was--Lady Sophia Huntington. He knew she had Mary's diary and for some reason he wanted it. That same closed-in, hunted feeling she had had when Lord Hammond tried to find her was descending on her again. Back then she had run to Paris. But she knew she couldn't run any longer, not from Dominic, not from herself.

She had to find out why he wanted that diary.

Nine

⌒⌒⌒

SOPHIA STARED out through the carriage window at the dazzling mansion as they rolled to a halt before the front doors. It was lit up like a Chinese lantern in the darkness, every window ablaze. The lights shimmered on the white stone walls and cast sparks off the guests' jewels as they climbed up the marble steps and poured through the open front doors. The faint strains of a lilting waltz could be heard even from outside.

It was all very elegant, the epitome of Parisian style. No doubt the champagne would be the best, the conversation the most intelligent, and the dancing would soon until dawn. It was exactly the sort of evening she had always enjoyed.

But tonight she found herself strangely reluctant to leave the shelter of the carriage and go inside. The long evenings at La Reine d'Argent, though undoubtedly fun and profitable, had left her feeling oddly hollow inside. As if there should be something-- more.

What that something could be she had no idea. She was just sure it had to be out there somewhere. But probably not in that house. It would surely be all the same people she had seen for the last few nights at the club.

For an instant she wondered if Lord Hammond would be there. She hadn't seen him since that day at the park, and she hoped he had left Paris for London already. She would certainly have to worry about him once she returned to England and tried to contact her family, but at least she would have some time to think before then.

If, however, he still lurked in Paris, their host tonight, who was a French duke, was surely just the sort of person he would know. Yet Sophia wasn't as worried about Hammond as she was about seeing Dominic again. She seemed to make a fool of herself whenever he was around.

"Are you ready, Sophie?" Camille asked.

Sophia suddenly realized the coach was at a complete stand-still and a liveried footman held open the door. She laughed, and smoothed her kid gloves over her wrists. "Yes, of course. I'm sorry, Camille, I must have been woolgathering."

Camille laughed in return as they stepped down from the carriage and joined the glittering line up the stairs. "I have the feeling you don't really want to be here tonight, my friend. Did you not like the duke when you met him at the club?"

"No, Monsieur le Due seemed perfectly charming,"

Sophia said, though in truth she couldn't quite remember exactly what the man looked like. They had all begun to look rather alike. Except for Dominic. She remembered every detail of him vividly.

"Then you have tired of parties?"

"Perhaps a bit," Sophia admitted. "But I know that socializing is an important part of your business."

"So it is, an enjoyable part. Yet I am sensing you do not relish it as I do right now." Camille's gaze was sympathetic as they gave their wraps to a waiting maid and turned toward the noise and sparkle of the ballroom. "You are still thinking of your family?"

"I do think of them," Sophia said, though she knew she hadn't been thinking of them enough, if she wanted to persuade them she was ready to return. She needed to formulate a plan to be respectable. "I must decide what to write them soon."

"You must do what pleases you, of course," Camille said. "But I still say you are not made for stuffy English respectability."

Sophia laughed, and they were swept into the very midst of the party. She had more dance partners than she could fit on her card, and was even enjoying herself as the evening went along.

But then as Sophia spun around in the last turn of the dance, she glimpsed a tall, dark, distinguished-looking figure standing in the doorway. At first she thought she had imagined him, but when she twirled to a stop facing the door he was still there, surveying the party with a cool smile on his face.

A footman offered him a glass of wine from a tray, but Hammond waved him off. He saw Sophia watching him, and his smile widened. He stepped into the glittering crowd, and for a moment he was lost to her view.

All of Sophia's senses seemed to sharpen. The room around her felt brighter, warmer; the laughter seemed louder. She knew she couldn't panic, not here.

After the dance ended, Sophia had her partner escort her to Camille's side. Her friend stood near the cooling breeze of the open terrace doors, sipping champagne and laughing with a few friends from the club.

"Sophie, you look flushed from the dance," Camille said with a merry laugh. She snatched another glass of champagne from a passing servant "Here, have a drink."

Sophia gratefully took the glass and gulped the bubbling liquid quickly, in a way that certainly didn't do it justice. Yet she still felt nervous.

"Are you quite all right, Sophie?" Camille asked.

Sophia nodded as she surveyed the swirling crowd in the ballroom. Only as the dancers turned did she glimpse Lord Hammond again. He stood across the dance floor, flanked by two very attentive ladies Sophia recognized as among the most expensive courtesans in Paris. His gaze caught hers, and he spoke a quiet word to the women. They hurried off in a flash of diamonds. One of them tossed him a wistful glance, but it was obvious they would do nothing to contradict his orders.

It seemed he held that strange power over many people. Then he moved away and disappeared into the crowd again.

"Do you know that man?" Camille said.

Sophia turned to her, still tense at the knowledge that Hammond was out there, watching her. "Which man?"

"The one who was staring at you, of course. He looked like a hawk with a mouse."

And that was exactly how he made Sophia feel--like a mouse. She didn't like that sensation at all. "We have met once or twice in Baden-Baden. Do you know him, Camille?"

"I have heard of him," Camille said with a weirdly bitter note in her voice. It seemed she really had heard tales, unsavory ones. "His name is Lord Hammond, yes?"

"Yes," Sophia answered in surprise.

"He seldom comes to Paris, but I know he has his finger in many businesses in the city. All across Europe, really. He claims it is in his role as agent for his cousin, an English duke, but I have my doubts. Men like him..." Camille frowned. "They thrive on power. They need it. And you say you know him?"

Camille suddenly took Sophia's arm and led her to a quiet corner behind a bank of flowering green plants. She opened her reticule and drew out a small gun.

Sophia gasped in surprise at the unexpected sight. "Camille, why do you have a pistol at a ball?"

"Because one never knows what might happen, or who might appear." Camille took Sophia's hand and pressed the gun into her palm. The delicate inlaid handle was cold through her glove. "I have others, though. You take this one."

"Camille, no," Sophia protested automatically, though the weight of it did feel reassuring in her clasp.

"Just in case, my friend," Camille said.

Sophie didn't want to take it. She had learned to shoot on her uncle's estate, but she had never liked guns, the noise and raw power of them. But Camille held it out insistently, and Sophia nodded and tucked the gun away in her own reticule. As Camille said, just in case. She could return it later.

Ten

THE THEATRE NATIONALE, where visiting companies from abroad presented plays and pantomimes for theater-mad Parisians, was one of the grandest establishments on the rue Vivienne, and as Sophia looked around her, she forgot where she was for a moment and just lost herself in the beauty. When she was a girl in England, she hadn't been allowed to see anything but the Italian opera. She avidly absorbed every chance to vanish into the world of a play.

She leaned her elbow on the gilt railing of Camille's rented box and studied the lush surroundings. The crimson velvet curtains at the stage were looped up with thick gold cords and trimmed with beaded fringe, which was echoed in the draperies at the boxes. Bright frescoes of the Muses, glowing with touches of lapis and gold leaf in the gaslights, looked out from above the proscenium, and the ceiling was a soaring dome painted to look like the summer sky.

And the audience was equally grand. A swirling mass of Parisians in their jewels and satins watched each other avidly from the shadowed depths of the boxes and filled the red velvet stalls below. There were whispers that some visiting German prince and his entourage were soon to appear, and there was a French duke or two as well. It was a sparkling, elegant scene.

Sophia looked down at the embossed program in her hand and saw Dominic St. Claire's name scrolled across the top. She had heard that in London he was best known for playing Shakespearean villains, but tonight's play was a modern romantic comedy, newly written just for this appearance in France, and he played the leading man. Sophia thought wryly that he was surely well-suited to such a part--so charming, so handsome, so attentive to the ladies. Yet there was also that flash of steel beneath, that sense that he hid things in his depths. She had seen that darkness when he came to her and demanded that she give him Mary's diary. Right after kissing her senseless.

And the terrible thing was he was such a very *good* kisser. He made her forget that she needed to be wary of him when his lips touched hers, when he touched her.

Was that all part of a role, too? The perfect lover, a villain underneath. Sophia sighed, and closed the program with a little snap. She felt as if the world was nothing but a series of masks, layers upon layers that hid the core of raw truth. Like a never-ending play. She wasn't sure she would even know the truth if she saw it now.

"You look pensive tonight, Sophie," Camille said. She had her opera glasses trained on a box further along the row, intently watching a handsome young man in a gleaming white-and-ivory uniform. "Is something worrying you?"

"Not at all," Sophia answered. "Perhaps I am just a bit tired."

"You have been working too hard. The maid said your light was burning very late last night."

"I was going over the ledgers," Sophia answered. "I will master how to do accounts yet!"

"I have told you, ma chère, you should not work so hard," Camille said. "If you would only..."

"I know, I know," Sophia said with a laugh. "If I only married a suitably rich gentleman, my troubles would be over." Or if she returned to her family.

"You should not dismiss such a scheme. It has worked for clever young French women for hundreds of years. And you have so many admirers here."

Sophia noticed the handsome young officer watching Camille, a soulful look on his face. "Not as many as you."

"Ah, yes! Monsieur le capitaine. He is a handsome devil. Though not quite so handsome as the freres St. Claire?" Before Sophia could answer, Camille gasped and turned her glasses down into the stalls. "Oh, look at Princesse d'Artignan's gown! Such a fright. I do hope that color is not the new style…"

Sophia peered down to try to glimpse the frightful couture, but her attention was caught by the group moving into the vacant box across the way. It was an Austrian duke she had seen at the Tuileries, along with his dowdy wife in poison-green satin and a few other people in their Viennese fashions. And one young lady who looked as if she had wandered into the wrong spot by mistake, a beautiful, ethereal creature, all silvery-blonde hair and pale blue tulle, who was smiling vaguely at something a young man was whispering into her ear. She seemed as if she was off in her own world, as she always did. Sophia knew that look well.

She was Sophia's cousin Elizabeth, who had been widowed soon after Sophia ran off with Jack, and she was the first member of her family she had seen in months.

Sophia's fist crumpled her program as she watched Elizabeth and remembered the last time they met. Elizabeth had been staying in the house the night Sophia left with Jack. She had glimpsed Elizabeth's blonde head peering down over the banisters as she ran from the house, her father shouting after her, her mother weeping but making no protest. Elizabeth had said nothing. She never did.

Yet somehow seeing her, a reminder of the past thrust suddenly into the present, made Sophia remember too sharply the wounded feelings of that night. That sense of being utterly rejected for her inability to be what they wanted, while Elizabeth drifted through life being so quiet, so perfect.

Sophia had thought that pain was gone, buried beneath the tumult of life as Mrs. Westman, of finding herself outside her family's insular world. But now it felt as if someone prodded at the old scar, and it stung.

"Sophia? Are you well? You look rather pale suddenly," Camille said.

Sophia turned away from her cousin and gave Camille what she hoped was a bright smile. "I am perfectly well. I just saw someone I know--my cousin Elizabeth, just over there."

"Your family?" Camille said. She knew something of Sophia's checkered past with the Huntingtons, and she gave Elizabeth's box a startled glance. "We can leave, if you wish. I know of a new cafe that just opened down the street. They are supposed to have lovely oysters..."

Sophia laughed. "Of course we can't leave, just because my cousin is here. She probably has not even noticed me. I'm looking forward to this play too much to miss it." She looked toward the other box and found that, on the contrary, Elizabeth *was* watching her, her beautiful, angelic face very pale and still. She gave Sophia a little nod, and Sophia smiled at her in return. The young man spoke to Elizabeth again and she turned away.

Sophia studied the stage, wishing the house lights would dim and the curtain would rise at last, so she could lose herself in the make-believe of the play and not in the past.

"Everyone is looking forward to the play!" Camille said brightly. "That handsome Monsieur Dominic is the romantic lead? This will give the ladies something to sigh about."

"I don't think he needs a stage role to make the ladies sigh," Sophia murmured.

Camille laughed. "Ah, no! Indeed not. And I heard the most romantic, sad tale about him today at the modiste that only adds to his allure. His poor, dead love..."

Sophia was startled. "His dead love? Are you sure this wasn't gossip about one of his plays?"

"Not at all. The lady relating the gossip was quite sure of it, and she has only just returned from London with all the on-dits. It seems he was engaged to marry a young lady called Jane Grant, after years of other amorous pursuits. It was said she was so good, almost an angel, and he has been quite elusive since she died." Camille sighed and waved her opera glasses in a dramatic gesture. "Is it not terribly romantic? You are quite right--it could almost be a play. The handsome, dashing hero brought low by the tragic loss of his beautiful, fragile heroine."

Brought low? Sophia stared down blindly at the stage as thoughts raced through her mind. She remembered how Dominic had kissed her, how his hands felt when he touched her--how she wanted more and more. And he had wanted her, too. Was she merely some fleeting distraction from his grief over his "beautiful, fragile" love?

Sophia had no desire to be someone's distraction. Not when she needed to get her own life in order again.

"A man who has found love once could easily find it again," Camille said. "He spoke with you for a long time at the park."

"Only about the club. There were no whispers of romantic yearnings," Sophia said.

"Are you quite sure that is all?"

Sophia was saved from answering by a knock at the box door. "One of your admirers, Camille? Monsieur le capitaine, perhaps?"

Camille laughed as she glanced back over her shoulder. "Ah, no. More likely someone wanting to meet you, the mysterious lady in black. Come in!"

A footman in the red livery of the theater presented a note to Camille, which she quickly read. A smile broke over her face. "An invitation from my old friend Monsieur DuLac, the Nationale owner! He has asked us to a supper party backstage after the play, to meet the actors. You can have more conversation with the oh-so-intriguing Monsieur Dominic. Such fun."

Sophia sighed as she studied her cousin's pale, cameo profile across the theater and thought about an evening spent trying to find something innocent to say to Dominic. *Fun* was not exactly the word she would choose...

* * *

"Are you still enjoying your time in Paris, Mrs. Westman?"

Sophia smiled at James St. Claire, who sat next to her at the long supper table. The lavish meal was nearing its end. An array of cheeses and sweets had been laid out on the damask-draped table, and rich red wines were being poured into sparkling crystal goblets. The conversation was louder than before, echoing with merriment and high spirits after the play. It was extraordinary to dine backstage at a grand theater, under the soaring walkways and in the midst of vivid scenery and a jumble of props. Like an Aladdin's cave, full of shadows and mysteries.

She hadn't spoken much with James after the initial pleasantries when they sat down and found themselves dinner partners. She had mostly conversed with the actor who sat on her other side, an older gentleman filled with fascinating tales of his years in the theater and gossip about London matters, and James was being flirted with by the pretty young redhead next to him. But he had made sure Sophia always had wine in her glass and occasionally whispered a teasing comment in her ear to make her laugh. Whenever he did that, she would notice Dominic watching them from down the table, his face expressionless, and it made her inexplicably want to giggle.

"I'm enjoying it very much indeed, Mr. St. Claire," she said. She glanced up at him and saw that his eyes were the same vivid green as Dominic's. He really was a handsome young man, his features lean and sculpted, his smile open and charmingly shy. Just as handsome as Dominic, objectively speaking. Yet there was no spark within her when she looked at him, nothing like the flame that kindled whenever Dominic smiled at her.

"Don't you miss the adventure of traveling the Continent, moving from place to place?" James said. "I would love to travel, see new places and new people."

"Certainly Germany and Italy have their beauties, and I am not one to say no to adventure," Sophia said with a laugh. "But being settled in one place has advantages, too. And one day I may return to London. It can be interesting there, if one knows where to look."

James made a scoffing sound as he reached for one of the bottles on the table and refilled her glass. "If one likes rain and fog, I suppose. I am not looking forward to returning there after our play ends its run here."

"But surely being in the theater must make it feel like you are in a new place every day," Sophia said. She took a sip of wine, and her gaze caught on Dominic over the gilded edge of her glass. He was listening to the chatter of the lady who sat beside him, that half-smile on his face that Sophia knew very well now. It was one of his masks to hide his real thoughts.

For a while that night, as she watched him onstage, she had forgotten he was Dominic. He had drawn her into his magic and convinced her completely that he was someone else. He drew her into the narrative he chose to tell. Surely he did that offstage as well, playing parts in real life that kept his true self hidden, just as she did.

Had Jane Grant seen behind all that? Had Dominic let her glimpse his true self? Sophia felt a flutter of something unpleasantly like jealousy, and she pushed it away. It was absurd to be jealous of a lady she had never known, a lady who was gone. But from what Camille had said, Dominic had cared for this Jane Grant, and Sophia couldn't help but wonder what that would be like.

What it would be like to glimpse Dominic's secrets.

He glanced up and caught her staring at him. He raised his glass to her in a mocking salute, and Sophia turned away. She didn't need to know Dominic's secrets. That would mean he might see hers in return. She drained the last of her wine and smiled brightly at James.

His eyes widened at her smile. "To tell you truthfully, Mrs. Westman, I am not sure the theater is really for me. But I hope you won't tell my family that!"

"Certainly not, Mr. St. Claire. Does your father want all his children to go into the theater business, then?" Sophia could certainly sympathize with longing to be free of the weight of parental expectations. Being a Huntington had constrained every part of her life, pressing down on her until she was sure she would be crushed. Only running away had freed her.

She would have thought the theater was a sort of freedom. But maybe it was just another kind of cage.

"We are all in the business already, in one form or another," James said. "Dominic and Isabel act, as our parents once did. My eldest sister, Lily, took care of the business side of things, before she married and moved away. Now she and her husband run another theater in Edinburgh." He paused suddenly and gave a wry laugh. "But you know that, of course. Aidan is your cousin."

"So he is, but I fear I haven't heard from him in a while. I hope he and Lily are happy." Aidan had once been one of her favorite cousins, a wild spirit who could understand her. When he broke away from her uncle and married Lily St. Claire, he had inspired her to make a bid for freedom, too. But hers had not ended as well as his.

"They are very happy. Expecting a baby in the winter, even."

"A baby!" Sophia cried. "How splendid."

"Yes. My mother is ecstatic for her first grandchild." James took a long drink of his wine. "And I have to apologize to you for my reaction to your conversation the other night, Mrs. Westman. I was merely startled to learn you had been Lady Sophia Hunting-ton. I never meant for Dominic to make such a big thing of it all."

"That is quite all right, Mr. St. Claire. It's not every day one discovers a lost family connection, I suppose, even a distant one. And I don't really consider myself a Huntington any longer."

"Do you not?"

She shook her head. "Not since I left to marry. I longed for freedom, just as you do. But freedom has a price, too."

James gave her a searching glance. "What do you mean, Mrs. Westman?"

Sophia laughed. How could she tell this young man, so secure in his family, who so obviously looked out for each other, what it felt like to be adrift in the world? To be alone, even if it was by choice? "I don't mean anything at all. Tell me then, Mr. St. Claire, have you acted yourself? Have you had many roles?"

They went on to talk about the theater, and about the sights of Paris. Before she knew it, the dinner was over, and Monsieur DuLac, the theater owner, offered to lead everyone on a backstage tour. The walkways behind the scenery were narrow and dark, and everyone laughed and stumbled together, turning one way and then another as if at a carnival.

Once they made their way up into the rafters high above the stage, Sophia found herself trailing behind the others until she was alone in the silent darkness. It seemed like something in a storybook, something perfect and strange, and she didn't want to hurry to catch up too fast. She didn't want to lose the enchantment of the theater.

She tilted her head back and stared up into the soaring space above the walkway. The darkness was crisscrossed by an elaborate web of ropes and pulleys for the scenery, and they swayed gently in the shadows like ghosts. Far below she could see the stage set, the shapes of sofas and chairs and false fireplaces, the facade that mimicked real life. From here she could see how hollow it all was. From here, everything was dark and half-seen, half-understood.

Just like life itself. Just like Dominic.

Sophia wrapped her fingers around the railing and sighed. She knew she should catch up to the others. She could hear their voices from somewhere in the wings, a weird, dreamlike echo. But she didn't want to be in a crowd again just yet. She moved slowly along the walkway, the heels of her shoes clicking on the planks. Even that seemed strangely loud in the soaring, hollow space.

A man suddenly moved out of the shadows, blocking her path into the wings. She gasped and fell back a step as she felt her heart pound in surprise. For an instant, she remembered Lord Hammond and how he had reached for her in the casino, his eyes filled with that burning possession. His threats.

But then she saw it was Dominic, his hair like a golden flame in the shadows, and she drew in a deep breath. Yet Dominic was just as fearsome as Hammond, in his different way. He threatened her in ways Hammond never could.

"You startled me," she whispered.

"I'm sorry. I didn't mean to," he answered quietly. But Sophia couldn't hear anything contrite in his tone. He took a slow step toward her, and she reached out to hold on to the railing. "Madame Martine was worried you had fallen behind, and I told her I would find you."

"I'm fine. I just wanted to explore a bit. I've never been backstage at a theater before." Sophia glanced over her shoulder at the soaring space beyond them. It felt as if she and Dominic were suddenly all alone in the darkness, suspended high above the world where no one could find them. She had the sudden, strongest urge to reach out for him. She wanted to wrap her arms around his strength and hold on so she would know there was one real thing in this dream-world.

But she knew if she touched him, that fire inside her would ignite and she couldn't hide it again.

She glanced down at the stage below. "It's amazing up here," she said.

"Yes. Like a different world," Dominic said, as if he knew her thoughts. He took another step until he stood beside her, and he braced his hands on the railing next to hers. He didn't touch her, didn't look at her, but she was very aware of him close to her. The smell of his skin, the heat of him, made her remember their kiss vividly.

"When I was a boy," he said as he looked down at the stage, "I used to hide up in the walkways of the theater all the time. It was my favorite place, for there I could pretend I was anywhere, anyone. No one could see the real me. That's how I learned that the theater meant freedom, the only real freedom I could find."

"So you loved acting from the beginning?" Sophia asked softly. She couldn't look away from Dominic, from the fascination of this rare glimpse into his thoughts. He drew her in so easily.

He shot her a quick, flashing smile. "How could I not love the theater? It's in our St. Claire blood. We spouted Shakespeare quotations as our first words. Who wouldn't want the gift of being someone else, if only for an hour?"

"Yes, indeed." Sophia murmured. Yet his brother found the theater a trap of family expectations. How strange clans were; how easily one could be lost in them. She would love to be someone else for a moment, someone who didn't have that wild impulse deep inside that always drove her to trouble even when she only wanted to avoid it. Someone who had a net to catch her when that recklessness overtook her. Someone whose play had a happy ending, no matter what chaos ensued in the midst of the action.

But that was the theater, not real life. In real life there was nothing to catch her, or anyone else. "What is your favorite role?" she asked. "Romeo? Hamlet? Some dashing, romantic rake?"

"Iago," Dominic answered.

Sophia gave him a startled glance. She wouldn't have expected him to choose a villain, a man tormented and driven to incite another to murder by blackest jealousy. "Iago? But he is so..."

"Scheming? Evil? Cruel?" Dominic said with a laugh. "Yes, all those things. His demons eat him up inside until he has no choice but to destroy everything around him, even when that thing is the personification of sweetness and light. It's better to let such things out on the stage, wouldn't you say--Lady Sophia?"

Somehow he put a world of hidden meaning into those two

words. Sophia studied him in the faint, murky light. His handsome face looked harsh, his cheekbones sharp enough to cut. His eyes darkened as he looked down at her. She could see him as a villain, so beautiful he drew people closer and closer before he destroyed them because he could not help it. Because he was driven on by demons, just as she was.

She thought about Jane Grant, the lost fiancée, and wondered if she was something of sweetness and light. If he still mourned for her and what she had meant in his life. She wondered what had driven him to hide in the theater rafters as a boy, what drove him to the million deceptions of the stage and the card table.

But she couldn't ask him. She didn't have the words, and she suspected he would never share his secrets, his deepest self. Perhaps, like her, he didn't even know.

"That sounds strange to me," she said. "I haven't been Lady Sophia in a long time."

"Have you not?" he said, a touch of some dark amusement in his voice. "But it suits you. Mrs. Westman sounds too prosaic for such an exotic princess."

Sophia laughed. "A penniless princess, cast away from the palace. Yet I wouldn't trade what I have now for an ivory tower. Nor do I think you would trade the theater for the grandest of castles."

"You're right. Only the theater suits me, I fear. I'm no good at anything else." Suddenly, he turned to her in one quick, lithe movement. He drew her close, the soft curves of her body molded to the hardness of his. And she knew his words weren't true--there was surely at least one other thing he was very good at indeed.

She grasped at his shoulders to keep from falling and his arm tightened around her.

His head bent down to hers, his kiss brushing against her brow. "It was you, wasn't it?" he said, his voice low and rough.

For a moment she was confused; all she could make sense of was his touch around her. "What was me?"

"That night at the Devil's Fancy," he said, and she felt his lips curve in a smile against her temple. "You kicked me in the balls. I was furious about that for weeks after."

"Were you really?" Sophia laughed at the memory, a memory that had haunted her as well. "It was rather clever of me, though I had never tried such a thing before. My old nanny told me to do that if any man ever grew overly bold with me."

"Was I too bold with you? You seemed to like it--at least until you ran off and left me in agony."

"I did rather like it," she admitted reluctantly. She could hardly deny it after what had happened between them in her bedchamber. The sparks that crackled between them were too bright to be dismissed. "But it frightened me as well"

"I frightened you?" he said tightly, and she wished she could see his face and read what was in his eyes.

"I-well, I think I frightened myself," she said. "I was a silly, naive girl back then, but I thought myself so bold and brave to be sneaking into your club. I was in over my head."

"And now?"

"Now I am not so naive any longer. I have traveled a great deal and met many men." Men like Lord Hammond, who were angry when they were denied, and men like

Jack, handsome and foolish. Men weak, and men so strong they ran over everyone in their path. But she still felt just as silly as ever when it came to Dominic. "You should stay away from me."

He shook his head, and his lips brushed softly over her skin. "What role do you play now, Sophia?" he whispered against her hair. "What secrets do you keep?"

"I-I am only myself," she answered, even though she often had no idea what that meant. "I am no Desdemona, no Ophelia."

"You definitely are not. You're the enchantress in her dark palace, concocting spells, mixing up your potions and poisons." His mouth trailed a light path over her temple and the curve of her cheek, the merest, softest brush. Her eyes drifted closed, and she shivered.

"I have no magic spells," she said shakily. If she did, she

wouldn't be where she was, alone in the world. Unsure of what to do next.

"That's where you are wrong," he said. His mouth trailed down to her throat, open and hungry as her head fell back, and he traced a ribbon of burning kisses over her skin. "You have a spell that makes me keep coming back to your side even when I know very well I should not. That Huntingtons are always trouble."

Sophia gasped as his tongue tasted the pulse that beat frantically at the base of her throat. She held on tighter to his shoulders, her nails digging into him through the fabric of his velvet coat. She wished it was his bare skin, hot and damp under her hands. She wanted to feel him, all of him, as he rose above her and filled the whole world with only him, only that moment between them.

"No, you shouldn't," she whispered. His mouth trailed over the curve of her bare shoulder as his strong hand held her hard around the waist. "But I do like it when you do..."

"You taste like sunshine," he said hoarsely against her skin. "Do you want me to stop?"

Sophia shook her head. Then she forgot everything completely when his other hand slid up her waist and cupped her breast through the satin of her gown.

His fingers curled around her, and she felt his thumb trace lightly over her nipple. It hardened under his touch, and her head fell back as she let the sensations rush over her. The hot pleasure of his touch was delicious, and she craved more and more of it. What would it feel like if his mouth closed over her bare breast? If he touched her with nothing between them?

His thumb and forefinger closed over her nipple and plucked at it lightly, and she whispered his name. His teeth set to her shoulder and she felt him smile against her.

"Sophia," he said, his voice so rough she could barely recognize it. "You are so beautiful."

So are you, she thought as she looked down at his golden head against her. He was like a bright god. She twined her fingers in his hair and felt its silk shift through her touch. She tugged at it as he plucked at her nipple again, pulling his hair hard enough to hurt, but he said nothing. He just scraped his teeth against her and drew her even tighter to his body. His palm slid under the curve of her buttocks, and she felt the press of his erection against her through their clothes.

She had never wanted anything like she wanted Dominic now. It was a dark abyss that would consume her, yet she couldn't help but leap into it head-first.

As Sophia watched in dazed shock, he fell to his knees in front of her and her skirts fell back over him. She tried to kick him away, but his hands closed hard over the soft, bare skin of her thighs above her stockings. His fingertips caressed her there, feather-light just on the tender crease at the top of her leg, and he pressed her legs apart.

She felt the hot touch of his breath on her most intimate place, light as a sigh, just before his tongue plunged deep inside.

Damn it all! Her eyes fluttered shut, and she held tight to the railing as a trembling, burning rush of pure sensation shot through her body. He seemed to know instinctively just how she liked to be kissed, how she liked to be touched--just *there*.

He licked one slow, languid stroke then another, before he flicked at that tiny, sensitive spot with the tip of his tongue. She felt herself contract at that touch, felt a rush of wetness trickle onto her inner thigh, and he groaned at the taste.

How savagely she wanted him! How she had missed this feeling of being so vitally alive, so aware of her body. For just an instant, she let herself feel it, let him pleasure her.

A sudden burst of raucous laughter broke into her sensual dream. Her eyes flew open, and she found that they had not actually jumped together into some new world. They were still on the theater walkway, and there were other people nearby. Including his family.

Oh, damn it all, she thought again in a hot rush of panic. She had been reckless before in her life, but never quite like this. Dominic let her go and rose to his feet, and she backed away from him as she tried to draw in a breath. Her skirts fell around her again, and she pulled up the cap sleeve of her bodice. Her hand trembled on the slippery fabric.

Dominic leaned toward her as if he would reach for her again. His face was taut with lust, his eyes hooded, but then he turned away. As Sophia watched, confused, he crossed his arms over his chest, and his shoulders rose with a deep breath.

"I should rejoin the others," she said softly. Camille would be looking for her soon, if she hadn't been distracted by some new flirtation. But Sophia felt too flushed and shaky to face anyone.

"I'll take you," he said. His voice sounded very far away, and he didn't turn to face her.

How could he move from the hot rush of passion to this chilly distance so fast? Sophia wished she knew how to do that, too. Perhaps she was out of practice with her own acting skills.

"I think it's best if I go alone for the moment," she said. She heard another burst of laughter, louder and closer this time. "They can't be far."

Dominic slowly turned to face her, and his expression was as cool and blank as a classical statue. A handsome Apollo. "At least let me watch until you are safe," he said. "I won't let them see that we're together."

At first, Sophia had the irrational flash of thought that Dominic was ashamed to be seen with her. Then she laughed at her hurt. Of course they should not be seen together. She was at a crossroads in her life, trying to see where she should go next. The last thing she needed at this moment was another scandal, another wave of gossip, especially with her cousin Elizabeth in Paris. That could be her way back to her family.

She nodded. "Very well. But really, what trouble could I get into here at a theater?" Beyond the trouble she had already found...

Dominic laughed. "More trouble than anywhere else, I fear."

Sophia nodded. She began to turn away, but suddenly Dominic reached out and caught her gloved hand in his. She spun around and found him watching her, smiling. She distrusted that smile more than anything else.

"I haven't forgotten that diary, Lady Sophia," he said, a thread of steel running through his quiet voice. "I still would like to buy it from you."

The diary. What strange hold did it have over him? Why would someone like Dominic want a long-dead woman's crumbling journal? The mystery just made Sophia want to hold on to it, to hold on to Mary, even more.

She slid her hand out of his. She could think so much more clearly when he wasn't touching her. "It's not for sale. And why would you want it, anyway?"

Dominic gave a careless shrug, but Sophia wasn't fooled. She could see the dark, determined glint in his eyes.

"I am interested in old family history," he said. "Perhaps there is something there I could turn into a play."

"I doubt it. Mary Huntington led a quiet life, from what I've read so far." A quiet, sad life, slowly destroyed by unrequited love. Heartbreaking, yes, but not the stuff of great drama.

"I would still like to read it," Dominic said. "If you won't sell it to me, may I at least take a look at it?"

Sophia studied Dominic's face. She wondered if he looked anything like Mary's husband. If he did, surely Mary's heart had broken all over again every time she looked into his beautiful eyes and didn't see what she longed for there. Sophia suddenly wanted to be away from Dominic, to be away from herself when she looked at him. "Perhaps," she said quickly. "Now I really must go and find the others."

She hurried away, hardly seeing where she was going until she found a narrow flight of stairs leading down from the walkway. She could hear laughter again, but it had moved further away. As she climbed down to the stage below, she was suddenly surrounded by looming scenery, painted images of meadows and drawing rooms that created a confusing vista that closed in around her.

Sophia twirled in a circle, disoriented and breathless. She could still hear voices, but they seemed at once nearby and very far away. As she stared up into the darkness of the walkways, the back of her neck suddenly tingled, as if someone watched her.

Her heart pounding, she swung around, only to be confronted by more shadows. There was a flash of movement, like a break in dark storm clouds that rippled around her.

"Who is there?" she called. "I think I'm lost..."

But there was no answer. Sophia stood very still, and as she listened closely, she heard the faint sound of footsteps hurrying away.

I must be imagining things, she thought, rubbing her hand over her brow. Surely she was just tired, and the fantastical atmosphere of the theater was overcoming her senses. She was beginning to imagine her life was a play, with mysterious, dark heroes and villains watching from the night.

She rushed between the scenery, hurrying forward blindly, until at last she heard Camille calling out to her. "Sophie! There you are. Wherever did you vanish to? Monsieur Caville is taking us to that little cafe I told you about, it should be such fun..."

From the Diary of Mary St. Claire Huntington

I miss my family most desperately since I lost the child. There, I have written it, I can see the words here in blackest ink, so everyone may know they are true. My sister and mother write to me every week, and I sit here by this window and wait for their letters as if they were fragments of the real world flung into the recesses of my lonely tower. They write of such ordinary things-- the garden, a marriage in the village, a new dress, but to me every word is manna from Heaven. I used to think my family so dull, so ordinary! But now I miss them, and I think they are exactly what a family should be.

My husband's family--they are nothing like that, even when they come to visit us here. And they seem to frown every time they look at me, as if they expect something from me I cannot give, I cannot be. John says I imagine things, that our love should be enough to make me happy, and I used to think that as well.

But perhaps things are looking brighter for us. Word has come that the king's brother, the Duke of York himself, is to visit us on a hunting trip! John seems excited to think our position at Court is improving, and I spend all my time planning the visit. I pray this works out as my husband hopes it will.

Eleven

A CHOCOLATE SHOP. How difficult could it be to work there? And yet they had turned her down when she tried to apply, saying she was too fine a lady to be behind the counter

Sophia stood outside the large, gleaming window of the chocolatier and examined the tempting array of elaborate sweet treats laid out there. The Aide Demande sign in the door was still there, but they had not wanted *her* help. Could she really find some way to be useful?

"Excusez, madame," a couple said as they brushed past her into the store. She stepped back out of their way, and suddenly caught a glimpse of a man's reflection in the window. He was watching her intently with a half-smile on his lips.

A smile she knew all too well now. Dominic St. Claire. "Considering new employment, Sophia?" he said. "Or do you just have a sweet tooth today?"

Sophia was caught between anger and the desire to laugh. He always seemed to catch her in her most off-guard moments. "Both, I suppose," she answered. She turned to him with a polite smile, hoping she could maintain her facade with him today. "Who doesn't like chocolate?"

"I am not so fond of it, I confess, but my sister Isabel loves it," he said. "I thought I might fetch her a little treat today."

"Don't let me keep you then," Sophia said quickly.

"There is no hurry. If you intend to apply for another position, you may need assistance."

Sophia shook her head. "I don't think I will be making any inquiries today."

"Then maybe you would do me the honor of walking with me for a while? It's a very fine day."

It was a fine day, sunny and warm, the streets crowded with people enjoying themselves. Sophia was even tempted to go with him, too much so. She knew she shouldn't be with him, that he was too dangerous for a woman's good sense, but she couldn't seem to help herself.

"Why?" she asked with a teasing smile. "To warn me away from your brother again? Or perhaps to try to buy the old diary-- which still is not for sale."

Dominic threw back his head and laughed. The sunlight caught on his bright hair, and several passing ladies faltered in their steps to watch him.

"No more, Mrs. Westman," he said. "I think we understand each other on those scores now."

"Indeed we do."

"Then let me make amends for my behavior. Let me buy you a cup of tea in that cafe over there. I think we do still have things to talk about."

Sophia glanced over at the cafe. It looked crowded, noisy, and affable, not a place where much trouble could happen. It was such a lovely afternoon, just begging to be wasted away at a cafe with a handsome man. And if she was to be honest with herself, she had to admit she wanted to know more about Dominic.

"Very well, one cup of tea," she said. He gave her a brilliant smile and led her to the tables arrayed outside, where they found a quiet spot in the shade of a red awning. Dominic summoned a pretty waitress with one flashing smile, and she seemed to spend an inordinate time giggling at him until she brought the tea.

"So why do you want to work in a chocolate shop?" Dominic asked when the waitress sashayed away. "Do you enjoy working so much?"

Sophia slowly removed her gloves before she answered. "I would enjoy working at something, I think. But my experience of the culinary arts is rather...limited, I confess."

Dominic laughed. "I would never have guessed," he said.

Sophia smiled and studied him closely for any sign that she was boring him, but he watched her closely, attentively. "But when I was a child I would often sneak down to the kitchens, where our cook would give me treats. She taught me how to make a cup of chocolate by careful stirring and measuring, and--well, it sounds odd, but those were some of my happiest moments. The smell of the chocolate, the warmth, the patient attention of the cook, who never belittled my efforts even when I spilled or burned the chocolate."

"A duke's niece taking refuge in the kitchen?"

"Yes, exactly. Those days ended when my mother found out what was happening and forbade me to go to the kitchens," Sophia said. She still felt a pang of that old disappointment. "I still make a very fine cup of chocolate, though."

Dominic laughed, and somehow she sensed he was in a light-hearted mood today. Usually, even though he smiled and was charming, there was some sort of cloudy watchfulness behind his eyes. Maybe his play was going very well.

Then she noticed the waitress smiling at him through the window, her pretty dimples flashing. Maybe his good mood was due to something else entirely.

Sophia stirred slowly at her tea, not looking up at him. "I'm surprised you wanted to spend so much time in the kitchens," he said teasingly. "Aren't duke's nieces usually tied up in ribbons and lace in the drawing room?"

Sophia had to laugh. If only he knew how true those words

were. "Something like that. But I was always interested in talking to people, all sorts of people. Finding out about their lives. I couldn't always do that trussed up like a porcelain doll by my family."

"You like to build characters in your mind," he said.

Sophia peeked up at him from beneath her hat brim. "Yes," she said. "Exactly. I liked making pictures of their days in my imagination. What they did, what they thought. Like a play, I suppose."

"People are endlessly fascinating, I agree," Dominic said. "And the theater is like life amplified, explained. Have you ever thought of becoming an actress?"

Sophia was startled. "I-no, never. An actress?"

"You said you were looking for work. The milliner, the chocolate shop. Why not a theater?"

Sophia could feel herself blushing. He, Dominic St. Claire, thought she could be an actress? For one wild moment she let herself imagine it. "I am so flattered you think so, but I've only done some amateur theatricals at family house parties. I've never learned how to really act."

Dominic shrugged. "There are things you can be taught, like projecting your voice and stage movement. But some things can't be taught. Natural interest and insight into people, for one. Presence is another. You must know how beautiful you are."

Sophia laughed. She could feel her blush deepening, turning hotter as it spread across her cheeks. "You are too kind."

"Not at all. I'm always honest about the theater. You should try acting."

"I think I would enjoy that, but..."

"But what?"

"But I am sure my family would not like that, if I am ever to be reconciled to them." Even as Sophia said the words, she could see that her hopes of returning to the security of the Huntingtons seemed further away than ever. "All my attempts at respectability seem to fail!"

Dominic leaned back lazily in his chair. "Respectability is overrated, I think," he said. "Yet you wish to go back to your family?"

Sophia shrugged and took a sip of her tea. "It seems like the right thing to do at this point in my life. Even black sheep must settle down eventually. I have surely caused them enough trouble."

"Have you indeed?" Dominic said quietly. He was silent for a long moment, as the laughter of the other patrons flowed around them. He studied her closely until she feared she would start to fidget, and then suddenly he smiled again. "How very interesting you are, Sophia Westman."

"Not as interesting as *you*, I think," she said. "Tell me more about your play."

Dominic nodded and followed her lead in the change in subject. But even as they chatted lightly about the theater, she couldn't shake the sense that something between them had changed.

* * *

Sophia Westman really was a great beauty, Dominic thought as he watched her laughing in the sunlight. Her black hair, coiled neatly beneath her hat, gleamed like rare ebony, and her pale skin was touched with rose-pink over her high, sculpted cheekbones. He had never seen eyes quite the color of hers before, almost like the sugared violets in a patisserie window.

Even as she tried to hide under her drab, dark clothes, that beauty showed through. He hadn't lied to her. If she could recite a line with any conviction at all, she would be a sensation on the stage.

And if her being an acclaimed actress shocked her family, all the better. A woman like her *should* shun convention, shun anyone who tried to stifle her.

Surely she had once thought that, too, or she wouldn't have

eloped with Westman. But she wanted to return to her family now.

His mind often seemed to work like the plot of a play, and now one was forming in his imagination as he watched Sophia smile at him. The beautiful, disgraced daughter of an ancient family, thrown out onto a cold world. All her efforts at reconciliation rebuffed, until her heart hardened toward them and she threw herself into a life of scandal.

Or perhaps a future life on the stage? With a notorious family like the St. Claires? Perhaps even as his mistress? How the Huntingtons would hate that.

Twelve

SOPHIA RUBBED her hand over her eyes and stared down at the column of numbers in the account book. Surely they hadn't moved, but they seemed to swim in front of her. Her skill at book-keeping obviously had not improved, but after her failed attempt at finding other employment she needed to find a way to earn her keep. She kept remembering Dominic's words, that she could be an actress, and she was intrigued by them. She had always loved the theater. But how her family would hate that.

After she returned from the cafe, Sophia had reluctantly gone along with Camille and her friends to a new restaurant. She hadn't been in the mood for champagne and oysters, but after all that had happened that day, she hadn't wanted to be alone. Thinking too much was obviously not good for her. Among that noisy, convivial company, she had begun to forget.

And neither was too much champagne good for her. Sophia reached for her glass of soda water and took a long sip, yet it didn't seem to help much. The numbers still persisted in wriggling around on the page.

Suddenly there was a knock at the office door. "Yes?" Sophia called, glad of the distraction.

Makepeace, the English butler, stepped into the room. Sophia wasn't sure where Camille had found him, but he was the perfect major-domo for an exclusive gaming club. Quiet, watchful, and unfailingly discreet. He saw everything and revealed nothing, including his own thoughts.

Sophia wished she could be more like him.

"You have a visitor, Madame Westman," Makepeace said. "In the salon."

"A visitor? At this time of day?" Sophia said. So early in the afternoon, everyone she knew was either still sequestered in their chambers, as Camille was, or out buying flowers to apologize for whatever had happened the night before. They were seldom paying calls.

Perhaps it was Dominic? Sophia's heart beat a little faster at the thought even as she told herself she was being ridiculous. She had just seen him yesterday at the cafe; he wouldn't be calling on her now.

"She won't give her card, or even a name," Makepeace said with a sniff at such a breach of etiquette. "But she was rather insistent that she must see you."

A woman. Not Dominic after all--of course. Whoever it was, Sophia had to see her off quickly and then try to get back to the accounts. Perhaps it would be something interesting to break up the quiet day and distract her.

"Thank you, Makepeace. I will be down in a moment." As the butler bowed and left, Sophia quickly smoothed her hair and snatched up a shawl to wrap around her shoulders. The day had grown chilly, and no fires were lit. With the club closed and all the merrymakers gone, the old rooms were silent and cold. The main salon seemed cavernous and echoing, almost ghostly in the faint light that streamed from the one uncurtained window. A woman in a short, jet-beaded black velvet cape and a veiled bonnet sat on a sofa at the far end of the room with her back to the door, and she was so very still she could have been a ghost herself. Sophia saw that the butler, ever efficient, had left a tea tray on a table, but the woman hadn't touched it.

Oh, dear, Sophia thought. She hoped this was not some disgruntled wife whose husband had lost too much at the faro tables or flirted too obviously with one of the pretty dealers. Whatever it was, surely it was best to deal with it quickly. Sophia pasted on her brightest, most charming smile despite her aching head and hurried across the room. "I am so sorry to keep you waiting, madame. How may I help you?"

The woman slowly turned around. The heavy veil was tucked back to frame a pale, perfect oval face and silvery-blonde curls. Sophia froze in her tracks. It was her cousin Elizabeth.

"Hello, Sophia. It's good to see you again," Elizabeth answered as she rose to her feet. The rustle of her silk gown seemed inordinately loud in the silent room. A tentative smile touched her lips, and for an instant, Sophia glimpsed the Elizabeth she had known long ago.

When they were girls, Elizabeth had been sweet and a little shy, a beautiful example for Sophia's parents to hold up as model behavior for a Huntington female--a model Sophia, with her wildness, simply couldn't follow. But there had been a hidden streak of mischief to Elizabeth as well, and a wonderful silvery bell of a laugh that made everyone want to laugh with her. Elizabeth, Sophia, and their cousin Aidan had come up with many ridiculous larks during stuffy family holidays.

Then, when Elizabeth was only eighteen and Sophia sixteen, all that had ended. Elizabeth suddenly vanished for several weeks and then was quickly married to Lord Severn, a man decades her senior. She'd appeared at the ducal estate for family occasions again, but the laughter was gone. Elizabeth had become silent and vague, as if she was off in her own little world where no one could follow.

Sophia hadn't seen Elizabeth since before she married Jack, though she'd heard that Lord Severn had died. Now here Elizabeth was, in Paris, sitting in Sophia's own salon. Her blue eyes were bright as a summer sky, with flashes of the old Elizabeth. But her smile slowly faded when Sophia couldn't move.

She felt frozen and awkward with surprise. "Cousin Elizabeth," she finally managed to say. "What a surprise."

"Yes, I suppose it must be," Elizabeth answered. "I didn't know you were in Paris until I saw you at the theater last night. You are looking well."

"So are you," Sophia said truthfully. Elizabeth had always been beautiful, but now she'd lost that doll-like stillness. It reminded Sophia of the days when they were girls together, of times with her family when it hadn't been all battles or frosty silences. She had no idea what she should feel in that moment, as she stood there looking at the only member of her family she had seen in months. Part of her longed to rush forward and hug Elizabeth. Yet part of her wanted to turn and run, to deny that she was a Huntington.

"I heard about Lord Severn," Sophia said. "I am sorry."

Elizabeth nodded. "It was mercifully quick, at least. I'm also sorry about Captain Westman. You hadn't been married very long."

"No. Not long."

"Yet you must have loved him a great deal, to be brave enough to do what you did."

Sophia wasn't sure what to say to that. Love Jack? Once she had thought she loved him, that he would rescue her from her family and from herself. Instead he'd taught her only that she had to rely on herself alone.

"Yes," she said simply. "How-how is everyone? I have heard from no one but Aidan in a long while."

Elizabeth smiled, and her beautiful face became transcendent, like a sunbeam, an angel. "Ah, yes, Aidan. He is disgustingly happy, writing his plays and living with his new wife, as he deserves to be, even though he is quite ostracized by the family. And everyone else is much the same. Edward is engaged to be married any day now."

"Edward is engaged?" Sophia said. She could hardly be surprised. After a series of youthful peccadilloes, her brother had learned to toe the family line. He had always ended up doing what was expected of a Huntington, outwardly anyway.

"Yes, to the daughter of one of your father's neighbors. Our uncle the duke is quite happy about it."

Sophia nodded. So, since her brother was properly engaged and the two black sheep, Sophia and Aidan, were in exile and out of sight, all was well in the Huntington world again. But what had brought Elizabeth here? "Why are you in Paris, Elizabeth?"

There was a tiny flicker of unease in Elizabeth's eyes. "I thought a little holiday might help me get some things in order."

In order? As far as Sophia knew, nothing in Elizabeth's calm life had ever been in the slightest bit disordered. "What sort of things?"

Elizabeth shrugged. "I'm just learning to manage widowhood, I suppose. I have never had to be on my own before. And Paris seemed like the best place to do that. I was glad to see you were here. You seem to be doing well with your-your business ventures." She gestured around the room at the card tables and roulette wheels. "So very exciting."

"It's a living," Sophia answered. She reached for the tea tray for something to do and carefully poured out two cups.

"I envy you," Elizabeth said, drawing off her kid gloves. As she took the cup from Sophia, the dim light caught on her large diamond wedding ring--and on a

long scar that bisected the back of her hand.

It was something Sophia had never seen before, that stark pink flaw on her cousin's perfect skin, and it startled her. But Elizabeth was sipping at her tea as if nothing was amiss at all.

"Why should you envy me?" Sophia murmured. "You were always the perfect one, the one who knew exactly what to do and how to behave." Who was content with her life, while Sophia was always leaping before she looked.

Elizabeth gave a bitter little laugh. "I am only a good actress. I have had to be. But you, Sophia--you know yourself. You stand up for what you want." She studied the room over the edge of the china cup, an unreadable expression on her face. "You are free."

Sophia hardly knew what to say in the silence that hung between them after those strange words. "Anyone could do what I did."

Elizabeth shook her head. "No. A coward like me could never run away like that. Whenever I try to be free, it ends up in something very bad. I am trapped where I was born."

"Is your life so very terrible, Elizabeth?" Sophia asked quietly, concerned. "What has happened?"

"My life is not bad at all. Especially now," Elizabeth said with another sudden, sunny smile. "It is the strangest thing, Sophia. I had a letter from your mother only a few days ago."

"My mother?" Sophia was dizzy with the sudden change in subject.

"Yes. She thought I might run into you here in Paris. She had heard you were traveling again."

"I am quite sure she did not send her love," Sophia said with a wry laugh.

"Oh, you are wrong, cousin. Your mother misses you a great deal."

That was even more surprising. For an instant, Sophia remembered when she was a child, and the echo of her mother's rare laughter as she walked through the gardens of their country home with Sophia and Edward, chasing them around the flowerbeds and through the old maze. The smell of her lily of the valley perfume in the air when she knelt and hugged them. Such moments had seldom lasted long--Sophia's father disliked the noise of children playing, and her mother was very busy with her social obligations. But they had been sweet moments nonetheless.

And then when Sophia's father had cast her out when she wanted to marry Jack, her mother had cried but done nothing. The family always came first with her, even above her daughter.

But Elizabeth said her mother was asking about her now.

Against her better judgment, Sophia felt a rush of hope. Could this be what she had been waiting for?

"What did she write to you?" Sophia said carefully, stirring her tea.

"Merely that she thought perhaps you might have married again."

"I have hardly had time to think of such things."

"I know. Neither of us has been widowed long, and really who would want to jump back into the matrimonial state when it has barely been escaped? But your mother..." Elizabeth hesitated.

"My mother what?"

"She asked me to see if you had any new suitors. Anyone--well, I believe her word was 'suitable.'"

Sophia had to laugh. Her mother, who'd abandoned her, was worried about her suitors? "Mama asked you to spy on my love life?"

A touch of pink bloomed in Elizabeth's pale cheeks. "Not spy! Just find out how you are doing. Since we're family."

"And did she have any candidates in mind?"

"Not at all. She merely hinted that a husband who was accept-able to your father might--facilitate your return home. She does miss you, Sophia, I am sure of it. And I've missed you, too. With you and Aidan gone, life in the family is very quiet."

"I see," Sophia murmured, though in truth she didn't see at all. Was this some sort of olive branch being extended, however obliquely, through her cousin? The possibility of a return home, to her old life, no longer alone in the world--if she married prop-erly and mended her ways. If she caused no more trouble.

"I miss you as well, Elizabeth," Sophia said carefully. "I miss how things once were. But I fear I have no suitors, respectable or otherwise, at the moment. And even if I did, it is probably much too late for me to change my ways."

Elizabeth nodded, a sad smile on her lips. "I have done what I told your mother I would do, and I've given you her message. But if I were you, Sophia, I would not go back. What you have here is quite extraordinary. You shouldn't trade it for something cold and airless. It would suffocate you."

Before Sophia could ask Elizabeth what she meant and demand to know what had really happened to her cousin, Elizabeth suddenly put down her teacup and rose to her feet. She leaned over to kiss Sophia's cheek.

"I must go now," she said. "But I hope we will see each other again before I leave Paris. You don't need to see me out. I remember the way."

She lowered the veil on her bonnet and hurried out of the room, leaving only a trace of violet perfume in the air. Sophia went to the window and glanced out to see Elizabeth being handed into her carriage on the street below.

For a moment, Sophia wondered if she had imagined the whole encounter. It had been so long since she saw any member of her family. Now there was the hint that she could be welcomed back as she had hoped, if only she did what a Huntington should. If she found a staid, dull husband and settled down.

But *staid and dull* never seemed to be interested in her. All she seemed to find were men as complicated and difficult as Jack, Lord Hammond--and Dominic.

Dominic St. Claire was definitely *not* staid. And a St. Claire would be the last person her family would consider acceptable. Aidan left the family when he married Lily St. Claire, and Sophia envied him. He'd found himself, found happiness, when he found love. But she would never be so lucky as Aidan. Surely it was better to take this opening and find a way to return to her family, as she had hoped.

The salon door opened and Camille hurried in amid a rustle of feathers and organdy ruffles. "Sophie, did you have a caller?" she asked as she poured herself some tea. "I saw a grand carriage pulling away. It must have been someone terribly interesting."

"Yes, but I am sorry to disappoint you and your matchmaking, Camille," Sophia said with a laugh. "It was not a gentleman admirer, but my cousin Elizabeth, Lady Severn."

"Ah, so sad! I was sure it was a fascinating man. But I thought you said you were estranged from your family now?" Camille nibbled at one of the untouched sandwiches.

"I am. I haven't see Elizabeth in ages, but she happened to catch a glimpse of me at the theater."

"Oh, yes, the theater." Camille gave her a mischievous smile. "You quite vanished there for a while, Sophie. As did the handsome Monsieur Dominic."

"I got lost amid all the scenery backstage," Sophia said, trying to sound careless. Trying not to remember what had really happened there on the walkway. "He helped me find my way."

"Did he indeed?" Camille said, much too innocently. "How kind of him."

"Yes. Very kind."

"Well, then, c'est vrai. At least you are not still wandering around lost backstage, or you could not attend our little al fresco luncheon tomorrow."

"Al fresco luncheon?" Sophia said, glad of the change of subject. She left the window and went to see if there was any tea left. "Are we having a party?"

"We are not, but my friend Madame Dumas is. I saw her while I was out shopping yesterday, and she invited us to accompany a group to Montmartre for a little country outing. Count Danilov, that Russian who has been courting me so charmingly, will be there, and he is bringing friends. And I think the fresh air would do you good."

"Who else will be there?" Sophia asked suspiciously. Camille had let the topic of Dominic drop a bit too easily.

Camille shrugged. "No one in particular, I suppose. Just some friends. Do say you will come, Sophie! It will be such fun."

Sophia laughed. *Such fun*--like when she indulged in too much champagne last night, trying to forget what had happened with Dominic? But she had to admit a country picnic did sound lovely. She had been in the city for too long. "Very well, then, I will go. But I warn you, no matchmaking..."

* * *

"Is everything all right, my lady?"

Elizabeth smiled wearily at her maid as she handed her the veiled bonnet. Meg had been with her for a long time, through all the painful years with Severn, and she seemed to have a sense for when Elizabeth was feeling low.

For when the evil lure of the opium called to her again. But this was not one of those times. "Quite all right, Meg. I am just a bit tired."

"Were you shopping today?"

"No, I had a better errand than that. I called on a family member I have not seen in a long while."

"A family member, my lady? Here in Paris?"

"Yes. Perhaps you remember her? Lady Sophia. She is Mrs. Westman now." As the maid bustled around putting things into wardrobes, Elizabeth sat down at her vanity and drew the pins from her hair. She sighed as the heavy mass tumbled down, easing her headache.

"Lady Sophia? Of course I remember her," Meg exclaimed. "Why, the two of you used to run wild over the duke's estate. It has been ever so long since you saw her, my lady."

"Yes. Much too long." Elizabeth closed her eyes against the image in her mirror, and for a moment she was sixteen again, riding across her uncle's land with Sophia. The two of them laughing as their horses hurtled over jumps and they raced each other through the woods, as if they hadn't a care in the world.

And back then they hadn't. They were young, spoiled, free, the best of friends, as they giggled together over romantic poetry. Before the real world closed in on them, the expectations and obligations of being Huntingtons. Before her parents arranged her disastrous marriage to Severn.

Before she lost the man she really loved, Brendan St. Claire, in such a horrible way.

Elizabeth opened her eyes and found herself staring back from the glass. That all seemed so very long ago, and yet sometimes it seemed only a brief moment back in time. She could see his face so clearly, feel his kiss. But Brendan was gone completely from her life. Surely she would never see him again except from a distance.

And Severn was gone, too, the long nightmare of their marriage over at last. She hadn't touched a drop of opium in months, and she was beginning to make a new start in her life. A good first step would be to renew her lost friendship with Sophia, so she had leaped at the chance to intercede when Sophia's mother asked for her help.

Not that being in the smothering embrace of the Huntington fold was always such a good thing. Maybe Sophia was happy to have escaped. But at least they could be together again, as they were when they were girls. Elizabeth wanted to make amends for not being there when Sophia needed her.

Meg finished putting the clothes away and came to take up the brush to run it through Elizabeth's hair, gently smoothing the tangled waves. "How is Lady Sophia? She must have been happy to see you, my lady."

Elizabeth hoped she was, yet all she could sense from Sophia had been wariness. "I hope so. I only wish I could be of some help to her."

"Help, my lady?"

"I'd like for her to come back to England with me, but I'm not sure she will." If only Sophia would just let her try, she was sure that she could be of help. That they could be friends again.

"I hope she will, my lady. It would be good for you to have a friend like Lady Sophia again."

Elizabeth nodded, but she was afraid it was all much too late.

From the Diary of Mary St. Claire Huntington

The preparations for the duke's visit have been a wonderful distraction for me, and everything seems to be going well. I have ordered most of the provisions, and the house is being scoured from the attics to the root cellars. At last the grand state bed John's parents ordered so long ago will be used! John seems to think this visit means new favors for us at Court, though I fear that will mean he will be gone from me even more.

My brother is also coming to visit in the next few days, and I am sure I can persuade him to stay for the royal visit. I want to help my family any way I can, and Nick declares he has some fine news for me. I cannot wait to see him again. This is surely a new, better day in my life...

Thirteen

"MONSIEUR DOMINIC! Monsieur Brendan! You must come quickly."

Dominic glanced up from the script he was studying with a flash of irritation at the interruption. A quiet evening with no performances or engagements was rare indeed, and he needed the chance to get caught up on reviewing plays for next season at the Majestic. He had spent too much time thinking about Sophia and their conversation at the cafe. But he took one look at the red-faced actor who had just run up the stairs, and he knew it wasn't a frivolous interruption. The man looked truly frantic.

Brendan pushed himself up from the sofa where he had been lounging and reading. "What is it, Marcel?" he asked tightly. "Has there been an accident? Is someone hurt?"

Marcel shook his head, struggling to catch his breath. Dominic noticed that the man looked as if he had been through a storm, his clothes pulled askew and his hair standing on end. A bruise stood out on his cheek. "No, no, but someone will be very soon if you don't hurry! It is Monsieur James. He came with us to Madame Brancusi's establishment tonight and has been drinking. There was this man, he said Monsieur James was cheating at cards..."

Dominic exchanged alarmed glances with Brendan. James and brothels were a dangerous combination. He seemed to find trouble lurking every time he entered one, and he was ripe for fights and cons. And when one added in drink...

"Let's go," Dominic said, and snatched up his coat from the back of his chair.

They'd visited Madame Brancusi's when they first arrived in Paris. It had a reputation even in London as a place of luxury and elegance. But tonight it looked as if a dockside brawl had suddenly been transported to a gilt and brocade haven. When Dominic ducked through the door and saw the havoc of Madame Brancusi's salon, he almost laughed at the farcical scene. Girls stood on velvet sofas and atop marble tables, shrieking, sobbing, or calling out encouragement to the men fighting on the fine silk carpets. One of the whores threw a glass at the velvet-covered wall. It cracked and splattered amber liquid down a marble sculpture of a couple entwined in anal coitus, but it didn't deter the fighting one bit.

The air, thick with the scents of cigar smoke, expensive perfumes, and brandy, rang with shouts and grunts and the sounds of fists connecting with flesh. Bodies clad in fashionable black evening coats, now torn and ripped, rolled atop overturned card tables.

"The world has obviously gone mad," Brendan shouted.

Dominic had to agree. He was used to tempers flaring out of control--it happened every week at the Devil's Fancy, a potent combination of drink, money, and women. But there were ways to defuse such situations. Madame Brancusi was a professional. He was surprised she'd let things get so out of hand.

"Never mind that," Dominic shouted back to Brendan. "We need to find James and get him out of here."

They waded into the fray, pushing heaving bodies out of the way as they searched each face for their brother's. Dominic drove a fist into one man's jaw. One of the girls leaped onto his back as he pushed past her table. He neatly deposited her on a sofa and ignored her screams.

Brendan was right. This was a madhouse. And he wished he had time to leap right into the fray, to lose himself in the blood-lust of a good fight. He needed to free some of the frustration he had kept locked inside him ever since he met Sophia Westman again.

But James had to be his first mission now, not brawling. James was no good in a fight, and yet he very often seemed to find himself in trouble just like this.

Dominic drove an elbow back into another assailant's midsection as the man tried to choke him. As Dominic shoved him away, he finally glimpsed James. His brother lay in a dark corner, sprawled out on a carpet of scattered cards. His coat and cravat were gone, brandy spilled on his shirt, and there was a bruise blooming on his jaw.

Dominic glanced over his shoulder to wave at Brendan, who had a man in a headlock. Brendan calmly nodded and shoved his opponent away to wend his way across the room.

Dominic knelt and grabbed James's arm to pull him to his feet. James groaned, and his head lolled back as his eyes fluttered open.

"Wha' happened?" he muttered.

"That's what we would like to know," Dominic said. "How do you find yourself in such fixes, James? Surely a monastery would erupt in a brawl if you set foot in it."

"Not my fault!" James cried, then moaned as if at the loud noise in his head. "I don't even know how this started. I was just having a game of cards, and the next thing I knew there was this man…"

"And you were unconscious on the floor, covered in spilled brandy?"

"Lost all my money," James grumbled.

"We need to get out of here," Brendan said as he reached their corner at last. "I think I saw a back door the last time we were here."

"You always do know all the exits," Dominic said, trying to hold on to James as his brother listed to one side.

"One never knows," Brendan said tightly. He looped James's other arm around his shoulders and led them through a doorway half-hidden behind a velvet curtain.

Dominic saw that it led to a steep, narrow flight of stairs twisting up to a dimly lit corridor. A thick carpet muffled their footsteps, and a series of small peepholes lined the dark-painted walls. Tiny points of light shone from behind them, and Dominic could hear soft groans and gasps, the crack of a whip, a shout.

So not everyone was involved in the fight downstairs.

"A spy system," Dominic said with a grin. "Most ingenious."

"Perhaps we should install something similar in the Devil's Fancy when we get home," Brendan said. "But there's no time to examine Madame Brancusi's interior design right now. We need to get James out of here and sobered up."

The words were barely out of Brendan's mouth when a door flew open at the end of the corridor. It bounced back against the wall, and Madame Brancusi herself appeared there.

The proprietress of the place was an imposing woman under any circumstances, tall and buxom, with dyed black hair piled high atop her head and an imperious glint in her eyes. Tonight she looked like a classical Fury, with a whip in her hand, her hair falling from its pins, her elaborate velvet gown the color of fresh blood.

"Allez!" she shouted to the hulking, muscle-bound guards who appeared behind her. "Get downstairs now and take care of that rabble. I won't have such merde in my place."

As the guards ran past, Dominic exchanged a quick glance with Brendan over James's slumped head. They started to follow the guards back down the stairs to beat a retreat, but Madame Brancusi stopped them with a shout and a crack of her whip.

"You! Get back here," she called. "You English are nothing but trouble. Don't think I don't know what happened down there."

"Then you know more than us, chère madame," Dominic said in his calmest, most soothing voice. "We only just arrived."

But she wouldn't be calmed. She stalked toward them, her eyes glittering. "You can't fool me. And I know you are his brother." She spat out the word "his," gesturing toward the half-comatose James with her whip. "He began this mess."

"I'm sure there was some misunderstanding," Brendan said carefully. "Our brother is young and can be rash at times, but he doesn't *start* trouble."

Madame Brancusi shook her head. "I have a man in my office, one of my best customers, who says Monsieur James was drinking heavily and accused him of cheating. When he tried to talk with Monsieur James to calm him, Monsieur James hit him. I cannot have such behavior in my place. You see how one drunken cochon throwing a punch is like a domino. It becomes out of control in a second."

James sagged against Dominic's side, and Dominic scowled. He definitely did not need this right now--or ever. His own life was enough of a mess without James messing up his own in the bargain. "Tell that man to call on us tomorrow with his complaints," he said brusquely.

"Non! You will tell him yourself, right now," Madame Brancusi shouted with another crack of her whip. "In my office. Allez vous en."

"I think we should take care of this right now," Brendan muttered. Dominic nodded, and between them they hauled James after her through the open doorway.

Where the rest of the house was plush and luxurious, covered with velvet and gilt, the office was small and utilitarian, with only the desk and a few straight-backed chairs. The only sign that the room belonged to a bawdy house was a series of framed prints on the walls--couples in vaguely classical draperies involved in coitus in various positions. It was obviously a place where patrons who had misbehaved were brought to be reprimanded, and not in a fun way.

Or there were those with a grievance. A man who sat in the shadows at the far end of the room rose to his feet as they entered.

Dominic's eyes narrowed as he studied the man. He looked a bit familiar, as if he had seen him somewhere in London long ago, but Dominic couldn't quite place him. He was tall, well-built, with graying dark hair and sharp dark eyes, obviously a man of breeding and confidence.

The man smiled, all polite and correct, perfectly calm. Yet there was something in his demeanor, in that very stillness, that Dominic instinctively did not like. Some watchful, chilly air. The man's clothes and hair were not even mussed, as if he'd not dirtied his hands in the business outside, as if the chaos had been created for some other purpose and he had merely watched it from afar.

"This is Lord Hammond," Madame Brancusi said. "And these are Monsieur James's brothers."

She kicked out a chair, and Dominic carefully lowered James onto its wooden seat, never taking his attention from the cold-eyed Lord Hammond.

"Ah, yes. The famous St. Claire brothers," Lord Hammond said, his smile widening. But it never reached his eyes. "I saw you perform at the Theatre Nationale last week. Very entertaining."

"Not as entertaining as tonight, it would seem," Dominic said.

Lord Hammond laughed. "Indeed not. It appears your brother cannot hold his drink. You should keep a better eye on him, a poor little cub like that."

At these seemingly sympathetic, affable words, James suddenly lunged up from his chair. Dominic was caught by surprise at the quick move--his attention hadn't been on his brother, but on this strange man who suddenly seemed to have some sort of problem with the St. Claires.

"You bastard! You know it wasn't like that," James shouted. He clumsily lurched toward Lord Hammond, but Dominic caught him by the back of his collar and shoved him toward Brendan, who caught and held him neatly. "He put something in my drink. I'm sure of it."

Lord Hammond shook his head sadly. "I see the theatrics are not confined to the stage. I fear your brother was in his cups and attempted to cheat at cards. Rather clumsily, I might add."

"So that's how that brawl outside started?" Dominic said. That was a serious charge indeed, and if Hammond had something to back those words up, James was surely in trouble. "When you accused James of cheating?"

"I'm afraid that was something of an unfortunate accident," Lord Hammond answered, still infuriatingly calm. A small smile hovered around his lips, as if these proceedings pleased him very much. As if they were all acting according to some hidden script of his own. Dominic didn't care to be manipulated, not by anyone.

He glanced over at Brendan, who still held James as he watched the scene. His gaze flicked to Dominic, and Dominic saw that his brother felt the same way. Something strange was going on here, something beyond a simple brawl.

"I merely pointed out to your brother his error," Lord Hammond continued, "and he attempted to hit me. His fist went astray and landed on some other poor fellow's jaw, and--well, forgive me, chère madame." He gave Madame Brancusi a bow. "I am sorry to have marred a most pleasant evening at your exemplary establishment."

"Never mind all that," Madame Brancusi said shrilly. "I want to know who will pay for the repairs. I can't be closed to business very long, you know."

"James will." Brendan said. James turned red and opened his mouth as if to protest, only to fall silent at a cold glance from Brendan.

"I would be within my rights to call him out, of course," Lord Hammond said. "Such a slur on my honor should not be allowed to pass unchallenged."

"This isn't 1750," Brendan said. "Dueling is illegal."

"Ah, but what is such a trifle as the law to men like us?" Lord Hammond stepped closer, a muscle ticking in his lean jaw the only flaw in his cold demeanor. Dominic could clearly see that the man's smooth, polished facade was just that--a wall put up to obscure a deep well of primitive violence.

Dominic knew such a feeling because it was in him as well, far too often. That dark, wild anger that needed a place to go or it would explode. He poured it into stage villains, Iago, Don Juan, dark dukes and princes, but often it felt as if it had nowhere to go but into a storm of violence and passion. He hoped he hid it as well as this man, but that darkness still lurked there, just as it seemed to for Lord Hammond.

But what he didn't understand was why Hammond's fury would be turned on James at all. James, who fumbled through life never hurting anyone but himself. It was like a Renaissance revenge tragedy, played out on the innocent, but surely a man who didn't even know them could have no quarrel with them.

"I have heard of your family," Lord Hammond said. "The famous St. Claires, fallen from grace so long ago."

"I am sorry to say we can't return the favor," Brendan said. "We have never heard of you."

"Ah, well, unlike you and your relations, I live quietly. I have been gone from England for many months, on work for my uncle," Hammond said. "The Duke of Pendrake. Perhaps you have heard of him?"

Everyone knew of the Duke of Pendrake. He was one of the wealthiest, and most ruthless, men in England and was said to have a hand in almost every business endeavor in the Empire.

"I see you have," Hammond said, smiling again. "Perhaps then you could see why a duel would be easily overlooked, even here in France. But I see no need for such extreme action at present. It seems clear your brother is just a young pup on a spree. I hope this has taught him a small lesson."

Hammond stepped closer to Dominic and, still smiling, said quietly, "I am a good friend, but a terrible enemy, Mr. St. Claire. I don't care to be thwarted when there is something I want. You would do well to remember that, should we ever meet in the future."

Before Dominic could answer, Hammond moved away and made his farewell to the slightly appeased Madame Brancusi. After leaving a hefty payment, Dominic and Brendan hauled James out of the now-silent house and bundled him into a cab.

"How did you manage to run afoul of a man like that?" Brendan demanded. "We leave you alone for one night..."

James groaned and buried his face in his hands. "I don't know! He was the one who sat down at my table, sought me out. I have never seen him before. I didn't know he was a relative of the Duke of Pendrake."

A relation of the Duke of Pendrake--and he seemed to have a grudge against the St. Claires. Dominic frowned as he stared out the window at the dark streets flashing by.

He was sure he'd never met Hammond before, yet that glint in the man's eyes, the hard note to his strange words, said that he knew them. And he had something against them.

Dominic resolved to find out as much as he could about this Hammond. The man would discover that the St. Claires were not without resources of their own. Resources those in polite Society didn't have.

That was the one advantage of living on the shadowy margins. Of being, as Hammond had put it, "fallen from grace so long ago."

"Perhaps it would be best if you went home soon, James," Dominic said. "To London."

"No!" James cried. "I can't go home alone. Our parents would think I disgraced myself."

Brendan snorted. "And you surely will if you keep going on this way. Would you rather explain to our parents--or to Isabel?"

James sank back against the seat. It was clear he wouldn't want to talk about tonight's debacle with his twin sister. "Why does this keep happening to me?"

"Because you are young and green," Brendan said in a hard voice. "You will learn soon enough, as we've all had to."

Dominic almost laughed aloud. Once he would have agreed with Brendan; life was a stern teacher indeed, and no one in their position could afford to remain innocent for long. But some lessons it seemed would never be learned.

Why else would he keep going back to Sophia Westman, when she was the last woman in the world he should want?

Fourteen

⤲

SOPHIA LEANED her hands back on the grass and gazed up into the pure blue sky above her. She had been reluctant to go with Camille and her friends to this picnic in the hilly village of Montmartre, but now she was glad she had. A lazy afternoon was just what she needed, and this was a most unexpectedly pretty spot. A pastoral little place high above Paris, dotted with windmills and an abandoned shepherd's hut at the foot of the hill. An afternoon of laughter and good conversation--and watching Dominic.

Now they were all content with languor, resting on the picnic blankets as the afternoon slowly waned away.

"I say, you are all being far too quiet now," Camille's Russian count said, his voice slurred due to the wine they had been consuming. "I suggest we play a game."

Sophia laughed to think of anyone in the party being "quiet," especially after all the wine and brandy, the oysters and music. She felt dizzy with the sunshine and the alcohol, almost reckless-- which was never a good sign. That was always when she got into the most trouble. But if she was able to return to her family there wouldn't be many more days like this one.

She leaned back against the rough trunk of the tree and

looked across the clearing to where Dominic lolled on the grass. His face was turned up to the sunshine, his hair burning in the light, and a faint smile touched his lips. How very handsome he was. She wanted to be closer to him, to let some of that warmth into herself.

"Charades, maybe?" Camille suggested as she collapsed onto the blanket next to Count Danilov, her pale green skirts puffed out around her like a flower.

"Or cards?" someone else suggested. "We could play whist."

"We play cards all the time," Camille protested.

Count Danilov laughed. "And we are not a group of creaky old ladies waiting on your English queen, are we? No, I propose something much more fun. A way for everyone to get to know each other better."

Camille laughed and leaned on Danilov's arm. "I think we all know each other too well already," she said. "And as hostess today, I really should discourage your mischief, mon cher comte."

"Are you going to discourage *me*?" Danilov said with a teasing grin, plucking at the ruffles of Camille's skirt.

Camille giggled. "Certainly not! Mischief is what this party is all about, non? So what game do you suggest?"

"Blindman's Buff!" one tipsy lady cried.

"No, better." Danilov paused to sweep an arch glance over the lazy company. "A game that is quite popular at house parties in St. Petersburg. Hide and seek."

A wave of laughter swept over the group, like a small breath of life in their laziness. "What fun!" the tipsy lady cried, then shrieked as someone secretly pinched her.

"A nursery game?" someone else protested.

Sophia laughed. She had the feeling this wouldn't be quite like the games of nursery days. She peeked over at Dominic and saw that he still lay in the sun, his eyes closed. Something in her wanted to wake him up. "Who shall hide and who shall seek?" she said.

"The ladies shall hide, and the gentlemen seek," Danilov declared.

"Ah, isn't that how it always is?" another man said ruefully.

Sophia scrambled to her feet with the other ladies, all of them giggling as they gathered at the edge of the clearing. She gathered up her hem as Danilov began counting.

"And--now!" he shouted, and there was a burst of chaos as the women dashed away and scattered in all directions, down the hill and into the clusters of trees. For an instant, Sophia spun around, disoriented and unsure where to go, then she remembered the abandoned-looking hut she'd seen when they arrived. She lifted her skirts and ran as fast as she could down the hill, sliding a bit on the grass.

The shrieks and laughter of the others faded behind her as she kept running, gasping for breath in her tight bodice. She turned at the base of the hill and dashed to the gates. The hut loomed just beyond in the shade of a windmill, silent and dark.

She ducked through the door and let it squeak closed behind her on its rusted hinges. Suddenly she was wrapped in a blanket of silence and dusty darkness. The only light were the chalky-yellow rays of sun through the cracks in the old wooden walls, illuminating broken cabinets lining one wall and shards of crockery littering the corners. Her shoes skidded on the cracked floor, and she could

smell old woodsmoke and the heat from the day outside, as well as the pungent odor of gin. It seemed someone still used the hut for something, if only for drinking.

The quiet after all the wine and laughter made her feel dizzy. She found a small space behind one of the cabinets, and slipped between it and the wall to wait out the game. Her foot nudged a pile of tattered blankets, and she leaned back against it as she closed her eyes and let the silence wrap around her. But even there, in that solitude, she saw Dominic. She thought about the way she had tried not to watch him during the picnic, the way she would peek at him only to find him watching her, that unreadable intensity in his eyes.

The soft squeak of the door opening made her eyes fly open. Holding her breath, she peeked around the cabinet. For an instant, she saw a man's tall figure silhouetted against the light outside. Then he stepped inside, and the door shut behind him.

"I know you're here," he called quietly, too quietly for her to recognize his voice. She could only tell he was English. "I can smell your perfume."

Suddenly, Sophia had a sharp memory of Lord Hammond, how he followed her, stalked her. How he made her feel trapped, as if she couldn't breathe. She knew it was foolish, that Lord Hammond couldn't be at their party, yet still that choking fear remained. She pressed her hand to her mouth to keep from crying out and tried to make herself breathe. She could hear the man moving around the small room, steadily, stealthily. Any moment he would find her.

The darkness around her was disorienting, making those memories rush over her even more. Even stronger.

She ducked out from behind the cabinet and dashed for the door.

Suddenly hard, muscled arms closed around her waist like iron bands, and she was caught. For a second, the panic that had been growing within her broke free, cold and paralyzing. She twisted in the man's arms and kicked back at his legs, wishing she wore something sturdier than her kid shoes.

The man grunted when her foot connected with his shin, and his arms closed even harder around her. Then she smelled him, that scent of expensive, lemony cologne and clean linen that she remembered from when he lay in her bed. It was Dominic who'd caught her, not some nightmare stranger. The warm relief that washed away her panic made her laugh, at herself and her old fears, at the strange tension the drinking and the game had created. Memories of Dominic overcame the old memories of Baden-Baden, stronger and brighter.

But no less frightening.

He drew her back tighter against his chest, until she felt the softness of his fine wool coat slide against her body through the thin muslin of her gown. His lips touched the side of her neck, open and hot, trailing slowly over her skin until her eyes closed, and she sighed at the heated rush of pleasure.

"Damn it all, Dominic, you scared me," she gasped.

She felt him smile against her, just before he bit down lightly on the soft curve of her shoulder. "Cursing, Lady Sophia? So unladylike. Shocking."

Sophia slapped at his hand where it lay on her waist, but that only made him pull her closer. She felt the length of his tall, hard body all along hers. His erection was hard against her backside, and it made her desire flare even hotter.

Had she been drinking too much of the wine? Had she been overcome by the party atmosphere, the Frenchness of her Parisian life? Was that what made her wild spirit beat against the prison of good sense all over again? Or was it just Dominic who made her feel this way? As if she would burst from all the emotions and needs swirling inside of her.

"I wouldn't have to curse if you weren't so maddening, Dominic St. Claire," she said. She traced her fingertips over his hand, the bare skin of his knuckles, and his long, elegant fingers, and she wondered at the scrapes and calluses she felt there. A man who was an actor and a gamester should surely have soft hands, not ones that felt as if they'd been doing hard labor.

But she had no time to ponder that intriguing puzzle. He touched the tip of his tongue to her bare shoulder and then blew on it lightly until she shivered. That wild, yearning feeling inside her expanded until she thought she might burst out of her skin. He did that to her, Dominic. He drew out the dark recklessness that had always been her undoing.

Dominic scraped the edge of his teeth gently along her skin, making her shiver again, before he pressed an open-mouthed kiss on her skin just where her sleeve fell from her shoulder. His hand flattened against her waist and slid down over her abdomen, lower and lower, gathering up the heavy folds of her skirt as he went. Sophia sighed and let her head fall back on his shoulder.

He caught her lacy petticoats up with the skirt, and she felt the heat of his touch through the thin silk of her drawers. One fingertip traced her damp slit over the fabric, and she heard him groan when he felt how wet she was there.

Sophia spun around in his arms and stared up into his eyes. His face was chiseled and half-shadowed in the faint light that poured from the cracks in the wall. His eyes glittered with passion, and his lips curved in a wry half-smile as he looked down at her.

She traced a light touch slowly up the front of his linen shirt and felt the hard heat of his body under the soft fabric. Unable to stop herself, she slipped the pearl buttons free and slid her hand inside to trace his naked skin. She loved the way he felt, so strong and warm. So very *alive*, the most alive person she had ever known.

And he made her feel alive, too, after she had felt cold and numb for so long. After she had shut off her emotions just in order to survive. That feeling was more intoxicating than any wine could be.

She felt his stomach muscles tighten as her hand slid lower and lower. The tips of her fingers brushed the band of his trousers, and she felt his erection harden even more. "Sophia..." he said tightly, but he didn't move. He just watched her closely with those jewel-like eyes.

Sophia smiled. She liked having Dominic under her touch, under her control, even as she knew it was only an illusion. She knew that he surely never gave up his power to anyone. She slid her palms up over his chest and pushed the coat back from his shoulders. He shrugged it off and let it fall to the floor, still watching as she untied his cravat and wound the length of fabric around her hand.

He unfastened his trousers and pushed them down, and

suddenly he stood before her naked in the shadows. He was so handsome it was almost unreal, Sophia thought in a daze as she traced a soft caress over his shoulders, down his arms, her fingertips fluttering over the lean planes of his chest. Suddenly nothing else mattered but touching him, feeling him. Forgetting everything else.

But even as she let herself dive deeper into that swirling pool of desire, she knew how very dangerous this could all be. A woman in her position, so uncertain and alone, couldn't afford to forget. Look where letting her passions rule had taken her before-- married to the wrong person and at the mercy of unscrupulous men like Lord Hammond. Yet somehow today felt like one small, too-brief moment out of time. Just for this moment she could be herself, with Dominic. The man she wanted like no one else she had ever met.

And he seemed to sense what she needed. His breath was harsh, his jaw tight, but he stood still and let her explore.

She closed her eyes and leaned closer to him. Every breath she took was filled with the scent of him and seemed to draw him into her even more. She pressed her parted lips to his bare chest and tasted the warm, damp salt of his skin. She could feel his heartbeat against her, fast and frantic, echoing her own. She let the tip of her tongue swirl around his flat nipple.

She had never been able to explore a man's body like this. With Jack, there had always been a quick explosion of passion then a swift fall. It was fascinating. She curled her arms around him and traced her palms down his spine to pull him closer. Her hands moved down, slowly, teasingly, until she traced her fingers over his ass. He was so hard and tight, and she moaned against him.

And with that his iron control shattered. "Sophia," he groaned, and his hands closed around her waist to lift her up against him. Sophia laughed as he carried her across the room to tumble her back onto the pile of old blankets behind the cabinet. He kissed her, hard and hot and wet, full of raw, burning need. She arched her hips up into his, and she felt his tongue slide into her mouth. The blurry haze of sexual need closed in around her, and she held on to him tight as she fell down into it.

What was it about *this* man that made her feel this way? She didn't know, and at the moment, she didn't care. That reckless-ness was taking over again.

"Sophia." His mouth slid lower along her jaw, her shoulder, to linger on that sensitive spot on her neck. When she sighed and let her head fall back, he reached up to curl his fingers around the satin edge of her bodice and tugged it down. He nudged aside the lace of her corset and bared her breast to his avid, bright green gaze. In the faint light she could see that her nipple was already erect, dark pink, and aching for his kiss.

"You are so beautiful," he whispered darkly. "An enchantress." He traced the tip of his tongue along the soft underside of her breast, teasing her.

Sophia reached up to tangle her fingers in the rough silk of his hair and held him against her. Finally, as she murmured wordless entreaties, he gave her what she begged for and took her nipple deep into his mouth. As his tongue swirled around it, his fingers caressed her other breast, gently, expertly. He rolled and plucked at the nipple until she cried out his name.

His mouth traced a ribbon of kisses on the soft skin between her breasts, and Sophia reached out blindly between their bodies. His cock sprang into her hand, hard, hot, the veins throbbing under her touch, and she felt a surge of triumph that he wanted her as much as she wanted him.

She ran a slow, caressing touch up the full length of his manhood, then pressed closer as he moaned. He pulled her skirts higher, and there was a sudden, short ripping sound as he tore the delicate silk drawers out of his way. His finger lightly traced her slit before sliding deep inside her. The rough friction of his touch against the soft wetness made her cry out. Her back arched up from the quilts and her eyes closed as the feelings washed over her.

His thumb rubbed hard against that tiny, hidden spot up high inside her, and it felt as if white-hot sparks raced through her.

"Sophia," he whispered against her neck as he kissed her there again and again. "Tell me you want me."

For an instant, she thought there was a strange, yearning note in his deep voice, but when she opened her eyes to look up at him, his face was drawn taut into inscrutable, unreadable lines.

"I-I want you," she gasped. And she did want him, in the most fundamental way a woman could want a man. She wanted his touch on her skin, his body inside hers. But there was more she wanted, longings she didn't even understand. Things she didn't want to understand.

Dominic nodded, and his hand slid down her body to press her legs open. Then with a sharp twist of his hips, he thrust deeply into her.

Sophia gasped at the sensation of being joined with him. She wrapped her legs tighter around him and let the fire of pleasure close in around her. Pleasure only *he* could bring. She held on to him as he drew back and lunged forward again and again, deeper, harder, pounding into her. The scent and burning heat of him surrounded her and she moved with him instinctively, seeking her own pleasure. Their bodies and their breath were like one.

The sparkling, tingling pressure built and built deep inside her, growing and expanding like the night sky until it exploded in a shower of white-hot stars.

"Dominic!" she cried, clinging to him as if he was the only rescue left in a drowning world.

He threw his head back, his whole body taut above her as he found his climax. "Sophia," he shouted, and then slowly collapsed beside her on the blankets, his shoulders shaking, his skin damp as it slid over hers. His breath sounded harsh in the sudden silence, and Sophia feared she couldn't breathe either. She closed her eyes to try and hold on to the feelings as long as she could.

"Sophia," Dominic whispered, and she felt him shift against her to rest his head on her midriff, just below her bare breasts. His tousled hair brushed softly against her skin, and she reached down to thread her fingers through it.

A strange kind of peace flowed through her as she lay there with Dominic, and at first she was confused. What was that feeling? She'd never known such a moment of warmth and contentment, as if that was exactly where she was meant to be. The restlessness that always seemed to drive her onward was gone. She felt him press a soft kiss against her skin, and she smiled.

But that rare, shimmering moment was suddenly shattered when there was a burst of loud laughter outside their rickety sanctuary. Dominic sat up, his whole body tense as he looked toward the door.

Sophia heard the patter of footsteps running over grass, a shriek as someone was caught in the game that she had forgotten. An inexplicable sadness came over her as she felt her time with Dominic dissolve around her like a bubble. She pushed herself to her feet and straightened her rumpled gown as she turned her back to him.

She heard the rustle of cloth as he pulled on his discarded clothes. His booted footsteps sounded on the wooden floor behind her, and she closed her eyes as he moved close to her. She knew she should leave and slip back into the party, but a part of her wanted only to cling to this moment. She felt his hands brush lightly over her shoulders, and she pressed back a sob at the touch.

He gently swept the loose hair off her neck and smoothed it back into the combs that had held her coiffure in place. He didn't say anything, but his touch was careful and tender, and Sophia was glad he didn't speak. She was afraid she *couldn't* speak, or that she would start crying and embarrass herself in front of him. He was the last person she wanted to see any weakness.

"I should go," she said.

She felt him nod. He pressed one light, fleeting kiss to the nape of her neck and let her go. Without looking back, she tiptoed to the door and peeked out at the sun-washed meadow. For an instant, the light dazzled her eyes, but she could hear the laughter and shrieks.

"Sophia..." Dominic said. She held up her hand, still afraid she might shatter if he apologized now.

He said nothing else, and she slipped out of the hut, letting the door squeak closed behind her. She saw a group just at the top of the hill, the women running as the men chased them, a flock of bright butterflies in the sunshine. She made her way toward them to slip into their midst, but part of her desperately wanted to run back to Dominic and that one fleeting moment of peace she'd found in his arms.

Fifteen

THE SMELL of sweat and blood hung thick and choking in the humid air. Dominic could hear the rabid shouts and cries, the howls of derision and encouragement, but it all seemed very far away. All he could see were his opponent's eyes, dark and feral beyond the pall of smoke that hung between them. All he could feel was the rush of pure exhilaration through his veins, bringing the pulse of raw, real life.

That feeling of being alive had been hard to find lately, no matter where he looked for it. Onstage, in women's beds, in alcohol--all the places that once gave him pleasure held no spark for him now, and hadn't for a long time. Only here, with the noise and the blood, the pain, could he almost grasp it again.

Here--and when he was with Sophia. When he touched her, smelled her perfume, had sex with her, it was like life again. Pain and pleasure mingled until he couldn't tell one from the other. He only knew he wanted her, *needed* her, in a way he never had anything else before.

And he hated that feeling. He couldn't want a Huntington, not after a lifetime spent hating them. He couldn't let tender emotions take over his life, not with Sophia.

So he had come here, to this dingy, dark basement under a

cheap gin-joint in Pigalle. Here there were no rules, no veneer of civilization, only pure instinct. Only pain that made him feel alive again for a moment.

Dominic slowly circled his opponent, his fists up as he studied the man's every movement, every flicker in his eyes. So far the man was something of a disappointment. He was a huge, hulking bargeman off the Seine, far outweighing Dominic, and from what Dominic had heard, he had something of a reputation on the Paris fight circuit. Dominic had looked forward to taking him on, but the man had no strategy, no speed or grace. None of the challenge that would offer a real escape.

The man gave a great roar and ran headlong at Dominic. For an instant, Dominic was caught off-guard and staggered back, but he regained his lithe footwork and let loose with a punishing flurry of blows. His opponent couldn't keep up, and at last he went reeling and fell to the floor amid a roar of derision.

Dominic stared down at his fallen opponent. A mountain of rock-hard muscle laid flat and unmoving on the sawdust-covered floor. Such a pity; it had been over much too quickly.

As the crowd surged around him with a roar, Dominic laughed. Coming here tonight had been meant to banish something inside him that had been plaguing him ever since he had sex with Sophia, yet it still lurked there. That dark need that could never be banished no matter what he did, that had only left him when he was inside her.

He broke free of the tangle of people and spun toward the bar. The barkeep slid a generous portion of cheap gin in front of him, and Dominic drank it down in one swallow. The burn of it revived him, but it still couldn't put out that fire inside him. He gestured for another.

"Better be careful," he heard Brendan say. "You'll ruin that pretty face of yours, and the ladies won't chase after you anymore."

Dominic glanced over at his brother. Brendan lounged on one of the bar stools in his shirtsleeves, a half-full glass in front of him.

He rarely imbibed much in places like these and never fought, even though he'd once had quite a fierce reputation for it. He just watched, silent and unreadable, as if he waited for something.

In the smoky darkness, Brendan's scars could hardly be seen. But Dominic knew they were always there, an outward manifestation of something dark and hidden in his brother's soul. Neither of them could ever be content. It was part of what made them St. Claires.

"It hasn't stopped your success with the fair sex," Dominic said. He gestured with his glass at one of the barmaids, a buxom blonde in cheap red satin who had been sending Brendan coy smiles and lingering glances all night.

Brendan shrugged. "I do have other talents. But you won't if you keep letting yourself get pounded like that."

"I'm not the one passed out on the floor." Dominic gestured for another gin. The numbness hadn't come over him yet, but he hoped that soon it would. Maybe then he wouldn't keep seeing Sophia's face in his mind, her eyes closed as her head arched back in pleasurable abandon.

"Not tonight maybe. But your next opponent may very well be more skilled than that behemoth. If you were to kill yourself doing these things, the rest of us would never hear the end of it from our mother. You are her favorite darling."

Dominic laughed. "No, indeed. That would be James, and it's a good thing we sent him home before he got into any more trouble."

"Paris seems dangerous for impressionable young men," Brendan said.

And not-so-young men who shouldn't be impressionable any longer? But Dominic knew it wasn't Paris that was making him crazy. It was Sophia Westman.

He tossed back the last of his gin. "I think I might try Madame Brancusi's tonight," he said.

"After what happened with James?"

Dominic shrugged. "They say her girls are beautiful and

highly skilled. Perhaps if I spend enough money there, she will be in a forgiving mood. She is a businesswoman, after all."

"Perhaps, if that Lord Hammond isn't there. I didn't trust that man."

And neither had Dominic. The St. Claires were often unscrupulous in their business dealings, but they did have hearts. Hammond's eyes had been the coldest Dominic had ever seen. "He won't be."

"Then I'll go with you," Brendan said as he reached for the last of his drink.

"You have no need of Madame Brancusi's girls tonight," Dominic answered, gesturing toward the barmaid.

A rare smile flickered over Brendan's scarred face. "She does have some rather-interesting attributes. But you don't seem to be in any fit state to be wandering the streets of Paris alone."

"I don't need a nursemaid, Brendan. Stay, enjoy your barmaid. I will see you at the theater tomorrow for rehearsal."

"I don't trust that look in your eyes."

"Think I might get into some trouble?" Dominic laughed as he reached for his coat. "Damn it, I do hope so."

He left Brendan to his pretty barmaid and made his way up the stairs to the public rooms above the basement. It was slightly cleaner there, the air free of the thick tang of blood and sweat, but it was no less noisy. A band played a boisterous polka as couples galloped across the floor, fueled by the music and the cheap gin. No one looked twice at his bruised face; it was late and the night's merriment was reaching its deafening, drunken crescendo. It was all fun now, but Dominic knew places like this, and he knew how quickly the laughter could cross over into violence.

He considered staying, but he'd had his fill of fistfights for the night. It was time for other distractions. He ducked past the knot of people blocking the front doors and made his way out into the street. It was a colorful neighborhood, teeming with drunken, shrieking people reeling along the walkways together, light spilling out of windows and doorways, prostitutes beckoning from alleyways. But Dominic turned at the end of the street and found a quieter, narrower lane, one where people usually sought more clandestine pleasures. Tonight it was nearly deserted, even more so when he got near the river.

Suddenly he heard a click on the pavement somewhere behind him. It was a small thing, a tiny sound that fell in the nighttime quiet like a raindrop in a pond. But he was still on edge after the fight, and every sound echoed around him.

He kept walking, never breaking his stride, but his fingers tightened into fists and he smiled. If anyone wanted to rob him tonight, they had best be ready for a brawl, because he had no intention of going down easy.

As he turned the corner, he glanced in a shop window and caught the ghostly reflection of a black-clad man several feet behind him. A knife gleamed in the man's hand. Dominic suddenly spun around and saw the flicker of surprise on the man's bearded face just before Dominic's fist shot out and caught him on the jaw. He staggered back and crashed into the wall.

But he recovered quickly, and with a roar, launched himself at Dominic. He was a big man, bulky with muscles and fat under a rough wool coat, but Dominic was used to fighting such men, just like his opponent in the gin-joint. They tended to rely on their sheer size, while years of stage sword fighting and acrobatics taught Dominic speed and agility. He ducked out of the way as the man's meaty fist shot toward him, and he came back with a blow to his opponent's midsection.

His blood was still up after the fight in the gin bar, and he knocked his attacker to the ground. But as he turned to leave, a group of men came running around the corner.

This is not good, he thought wryly, just as the first man reached him and felled him with a hard blow to the jaw. More blows rained down as Dominic fell to his knees on the pavement, but he felt only the first of them as darkness closed around him.

* * *

Sophia sat straight up in bed, her heart pounding. For an instant, she was completely confused, caught halfway between dreams and waking, and she didn't know quite where she was. Not in her girlhood chamber in her father's house, with its abundance of frills and ruffles; not in one of the endless shabby hotel rooms she and Jack called home. She was lost.

Then she drew in a deep breath and watched as a ray of fading gaslight from the street outside fell across the bare wood floor, and she remembered. She was in her little apartment at La Reine d'Argent, and it must be very late indeed. It felt as if she'd just fallen asleep, exhausted after chasing out the last of the drunken customers and seeing Camille and Count Danilov off to a late supper, but the night was still deepest purple-black outside. Not yet near dawn.

What awakened her? Sophia rubbed her hand over her face and tried to chase away the last cobwebs of her dreams. Had it been some nightmare? She'd thought those bad dreams would be gone once she was safe, away from men like Lord Hammond and in charge of her own life. Or had she forgotten something she was supposed to do, something important?

Or was she just thinking about that day in Montmartre with Dominic yet again? Memories of it had come back to haunt her in the days since then, usually when she least wanted them. Least wanted to remember how much she had loved his body over hers; how much she wanted to see him again. She knew he was still at the Theatre Nationale, but he hadn't appeared again at the club.

"Oh, just go back to sleep," she murmured. She lay back down and rolled onto her side. Her worries would surely keep until morning.

A sudden pounding noise from downstairs made her sit up straight again. Someone was at her door, and the cold pit of feeling deep in her stomach told her it was not good. Only ill could come to the door so late at night, a lesson she'd learned too well in her life with Jack. As a knock echoed again, Sophia slowly slid out of bed and reached for her dressing gown. As she eased her feet into her slippers, she opened the drawer of her bedside table and took out the small pistol Camille had given her.

Holding its reassuring, chilly weight balanced in her hand, she crept down the stairs and paused to light a lamp on the landing. There wasn't another knock, and Sophia half-hoped whoever it was had gone. That it was merely some confused drunk stumbling past. But somehow she knew that wouldn't be the case tonight.

She crossed the foyer and pressed her ear carefully to the front door. She could hear only the soft rush of the wind sweeping leaves and debris down the street, and she leaned back as she let out the breath she was holding. She started to turn away, but a sudden sound, a scratch on the wood like a cat's claws, brought her back again. Somehow that soft noise was more ominous than the pounding knocks.

Clutching at the pistol with one hand, she threw back the locks and opened the door a mere crack to peer outside. For a second, she could see nothing but the quiet, darkened houses across the street, their stones pale in the moonlight. Suddenly a strong grasp closed on the hem of her nightdress, and she screamed in shock.

"Bloody hell, woman, you will make my head explode," a man said hoarsely.

Sophia looked down at the shocking sight of Dominic St. Claire lying on her doorstep, his hair bright in the moonlight. "I must still be dreaming," she whispered, and gave her head a hard shake. Because otherwise it simply made no sense at all that he would be there.

She stepped back to try to slam the door, and his fist tightened on her hem. She tried to pull herself free, and that was when she saw it. Blood dripped down his hand and stained the white muslin of her gown. She knew it was no dream.

"Dominic!" she cried. She fell down on her knees beside him and dropped the gun to the pavement with a metallic clatter. In the gaslight, she could see that his head was bleeding as well, a stain spreading along his temple into his beautiful hair. She reached out with her trembling fingertips to carefully touch his cheek, and he pulled away with a hissing breath.

"Dominic, what happened to you?" she said. She brushed away his protests and gently turned his face into the light. She could see bruises, and a cut under one eye, as well as the bleeding wound on his temple. The sleeve of his coat had ripped away where another wound had started to clot and dry. "You are in a rare mess," she said, her heart aching.

"Part of it is from the gin palace earlier tonight," he said. He tried to laugh, but it ended in a choking cough that made him wince with pain.

Sophia thought it best not to ask what he had been doing brawling in a gin palace. She had to concentrate on helping him now. "And the other part?"

"Some men attacked me when I left there. At least I think that is what happened, from what I remember, which I admit is a trifle hazy."

She studied his wounds again and saw the gleam of his watch chain, the gold signet ring on his finger. "Was it a robbery? They don't seem to have been very thorough," she said, trying to stay as careless as he was trying to be. She feared she couldn't, not when her heart was pounding with fear for him.

"Not a robbery. It seems they were looking specifically for me."

"Indeed?" Sophia held his face gently between her hands and searched his eyes. The pupils were dilated, nearly obscuring the green, and she knew enough to be sure she needed to keep him awake, keep him talking. "Was it a rival theater owner? A disgruntled husband?"

He gave another groaning laugh. "Who knows? I didn't have much conversation with them. I wondered if it was you, taking your revenge on me for my piss-poor behavior toward you."

Sophia had to laugh, too, despite her fear. "I would take my revenge myself, you can be sure. But how did you get here?"

"Now that I couldn't say. I was sadly knocked unconscious,

and when I woke, I was here. A parcel I'm sure you have no use for."

Sophia sighed. It was true she'd hoped to be done with trouble, to find some peace somewhere. To make a new life. But trouble always knew where to find her. And Dominic, too, it seemed. They were two of a kind.

She glanced down the street, half-afraid his attackers still might linger there, but everything seemed quiet. When she turned back to Dominic, his eyes were closed, and his head was heavy in her lap. "No, don't go to sleep," she said urgently. "We must get you inside, and I certainly can't carry you."

"Then leave me here," he said. He didn't open his eyes. "Your doorstep is quite comfortable."

"It's also quite damp, and I can't let you catch a chill on top of everything else."

"Why, Sophia." A smile drifted over his lips. "I didn't realize you cared so much."

"I don't want the trouble of explaining to Camille how you happened to die outside her house." Sophia took his uninjured arm and slid it around her shoulders as she tried to tug him upright. It was like trying to move a boulder. "Come along now, Dominic. We need to get you somewhere that I can take a proper look at your wounds."

"Into your bed, perhaps? Mrs. Westman, how terribly shocking you are being tonight. I must say I am flattered."

"Half-dead and still trying to flirt. Of course." Sophia gave his arm an impatient tug, and he finally sat up. She felt his body tense, his breath catch, and she knew he was truly in pain, no matter how much he tried to conceal it.

That made her even more frightened.

She helped him stagger to his feet and into the foyer of the house. She propped him carefully against a marble table while she fetched her gun and relocked the door, and when she hurried back, he was listing badly to one side.

"Come along," she said briskly as she put her arms around

him. She tried to remember the reassuring way her old nanny used to deal with nursery wounds and to not give in to her own panic. "I'll help you upstairs."

"You are being much too nice to me, Sophia my dear," he answered. He leaned on her as they made their slow way up the stairs. "I must be in bad shape indeed."

"Yes, you are," Sophia said, breathless from holding him upright.

"I don't deserve it. Not after the way I behaved," he said. "Not after the way I think about you all the time…"

How did he think about her? Sophia very much wanted to know, but this didn't seem like the right time to press. "No, you don't. But I'll send for the doctor. Should I find your family, too? Your brothers and sister?"

"Certainly not," Dominic answered. His voice was stronger, more adamant, as they stumbled over the last step. "My sister would be in hysterics if she knew, which would not be helpful, and Brendan is--occupied tonight. I'll be fine in an hour or two and out of your house."

Sophia wasn't so sure about that. The bruises on his face looked alarmingly vivid, no matter how he had gotten them, and he winced when her hand accidentally slid over his ribs. She didn't need this kind of trouble. But she could never turn him away, not when he needed her. He seemed like the kind of man who never needed anyone.

She nudged open her bedroom door and led him to the rumpled bed. "What makes you think *I* won't go into hysterics?"

He gave another laugh that ended in a worrying, hacking cough. He slowly lowered himself to the edge of the mattress, his arm wrapped tight around himself. "You haven't had hysterics yet. You seem much too cool-headed for that sort of thing. I doubt you would faint at the sight of a little blood."

"Me? Cool-headed?" Sophia laughed as she knelt to help him remove his boots. "My family would surely disagree with you. They always declared me to be wild and flighty."

"Did they?" Dominic murmured, as if he grew sleepy. "Why would they say that?"

"Because I was trouble from the day I was born, at least according to my father. And I proved him right in the end, running away with Jack like I did." She tossed aside the boots and sat back on her heels to look up at him. In the light of only one lamp, she could barely see the bruises that marred his handsome face. His hair was tangled over his brow, and he watched her closely with his darkened eyes. He always seemed to have that power to focus so closely, to see so much. It made her want to turn away, to not let him see. To protect herself from being hurt again.

But it also gave her the strangest, strongest urge to tell him all her secrets, all the doubts and hurts she kept hidden. As if he could really be the powerful, golden angel he appeared to be.

Yet he was *not* an angel, she reminded herself sternly. He was a man who had made love to her, given her the greatest pleasure, then vanished. He was a man who'd gotten into a vicious fight and found his way to her doorstep in the middle of the night.

"What did you do that was so much trouble, Sophia?" he said gently. "Why do you live alone now, so far from your family? Just because of your marriage?"

"That is too long a tale for tonight, and you're in no condition to listen to my stories anyway." Sophia pushed herself to her feet and busied herself with pulling down the bedclothes and piling up the pillows.

Dominic suddenly reached out and caught her hand. He was shockingly fast and strong for someone who had just been in a brawl, and he held her there until she looked at him. "I like stories," he said. "I want to know yours, Sophia. Very much."

"I'm very dull," she answered. She gave her wrist a twist, and he let her go. Avoiding his gaze, she went behind him to help him ease out of his coat. Surely he didn't really want to know about her; no one did, especially men who wanted to sleep with her. But she found she did want to tell him. Too much. "Especially compared with the dashing actresses and Society beauties you see every day."

"I suspect there is nothing dull about you at all, Sophia. And you must know you could outshine any other Society beauty you wanted to."

He thought her beautiful? "What do you want to know then?" Sophia folded his ruined coat over the foot of the bed and turned to look for her box of salves and bandages in the cupboard. In her life with Jack, she'd learned never to be without them, but she wouldn't have expected to need them for Dominic St. Claire.

"I want to know everything," he said. She heard the soft shift of cloth, and she glanced over her shoulder to see that he had pulled off his shirt. The lamplight poured a soft glow over his bare skin, gilding the lean planes of his chest and his ridged abdomen. He stretched his neck from side to side, and Sophia swallowed at the sight of him. He was so gloriously handsome, even in this sad condition.

"Everything?" she said. She laid the box on the bedside table and poured out water into a basin. "That might take some time."

"It appears I'm not going anywhere."

Sophia laughed wryly. "Is this a ploy to persuade me to let you read Mary's diary?"

Dominic shook his head, his eyes never leaving her face as she worked. "I have no interest in long-dead people tonight, no matter how they are related to me. I want to know about *you*. What brought you here. What you want next in your life."

"Well, I would rather hear about you, I think." As Sophia leaned closer to him, she saw that his perfection was an illusion of the night's shadows. It was marred by darkening bruises and by the cut on his arm that was oozing blood again. He would have to use a great deal of stage makeup before his next performance, she feared. But the wounds seemed only to enhance his strange magic, carving a dimension of vulnerability to him that was otherwise never there. A rare glimpse behind his armor, the primitive allure of a warrior.

"Ah, now I really am dull," he said with a smile.

"I can't believe that," Sophia answered. She tucked the blankets around him and lay down by his side. The rush of fear and danger that had sustained her when she discovered him had faded, and now she was tired. But she knew she couldn't sleep yet. "The life of an actor could never be dull. Isn't it exciting when hundreds of people are applauding you?"

Dominic laughed wryly. "I do admit I like the applause. But that only lasts a few minutes. There are hours and hours of practice that lead up to it. Repeating the same words, the same actions, over and over until you're sick of them. There's playing peacemaker in quarrels between other actors, doing accounts, ordering costumes, planning seasons years in advance, worrying about what other theaters are doing--all very dull. And the work never ends."

Sophia shook her head. "It still sounds wonderful to me. Doing something you love, in the company of other people who love it. Having the support of your family. Being part of something that makes so many people happy."

"You're right. It's not so bad." Dominic closed his eyes. "I can't imagine doing anything else. Yet it can be hard to maintain a balance between the theater and a personal life, if someone hasn't been born to the acting life and thus understands it."

Sophia remembered the snippet of gossip she had heard from Camille, that Dominic had lost his fiancée. "I heard you were once engaged, though."

A frown flickered over his brow. "Yes. Once."

"To a woman named Jane Grant?"

"That was her name. I see gossip can fly fast over the Channel."

"Camille knows everything about everyone. She mentioned it when we attended your play."

"Did she tell you Jane died?" he asked.

"Yes," Sophia said, feeling terrible that she had even brought it up. She hated it when people tried to pry about Jack. "I am so sorry."

"We were probably not a good match, even if she had lived."

"Did she not like the theater?"

"She didn't fully understand what I did there, why I needed it so much. But she wanted to understand. She was a sweet, kind lady who wanted everyone to be happy."

Sweet and kind. Two words Sophia feared could never be used to describe herself. "So she would have tried to understand what happened to you tonight?"

Dominic started to laugh again and winced with pain. "She might have tried, but I fear she never would have. There are things inside me she could never have fathomed."

"Where did you meet her?" Sophia asked.

"She was the daughter of an old school friend of my mother's. Her father owned a textile import business, very respectable. I had known her since I was young, and when we got older we met at parties more often, and it felt like time for me to settle down. To mend my wild ways. Or try to, at least. And Jane and I liked each other. It seemed a good fit, a way to build a suitable future."

It didn't sound like a grand passion to Sophia, the kind she would expect with a man like Dominic, who was obviously a man of fire. But it did sound like something she herself would try to seek, and would surely never find, because it simply wasn't in her. "Do you miss her?"

"Yes," he said simply. "For a while, I didn't know what to do next. She had been like an anchor to me and suddenly I was adrift again."

"What did you do after?"

"I found the theater again. It's always been what I come back to in the end."

Sophia closed her eyes against a sudden wave of longing. "I don't think I have anything like that."

"Like what?"

"A home. An anchor."

Dominic was quiet for a long moment. Sophia wondered if he had drifted to sleep when he suddenly spoke again. "What was your marriage like?"

"I don't really like talking about myself," Sophia said with a laugh. "My marriage was just a mistake."

"What sort of mistake?"

"My reasons for marrying Jack were almost entirely the opposite of yours with Jane. I knew very well it was no way to a stable, respectable future."

"Then why did you do it?" Dominic asked. He sounded as if he genuinely wanted to know.

But Sophia wasn't going to tell him the truth--that after her encounter with him at the Devil's Fancy, she'd been feeling even more reckless. "Jack was a half-pay officer, very handsome and dashing. He came from a respectable enough family, but there was no money there, no estate. My family couldn't approve of him. I met him out riding at the park one day, and he flirted with me. He was so charming. And when he wanted to call on me and my mother forbade it, I couldn't resist. So I started writing to him in secret."

"It sounds like a play," Dominic said. He seemed amused rather than shocked by her tale.

"It was a young girl's romantic folly, that's all. I just took it much too far."

"Were you sorry you married him?"

"At first I was. After the excitement of the elopement and going to live abroad, I realized that housekeeping on almost no money was not much fun. And Jack was quite fond of his drink. That was what killed him in the end. We'd only been married a few months."

"But you're not sorry now?"

Sophia thought about his words for a moment. "No, I'm not. I've learned so much about myself now. I've learned I can be strong when I must. I sometimes do wish I had a family like yours, Dominic. But I do well enough on my own."

"Do you think you'll marry again?"

"Probably not," she said with a laugh. "And I think we have talked enough for tonight. You need your rest."

"I'm not so tired," he protested. "I want to hear more."

Sophia propped herself up on her elbow to study his face. She could see that, despite his protests, he was struggling to stay awake. His eyes were closed, and she could see the strain of everything that had happened that night in the lean lines of his face.

"Sleep now," she said. "I'll tell you more tomorrow, though I fear there is little more to say about my pitiful marriage."

Dominic nodded, and as Sophia watched, he slowly drifted down into sleep. Despite her tiredness, though, she couldn't find rest herself. She lay there as the candle sputtered lower and lower, listening to Dominic's breath become deep and even in sleep. At least he could rest and start to mend.

She reached for a book on her bedside table, an English novel she hadn't had time to begin yet, and started reading as she kept vigil over Dominic. He slept for a time as she lost herself in the story, a romantic tale of pastoral love between a marquess in disguise as a shepherd and a pretty, virtuous milkmaid who was actually a runaway princess. Sophia thought it would make a good play for Dominic.

But as she replaced the burned-down candle, Dominic started to mutter in his sleep. Sophia turned back to him just as his fist shot out, and he shouted an incoherent curse.

"No, Dominic!" she cried. "You'll open your wounds again."

She tried to pin his arms down, half-lying on top of him, but he was too strong for her. In his nightmare, he had no gentleness or care. He tossed her off and she landed hard on the floor.

As Sophia pulled herself to her feet, she glimpsed the tied-back curtains at the window and had an idea. She had to keep him from hurting himself all over again. She took the gold cords from the hooks of the draperies and came back to the bed to resolutely press him down to the mattress.

He still cried out in his sleep, obviously having a terrible dream, but Sophia straddled him and held his arms down with her legs. She took first one hand, then the other, and tied them as tightly as she could to the bedposts.

When she finished she was exhausted with the effort, but he seemed quieter. He fell back down into sleep, still frowning but not shouting out. Sophia lay down beside him and tumbled into a troubled sleep of her own, Dominic bound at her side.

It's too bad he's asleep, she thought ruefully as the darkness closed around her. Otherwise it could be rather fun.

From the Diary of Mary St. Claire Huntington

My brother Nick has come to visit, and he did indeed bring news. He has recently been at Court himself, and he thinks he knows the reason why the Duke of York is coming to visit. The duke has recently found himself in need of funds, and he has become involved in a plan to raise money on foreign notes. I cannot understand it myself, but Nick is very excited about the idea. He has always been in need of more coin himself.

I admit that anything that has royal approval would appeal to my John, but I can't help but feel some disquiet at this idea. Yet I will not be consulted, and I must finish the preparations for the visit.

Sixteen

"SOPHIA, SOPHIA. UNTIE ME."

"What..." Sophia pulled herself up out of sleep at the sound of Dominic's voice. She rolled onto her side to find that he was awake now, his eyes open and bright, free of the nightmares that had caused her to bind him to the bed. But his hands were still tied.

She smiled and sat up slowly to swing one of her legs over his hips so she straddled him again. "I'm so sorry, Dominic, but I had to tie you. You were thrashing around too much with your nightmares."

"I'm awake now," he argued, watching her with narrowed eyes.

"Are you? I'm not quite sure..." Sophia slowly leaned over to kiss the side of his neck. She parted her lips and savored the sweet-salty taste of him, the way his breath turned harsh at her touch.

His body grew tense under hers. "Untie me," he demanded. "Now."

Sophia laughed and reached up to loosen the cords around his wrists. "Are you sure you want me to let you go just yet? There's so much else we could do..."

Before she could say anything else, he rose to meet her and his mouth swooped down over hers. Open, hot, hungry, as if he wanted to devour her. The thought flickered through her mind that he must be still dreaming, but as always when she was with him, it awakened something deep inside her, that flame of longing and pure need. When he kissed her, he swept her away on a river of fire, swept her away to her true self.

Sophia opened her lips to his and drew her tongue over his. His taste filled her, brandy and darkness, and she moaned.

As they kissed, deeper, hungrier, their tongues entwining, she laid her hands flat on his hard shoulders and felt the damp heat of his skin. He groaned deep in his throat, and his hands fisted in the ropes as if he wanted rip her chemise off her.

His passion made her feel bold. She slid her caress lower, slowly, savoring the delicious way his nearly-naked body felt against hers. So strong, so hard, so hot. This was what she craved, what she needed. It made her feel alive at last.

She traced her fingertips over his flat nipples and felt them pebble under her touch. She scraped the edge of her thumbnail over one, and he growled low in his throat. She pressed slightly harder, hard enough to give just the slightest edge of pain. His body shuddered, but he went on kissing her as if he was starved for the taste of her.

Sophia slid her touch even lower, feeling every inch of his taut, damp chest, his bare skin. He felt like hot satin stretched over iron muscles, and the light whorls of golden hair tickled her palms. She dipped the tip of her smallest finger into his navel before she moved even lower to the band of his trousers.

And suddenly she felt her newfound boldness, the temptress inside her, flee as his rock-hard erection brushed against her hand. She drew away.

"Fuck it, Sophia, don't stop now," he whispered fiercely as his mouth tore away from hers. He pressed hot, openmouthed kisses to her jaw and the soft curve of her throat. He bit at her there, drawing her skin lightly between his teeth.

Sophia gasped and let her head fall back as she caught at his shoulders. His mouth opened on the pulse that beat frantically at the hollow of her neck. He licked at it, swirling the tip of his tongue just there.

"Dominic!" she cried. She felt his hand twist in the loose braid of her hair and he wound its length around his wrist as if he would bind her to him.

He didn't raise his head. His open mouth swept over her collarbone, the little hollows just at her shoulders, until the tip of his tongue traced the upper swell of her breast. The edge of his teeth scraped over her tender skin, and her hand curled against him.

"You like that?" he whispered.

"Do you like *this*?" Sophia moved her hand lower and lower, a slow slide until she covered the hard ridge behind the wool fabric. She slid her fingers down in a soft caress until he groaned. She pressed the pad of her thumb to that sensitive spot just at the head of his penis, and he seemed to grow even harder in her touch. She reached up and untied his hands, longing to feel his touch on her.

"Sophia," he whispered darkly. Suddenly he pulled her chemise over her head, tearing her hand away from him. She knelt on the bed in front of him, her body naked for a man as it hadn't been in so long. Not since those first heady days of her marriage to Jack. A wave of sudden cold shyness swept over her as she remembered how many women Dominic must have seen this way, women taller, thinner, with bigger bosoms than hers. Lack of confidence had never been something that troubled Sophia, but she had never cared so much what a man thought of her before.

When he just looked at her with those beautiful green eyes, silent, she tried to turn away and reach for her discarded chemise. But his hands were already on her again, and he spun her back into his arms.

"So beautiful, Sophia," he said roughly as his head lowered to her breast. "You are so damnably beautiful."

Sophia smiled. Yes--when he looked at her and touched her like this, that strange shyness fled, and she felt beautiful again, in a way she hadn't in so long. Desirable. Wanted, and not in that way she had felt her beauty used in gaming rooms with Jack, as a commodity, a distraction. Truly beautiful. As his mouth closed hard on her nipple, drawing her in deep, her head fell back and her eyes closed. She felt the braid of her hair fall down her back, and the heat of his lips on her aching breast. She bit her lip to keep from crying out. Her whole body, which had felt frozen and numb for too long, roared back to burning life again.

He covered her breast with his palm, his fingers spread wide to caress her. One fingertip brushed over her engorged nipple, and a cry burst from her lips. She felt him smile against her, just before his teeth bit down lightly.

She reached desperately between their bodies to unfasten his trousers and push them down over his lean hips. His hard cock sprang free against her abdomen, and as she held it naked in her hand at last he groaned. His teeth tightened on her nipple before he arched his head back to stare up at her.

Sophia looked down into his eyes and saw that they were burning and dark, the green almost swallowed in black lust. She bent to kiss the side of his neck, to bite at him as he had with her. He tasted salty and sweet, intoxicating.

As she kissed him, she ran her open palm up his penis to its swollen tip. There was a drop of moisture there, and she caught it on her finger to spread it up again, slow, steady, hard. Dominic's hands suddenly tightened on her backside, his fingers digging into the soft skin as he dragged her even closer. Her hand dropped away from him, and he slowly pressed the tip of his cock against the soft nest of damp curls between her thighs. He moved up and down, lightly teasing at her swollen cleft.

"Dominic," she whispered against his neck.

"So wet, so hot," he answered, in a voice so deep she didn't recognize it. He pulled her flush against his hips, and then suddenly they tumbled back together to the bed. He came down on top of her, his hips between her spread legs, his lips taking hers in another wild, desperate kiss.

Sophia wrapped her legs around his waist and arched up into him. He was large, strong, and completely overwhelming. She felt surrounded completely by his heat and power. She couldn't breathe, couldn't think. She tore her lips from his kiss and tilted her head back to try to gulp in a breath, to try to find a particle of sanity. Her hands dug into his shoulders as if she would push him away--or cling to him tighter.

Dominic seemed to sense something was wrong. His hands slid around her waist, and in one swift movement, he lay on his back with her on top of him. She straddled him, her legs tight to either side of his lean hips. He stared up at her with an almost feral gleam in those extraordinary eyes, as if he was so hungry he would devour her. Yet he made no move; his body was taut and still with perfect restraint.

Sophia braced her hands on his chest, letting him support her. She slid them down, a slow, hard glide over is warm skin. He felt tense under her caress, as if he waited for what she wanted to do. It made her want him even more when she saw he would give her control like that

She reached up and released the tie on the end of her braid to shake her hair free as she smiled down at him. A muscle tightened in his jaw, but his stare never wavered from her face. She took his hands and moved them from her waist to hold them to the mattress. She leaned down and laid her open mouth on his naked chest. His hands jerked but he didn't push her away.

She tasted him with the tip of her tongue, swirling it lightly over his flat, brown nipple. It hardened under her kiss, and she felt him draw in a sharp breath of air. She nipped her teeth over him.

Surely she would always remember this, no matter what came tomorrow. It was like a dream, a lustful fantasy before she had to go back to her real life. His taste, his smell, the way his body felt as it slid against hers--she would remember it all.

She licked at the indentation along his hip, that enticing masculine line of muscle that dipped toward his erect cock. She breathed softly over the base of his penis, touched him once with her tongue, and sat upright atop him again.

"Witch," he groaned. "How do you do this to me?"

"What do I do to you?" Sophia closed her eyes and laid her hand lightly between her bare breasts. Slowly, very slowly, she traced her touch down her own body, over her abdomen, until her fingers lay over the place that was so wet for him she ached with it. She slid one fingertip between her damp folds, and then his perfect stillness shattered.

"Bloody hell, Sophia!" he shouted. Her eyes flew open as his hands closed hard around her hips. He pulled her body up along his until his mouth closed over her womanhood just where her hand had been. She knelt over his face as his tongue plunged deep into her.

Sophia cried out and grabbed the scarred wood of the bed as his mouth claimed every intimate part of her. His fingers dug into her buttocks as he kissed her, licked her, tasted her skillfully. She was no longer the one in control, but she didn't even care. She only wanted his mouth on her, his touch.

His tongue flicked at that tiny spot high inside her, and she moaned. One of his hands let go of her, and he drove one long finger into her as he kept licking. He moved it slowly in and out, pressing, sliding, until she cried out his name over and over.

"Oh, Dominic," she moaned. "How do you do this to me?"

"Just let go," he whispered against her. "Let go for me..."

Another finger slid into her, and she felt the pressure building up low in her abdomen. He had done this to her in that warm, dusty hut, too--it didn't seem to matter where they were, who they were, only that they were a man and a woman drawn together by a deep need. That heat built and built, expanding inside her like a fire out of control. Her whole body seemed to soar upward. Dominic's tongue pressed harder as his fingers curled inside her, and she shattered completely. She screamed out loud and clutched at the bed to keep from falling.

But he wasn't done. He lifted her off him and pushed himself up to sit against the bedpost. He drew her body down until she straddled his hips again and was spread open over his iron-hard cock.

"Ride me, Sophia," he commanded.

She could hardly focus through her pleasure-dazed mind. She stared down at him as she held onto his sweat-slick shoulders. His eyes were still dark with lust, and she could smell herself on him. It made her want him, need him, all over again.

She raised herself slightly until she felt his tip nudge at her opening, and then she held on to him tight as she slid down. Lower, lower, until he was completely inside her. His head fell back as his hands closed hard on her waist.

"Sophia," he groaned. "You're so tight, so perfect. I can't..."

She raised up again and sank back down, over and over, faster, until she found her rhythm. His hips arched up to meet hers, and they moved together, harder, faster. Until she felt her climax building all over again.

She leaned back and braced her hands on his thighs as he thrust up into her. She closed her eyes and saw whirling, fiery stars in the darkness, exploding around her in showers of green and white as she cried out his name. He shouted out a flood of incoherent curses as his whole body went rigid. She felt him go still deep inside her as he let go and soared free with her.

Sophia sobbed and let herself fall to the bed. Her legs were too weak to hold her up any longer. She trembled as she let the bone-deep exhaustion claim her. The ceiling above her spun around and around as she tried to catch her breath, to make sense of what madness had just happened.

Beside her, Dominic had collapsed to the pillows.

They didn't touch, but she could feel the heat of his body close to hers. His breath sounded rough and uneven, and suddenly she remembered the injuries that had brought him to her door in the first place. She sat up to frantically examine him, worry replacing the languor of sexual pleasure. Had she hurt him? What craziness had come over them to do something like that?

But he looked well enough. His arm was still bandaged in clean white linen, and the cloth wasn't spotted with blood. His eyes were closed, his hair falling in damp waves over his brow. She gently brushed it back, and he caught her hand in his to kiss her palm. Sophia felt a sudden wave of unwanted tenderness wash over her. Tenderness--for Dominic St. Claire of all people! Her head was spinning, as if the reality of what had happened could hardly sink in. She'd never felt quite that way before. The heat of sex and need was all tangled up with the past, and she didn't know what would happen next.

She didn't even know what she wanted to happen now. She was so close to getting back with her family. There was only this one unreal moment, here alone with him.

She laid her hand gently against the side of Dominic's cheek. In the dying candlelight she could hardly see his bruises now, but she knew they were still there, and her heart ached at the pain he had suffered. He had said some of them weren't inflicted by his attackers, but from an organized prize fight in some cheap gin palace. It even sounded like a regular event for him. There was so very much she didn't know about him.

Sophia traced the hard line of his roughened jaw and the softness of his sensual lips. He was so very handsome; why would he do such things to himself? What drove him to seek out such pain? Was it his lost love? Did he do it to drown memories of her?

Her touch drifted over his closed eyelids, and she felt his breath drift softly over her skin. His arm wrapped around her waist, and he drew her down to the bed beside him.

"Sophia," he whispered hoarsely, his voice distant as if he was drifting into sleep. "What is it that you do to me?" She shook her head. What did they do to each other?

He made her crazy, made her forget everything else when she was with him. She'd gone down the winding path of mad infatuation before. And even though she knew Dominic was not really much like Jack, he did have a wild streak to him that led him to fighting and gaming. A wild streak that would only encourage her own. She couldn't fall for someone like that again.

But she couldn't make sense of any of it, not now with sleep and the languorous pleasure of sexual satisfaction weighing down on her. Not here in Dominic's arms, where she felt so warm, so deceptively secure. Sophia rested her head on the pillow next to his and closed her eyes. She would let herself sleep here, just for a moment. And in the morning, when things were bright and clear again, she would talk to Dominic and try to decipher what it was about him that had such a hold on her.

But Sophia slept deeply and dreamlessly, and when she woke, the sun was already splashing through her window. Its bright rays illuminated the tangle of ropes and bandages on the bedside table, the twisted cord of sheets over the bed. She heard the stirring of the house outside her door, the clatter of the maid walking down the corridor with her coal bucket, and the traffic from the street below. Sophia rubbed at her itchy eyes, and for an instant she was disoriented. Was she still half-caught in sleep, or was this really the day beginning? She rolled over on the bed, and as her aching body gave a twinge, she suddenly remembered everything. Dominic, his injuries--their lovemaking.

She sat straight up on the bed and looked around frantically, only to find that she was alone. Dominic was gone. Only those ropes and bandages told her she hadn't imagined the whole thing.

And now she was alone. Sophia pushed away a sharp pang of disappointment. She shouldn't be hurt that Dominic was gone. This was merely what happened when the illusions of the night were burned away by the daylight.

Yet she *did* feel disappointed. And worried. How had he even made it home in his condition? The ungrateful wretch.

"Men," she muttered. She swung her aching legs off the bed and looked around for her chemise.

She found it on a chair, neatly folded. On top of it was a slip of paper, covered with bold, slashing black handwriting. Sophia's cynical disappointment was suddenly cut by a slash of ridiculous hope, and she reached for the note.

"Sophia," it read. *"A thousand thanks for your kind nursing last night. I'm sorry I have to leave so early, but I have rehearsal, and you are sleeping so peacefully. Please let me show my gratitude by taking you to supper tonight at the Cafe de Paris--if you can bear to be seen with such a battered fool. Dominic St. Claire"*

Sophia smiled as she carefully refolded the note. She knew she should refuse. Last night had shown her just how weak she was when it came to Dominic. Yet an elegant supper out with him, in public at the Cafe de Paris...

How dangerous could that be?

* * *

No matter how many times Dominic tried to read the scene in front of him, the words simply wouldn't come together. He couldn't concentrate at all on his work.

This new play was meant to open at the Majestic Theater as soon as they returned to London, but every quiet moment when he should be working was filled with thoughts of Sophia. Thoughts of her black hair spilling over her bare white shoulders, filling his hands. The taste of her skin under his lips, the smell of the curve of her neck. The way her body felt against his in the darkness. *Sophia, Sophia.*

"Damn it all!" Dominic threw down his pencil and slumped back in his chair. He could hear the sounds of the rehearsal echoing from the stage, through the warren of walkways and corridors to his small office, but no one had dared approach him there yet.

He ran his hands through his already disheveled hair and resisted the urge to hit the wall. Destroying the office would solve nothing. After last night he was done with fighting.

Dominic buried his face in his hands and closed his eyes. Making love to Sophia again had seemed like a hot, feverish dream. Here amid the grubby, colorful, familiar world of the theater, he was almost sure it hadn't happened. As if his potent craving for her and the pain of his injuries had caused an illusion. A vivid, glorious dream. He had thought about her for too long, ever since that night at the Devil's Fancy, and their frantic coupling at the picnic had only made him want her even more.

Behind his closed eyes he saw her again. She'd lain on her side away from him, with her hair spread over the pillows and wrapped around his arm, as if she would hold him to her. Her bare skin was pale and perfect in the rosy sunrise light, and all he had wanted was to touch her again. To wrap his arms around her and know she was real.

That feeling of tenderness--toward Sophia, a Huntington-- had shocked him to his very core. All his life he'd been told that the Huntingtons had ruined the St. Claires, stolen their rightful place in Society and cast them out to the underworld margins. That his first duty was always to his family, always to remember. And now he was literally in bed with a Huntington, and what was worse, he wanted only to stay there.

His life was good as it was. He had his work, his family. He'd rebuilt after Jane died, come to terms with the knowledge that he was better off alone. That he was too hardened, too marred, for a lady to ever understand him.

But when he looked down at Sophia asleep next to him, when he saw her beautiful face and the soft smile on her lips, he wanted only to stay with her. So he'd left. Gathered his clothes and crept out of her room, afraid that if he stayed until she woke, if she looked at him with those deep violet eyes, he would never leave. Yet once he made it to the front door, something deep inside him, some spark of chivalry he had thought long dead, made him go back and leave her a note asking her to supper.

He hadn't yet heard from her. Perhaps she had more sense than he did and was resolved to stay away from him. They should stay away from each other.

Once he had been able to see her as only a Huntington, albeit one of their more scandalous family members among the more stiff-necked dukes and ladies. She'd seemed ripe for trifling with, a small revenge against her family. A weapon against them.

But after last night, he feared he saw her as far more than a beautiful, rebellious girl he could use. Her sad words about her short-lived marriage, her laughing dismissal of her troubles, the quickly hidden tears--they'd all given him a glimpse of her inner heart he almost wished he hadn't seen.

He saw the person who didn't want to be hurt again. Who refused to trust--and he recognized that, because he hid just such emotions in himself.

Emotions were of no use to anyone. They only caused trouble, caused pain. It was better to push them away and hide them until they vanished, leaving only toughened scar tissue behind. He had long known that, and Sophia was learning it. And that was why it was better not see each other.

If only he could quit thinking about her...

He was shaken out of his brooding by the sound of light footsteps hurrying along the corridor outside. The office door flew open, and his sister Isabel rushed in amid a flurry of lace ruffles, ribbons, and red-gold curls. Her cheeks were pink from the bright day outside, and her green eyes sparkled. They'd thought about sending her back to London with James, but she had a leading role in two plays here and no reliable understudy, so she'd stayed.

Dominic had felt uneasy at her staying after what happened to James, but he was glad she was there now. His spirits revived at the sight of her, as they always did. Isabel was the family's baby, their pride, their bright spirit.

"Issy," he said as he pushed back from the desk and stood up. "What a nice surprise. I thought you weren't scheduled to rehearse until later this afternoon."

"I've come to tear you and Brendan away from your never-ending work. You haven't had time to enjoy Paris at all," Isabel said happily. She went up on tiptoe to kiss his cheek, and the feathers on her bonnet tickled his chin. "Good heavens, but you do look a fright today, Dominic! Whatever were you doing last night?"

"Issy..." Dominic began sternly. But he was saved from making up some elaborate lie to explain his bruises when Isabel stepped back and laughed.

"Never mind," she said. "I'm quite sure I don't want to know. But I think it's terribly unfair you all get to have adventures when I am stuck at the hotel embroidering with Mrs. Smythe."

"Mrs. Smythe is meant to be your companion while you're here, since Mama couldn't come," Dominic said. "She came very highly recommended."

"Recommended as what? A jailer at Newgate?" Isabel protested. "I am in Paris! I want to have some fun, just a little bit, before we go home. So I need your help." She gently touched the lapel of his waistcoat, a coaxing smile on her face.

Dominic laughed and wrapped his arm around her shoulders to hug her. "I always have time to help you. As long as what you want isn't too scandalous."

"Of course it isn't. I leave the scandal to my brothers, as you all seem so good at it. I only want you to take me shopping before rehearsal this afternoon. I need to find gifts for Mama and Lily."

"And perhaps a hat or two for yourself?"

Isabel laughed. "Of course. I want all my friends to be wild with envy over my new French couture when we get home."

"I suppose a shopping trip is in order then," Dominic said. He wasn't getting any work done anyway. Perhaps Isabel's company would distract him.

Isabel clapped her hands. "And tea while we're out? Somewhere nice? Without Mrs. Smythe?"

"Very well, tea also. Perhaps Brendan will join us."

"Only for tea. He's such an impatient bear when it comes to shopping. Oh, I almost forgot! The concierge gave me this to give to you. It was delivered a little while ago." Isabel reached into her beaded reticule and took out a letter to hand to him.

Dominic took it from her slowly, almost as if it could come

alive and bite him. Only his name was written across the front in a small, neat, anonymous script, but it smelled faintly of Sophia's perfume.

He tore it open and quickly read the words printed there. *"Thank you for your invitation. I will meet you at the Cafe de Paris on the Boulevard Italiens at nine, if that is convenient for you. Sophia Westman"*

Dominic laughed ruefully. So Sophia *didn't* have any sense when it came to seeing him again. And it seemed they had both gone mad, because he knew he would definitely be there to see her at nine.

Luckily he wasn't performing that night, but Isabel was. And Brendan would have to be at the theater to keep an eye on her, so both of them would be far away from the Boulevard Italiens.

"Who is it from?" Isabel asked, trying to peek at the note.

Dominic refolded it and stuffed it quickly into a desk drawer. "None of your business, Issy."

Isabel laughed and spun away to peer out the grimy office window. "One of your amours, then. I hope she's very pretty." Suddenly a frown flickered over her face. "How very strange."

"Strange?" Dominic said, pausing as she shrugged into his coat.

"Yes. That same man was standing out there when I came in."

Dominic peered over Isabel's shoulder to the street below. It was the usual Parisian daytime tangle of horses and carriages, servants hurrying on errands, well-dressed couples, and yapping dogs on leads. But amid all the color and movement was one dark spot of stillness. A man leaned against the railing of the wrought-iron park fence across the street.

He was a tall, portly figure swathed in a brown tweed coat, with a cap pulled low over his brow. A rolled-up newspaper was tucked under his arm, but he made no move to read it. He seemed to be watching the crowds as they flowed around him. And watching the theater.

Dominic's hand instinctively curled into a tight fist, and he slid Isabel away from the window. There was no law against just standing on the pavement, of course, but after what had happened to him last night and Lord Hammond's strange threats, he was wary of any odd behavior.

"Do you know who he is?" Isabel asked.

"I've never seen him before," Dominic answered, still studying the man. He was very still, as if he was carved from stone, but Dominic somehow sensed he was indeed watching the theater. Dominic's instincts hummed on alert.

"Maybe he's a spy from another theater," Isabel said. She sounded far too excited at the prospect of thespian espionage. "He's going to break in tonight after everyone leaves and steal our scripts for the next show. And then..."

"Issy!" Dominic interrupted. He had to laugh, despite his suspicion of the man lurking outside. "You're much too blood-thirsty, you know."

Isabel pouted. "What do you expect? I'm an actress. I need excitement. And judging by your very colorful bruises, Dominic, I'm not the only one. Is he still there?"

Dominic glanced back out the window. The man was indeed still there, chatting with a maidservant. The girl pointed at the stage door, and the man nodded.

"Yes," Dominic said grimly. "Wait here for a minute, Issy. I'll be right back."

Isabel caught his arm as he turned away. "Are you going to confront him? Oh, let me come, too!"

"Certainly not. You'll stay here and wait for Brendan. And I'm hardly going to confront anyone. I'm merely going to see if the man requires directions."

"I always miss out on the fun." Isabel frowned, but she did plop herself down on a chair by the desk and crossed her arms as if settling in to wait. "At least I can see from the window if there's a fight."

"There won't be a fight," Dominic said. Not another one. Not on a public street right outside the theater in broad daylight. He wasn't that much of a barbarian.

He made his way out of the theater and onto the busy street. It was a beautiful day, sunny and warm, and everyone was hurrying past on their errands. Except for the man leaning against the park fence, the newspaper under his arm. Dominic saw his gaze flicker toward him as he stalked closer.

Dominic leaned against the fence next to the man and folded his arms across his chest. "You have some errand at that theater?" he said casually, as if he was merely making idle conversation.

"Non," the man said briefly, but Dominic could hear the man's flat English accent. He looked burly and muscular under his cheap tweed jacket, like many of the boxers Dominic faced in the ring.

"Just enjoying the day?"

"Something like that. You have a problem with that?"

Dominic suddenly swung around to face the man, not backing down. "Just as long as you don't enjoy yourself in the vicinity of my sister or any of my family."

"I don't know what you mean, monsieur," the man said sullenly. But Dominic saw the tick of the muscle in his jaw.

"I have seen you before," Dominic said quietly. "And you have the look of a hired man about you. But I warn you, hired or not--I will take down anyone who hurts my family. Just so we are clear."

Dominic started to turn away, but out of the corner of his eye he saw a sudden movement. The man's beefy fist started to swing up, but Dominic spun around on the balls of his feet and caught him with an uppercut to the jaw that sent him reeling back into the fence. A passing lady shrieked. Maybe he *was* a bit of a barbarian.

"I mean what I say," Dominic said. "Tell your master that as well."

Then he strode back into the hotel, leaving the hired thug bleeding and cursing behind him.

Seventeen

SOPHIA CLIMBED the marble front steps of the Cafe de Paris and stepped through the etched glass doors, feeling unaccountably nervous as she left the rain-swept streets behind. The sunny day had suddenly turned wet late in the afternoon, and she'd briefly had the wild thought to use the weather as an excuse to beg off this supper engagement.

Which was utterly ridiculous. She'd been attending social occasions since she was a child, had met and talked with any number of people, had learned to deal with any awkwardness. Why would she worry about going out now? Because she was meeting with Dominic, of course.

The man she'd made love with, twice, in a rush of hot, thoughtless need. Dominic, whom she had been so intimate with, as intimate as two people could be, yet who stayed so unknown to her. She wished she could read him better, as she could her opponents at cards.

This supper seemed like a sort of olive branch on his part, a chance to be with each other, maybe come to know each other a little better. No wonder she was rather nervous.

She felt as if she stood poised on the precipice of some steep, rocky cliff rather than on the threshold of a luxurious restaurant.

She was about to jump down into something completely unknown, something she'd never seen before.

"May I take your wrap, madame?" a maid asked, as Sophia paused just inside the door of the foyer.

"Oui, merci," Sophia said, letting the girl take away her hooded cloak. As she turned, she glimpsed herself in one of the tall, gilt-framed mirrors. For a second, she didn't recognize herself.

Camille had persuaded her to leave off her black for the first time since Jack died and splurge on a new gown from one of the shops on the Champs-Elysees. It was a vivid rose-pink silk, cut low off the shoulders and trimmed with loops of ivory satin ribbon and silk flowers. Her hair was piled high on her head and pinned with more roses. Since she had no diamonds or pearls, she'd tied a pink velvet ribbon around her neck.

She looked at the same time like her old self, the Lady Sophia Huntington who danced at London assemblies and debutante balls, and like someone completely new. Someone she didn't yet fully know, but whom she seemed to glimpse in Dominic's eyes when he looked at her.

Sophia smiled at her reflection and spun around to hurry toward the dining room doors. It was time to jump, to see what the future might hold if she could dare to be bold again.

Two liveried footmen opened the glass doors for her, and she stepped out onto the top of a short flight of red-carpeted stairs that led down to the main room. It was a beautiful, plush space, a deep cave of dark red velvet and gilt, lit softly by gaslight, that spoke of discreet pleasures and quiet comforts. An orchestra played on a small balcony above, a soft concerto that blended seamlessly with the environment.

Everywhere there was the gleam of diamonds, the soft sound of laughter, the clink of heavy silver on china, and the smell of gardenias and champagne.

It was its own small, luxurious world, and as Sophia studied it all, she could see how Dominic would belong there. Just as he belonged in the theater, or even in her bedchamber. He was changeable, just as she was, and no one space could contain all of him.

"Madame?" The major-domo, a tall, sternly thin man in dark evening clothes, stepped forward with a bow. "How may I assist you?"

Sophia suddenly realized that several of the people seated near the doors had turned to look at her, curiosity written on their faces. She could no longer hide behind her black clothes.

She didn't even want to hide, not any longer. She wanted to be free to be herself again. Dominic had given her that.

Sophia tilted up her chin and smiled at the major-domo. "I am here to meet Monsieur Dominic St. Claire."

"Of course, madame. He is already seated, if you care to follow me."

As Sophia trailed behind the man through the dining room, she noticed other people watching her and heard the soft murmur of their whispers. She nodded and smiled at groups she knew from Camille's club, and for an instant, some of them looked stunned, as if they had not quite recognized her.

But Dominic knew her immediately. She saw him rise from behind a table tucked into an intimate little corner, and he watched her as she moved closer. For a moment, his face was completely expressionless, his eyes shadowed, and her confidence faltered. Was this going to be the awkwardly polite supper she had feared? The overly drawn-out farewell to something that had barely begun?

Then he smiled. Not a polite, careful smile, but a wide, piratical grin that seemed to draw them together in their own little secret circle. He stepped around the table and held his hand out to her as she approached.

Sophia slipped her gloved fingers into his, and he raised them to his lips. And suddenly she realized there was nowhere she would rather be than here with him. She knew it was most imprudent to feel safe with him, of all people, but she couldn't seem to help it. He made her feel fun again; alive again.

"Thank you for meeting me tonight, Sophia," Dominic said as he drew out a chair for her. "You look very beautiful. Pink suits you."

"Thank you for inviting me," Sophia answered. She carefully arranged her silk skirts around her and gave him a smile as he reached for a bottle of champagne resting in a silver bucket. He filled her waiting glass with the pale golden liquid. "I have heard such good things about the Cafe de Paris. Camille quite raves about it."

"You haven't been here before?" Dominic sat down again across from her. A half-smile hovered around his lips as he watched her.

"I've been too busy working since I arrived in Paris. I haven't been able to see many of the sights."

"We must try to remedy that then."

Sophia laughed. "Are you not busy yourself? Surely the theater keeps you much too occupied for visiting museums and palaces."

Dominic shrugged, still smiling at her. "There's always time for fun. Life is much too short for all work. Don't you agree?"

"Once I might have agreed in an instant," Sophia said. She leaned back in her chair and watched as waiters laid out silver platters on their table. "Until I found I had to make my own coin and learned how time-consuming such things can be. But I'm finding I want some fun again as well."

A frown flickered over Dominic's lips as he lifted the silver lids to reveal a succession of rich, aromatic dishes. "Has your life been so difficult lately, Sophia?"

Sophia shrugged. "I told you how it was with Jack. Our lives were constantly up and down in our short marriage, always traveling, always in a different hotel. But I don't want to think about that tonight."

"No? Then what do you want to think about?"

"This wonderful-looking food, for one thing. And the sights of Paris you might want to see. Perhaps gossip as well. Nothing in the least bit serious. Not tonight." She would have to be serious again all too soon.

Dominic laughed and poured more champagne into her glass. "Very well. Serious topics are banned for tonight. Tell me--have you had time to visit Versailles yet? I understand the restoration work is progressing there..."

As they savored the succession of fine dishes and consumed the bottle of champagne, they talked of the beauties of Paris and of other cities they had visited. Dominic told her the gossip of London she had been missing, and Sophia related some of the funnier tales of her life with Jack, such as the eccentric people she'd met in the spas and casinos of Europe, like the Austrian count who always wore his coat inside out for luck and the elderly Russian princess who traveled with a retinue of ten cats.

They didn't mention Mary's diary, and Dominic didn't try to buy it from her again.

Sophia felt ridiculously happy when Dominic laughed at her tales, and as the night went on, she found that she felt more comfortable than she had in a very long time. It seemed she could say any outrageous thing she liked to Dominic, be completely herself, and he wouldn't be shocked.

And she found she liked him as well. When he laughed like that, she could easily see why he had such a reputation for charming the ladies. Sophia had long thought herself immune to charming men; their charm so often masked a determination to get what they wanted at all costs.

And it was very likely that Dominic was the same. She'd seen his streak of ruthlessness, and his potential for a hot temper. He'd wanted Mary's diary from her; perhaps he wanted other things as well, things she knew nothing about yet. But she was enjoying their evening together far too much to worry about hidden motives. Not yet.

"And what was the very first play you appeared in?" she asked as the waiters laid out plates of cheese and pastries and opened a bottle of dessert wine.

"*Richard III*," Dominic said with a smile. "I was one of the princes in the Tower, and I had no lines since I only appeared in a vision."

"You must have been terribly young."

"I was seven, and Brendan was five. He was the other prince, and he was terrified. He wouldn't quit crying on opening night, and our mother, who played Lady Anne, nearly had to break character to get him to stop." Dominic laughed at the memory. "That was the beginning and the end of his acting career. He's been working behind the scenes ever since."

"But I wager *you* were not scared," Sophia said. She was sure he was never scared of anything.

"Not a bit. I fell in love with everything about the stage that night. The way the world vanished and became something entirely new as the houselights went down. The way *I* could become someone else."

Sophia laughed. "The attention you got when you realized you were good at acting?"

Dominic grinned at her across the table. "I admit that has never been impossible to bear either. To be told we're good at something we love to do--what could be better?"

"I'm not sure I know what that's like," Sophia said wistfully. "The things I am good at, like gambling or causing a scene, have never held much value for my family. Not that it ever stopped me from doing them, of course!"

Something dark and unreadable flashed in Dominic's eyes before he turned away to slide a slice of strawberry gateau onto her plate. "What did you do when you were seven?"

"When you were making your stage debut? I hardly recall," Sophia said with a laugh. "Crying to nanny because my brother broke my doll, perhaps. Or escaping the nursery to creep out and watch my parents departing for a ball. It was one of the few times I could catch a glimpse of them, and my mother always looked so beautiful."

"You didn't spend much time with your family?"

Sophia shook her head. "You seem to know rather a lot about my family, Dominic, so you must know my father is the brother of a duke. My parents were always very busy with their social duties."

"My parents have always been busy as well, with the theater and their business concerns. Yet they always had time for their children."

"Then you were very lucky. It's a good thing for children to know they're loved and accepted for who they are, and not..." Sophia suddenly turned away, blinking against a rush of unexpected and unwelcome tears. She didn't want to think about her family, or the past. Not tonight. "Tell me more about the theater! I sometimes think I should have been an actress, as you once suggested."

She popped a bite of the creamy cake into her mouth and smiled. His eyes darkened, and he leaned across the table to catch a tiny spot of cream from her lower lip onto his fingertip.

"You would be a sensation on the stage," he said hoarsely. "There would be sold-out houses every night just to see you."

Sophia couldn't breathe as she watched him taste the cream. It was almost as if his mouth touched her own skin, as if he took her in his arms and pulled her against his body. "My-my family would die at the scandal. A duke's niece treading the boards!"

Dominic laughed and reached out to slide his hand over hers. It was a quick, impulsive gesture, even more intimate for its casualness. "Do you care what they think any longer?"

"I shouldn't. We have been done with each other for so long."

"Then you should go on the stage, if that's what you want. There are fortunes to be made there for the right people."

"And you think I could be the-right people?"

"Sophia, I think you could do whatever you set your mind to. You are obviously a determined and brave woman."

Brave--no one had ever called her that before. Beautiful, head-strong, willful, foolish, all those things. But never brave. It made her feel suddenly shy, as did the intent gleam in Dominic's eyes as he looked at her. As if he really saw her.

She turned away to study the dining room. Over the course of the night, the crowds had lessened, but the wine was still flowing along with the sparkling laughter. The orchestra played a lively dance tune, and it made Sophia want to take Dominic in her arms and dance around the room with him. To move and laugh, and never stop.

Suddenly a new group of arrivals appeared on the red-carpeted stairs, and Sophia's attention was caught by one of them. It was her cousin Elizabeth, a delicate, fairy-like figure in sea-green silk and pearls. She was laughing with the man who stood beside her, and Sophia was struck again by the difference in Elizabeth now. Her silent diffidence of years past was gone, and she seemed more alive. Lighter.

Perhaps Paris had such an effect on everyone, Sophia thought. Or at least on Huntington women. Here, with a sea between them and their family, they could be free.

Elizabeth caught sight of Sophia and raised her gloved hand in greeting. She glided down the stairs and across the room to Sophia's table.

"Sophia, my dear, how lovely to see you again," Elizabeth said as Sophia rose to greet her. Dominic stood as well, and Sophia sensed him watching them carefully.

"It is good to see you as well, Elizabeth," Sophia said. "I would have thought you had left Paris by now."

"I'm returning to England in a few days, from Calais aboard the *Mary Louise*. I am getting in all the fun I can before then!" Elizabeth said with a curious glance toward Dominic.

"Elizabeth, you must remember Dominic St. Claire from the theater," Sophia said. "Dominic, this is my cousin, Elizabeth, Lady Severn."

To Sophia's shock, Elizabeth suddenly turned very pale. She swayed a bit on her feet, and Sophia held on to her arm for fear she might faint.

But Elizabeth stood up straighter and gave Dominic a shaky smile. "Mr. St. Claire, of course. I enjoyed your performance immensely at the Theatre Nationale. I didn't recognize you at first off the stage."

"I'm glad you had a good time at the play, Lady Severn," Dominic answered politely. "Do you often attend the theater in London as well?"

"Not as often as I would like, but I mostly lived in the country while my husband was alive. I hope to be in London more now." Elizabeth suddenly bit her lip in an uncharacteristic show of uncertainty. "Tell me, Mr. St. Claire--is all your family in Paris with you?"

Dominic's brow creased with a small, puzzled frown, but he answered in that same smooth, polite tone. "Only my sister and one of my brothers. My other brother, James, recently returned home."

"I see," Elizabeth said. "You must miss your family when you are not with them."

"I do. But work sometimes takes us away from each other."

"Of course." One of Elizabeth's companions called to her, and she turned back to Sophia with a smile. "I must go now, Sophia dear, but I hope we'll see each other again before I leave Paris."

"I hope so, too," Sophia said.

As Elizabeth gave her a quick hug, she whispered in Sophia's ear, "And if you want to return to England with me, you need only let me know."

Then Elizabeth was gone, hurrying away across the dining room, and Sophia slowly sat back down.

"So some of your family *do* speak to you," Dominic said.

Sophia glanced across the table to find him smiling at her. "Only Elizabeth, and only because she is here where no one can see her." She looked over to where Elizabeth sat with her friends. "It's most strange..."

"Strange?"

"Yes. Elizabeth and I were friends when we were girls, but

after she married we hardly spoke. But she came to see me a few days ago, and now she is being very sociable tonight."

Dominic poured the last of the wine into her glass. "What did she want when she came to see you?"

To tell me I should find a new husband to suit my family, Sophia thought. But she could hardly say that to Dominic, the very last man who would suit her family. And the last man she should ever marry.

She sipped the wine, sorry to see their evening drawing to a close. It had seemed almost magical. A moment out of time. "Just to say hello, I suppose. It's been a long time since we saw each other."

Dominic nodded, and a few minutes later, he took her arm to lead her out of the dining room. By the time she found her cloak and they stepped beyond the glass doors into the night, it had ceased raining, and the moon was peeking out from behind the gray clouds. The damp streets seemed to glisten under the gaslights, and the air smelled cool and clear. Sophia drew in a deep breath to clear away the wine and the sheer intoxication of just being with Dominic.

"Shall I see you home?" he said. He raised his arm to hail a cab, but Sophia caught his hand in hers.

"Let's walk for a while," she said. "It's such a lovely night. It seems such a shame to waste it."

Dominic frowned and glanced over his shoulder, and Sophia feared he was remembering how he had been attacked on the Paris streets. "Just to the end of the street?" she said. The fashionable Boulevard Italiens was crowded with people leaving the restaurants and cafes; surely there were no footpads there.

Dominic nodded and took her arm. Sophia leaned against him and smiled.

The street that housed the Cafe de Paris was lined with fine restaurants and glossy shops, all of them blazing with light and life even so late at night. Sophia paused to examine the beautiful window displays, the furls of richly colored fabrics, the feathers and flowers of fashionable hats, the luscious chocolates and pastel macaroons of patisseries and chocolate shops. They were all lit like fabulous jewels, sparkling in the night.

And it all seemed even more beautiful, more exotic, with Dominic beside her.

At the end of the street was a bookstore. Unlike the other establishments, its window display seemed slightly dusty and shabby. New volumes from England lay on a green cloth, their brown leather covers subdued. As Sophia peered through the glass, she saw that the place appeared dark, except for a ray of light far in the back recesses.

Across the glass scrolled faded gold letters--*Books and Fine Stationery, M. Petron Proprietor.*

"Monsieur Petron's!" Sophia exclaimed. "Camille told me about this place. It's quite the secret. We should go in."

"A bookstore?" Dominic said, laughing. "At this time of night? You did not quite strike me as a bluestocking, Sophia."

"It's not just any bookstore." She tugged on his arm, urging him to follow her to the door. "Just for a little while. I want to see it."

"Are you sure they're even open?" he said.

"Of course." Sophia pushed at the door latch, and it swung open with a jangling of bells. Dominic shook his head, but he followed her.

The shop appeared to be deserted. The haphazard piles of volumes on the shelves were covered with a light, snowy layer of dust, as if no one ever touched them. Library ladders leaned against the peeling paint of the walls, soaring up into cobwebbed shadows.

Sophia made her way to the doorway half-hidden in the corner, Dominic close beside her. When they stepped into the back room, it was like an entirely different place. Wall sconces cast a soft amber light over the shelves and the chairs scattered over a plain green carpet. There were several people there, well-dressed couples who could have just come from the Cafe de Paris, as well as shady-looking men in caps pulled low over their faces. A display just inside the door showed what appeared to be the newest, most popular volume--a thin, leather-bound tale called *Therese Awakening, or one girl's escape from the convent into a world of sin and riches.*

The pen-and-ink sketch under the title showed a slender young woman with an improbably large bosom well-displayed in a tight corset. She leaned over a stool, her petticoats tossed up as a masked man wielded a switch over her bare, and copiously striped, buttocks.

"I do hope the riches are great indeed," Sophia murmured. She scanned the shelves and found a neat row of similar titles.

Dominic laughed. "I see what you mean, Sophia. This is no ordinary bookstore."

"In London they would have been raided by now. But surely you've visited such places before." She drew out another volume, *A Guide to the Prevention of Vices*, and found that it showed a myriad of things a virtuous person should not do. In great, colorful detail.

"I have, in other cities," he answered. "There hasn't been much time for-exploration here."

"Nor for me. Goodness, but doesn't this look interesting! How is such a thing even possible?" She showed Dominic a two-page illustration of two men and three women in various poses, all of them extremely athletic.

Dominic laughed again. She was glad he seemed to be enjoying himself. "Oh, believe me, it's possible."

"Indeed? How intriguing. I definitely think I need this volume then. My education is quite lacking." She handed it to Dominic to carry and went on to the next display.

It was a low, flat glass case like in a jewelry store's, but rather than diamonds and pearls it showed a range of finely wrought restraints, wrist cuffs and chains, and a selection of beautiful glass and ivory dildos. One looked especially realistic, with a tracery of veins carved in the smooth, pale stone. A ring of tiny rubies curled around the head.

"I'm sure the author of *A Guide to the Prevention of Vices* would have a great deal to say about the use of these," Sophia said, tilting her head to examine them more closely.

"Would madame care to examine this one?" the proprietor of the shop, a tiny, gray-haired gnome of a man, asked softly.

"No, madame would not," Dominic said, taking Sophia's hand.

Sophia pulled away from him, laughing. "Of course I would! I quite like this one."

Dominic shook his head, but he stayed with her. Sophia had the distinct sense he was amused by her explorations. And she was having fun, too. She could hardly remember the last time she really had *fun*. Yet with Dominic, the world always seemed new and amusing. He didn't even draw away from her wilder fancies.

"An excellent choice, madame," the proprietor said approvingly. He drew it out of the case and laid it out on a piece of velvet, as if it were a necklace or a ring. "Seventeenth century, from Venice. Ivory and cabochon rubies. Perfectly carved from life, as you can see. You would never be disappointed with such a fine piece."

"I shouldn't think so." Sophia slowly ran her fingertip along the ridge and swirled it over the bead. "Lovely."

Beside her, she felt Dominic grow tense, his breath turn harsh. "The lady will take it," he said.

"Dominic," she murmured. "I can't afford it."

"It's my gift," he said firmly.

Sophia stared up at him. His face was smooth, smiling. He gave no clue why he would buy her such an extravagant gift. "Dominic, no," she whispered.

He just laughed. "Please, Sophia, let me. There are few experiences I have not had in life, but one of them is buying a beautiful lady a jeweled dildo. Consider it a thank-you for an amusing evening."

Sophia looked down at the gleaming ivory. All the wicked, alluring things that could be done with it flashed through her mind, and she was very tempted.

"Very well," she said finally. "Thank you."

"You won't be sorry, madame," the proprietor said. After he had wrapped up their purchases, Sophia let Dominic lead her out of the shop and back onto the street. It was just as crowded as earlier, and a quartet of fabulously dressed, bejeweled people brushed past them into the store.

"A very popular place," Sophia commented as they turned toward home.

"Justifiably so," Dominic answered. "His stock is quite extraordinary."

Sophia laughed and clutched at the paper-wrapped package. She still couldn't quite believe she had let him buy it for her. It seemed like the perfect, silly end to a wonderfully giddy evening. They didn't say anything on the walk back to the club, just strolled along arm-in-arm and let the evening swirl around them.

"Here it is," Sophia said when they came to the side door of La Reine d'Argent. They looked at each other in heavy silence for a moment, and suddenly it was as if they both knew what had to happen next. Dominic bent down and caught her up in his arms.

He carried her up the stairs and along the shadowed corridor, lit only by the lamp the maid had left on one table. It was so silent there, so dark, as if they were wrapped up alone in their own world.

Dominic nudged open her apartment door with his foot and slid inside before kicking it shut again. Sophia barely had time to drop her precious paper-wrapped parcel on the sofa before he carried her through to the waiting bedroom. He laid her lightly onto the bed, and Sophia laughed as she sank back into the piles of blankets. She tried to sit up, but Dominic fell on top of her, pinning her down with the hard, lean heat of his body. He braced his arms to either side of her, holding himself above her as if she was his prisoner.

His prisoner. It was a delicious thought, to be Dominic's to do with as he pleased.

"What were you thinking, Sophia, to drag me into a place like that?" he said roughly, as his fingers tangled in her hair and drew the strands free of their pins. The roses there scattered around them. "Were you trying to drive me crazy with lust?"

Sophia laughed. "Did I shock you with my knowledge that such shops exist?"

"Oh, Sophia." His hands slid closer, gently cradling her face between his palms. She looked up at him, and his eyes glowed with laughter, lust, and--admiration. Or perhaps she only wished for that, imagining it there.

"I doubt anything about you could shock me," he said. "Everything I discover only makes me want you more. Damn you."

Before Sophia could let those words sink in, Dominic bent his head to kiss the pulse that beat at her temple, the tip of her nose, her chin. "Your skin is so soft..." he whispered hoarsely.

And then his lips brushed her eyelids as they fluttered closed. In that perfect darkness, she fell down and down into a soft, velvet abyss where there was only pure sensation. Only Dominic.

His open mouth slid down her neck, hot and hungry as she arched back beneath him. He nipped lightly at the hollow of her throat, as if he would absorb the life that beat there into himself.

"Sophia..." he whispered, and she sat up so he could reach behind her to unfasten the tiny pearl buttons of her bodice. Halfway down, he lost patience. With a low growl, his hand twisted in the soft silk and tore the rest free. The pearls scattered across the floor, and Sophia laughed as she slid her arms free of the tight cap sleeves.

Dominic drew the gown away until she lay beneath him in her petticoats and corset. His mouth was suddenly back on her skin, his teeth lightly scraping over the curve of her bare shoulder. Sophia shivered at the sensations that danced through her, and she drew her knees up tight to either side of his hips as her petticoats fell back around them in a lacy white froth.

She pressed herself up against him and smiled when she felt how hard he was. But his kiss was too soft, too gentle. His tongue lightly circled the soft curve of her breast, closer and closer to her aching nipple, until he slid teasingly away again.

"Dominic," she moaned, and he lightly pressed one finger against her lips.

"Patience, Sophia," he said with an infuriating smile. "Be still, let me touch you. We have the rest of the night..."

She sucked the tip of his finger between her lips and caught it in her teeth to suck at it. His breath hissed in his throat, and he sat up between her legs.

"You are being very naughty, Sophia," he said. He slowly slid his hands up her legs, beneath her petticoats. His touch was hard and hot on her body, and she wanted more. So much more.

His fingers slid under her satin ribbon garter, and he untied it to draw her silk stocking down her leg. His caress lingered on the sensitive spot at the back of her knee.

"Dominic!" she cried. "Enough teasing. I want you inside me-- now."

He rose above her, and Sophia felt exultant that he was finally going to give her what she wanted, what had been building between them all night. But he didn't move. He suddenly grabbed her wrists and forced her hands above her head, binding them together with her stocking. He wound the loose end of it tightly around the bedpost, holding her still.

"Dominic," she protested. His name seemed to be the only word she had left. She tried to wrap her legs around his waist to pull him back to her but he slipped from the bed. He drew her other stocking slowly down her leg and tore it in half to tie her ankles to the other posts, her legs spread for him.

"I warned you to be still," he said, smiling as he quickly stripped away his own clothes. His skin gleamed in the candle-light, his face half-hidden in the shadows.

"Dominic..." she cried. She pulled at her bonds, longing to be free of them even as they kindled a strange excitement in her. "I want you now, damn it all!"

Dominic slowly lowered himself between her legs again, laughing at her struggle. "You have to learn patience, Sophia," he whispered, and took her aching nipple between his lips to suck at it hard until she moaned.

His tongue circled the erect, sensitive flesh, until he caught it between his teeth. He bit at it lightly, and then soothed the wonderful sting with the tip of his tongue. His hand flattened on her taut abdomen, just above her navel, and slowly slid lower and lower as she gasped with the pleasure of his touch.

"Tell me what you want, Sophia," he said against her breast. One fingertip lightly caressed the damp curls between her legs, teasing her. "Do you want me to touch you here?"

That finger delved gently past her slit, a rough touch that slid against her most sensitive spot. But it wasn't nearly enough.

"Yes," she said fiercely, her head arching back on the pillows as hot sparks of pure sensation shot through her body at his skillful touch.

A second finger slid deep inside her. "Would you like it if I kissed you here as well?"

"Yes..." Sophia sighed, remembering how his mouth had felt between her thighs. So perfect--so, so good. Her body ached for it again.

His open mouth, hot and wet, trailed along her skin. He nipped with his teeth over her hip, circled her navel with his tongue, his hand touching her harder, deeper, until she cried out wordlessly.

Then finally he moved between her legs, and she felt his mouth on that most intimate, sensitive spot. His fingers spread her wide for his kiss, and the tip of his tongue licked lightly up her wet seam before delving deeply.

She cried out his name. And suddenly her desire for him, that desire that blotted out everything else, frightened her. Her whole life had been marred by losing control; she didn't want that now, even as she wanted it more than anything.

"Dominic--stop!" she cried as the crashing waves of pleasure threatened to consume her.

But he gave her no mercy. He just tasted her deeply, giving her pleasure even as he seemed to take it. Sophia let the sensations explode within her.

Only as she sank back to the earth, the tremors of her climax slowly ebbing away, did he rise above her on his knees. He looked down at her as she lay there, helpless, and he smiled.

He finally released her from her bonds, and she surged up to wrap her arms around him, their damp heat winding around them, tying them together even more than the silk bonds. He kissed her, open-mouthed, as if he was as hungry as she was. She tasted the scent of herself on his lips, his tongue, and it made her excitement grow all over again.

He wrapped his hands around her hips and tried to drag her closer, but she slid away from him. She moved down his body, skin against skin, and reached between them to wrap her fingers around his hard cock. He throbbed under her touch, and she lowered her head to take him deep into her mouth.

"Sophia," he groaned. His fingers twined through her hair as if he would push her away. But she liked having him at her mercy for once, and she wouldn't let him go. She traced the length of him with her tongue, tasting the musk of him. She wrapped her hands around his tight backside and drew him closer to her eager mouth.

"No more," he said hoarsely. He pulled back from her and pushed her back down to the bed. He spread her legs wide and thrust inside her.

Sophia dug her nails into his strong shoulders as she silently urged him closer, faster--deeper. He drove into her again and again, and she couldn't breathe, couldn't think. Everything was only feeling. She wrapped her legs tightly around his waist and drew him even deeper.

She found her release again, a hot wave that washed over her and made her forget the whole world for an instant. Above her, Dominic's head flung back, and he shouted out her name. His body arched into hers, and there was nothing at all between them. Nothing keeping them apart.

He fell down onto the bed beside her, their limbs tangled together. Sophia trembled; she was completely exhausted. She curled herself around him and he wrapped his arm around her waist to hold her close. She pressed a soft kiss to his shoulder and listened to the steady, strong rhythm of his heartbeat.

And she couldn't help but wish the night could last just a little bit longer.

From the Diary of Mary St. Claire Huntington

The duke has arrived in suitably grand state, with a trail of carriages and mountains of luggage. Our house has never seen such business before, all noise and motion! It is terribly exciting, I have to admit, and has done much to lift me from my sadness. He has not brought the duchess, but there is a startlingly lovely woman who seems to be with him at every moment. Except when she is talking to John.

John is also much happier than I have seen him in a long time. At the banquet tonight, he was so charming, just like when we first met, so full of smiles. I hope this will continue when the duke leaves.

Eighteen

"YOU HAVE a visitor in the salon, Madame Westman," the footman announced.

Sophia looked up from the papers she was perusing with Camille, her heart suddenly leaping with excitement. Perhaps it was Dominic. She hadn't been able to stop thinking about him ever since he had kissed her at dawn and slipped out of her apartment before the house awoke. He'd said he would see her later. Surely it had to be him waiting in the salon.

"A visitor?" she said, surprised that her voice sounded so calm while inside she felt anything but.

"Oui. He was most urgent he had to see you," the footman answered. "But he did not give his card."

"Ah, a secret admirer!" Camille teased. "How very intriguing."

Sophia laughed. "How secret can it be if he came to see me in my own home?"

"But you have so many admirers! Which one can it be? Perhaps I can guess..."

Sophia shook her head. She was glad the curtains were half-drawn across the windows so her blush wasn't so obvious. It felt silly to actually blush after everything she had done with Dominic last night. But it also felt good to do something as normal, as feminine, as laughing about suitors with a girlfriend.

"Go on and talk to your suitor," Camille said. "I will finish up these accounts."

"Are you sure?"

"Of course--go, go! It is much too pretty a day to think about anything except romance."

Sophia laughed and hurried out of the office. She felt so light, so ridiculously giddy, that she wanted to run down the stairs. Maybe even to slide down the banisters and twirl around and around. But she made herself walk in a calm, ladylike fashion.

At the landing, she paused to glance in a mirror that hung there. She smoothed her hair, braided and looped in a knot in the latest fashion, and shook out her skirts. She hadn't been able to face wearing black again after her beautiful pink dress, so she wore her only other colored dress, the yellow muslin from the picnic. She was glad now that she had pulled it out of her wardrobe, for it matched her mood.

She spun around and hurried down the rest of the stairs to the foyer. Here the windows and doors were thrown open to the sunny day, and the maids worked at scrubbing the marble floor and dusting the giltwork before that night's guests came flooding back to the club. La Reine d'Argent had been a great success so far, as the numbers in the account books attested.

Yet another reason to feel hopeful, Sophia thought with a smile. She wasn't so very useless after all; she could be good at business.

She pushed open the door to the salon and rushed inside, wanting to invite Dominic to the club that night after the theater. But the man who stood silhouetted against the window was not Dominic at all. Sophia froze, unable to believe what she was seeing as Lord Hammond turned and gave her a smile.

"Mrs. Westman," he said, his words as warm and friendly as if they were long-lost friends. They did not match the chill of that smile. "How lovely it is to see you again."

Sophia softly closed the door behind her and leaned against it as she studied him warily. She had hoped that he'd returned to London, as he'd said he was going to do after their last meeting. But she should have known better. A man like him did not give up so easily. Sophia thought about the money she was carefully saving from working for Camille and wondered if she could return the money he had wagered.

But she knew it wasn't really the money he wanted.

Beyond the door she could hear the bustle of the servants, and it gave her a slight feeling of security. She remembered the way Lord Hammond used to look at her, as if she was a possession he had the right to claim, and part of her wanted to leave the door open as an escape route. But she was sure she wouldn't want anyone else to hear whatever he had to say.

He came slowly toward her, still with that chilly smile on his thin lips. He was just as impeccably dressed as she remembered, just as austerely handsome. Her skin prickled as she watched him come closer, and she rubbed her hands over her arms through the thin muslin sleeves.

Sophia realized something as she studied him. Dominic had a similar air of confidence, almost arrogance, but his sense of self seemed to exude from fun and laughter. He drew people to him because they wanted to be part of that sheer exuberant life. Hammond held people captive by the force of his will, like some ancient warlord.

Sophia had never wanted to be his prize. And she was no longer as scared and lost as she had been in Baden-Baden. She pushed herself away from the door and stood up straight as she forced herself to smile at him.

"Lord Hammond," she said. "What a surprise. I didn't know you were still in Paris."

"I couldn't leave yet, not with you still here." He stepped close to her, too close. She could smell his expensive cologne, and the cloying scent of it seemed to wrap around her like tentacles. He watched her closely, as if he tried to read her every flicker of thought and emotion.

Sophia summoned up every ounce of acting skill she had learned at the card tables and held out her hand to him. He raised it to his lips, his kiss lingering on her skin until she slid her fingers out of his grasp and turned toward the sofa near the fireplace.

"I hope you have not stayed in Paris merely to see me," she said. She sat down and arranged her skirts around her. Lord Hammond remained standing, leaning lazily against the marble mantel as he watched her. "I thought we said everything we needed to last time we met."

"I had some business to attend to for my cousin, the Duke of Pendrake," he said. "But I must confess I could have avoided the errand if I had not wanted to see you again, my dear Mrs. Westman. I don't care to play games with you any longer."

Sophia slowly rose to her feet, and she found that her legs were shaking. "Then let me see you out..."

Lord Hammond suddenly moved, quick as a striking cobra, and caught her wrist in his hand. His fingers tightened until Sophia was just at the edge of pain. She gasped and tried to wrench away, but she found she couldn't move.

"I know that you are in no position to be so haughty, Lady Sophia," he said quietly. "I have made inquiries about you. Your family has turned you out and you are alone in the world, a gambler, a wanderer. You should think twice before you turn me away again."

Sophia's mouth felt dry, and she swallowed hard as she looked up into his cold eyes. "It's true I no longer see my family, but I am not so friendless as that."

Lord Hammond laughed and tugged her an inch closer. "If you are thinking of the St. Claires, I wouldn't count on them, my dear. They are some of the biggest chancers in London, and they will always look after themselves first. They would abandon you without blinking. But I could be your very best friend in the world, if you would only be a smart girl and let me."

Sophia stared at him, appalled. How did he know about the St. Claires? About Dominic? Terrible images flashed through her mind, of Dominic bruised and bleeding on her doorstep, James suddenly and inexplicably shipped home. Did Lord Hammond have something to do with all that?

She made herself laugh carelessly. She gave her wrist a sharp twist, and he finally let her go. She fell back onto the sofa, her legs too weak to hold her up. "The St. Claires? What would I need with their friendship? They are only theater people. They could never help me get back into my family's good graces."

"I'm glad you can see that, my dear."

"Of course I can. My uncle is a duke. The St. Claires can do nothing for a Huntington."

"Is that what you want? To be accepted by your family again?"

"I-I have considered such a thing," Sophia said slowly. Better for him to talk about the Huntingtons than the St. Claires.

Lord Hammond sat down beside her and reached again for her hand. His touch was gentler this time, his fingers almost caressing her wrist. A cold nausea almost choked Sophia, but she forced herself to remain still.

"I could help you with that," he said. "I could give you so much, Sophia. You need only ask."

Sophia laughed bitterly. "My family would surely never speak to me again if I returned to London as your mistress."

"They wouldn't dare shun Lady Hammond."

"L-Lady Hammond? But I thought you were married," Sophia stammered. He had caught her off-guard. He had suddenly changed whatever this tug-of-war was between them, and she had to figure out how to respond to fend him off.

"My wife has sadly passed away in the last few weeks. She was never very well. I require a proper wife now. And if you were my wife, your family would accept you again. You would have your rightful place in Society again."

"But in Baden-Baden..."

"I asked you to be my mistress, to let me keep you in the lavish style your beauty deserves. But I can see now I was wrong. You are different." He frowned as if it pained him to confess he could possibly be wrong. "A man in my position needs a wife, someone to run his home properly and help him in Society. With your looks and breeding, you should do very well." He suddenly smiled, and that smile seemed even more terrible than his anger. "And you would have to be grateful. Yes, an excellent solution."

Sophia certainly didn't think it was any sort of solution. She felt frantic to escape him now, to get away from his cold, hard certainty. His arrogant expectation that she would be grateful for his benevolence. He was everything she had fought against all her life.

"I thank you for your great generosity, Lord Hammond," she said quietly, rising to her feet. "But I don't intend to ever marry again. I like my life just as it is." She rose to her feet. "And now I bid you good afternoon."

Lord Hammond stood up beside her, his face set in lines as hard as granite. Sophia felt afraid again, but she couldn't bear to be near him another instant, even to maintain her facade. As she spun around to flee, he caught her arm and dragged her against him. She was too frozen to struggle.

"You ungrateful, stupid little bitch," he growled. "I offer you everything, even my name, and you are too foolish to take it. Perhaps you require another lesson or two."

That frozen fear suddenly crumbled in a flash of burning temper. How dare he come here again, telling her what she would do with the rest of her life? He was just like her father, like Jack, pulling her every which way to suit their whims.

And she was sick to death of it.

"I require nothing from you," she said. "I told you--I will make my own way in the world now."

Lord Hammond's lips twisted in a hard smile. "As a gambling club dolly? But what if this lovely little establishment was closed--

and no other would hire you? Then what would you do? Your skills and attributes are limited, my dear, and while I am in a position to make use of them, most men are not."

"Lord Hammond, I must go..." Sophia gasped, and desperately tried to pull away from him.

His other arm came around her, and he held her unmoving as his lips brushed her hair. "Please don't make this unpleasant, my dear. I could be a good husband to you. I could give you everything. But you must obey me." Sophia twisted around hard and reached out for the bell pull that hung just within her grasp. She pulled it as hard as she could, and when there was the sound of footsteps outside the door, Lord Hammond at last moved away from her.

"Madame?" the maid said.

"His lordship is just leaving," Sophia said breathlessly. Lord Hammond tugged his coat into place and smoothed his hair, just as imperturbable as ever. He gave her a cool smile.

"I will go now. You need time to think about what I have said, my dear. I understand that. It has been unexpected, and you are of a very passionate nature.

I do enjoy that--to a point."

He reached for her hand. Sophia pulled it back before he could kiss it, and his smile tightened. "This is a lovely place," he said. "I should so hate to see a misfortune befall it. Which understandably would happen if Madame Martine continued to maintain unsuitable employees."

Unsuitable employees. Sophia watched him, letting his threat hang heavy in the silence between them.

He nodded. "I am staying at the Hotel des Etranger until the end of the week. I look forward to hearing from you there, my dear Mrs. Westman."

Once he was gone, Sophia stumbled to the window and watched until she saw him step into his waiting carriage and ride away. She leaned her forehead against the cool glass, dizzy with how fast the bright day had turned dark. She had spun from being hopeful, even giddy, to feeling trapped and alone all over again. Caught.

All the things she wanted to escape were right there around her again.

The salon door opened again, and Sophia spun around, half-afraid that Lord Hammond had returned. But it was only Camille, smiling at her brightly.

"So, who was it?" Camille said. "Your secret suitor?"

"I have to go out," Sophia managed to say. She felt as if the walls were closing in around her, and she needed to be out in the fresh air, to breathe and think.

"Is something amiss?" Camille asked, bewildered, as Sophia hurried out of the room.

"Not at all," she called back over her shoulder. She caught up her cloak from where she and Dominic had dropped it the night before. "I just recollected an errand I must perform..."

She made her way out onto the street and turned blindly away from the club. She hardly noticed the carriages and carts that clattered past, the laughing people who brushed by her. She only felt that too-familiar urge to run.

Sophia turned at the end of street and made her way to the river. She climbed to the peak of the old stone bridge and leaned on the railing as she stared down into the water below. Boats and barges floated beneath her, and she wondered what it would be like to leap down onto one of those gleaming decks and float away to some unknown place. Someplace where she wouldn't be Sophia Huntington Westman, but just--herself. Whoever that was.

But even as the thought drifted through her mind, she had to laugh. Running away never worked before; she always ran into herself. She had to stay and face Lord Hammond.

Yet how could she stay and let him hurt Camille, when all she had done was help Sophia when she needed it the most? How could she fight him?

"Sophia!" she heard someone call. She spun around to find

Dominic making his way toward her over the bridge. He didn't wear a hat, and the wind off the river tossed his bright hair over his brow. He smiled at her, but it looked wary.

Sophia suddenly wanted to run to him, to hold on to him and hear his laughter reassuring her. To feel that she wasn't alone.

But the truth was, she was alone. "*The St. Claires are chancers...they will always look after themselves first,*" she remembered Lord Hammond saying, and while she put no credence in his opinion, she did know Dominic owed her nothing. That they had made love, that she feared she had come to care for him far too much, didn't mean he cared for her in return.

If only he did...

"What's wrong?" he asked as he stopped by her side. He leaned his hand on the bridge railing, his body close to hers. She wanted to lean into him. "I came by Madame Martine's, but she said you had gone dashing off. Luckily I saw you come this way."

Sophia quickly swiped her hand over her eyes, hoping he couldn't see the tears that threatened to fall there, that she didn't look too haggard and confused. He was the last person she would ever want to see her that way.

"You came to see me?" she said.

"Of course. I might be an actor, but I'm not so completely ungentlemanly as to ignore a lady after what happened last night."

He held out his hand, and Sophia saw that he held a bouquet of violets and tiny lilies-of-the-valley tied up with white ribbons. They were beautiful, perfect, like a new beginning between them. Too late?

"For me?" Sophia murmured.

"Yes, of course. But if you don't like them, I could always give them to that lady over there."

He turned as if to give away her bouquet with an elaborate flourish, and Sophia had to laugh. She caught them out of his hand and inhaled the clean, earthy scent of the flowers. Despite her worries, the day suddenly seemed a little brighter.

"Thank you," she said. "They're very pretty."

"As are you," he answered. He took a step closer, watching her carefully. A frown creased his brow. "But you look worried today. What's happened?"

Sophia shook her head, suddenly remembering Lord Hammond's visit and his threats. How could she tell Dominic what had happened? It was not his problem.

"Madame Martine said you had another visitor this morning, that he was the one who upset you and made you run off so suddenly," Dominic said.

Sophia shrugged. "I have many visitors, not all of them welcome."

"Who was he?" Dominic asked quietly. He reached out to gently touch her hand, and even that light contact made her want to cry again.

"Did he hurt you?" Dominic said. "Please, Sophia, you can tell me. Let me help you."

Sophia looked up into his eyes to find whether she could trust him or not. She saw concern there, puzzlement. And suddenly she realized they stood on a crowded bridge, close together and holding hands. Anyone could see them there. She stumbled back from him and glanced back over her shoulder frantically, wondering if Lord Hammond or one of his minions was watching.

"I'm not sure anyone could help me," she said. "This is a hole I have dug myself into."

Dominic's eyes narrowed. He seemed to sense some of her fear of being watched, for he took her hand again and turned to lead her down the other side of the bridge.

"Where are we going?" Sophia asked.

"Somewhere we can talk," he answered. "It seems we haven't done nearly enough of that."

Sophia followed him past the riotous color of the flower markets and the bustle of cafes and shops, until they found themselves in the comparative quiet of the Île Saint-Louis. There were still people there, knots of tourists with their open guidebooks circling the soaring shadows of Notre Dame and strolling in the gardens. They took no notice of Dominic and Sophia as he led her through the arched doors and into the cool, shadowed church.

Sophia had visited Notre Dame when she first arrived in Paris, taken on a whirlwind tour by Camille and one of her gentlemen friends. The man had considered himself something of an architectural expert and had swept down the aisles and through the nave pointing out columns and buttresses, windows and altars. Sophia had considered the dark beauty of it all, but today it felt different. Today it felt like a hushed sanctuary.

Faint light streamed through the red and blue glass of the windows, beaming past arches to cast a glow on plaster saints' faces and a few living humans kneeling on the stone floors. The air was cool, faintly touched with the scent of incense. Sophia felt as if she could hide there in the light and dark, with only Dominic's hand on hers to bold her to the earth.

But they didn't stop in the church. He led her to a narrow, winding flight of stone steps, and they started climbing up and up.

"How many stairs are there?" Sophia said with a gasping laugh.

Dominic glanced at her over his shoulder, the corner of his lips quirked in a half-smile. "Four hundred. But at the top, we can talk with noone to hear us but the pigeons and the gargoyles."

Sophia followed him as they climbed onward, the only sounds their breath and the brush of their shoes on the stone. At last they emerged into the light, high above Paris.

"Good heavens," Sophia sighed, enraptured by. what she saw around her. Between the horns of the twisted, snarling gargoyles, the whole city was laid out before her like a silent, white, glittering fairyland dotted with the domes and tall steeples of churches.

Even the sky seemed closer here, an arch of pure blue so near she was sure she could reach out and touch it. And Dominic was right-they were completely alone.

"This is so beautiful," she said. She leaned past the stone balustrade to peer down at the cobbled forecourt, where the crowds of tourists looked Like scurrying ants. "How could I have not noticed it last time I was here?"

Dominic smiled at her. He rested his hand on the stone ledge next to her, not touching but close, keeping her safe. "Because you weren't with me before."

Sophia laughed. "Yes. I can believe that you always find the most beautiful, most dramatic places wherever you go."

"Ah, well, setting is everything." Dominic gazed out over the city as the wind caught at his hair. "We're alone here, Sophia. You can tell me whatever you like. Who was your visitor today?"

Sophia took a step back to lean against the cold wall. As she studied the tiny, faraway city, she twined the ribbon of the bouquet around her finger. It *did* feel safe up here, alone with Dominic as he watched her calmly. He didn't press her or hurry her, didn't tell her what to do. He was just there. With her.

And she was really very tired of being alone.

"Before I came to Paris, I was in Baden-Baden," she said. "That was where Jack died. I was alone there, no money, no place to go. And there was this man. Lord Hammond."

"Hammond?" Dominic said, his tone startled. "He was your visitor today?"

"Yes," Sophia said. "Do you know him?" *Oh, please, don't let him be friends with Hammond*, she thought frantically. But that made no sense. Hammond had threatened the St. Claires as well today.

A muscled flexed in Dominic's strong jaw. "I have had encounters with him. A rather unpleasant individual, quite happy to throw his weight around."

"Yes indeed," Sophia agreed with a humorless laugh. "Unpleasant is one term for him."

"Shit-eating bastard is another," Dominic said. "If he was your unwanted caller, I'm not surprised you ran. So, you met him in Baden-Baden."

Sophia nodded. She told him a shortened version of the tale of her encounters with Lord Hammond, winning his money in the card game, his pursuit of her. His unwelcome, and most insistent, marriage proposal. It felt unbelievably relieving just to say it aloud, to get it out of her mind and out into the world for a moment.

"How did you come to meet Lord Hammond?" she asked as she finished.

Dominic stared out thoughtfully over the city. His expression was calm and cool, not betraying any reaction to her story. "He was playing cards with my brother James at a bawdy house one night. There was a disagreement."

"I see," Sophia said slowly. "So that is why James returned to London?"

"Yes. And the rest of us are to follow next week." Dominic was silent for a moment longer, then he suddenly turned to her with a smile. "There is only one solution to your difficulty, Sophia."

Sophia wasn't sure she trusted that smile. "Oh? And what is that? Murder?"

"Worse. You should marry me."

Sophia choked out a laugh. Surely she hadn't imagined that! She had never heard more outrageous words. "You shouldn't joke about such things."

She turned away from him, but he caught her hand and drew her back to him. He looked down at her steadily, and to her shock, he looked perfectly serious.

"I'm not joking," he said. "Sophia Westman, will you do me the honor of marrying me?"

"But we haven't known each other very long!" she said, even as she knew that was a silly argument. She had known Jack a month when she eloped with him.

And that was a mistake she was determined never to repeat.

"If you count our first meeting, we've known each other a long time," he answered with a quirk of a smile.

"Our first meeting was hardly an auspicious one," Sophia scoffed. "And why would you want to marry me after I kneed you in the groin and ran away?"

"Because you could use my help right now, I think," he said. "And that is a rare thing for me, to be able to help someone."

"It's true I could use your help," she admitted, remembering how alone she had felt when she ran to the river. And now here was Dominic. Even though she was cautious of his sudden offer, part of her wanted to reach out for it.

"But," she went on, "marriage is for such a very long time. Once the threat of Lord Hammond is past, and I don't need your help with him any longer, you may be sorry."

Dominic laughed. "Sophia, I have the feeling that even after Hammond, you will need my help. Just as I will need yours."

Sophia studied his face, puzzled. "How can I help *you*?"

"Once we return to London, the Devil's Fancy will need a hostess again. No one has been able to fill the role since my sister left, and I think you would be excellent at it."

"Yet you hardly need to marry me for that," Sophia said.

"And you could make my family cease to worry over me," he added. "Ever since Jane died, they have been hovering around me with solemn looks on their faces. If they think I've found a proper lady to look after me, I won't have to put up with that any longer. They'll let us set up our own household in peace."

Sophia laughed. "Somehow I can't picture your brother Brendan hovering around, clucking in sympathy."

"Oh, he is the worst of the lot, I assure you."

"I admit having a house of my own sounds wonderful," she said. She was very tempted. But what he was offering so far sounded like a business arrangement. His protection for her hostessing and housekeeping skills. "Yet could we really live together?"

She thought about Mary's diary, about how her marriage

started with such hopes and ended so bleakly. She didn't want to end up like that.

"Sophia," he said, taking her hand in his. "I think we could live together very well. We understand each other, do we not? We could have so many adventures together."

Adventures. Yes, they did understand each other. With him, she wouldn't have to fight against her nature, as she had tried to do with her family and failed at so miserably. He wouldn't expect her to be what she was not.

He made no mention of love, yet surely understanding was more than most couples could expect. She would be a fool to look for anything more, especially when she had never looked for this at all. She should be sensible and take what Dominic offered.

Yet still, underneath it all, there was a pang of quickly-stifled longing.

"Yes," she said. "Our lives would certainly never be boring."

"I know I am not what your family must have once wanted for you, Sophia," he said quietly. "My family lost their place in Society long ago. But the St. Claires are not without their own kind of power. I can give you anything you want-houses, carriages, jewels. And men like Hammond won't be able to touch you. I'll always stand as your friend."

Her friend. Sophia nodded sadly. That should be all she could want-Dominic's friendship. "Just my friend?"

Dominic laughed. "And your lover, too. You have to admit, Sophia, we definitely have adventures in the bedroom."

"And we haven't even really begun."

"So you will marry me?"

Sophia stared back out over the vast city. It wasn't perfect, what Dominic was offering. But what was perfect in life? She was tired of being alone, of endlessly fighting battles a lady by herself had little hope of winning. She had hoped she could go back to her family and finally fit in with them, even as she realized that wouldn't be possible. A life of adventure with Dominic, of finding her own place in London again-it was too tempting to resist.

And she had never been good at resisting temptation. "Yes, Dominic," she said firmly. "I will marry you."

And she hoped to heaven she would never rue those words...

* * *

Dominic hadn't taken Sophia up the steps of Notre Dame with the intention of proposing marriage to her there. In fact, until that moment, he'd been sure that, after Jane, he would never want to marry again. But as soon as the words were out of his mouth, he realized he meant them. He'd always known that being with Sophia could be a revenge of sorts against the Huntingtons, but he saw now there was Sophia herself.

And now they were holding hands, laughing like two naughty schoolchildren playing truant as they ran back down the winding steps. The full impact of his impulsive actions hadn't yet hit him, but Dominic knew it soon would. And he would have to face his family with the fact that he was marrying a Huntington.

Yet this wasn't just any Huntington. This was Sophia, who was unlike any woman, any person, he had ever met They ran out of the dark church and onto the sun-splashed walkway along the Seine. The hood of Sophia's cloak had fallen back, and her dark hair glowed a glossy, burnished sable in the light. She smiled back at him over her shoulder, and when he saw that those shadows of fear and worry were gone from her eyes, he knew he couldn't be sorry.

He wanted to protect her, like those knights of old; he wanted to make her laugh, make her happy. He hadn't lied when he told her they could make a life together because they understood each other. They were two wild spirits, beating against the narrow expectations of the world, yearning to be free. He had cared about Jane very much, but now he could see that no matter how careful he might have been, her gentle soul would have been crushed by life as a St. Claire.

Surely nothing could crush Sophia.

He didn't love her. He wasn't sure he even knew how to love in that way. But he would gain a wife who understood him and wouldn't ask for more than he could give. A beautiful wife he liked and who would fit into his life. And he would also protect her from Lord Hammond, an odious, overly entitled bastard if there ever was one.

Above all, it would be a revenge against the Huntingtons. If they thought Sophia was a scandal now, they hadn't seen anything yet.

Yes, it was a fine situation all around. Why, then, did he feel the oddest, smallest touch of disquiet? The voice of reason told him he was jumping headfirst into trouble he did not need. But the voice of reason had never counted for much with Dominic. He easily pushed it away and laughed with Sophia as she spun around in his arms.

"Are you absolutely sure you want me to marry you?" she said. She tilted her head back and smiled up at him.

"Of course I'm sure," he said. He gently smoothed a wind-blown curl back from her forehead. "We'll have a marvelous life together, never-ending fun and excitement."

Sophia laughed. "I know we will. But... "

"But what?"

A frown cut across her laughter, and for an instant she looked away. Dominic was afraid he was losing her, that she was drifting off somewhere in that moment, and he tightened his arms around her until she smiled again.

"I was just thinking-what about your family? What will they think about me?" she said. "When my cousin Aidan married your sister ..."

"It was your family who refused to see them," Dominic reminded her. "My parents hosted their wedding breakfast and gave them a theater in Edinburgh to manage. They will surely accept you."

"True enough." Sophia laughed ruefully. "And I can hardly do anything to make my family turn away more."

"So you will still marry me?"

"And let the chips fall where they may!" Sophia said merrily. "Not that such a philosophy has worked for me very well in the past."

"It will work now. You'll see." Dominic looped Sophia's arm through his, and they strolled back over the river. The day was growing later, the sky turning amber at the edges and the wind crisper as evening set in. The walkways weren't as crowded, as everyone made their way home to prepare for the night's revels.

Dominic had to be back at the theater to get ready for that evening's play. And to tell his brother and sister what he had done. Isabel, with her sweet, romantic heart, would be thrilled.

Brendan would probably not be. But Dominic could make him come around, could make him see this as another humiliating shot across the bow of the Huntingtons' ducal ship.

"When should we get married?" Sophia asked as they walked.

"Our engagement at the theater here is over in a few days," he said. "We could marry on our way home, at Calais perhaps. I think there is a small English church there."

"Yes," Sophia said thoughtfully. "If we left from Calais, perhaps we could travel with my cousin Elizabeth. It would be nice to have a member of my family at the wedding." She gave a wry laugh. "None of them were at my first ceremony."

And that would surely make word of her union with a St. Claire go racing back to her uncle the duke that much faster. "I think that is a very good idea. I'll make the arrangements right away."

They reached the club just as the sun was starting to sink lower in the sky in a burst of rose-pink, the color of Sophia's gown at the Cafe de Paris. Dominic was sure he could never see that color again without thinking of her.

He took her in his arms on the doorstep, and she smiled up at him. As he bent his head to kiss her, he caught a glimpse of a man hovering in a doorway across the street. It was the same man who'd watched the theater and then vanished. He was studying Dominic and Sophia now. Dominic gave the man a smile before he kissed Sophia.

One shot fired. How many to come?

Nineteen

"THERE. YOU LOOK ABSOLUTELY BEAUTIFUL," Elizabeth said as she put the finishing touches on Sophia's hair. "The perfect bride."

Sophia laughed, turning her head to examine herself in the mirror. "I wouldn't say that. This is hardly the ideal wedding, is it? But you've done marvels here, Elizabeth. Where did you learn to dress hair like that?"

Elizabeth's crooked little smile reflected in the glass. "Well, I found out my lady's maid was a spy in the employment of my husband. After that, I wanted to spend as little time as possible in her company, so I learned to do my hair myself."

"A spy?" Sophia cried. She spun around on the dressing table stool to look up at Elizabeth. Her cousin's blue eyes were as hard as chips of ice, and in that one instant, they seemed to flash with a light that spoke of worlds of hidden pain.

But Elizabeth laughed and turned away, that glimpse of stark pain gone. She smoothed her own coiffure in the mirror and reached for her blue satin hat. "And she was complete rubbish at fixing stylish coiffures anyway."

Sophia nodded, and slowly rose to her feet to adjust her gown. There had been no time to order something new before leaving

Paris, so her rose-pink gown served as her wedding dress. Over it, she wore an exquisite lace shawl that Elizabeth gave her, and a wreath of pink and white flowers wound through her hair. It was a hasty bridal toilette, for a wedding that still didn't feel quite real.

"I'm glad you're here today, Elizabeth," she said. "No one was at my first wedding at all."

Elizabeth laughed and reached over to tweak one of the flowers in Sophia's hair. "Well, *everyone* was at my wedding. St. George's was absolutely packed. And you see how that turned out."

"My first didn't turn out so well, either," Sophia said ruefully.

"But this one will be better! It's so romantic. You're marrying a St. Claire. It will be the talk of London when you get back."

"As if I haven't caused enough scandal!"

"Oh, but this will be different. You will be the envy of every woman in town." Elizabeth drew back the curtains from the window, and sunlight flooded into the hotel room. "It's a beautiful day for a wedding."

Sophia went to lean against the window ledge and examine the scene outside. The harbor of Calais gleamed below, sunlight reflecting on the water that lapped around the ships. One of them would carry them home on the evening tide.

But first she was to be married.

Sophia glanced at the clock on the dressing table. It was almost time to meet Dominic at the church. Suddenly, as she realized this was truly about to happen, her stomach clenched with nerves. On the trip from Paris, laughing with Elizabeth over romantic poems and speculating on why Dominic had gone ahead to Calais to prepare the wedding, it had seemed like a fun lark. A solution to her difficulties that would also be most enjoyable.

Now she saw it was very real. She was about to leap into marriage again.

But Dominic is nothing like Jack, she told herself. Jack had been a charming weakling; Dominic was the strongest man she had ever met. A man who understood her, whom she could build a life with. Wasn't he?

"Are you well, Sophia?" she heard Elizabeth say. Sophia felt her cousin's kid-gloved hand on her arm. "Do you feel ill?"

"No, I-I'm fine," Sophia murmured. "Just a fit of bridal nerves, I think."

"Here, sit down. Let me get you some water." Elizabeth led Sophia back to the stool and poured out a glass from the refreshment tray the hotel maid left.

"Are you sure you want to do this?" Elizabeth asked. "It is terribly romantic, but if you aren't sure..."

Sophia shook her head. What else could she do? Keep running, her funds growing ever smaller, always hoping not to run into Lord Hammond again? Alone? No, that held no appeal.

And the thought of never seeing Dominic again, never hearing his laugh or feeling his touch...no. It was better to stay and see what came next. She *wanted* to stay with Dominic.

"I'm as sure as one can be," Sophia said. She drank the last of the water and felt stronger. "Shall we go? It's almost time."

"Of course, if you're quite sure." Elizabeth handed Sophia the bouquet, a bunch of pink hothouse roses tied with white satin that had been delivered just that morning. A gift from Dominic.

Sophia held on to them with one hand and picked up her purse with the other. Mary's diary was tucked in there safely, waiting to go back with her to England. Her fear faded as suddenly as it had come upon her as they made their way down the hotel staircase. She felt only excitement. A warm, fizzing hope for the future she hadn't known in so long.

The English church was near the hotel, a small white stone chapel perched high above the harbor. It shimmered in the sunlight, shards of color from the stained-glass windows reflecting back onto the few monuments of the small churchyard. As she and Elizabeth stepped through the gate, the door opened, and Dominic was standing there waiting for her.

The light shone on his golden hair, and on the brilliant smile he gave her as he held out his hand. He was the perfect image of a romantic bridegroom, dressed in a perfectly cut blue coat and pearl-gray satin waistcoat, a tall-crowned silk hat in his hand and a rose in his lapel. And Sophia knew this was the right thing to do. It had to be, because she was just about to leap. The future was uncertain, but it would surely never be boring.

"You look beautiful," he said, raising her hand to his lips for a quick kiss.

"So do you," Sophia answered. "I know men can't be beautiful, but I think that's the only word for you today."

Dominic laughed. He tucked her hand in the crook of his arm and turned to lead her into the cool dimness of the church. The vicar waited for them there, Brendan and Isabel St. Claire beside him. The church was silent, the shadows of the empty pews and the muted colors of the stained glass dazzling after the bright day outside. The altar was spread with a snowy white cloth and laid out with pink and white roses like her bouquet.

Suddenly Sophia heard Elizabeth gasp. She looked back over her shoulder to see that her cousin's face had suddenly turned very pale. Elizabeth pressed her gloved hand to her lips.

"Elizabeth, what's wrong?" Sophia whispered in concern.

Elizabeth shook her head, her wide-eyed stare aimed across the church. Sophia saw that she watched Brendan--and that he stared back at her, his face set in stark, harsh lines.

Sophia was utterly shocked. She'd never seen Dominic's handsome, scarred, taciturn brother reveal so much as a flicker of emotion. And she'd never seen her elegant cousin so discomposed. What was happening here?

Elizabeth shook her head. A red flush across her cheekbones cut through the paleness. "Nothing at all, Sophia. Just a moment of dizziness." She smiled bravely, but it looked shaky. Sophia saw that her hand was trembling as she reached up to straighten her hat.

"Elizabeth..." Sophia began, but her cousin cut her off.

"I'm fine. This is your wedding day, a happy day."

Sophia glanced at Brendan, but he'd turned his back to them to face the altar. Something was definitely going on between the two of them, but Elizabeth was right--this was her wedding day. She couldn't think about anything else.

She walked down the aisle with Dominic until they stood together in front of the altar. The vicar smiled and opened his prayer book.

"Dearly beloved..."

Twenty

"WELCOME ABOARD, Mrs. St. Claire. I hope we'll have a calm voyage for you across the channel. A bit of a honeymoon, eh?"

Sophia laughed as she remembered the affable captain's greeting as they stepped aboard the ship that would carry them home. *Mrs. St. Claire.* It sounded so strange. So brand-new and shiny. Would she ever become accustomed to it? She never had quite gotten used to Mrs. Westman. Now she had to be someone else entirely.

She looked around the small cabin where she'd been shown, alone. Dominic had to talk to his brother before they departed, since Brendan had decided to stay behind in France at the last moment, and Elizabeth had retired to her own cabin with a headache after being quiet and watchful all afternoon. But Sophia didn't mind. She needed a moment to gather her thoughts. It had been such a whirlwind day she still felt dizzy with it.

She examined the space where she was meant to spend her wedding night. It was small but comfortable, the wide berth made up with a quilted comforter and plump pillows, and a table and two chairs set up near the porthole. A plate of fruit and cheese was laid out there, along with a bottle of champagne in a silver bucket. Her trunk stood next to the wall, by a tall washstand laid out with linens.

Sophia set her bouquet and lace shawl on the table and went to unlatch the porthole. As she swung it open, a rush of cool, faintly salt-scented air swept into the cabin. The sun was setting over the town, a blaze of pink and orange-gold. Soon they would set sail for England and a new life. A new horizon.

Sophia rubbed at the back of her neck, which suddenly ached at holding up her heavy hairstyle. She turned to the small, round mirror on the wooden wall and loosened the myriad pins Elizabeth used to secure it all. She managed to unbutton a few inches of her bodice, and the pink silk slid away from her shoulders as her hair fell down her back. The sea breeze touched her skin, and she shivered.

Suddenly the cabin door opened, and Sophia glanced back to see Dominic standing there. He smiled at her and let the door swing shut behind him, enclosing them in their own quiet world.

"I thought it would be impossible for you to be more beautiful than when I saw you at the church," he said. "But right now you are."

Sophia laughed and turned away to shut the porthole against the encroaching night. The ship rocked softly under her feet, and she could feel Dominic watching her as her loosened gown slipped lower.

"It was a lovely wedding," she said. "Thank you for that."

"I'm glad you liked it. I'm just sorry there wasn't time to make it as grand as you deserve."

"I wouldn't have wanted anything else." Sophia turned around to face him again. "It was exactly right."

He crossed the small cabin in two strides, his green eyes dark with intent. Before Sophia could breathe, his arms came around her and drew her close. One hand deftly slipped the rest of her buttons free and drew her gown away until it fell into a silken puddle at her feet.

Sophia closed her eyes as she felt him draw down the edge of her corset and chemise, and his hand gently caressed her bare breast. One roughened fingertip circled her nipple, closer and closer until at last it brushed her soft, aching tip. Sophia moaned, her head falling back as she arched closer to his touch.

"No one could be more beautiful than you, Sophia," he whispered hoarsely, and he held on to her as his head lowered to take her nipple deep into his mouth. "My beautiful Mrs. St. Claire."

Sophia buried her fingers in his hair and held on to him as the tension inside her grew tighter and tighter, until she was sure she would snap.

"And I think that you are overdressed for the occasion, Mr. St. Claire."

She pushed his coat off his shoulders until he shrugged it off, then she reached for the buttons on his waistcoat. When it was gone, she moved back a step to let him discard his shirt as she undid the fastenings of his trousers.

She eased the soft wool down until his hot cock was free to her touch.

"Sophia," he said tightly.

She shook her head. "Shh, just be quiet now. Let me attend to my wifely duties." When he fell silent, his whole body held under rigid, still control, she slid down his tall, hard length until her knees rested on the soft carpet.

Lightly, teasingly, she fluttered her fingertips down his erect penis. It was heavy under her touch, pulsing with need, and something dark and secret deep within her responded to that primitive need. Everything around her turned blurry and hot, dreamlike.

Sophia eased the tip of her tongue over him, tasting the warm saltiness of his flesh. He groaned, and the deep sound seemed to shimmer through her. She felt his whole body go tense as she took him fully into her mouth and twined her tongue around him.

His hips jerked under her kiss. She felt his hands in her hair as he pressed her closer, but then suddenly he pulled away and fell back a step.

"Sophia, I can't stand it," he said, his voice deep and rough. "I need you right now."

"I need you, too," she whispered. Dominic fell to his knees beside her and caught her in his arms as their mouths met in a raw, hot kiss full of pure need.

She felt him pull her down, until their kiss broke and she lay on her elbows and knees. She felt him move behind her, his hands touching her breasts, the arch of her back. He drew away the layers of her petticoats and tore at her thin silk drawers until he could trace the soft, bare curve of her buttocks.

"Dominic," she cried, and he drew her hips up and back. She felt him thrust into her, deep and fast, deeper than ever before. His hands were hard on her waist, holding her still as he pumped into her.

Sophia moaned, the pressure too much to bear as he slid over that one sensitive spot, over and over. She threw her head back and arched into him. She felt his damp chest against her back, the tight joining of their bodies.

At last that taut pressure broke, like a shower of hot, unbearable pleasure pouring over her. She felt the warmth of him inside her as he shouted out her name.

She collapsed weakly down onto the floor. She felt him fall beside her, his legs tangled with hers as his chest heaved for breath. She couldn't think, couldn't reason; she could only feel. She traced her hand over his damp shoulder, the length of his muscled back, his hair, and an unbearable tenderness washed over her.

Sophia closed her eyes and felt her heartbeat slow. The ship seemed to shift beneath her, as if they were heading out to sea and turned toward home. But nothing seemed to matter in that moment except Dominic's body next to hers.

She felt him sit up beside her. She didn't even open her eyes as he wrapped his arms around her and lifted her up as he stood. She felt him reach down to draw back the covers on the berth, and he laid her gently down in the nest of cool, soft sheets. But he didn't lie down beside her. She heard him draw off his shoes and the rustle of cloth as he shed his trousers completely.

She opened her eyes to see him standing by the washstand, wringing out a cloth in the basin of water. The last golden rays of daylight played over his bare skin, making him gleam. Her bright god.

Sophia propped herself up on her elbow, watching him as he came back to her side. His face looked still and solemn as he reached for her foot. He removed her satin shoe and rolled away her stockings before he smoothed the damp cloth over her skin. He gently bathed her whole body.

She lay back on the pillows and closed her eyes to let the cool, gentle touch ease over her skin. When he set the cloth aside, Sophia drew him down to lie beside her. Her body curled around his in the nest of the berth. His hand reached for hers, their fingers twined together. But the peaceful moment couldn't last; they weren't sated with each other yet. Dominic turned in her arms, and his lips searched for hers in the darkness.

Their mouths met in a heated kiss, and the very air around her seemed to turn warm and heavy, like the sky before a storm. That storm still raged inside her, violent and powerful, as everything she had locked away and suppressed for so long broke free and threatened to drown her. She held on to Dominic again and let herself go under.

He pulled his mouth from hers, making her moan with the loss, but he didn't leave her. His hands held on to her hips, so tightly she felt almost bruised, yet she didn't care. She needed that hardness, that edge of pain and passion that told her he was with her. They were alive together.

They knelt facing each other in the middle of the bed, then he reached for her again and slid her close to his naked chest.

Sophia laid her palms over the curve of his shoulders.

"So beautiful," she whispered. That smooth, damp skin over his lean muscles, so perfect but for a small white scar arcing over his ribs. Did that come from his fighting? She let her hands slide slowly, slowly down his chest, feeling every inch of him, every taut shift and ripple of his skin. He held her lightly by her hips, letting her explore him.

The light whorls of blond hair sprinkled across his chest tickled her skin and made her smile. The smile faded as her fingertips slid over the flat discs of his nipples. Her nail scraped over one, and it went taut as he groaned. His head fell back, his eyes closed, and she felt his penis jerk where it pressed her abdomen.

She lowered her head and took that pebbled nipple into her mouth, sucking, biting as he held on to her. She could feel the heavy beat of his heart under her lips, the ragged rhythm of his breath. His hands convulsed on her hips. She let her fingers trace down his chest, lower, lower, over his ridged stomach, the arrow of hair from his navel to his manhood, the hard line of his hips.

Her open mouth followed the path of her touch, licking, caressing, tasting him. As she bit at the arc of his hip, she let her hand flutter over his penis. It was hot satin stretched taut over rigid steel, the veins etched on it pulsating with his need. His need for her, for what she was doing to him now, and that realization flooded her with a powerful pleasure.

She pressed her lips to his taut stomach as she ran her hand down the length of him and up again to its base. She caressed that spot just behind that she knew he liked.

"Sophia!" he shouted. He drove his hand into her hair and pressed her against him.

She smiled and trailed her mouth lower until she could slip the tip of him between her lips. He tasted sweet and musky, his skin burning as she slowly took him deeper. She could give him pleasure in return for what he gave her, and it felt glorious.

"Sophia," he said, his voice just a rough growl. His hand slid through her hair, and she ran her tongue over him. His hips twitched but he didn't push himself deeper. He let her do whatever she wanted.

She held him to her as she caressed his warm skin, the curve at the small of his back. His hips thrust against her.

Suddenly he caught her shoulders and pushed her back from him. Sophia tilted her head to look up at him, and in the shadows of their bed his face looked harsh, carved into hard lines with lustful need.

Sophia smiled and reached beneath the bed for her valise. Carefully folded in its depths was the dildo he had bought her in Paris. She pulled it out. "Remember this?" she said teasingly.

"Sophia..." he growled.

Watching him, she lay back on the bed and spread her legs. Slowly, teasingly, never taking her eyes from him, she traced its cool hardness down her body. She circled her breasts and slid it down lower, lower. Dominic never moved, never looked away from its path.

"This was a wonderful gift," she said. She closed her eyes and arched her head back, imagining it was his touch as she eased the tip of the toy between her legs. But as she slipped it inside her, he took it away and tossed it to the floor with a clatter.

"I can't bear it anymore, Sophia," he said, and pulled her up to kiss her. There was no seductive art to his kiss now, only hunger and raw lust that called out to her own need.

She wrapped her arms around him as they fell back onto the bed. Dominic rolled her beneath him, his hips between her spread thighs as he kissed the curve of her neck, and she cried out as she arched against him. The pain and pleasure sparkled through her.

He trailed his open-mouthed kiss lower, tasting her with his tongue until he captured her aching nipple between his lips and suckled her, rolling it between his teeth.

"Dominic," she cried. She cradled his head in her hands, holding him against her. Her whole body felt so alive, so burning with need for him and what he was doing to her. What only *he* could do to her.

His hand drove between their bodies and traced her wet seam before he dipped one finger inside her, pressing deep. His palm rotated over that tiny spot of pure sensation, moving over her as he slid in another finger. He plunged deeper, harder, just the way she needed right now. He always seemed to know just what she needed, what she wanted, as if he could see into her very heart.

She shook away that disturbing thought, that knowledge he could know her as no one else ever could, and just let herself feel. Let herself be with him.

His hand slid away from her, and he held on to her waist as he rolled beneath her and held her on top of him, strong and steady. He turned her away from him, astride his hips, and traced his touch down the length of her back, over her buttocks.

"Ride me, Sophia," he commanded.

She laughed at the heady rush of his words as she raised herself up and slowly lowered onto his erect cock, one inch at a time. She let him slide deeper, deeper, until he was fully inside her, joined to her. She closed her eyes and let her head drop back as she reveled in the sensation of being filled by him. Part of him. He wound the ends of her hair around his wrist and thrust his hips up beneath her.

She let her need take over and moved on top of him faster, harder, until they were moving as one. She felt that hot pressure build where he touched her, slid against her. It expanded inside her, up and up, until it exploded.

She cried out her pleasure, her back arching like a taut bowstring back over his body.

"Sophia!" he shouted, and she felt him go still and rigid beneath her, felt the beat of his release inside her.

The energy drained slowly out of her, leaving her weak and shivering. She collapsed beside him to the bed and listened to the harsh, unsteady rhythm of his breath.

He reached for her and drew her to his side as he covered them both with the bedclothes. And slowly sleep crept in to claim her.

* * *

Sophia leaned over Dominic's shoulder as he lay on his side next to her, asleep. The moonlight cast a bar of silver light over his face and the rumpled waves of his golden hair. He looked so peaceful as he slept, so young, as if for a moment dreams erased the cares of life and he was free. Sophia wished she could make it like that for him all the time. That she could give him what he gave her that day--a fresh beginning.

As she carefully smoothed back his hair, the light caught on the narrow gold band on her finger. It still didn't seem quite real that she could be married again, and to Dominic St. Claire of all people, but there was the gleaming proof.

Dominic turned over under the bedclothes but he still didn't wake. Sophia was sure she couldn't go back to sleep, not with the ship rolling beneath her. She climbed down from the berth, careful not to disturb Dominic from his dreams, and quickly dressed in a simple day gown and jacket from her trunk. She retrieved Mary's diary from her bag and went up on deck to try to read for a while.

But she wasn't the only one who couldn't sleep. Isabel St. Claire was already on deck, sitting in one of the lounge chairs with a blanket tucked around her and a fashion paper on her lap as she read by lamplight.

Sophia hesitated, wondering if she should go back to the cabin and leave her new sister-in-law to her reading. Isabel had been very friendly at the church, and even the time they had met at the Tuileries, but Sophia felt strangely shy around Dominic's family. Especially after the way Brendan had glared at her during the ceremony. She usually tried not to care what people thought; she couldn't afford to if she wanted to be herself. Yet she wanted the St. Claires to like her.

Isabel glanced up and saw her there in the cabin doorway. She smiled happily and waved.

"Oh, thank goodness someone else is awake!" she called. "I was going crazy with loneliness here all by myself."

Isabel's friendliness dispelled Sophia's qualms, and she smiled in return as she sat down in the other deck chair. "Surely one can't be completely alone on a ship."

"Perhaps not, but it certainly feels like it," Isabel said. "I know this is a very short voyage, but I always feel somehow sad on a sea journey. All that water and no end yet in sight--it's terribly lonely."

Sophia studied the horizon beyond the polished railing. It did seem like an endless expanse of purple-black, broken by ripples of cracked moonlight on the waves.

"It does seem rather melancholy," Sophia agreed.

"But not when you're here!" Isabel said happily. "You must think me silly for my lonesome fancies. Dominic says you've traveled a great deal."

"Yes. In France and Germany mostly, a little in Italy. It seems strange to be going back to England now."

"Especially as a new bride, with your husband's crazy family waiting to meet you?" Isabel said, a teasing lilt to her voice.

Sophia laughed. "Especially under those circumstances. But if they are all like you, I'm sure I have nothing to fear."

"My mother is always perfectly kind and correct. You have nothing to fear from her. And James already adores you, though I think he will be terribly jealous of Dominic," Isabel said. "My father might snap and snarl at first, but he will quickly be distracted by a new play and will forget all about you. And Brendan is still in France. So you have nothing to worry about."

Sophia's head spun thinking about all the new family dynamics she would have to learn. At least it all seemed completely different from her own family. They might not "snap and snarl" but they never forgot. "I'm glad to hear that."

"And I'm happy you're here. I've missed Lily so much since she left. It will be nice to have a new sister."

"And I've never had a sister at all," Sophia said, something warm and welcome touching her heart at Isabel's words. "It will all be very new to me."

"I'm glad for Dominic, too. When poor Jane died, we feared he would never marry. One wouldn't think it to look at him, as he is all smiles and charm, but he is really rather lonely. I'm afraid he keeps too much bottled up inside."

Sophia nodded. She had seen that as well, the flashes of some hidden emotion in Dominic's eyes, quickly suppressed and hidden by his beautiful smile. She wished she knew how to bring those emotions out. "I'll certainly do my best to make him happy."

"Well, if anyone can do it I'm sure it's you. I wish I could feel like that for someone." Isabel suddenly looked wistful.

"Have you never had romantic feelings for anyone?" Sophia asked softly. She well remembered what it felt like to be young, to have so many emotions swirling around in her heart that she couldn't make sense of them. And Isabel was beautiful, passionate, an actress.

"Perhaps once," Isabel said softly. "But it was nothing. Just a man I saw once at an assembly. I'm quite sure he didn't even notice me, and even if he did-well, it couldn't be. I am me, and he is someone far above an actress. A man with a great title, as I am sure you know in your family. But he was very handsome, and he seemed so different from all the silly young men I usually meet. He seemed so serious and intense." She laughed. "I sometimes keep him in my mind when I need to pretend love onstage. Isn't that silly?"

"No," Sophia answered. "That isn't silly at all." For hadn't she kept Dominic in her mind all that time after their kiss at the Devil's Fancy? It was surely no different for Isabel to harbor a dream of a man she once saw. Sophia wondered who it could be, to have caught the attention of such a remarkable young woman.

"But I fear my babble is keeping you from your reading!" Isabel gestured toward the book in Sophia's hand. "What is that? It looks terribly old."

"It is rather old, about two hundred years," Sophia answered as she held up Mary's diary. "It's a journal I found on a dusty shelf in my uncle's house years ago. I read a little bit at a time. It keeps me company when I'm feeling alone."

"How intriguing," Isabel said. "I do love old books and jour-nals. They're like discovering new characters in a play."

"She feels like an old friend to me now. Though I'm afraid her life was not always a happy one."

"Really? Who is it? What's her story?"

Sophia remembered how Dominic had tried to get the diary from her, how he had seemed so strangely interested in Mary's story. She could see why, now that she'd read further in the yellowed pages and seen the unfurling of a St. Claire woman's misery caused by a Huntington man. But the St. Claires were meant to be her family now, too, and Mary's history was also theirs.

"It belonged to an ancestress of yours," Sophia said. "A woman named Mary St. Claire Huntington."

"Mary St. Claire?" Isabel gasped. Her smile faded, her eyes wide as she looked down at the book. "That is her diary?"

"Yes. Do you know of her?"

Isabel gave a bitter little laugh. "I have heard of her since the day I was born. Our father drilled her story into all of us."

Sophia held on tighter to the book. Once, before she met Dominic, she'd thought Mary was hers alone. That she was forgotten by everyone else. But now it appeared she belonged to many other people. And that they used her story for reasons of their own.

"What story were you told?" Sophia asked quietly.

"That long ago, back in the 1600s, a young lady named Mary St. Claire fell in love with a man named John Huntington, whom Charles II made a duke. They were not of the same social station, as Mary's family was only country gentry, yet they fell passionately in love. They married, but it ended sadly. They separated for some reason--no one ever will tell me why, so it must be something terribly scandalous. Mary died of a broken heart at being rejected by her husband, and the duke used his social position to ruin the St. Claires. They were cast out of their country home and had to fend for themselves in the world. All because of a love affair gone so wrong. Is that not terribly sad?"

Isabel paused for a moment, staring out at the black sea before she finished, "And my family has never forgotten that. I think it is our theatrical natures."

"Yes," Sophia murmured. "Very sad." The St. Claires felt the Huntingtons had ruined their lives. No--they didn't seem to merely feel it. They felt it in their bones. It was part of their identity as a family, just as stories of ducal greatness and responsibility were part of the Huntingtons.

But the ruination of Mary St. Claire was not part of any Huntington legend. Sophia could hardly be shocked by that. To her family, the Huntington name, the ducal title, was everything. Anything could be sacrificed to it, and the hearts and minds of mere women could be destroyed in an instant if they stood in the way of family honor. Sophia had known there had to be a reason for Dominic's desire to get the diary from her. She saw the dark and powerful enmity his family bore for hers. It had perhaps been cracked by Aidan's marriage to Lily, but it was certainly not broken. Maybe it never could be. It had been rewoven and strengthened far too much over the years.

Could she be strong enough to break it? Sophia looked down at the book in her hands. Even Mary, with her great love for her husband, hadn't been able to do it. And it destroyed her in the end.

Sophia knew she had to find a way to be stronger than that. Yet she couldn't keep the doubts from creeping in like tiny hobgoblins to chip away at the rare happiness she had felt in Dominic's arms. His proposal had been so quick, so convenient, their marriage so hasty. Why had he really asked her to marry him? What could he plan for her in London?

And how could she face his family?

Isabel studied Sophia's face closely, her eyes--so very green, just like her brother's--wide. "Didn't Dominic tell you about all of this?"

"He told me something of it, I suppose," Sophia answered carefully. "He did seem quite interested in the diary. But I had no idea there was such a complicated tale."

"Oh, my brothers can be such fools sometimes!" Isabel suddenly burst out. "I blame the steady diet of Shakespeare we've been fed ever since the nursery."

Sophia had to laugh, despite all the dark worries and fears swirling in her head. "Shakespeare?"

"Yes. All those feuds and revenge. It's affected how they see everything. But they never remember how those things always turn out--with everyone dead or mad."

"Surely no one died because of this feud."

"Not yet. But I think heartbreak and lives wasted in sadness can be even worse."

Before Sophia could answer, the ship's captain strolled across the deck to tell them it shouldn't be much longer until they reached Dover.

So England, home, was very near. The place she had fled so many months ago, and had started to return to with a tentative spark of hope.

From the Diary of Mary St. Claire Huntington

My brother Nick was very right about why the duke came to visit. He broached the subject of his money-raising plan while he was out hunting with John today. John seems quite interested. It is something that has the royal backing, after all, and as John pointed out it also has the backing of my family since Nick has brought our father and uncle into the idea as well.

I told John I was not sure it is something we should be involved with, but he just laughed and said I should not worry myself about such things. That I must only concern myself with creating an heir again. Yet still I worry. I can't help it--he is my love, and I want our lives together to be all we envisioned when we wed.

Twenty-One

"THIS IS YOUR FAMILY'S HOUSE?" Sophia said as she peered out the carriage window at the residence that loomed into sight. "It isn't what I expected."

"What did you expect?" Dominic said. "That my parents lived backstage at the theater? That it would be painted red and hung with satin curtains and gold tassels?"

"I'm not really sure what I expected," Sophia said with a laugh. But she wouldn't have picked out this particular house, a tall, narrow, eminently respectable house of red brick and black-painted shutters on a quiet square, as belonging to the St. Claire family. "I must say I'm rather disappointed it's so ordinary."

Dominic smiled at her. "Then you can choose something as garish as you like when we go house-hunting."

"House-hunting?"

"We can't stay in my lodgings forever. And I doubt you would want to move in with my parents."

"No," Sophia murmured as she looked up at the house again. It was so stolid, so placid and quiet, giving away no clue to what might be hiding behind its walls. She doubted his parents would want her, a Huntington, to take up residence in their house. What Isabel told her about the St. Claires' long and bitter enmity

244

for the Huntingtons had nagged at her on the journey from Dover, and she couldn't quit thinking about it all.

Marrying Dominic had seemed so right, so natural, when he asked her in Paris. But would another hasty decision come to haunt her?

Sophia supposed she would know more once she met Dominic's parents, but the thought of that imminent encounter had her stomach in knots. "I rather like your lodgings, Dominic," she said.

"Do you? What is it you like so much? The faded rug with the burn marks?" he teased. "The ill-tempered landlady shouting up the stairs at us? The tiny fireplace that smokes?"

Sophia laughed. "The fact that there is little to keep clean. And there's a cupboard big enough for my clothes. And a large bed."

"It won't be nearly big enough when I'm done with you." He raised her gloved hand to his lips for a quick kiss. "I'm glad to hear you laugh, Sophia. You've been

much too quiet since we arrived in England."

"There's a lot to think about, I suppose," she said.

"Soon there won't be time to think at all," Dominic answered. "With Brendan gone for the time being, the Devil's Fancy is all ours for a while. There's much work to do there."

"I can't wait," Sophia said, and truly she couldn't. She wanted to work. She wanted to keep busy and feel useful. Thinking didn't seem to get her anywhere.

Dominic climbed down from the carriage and reached back to help her. As Sophia peeked up at the house from under her hat, she saw a curtain at an upstairs window twitch. Then all was still again. Dominic offered her his arm and led her up the polished marble steps just as the door swung open to reveal a black-coated butler.

"Welcome home, Mr. Dominic," he said with a bow. "I trust your journey was an enjoyable one."

"Most enjoyable, as you can see," Dominic answered. "I have brought home a new bride."

"We did hear the good news, Mr. Dominic. And all the staff wishes you every happiness," the butler said, a smile threatening to break through his stern facade.

"Dominic!" Isabel cried. Sophia looked up to see her running down the stairs in a cloud of white muslin. "Sophia! You are here at last. It seems we've been waiting ages for you to call since we got home."

Dominic laughed and kissed his sister's pink cheek. "We've only been back two days, Issy. Sophia needed time to settle in a bit."

"You needed time for Papa to calm down, more likely," Isabel said.

Sophia swallowed hard and forced herself to keep smiling at those words.

"And has he?" said Dominic.

"Oh, you know Papa," Isabel said vaguely. "And Mama is rather unhappy at being deprived of planning a grand wedding."

"Mama can wait for *your* nuptials," said Dominic. Isabel gave an unladylike snort, completely incongruous with her fairylike appearance. "That surely won't be

for quite some time. But Papa is waiting for you in the library, Dom. You go in and talk to him while I take Sophia to have tea with Mama."

Isabel took Sophia's hand and led her toward the stairs. Sophia threw a startled glance back at Dominic. She didn't want to meet her new mother-in-law for the first time all alone! On the other hand, William St. Claire sounded rather more fierce than his wife, so perhaps it was better she didn't have to meet him just yet.

Dominic's face looked shadowed and serious, but he gave her a quick smile. Just before he disappeared from her view, he turned toward a closed door just off the foyer. Isabel chattered away as they moved down a corridor, talking of the new play at the Majestic, a production of *The Tempest* where she was to play Miranda. Sophia hardly had time to think before she was swept in Isabel's wake into a pretty, sunny drawing room.

It was a welcoming space, all pale blue and white walls hung with portraits and pastoral landscapes, dotted with comfortable-looking sofas and chairs. There were china figurines clustered on the fireplace mantel and a writing desk littered with letters and invitations, but nothing like the newly fashionable clutter that took up every inch of her own mother's drawing room. This was a bright, airy space, welcoming, and Sophia felt a little less nervous as she looked around.

A table was set up by the window and laid out with tea things, fine china and polished silver gleaming in the sunlight. A lady rose from behind it, her blue plaid taffeta skirts rustling and a tentative smile on her lips. She looked rather like an older version of Isabel, her red-gold hair only lightly sprinkled with gray, her eyes very green in a delicate oval face.

"You must be Sophia," she said, coming slowly forward. "Dominic's new wife. Isabel has told us so much about you."

Sophia summoned up all her ingrained social training to give a smile and a nod. "Yes. I am Sophia."

"And I am Katherine St. Claire. Welcome to our home." Katherine gave her a gentle hug, and at first, Sophia was startled. She would never have expected such a thing from someone she had just met, and she stood stiffly for an instant, unsure of what to do.

But Katherine's smile was kind as she drew back. "Please, have some tea, my dear. Knowing Dominic and his father, and the way they are when they start talking about the theater, they won't be in for some time."

"Thank you very much, Mrs. St. Claire," Sophia said. She followed Katherine and Isabel to the table and sat down as Katherine reached for the silver teapot.

"Oh, please, do call me Katherine! Or we shall both be calling each other Mrs. St. Claire and it will be terribly confusing," she said. Though her smile was gentle, her green eyes were bright and probing as she looked across the table. Sophia remembered hearing that she was a trained actress, who surely missed little that went on around her. "You must tell me how you met Dominic in Paris. I'm sure it is terribly romantic."

"I told you, Mama! She came to the theater," Isabel said, helping herself to a cucumber sandwich. "When we had the dinner backstage. They couldn't quit staring at each other."

"My dear," Katherine said gently. "You should let Sophia tell her own story."

Sophia laughed.

"No, that is the tale. We met at the theater, and at my friend Madame Martine's home, and--well, I had never met anyone quite like Dominic before. He is most extraordinary."

Katherine smiled, and for a moment, she looked very much like her son as well as her daughter. "So he is, though I confess I'm prejudiced. He must have found you quite extraordinary, as well. We thought he would never marry, and now--well, this has all been so sudden."

"It was sudden for me, as well, I confess," Sophia said carefully. "But it felt like the right thing to do."

"I did not know my husband very long when we married, either." Katherine offered a plate of cakes. "I was seventeen and appearing in my first play, as Cordelia opposite my father at Covent Garden. William saw me there one night and wanted me to play Juliet at his new theater, and one thing led to another. My parents didn't care for him, didn't think I was ready to be married, but I couldn't quit seeing him. It was terribly romantic, and I have never regretted my choice."

"I hope I never will, either," Sophia said. Katherine's kind welcome had assuaged some of her doubts, but she still didn't know what Dominic's real motives in their marriage were. She feared they were not quite as "romantic" as his mother supposed.

"You were married before, were you not?" Katherine asked.

"Yes. My first husband, Captain Westman, died last year," Sophia said. "We were not married very long."

"And before that you were Lady Sophia Huntington."

"Mama!" Isabel protested. "That was a long time ago. It doesn't matter now."

"No, it is true," Sophia said, watching Katherine steadily, wondering if this was some sort of test. "I was Lady Sophia Huntington. But I haven't lived with my family since I married Captain Westman."

Katherine nodded, her expression serene. She gave away no clue to her feelings. "And Dominic knew this."

"Yes, of course."

"Well then, I was right. It *was* romantic. Love conquers all," Katherine said with a smile. "Now, tell me, Sophia, do you enjoy the theater? You shall certainly have to, now that you are a St. Claire!"

They went on to talk about the London theater scene and new plays to be presented that season, light, innocuous chatter that set Sophia at ease again. She was good at being sociable, at knowing about fashion and gossip. But playing cards had also taught her to sense hidden meanings, to know when something unsaid and unacknowledged lurked beneath.

Once they finished their tea, Dominic had still not appeared. Sophia tried not to worry about what he and his father were talking about and listened to Katherine as she pointed out portraits around the room. There were images of Katherine and her husband as Romeo and Juliet, charming pastels of all the St. Claires as children, and a new one of Lily St. Claire as a bride.

And hanging in one shadowed corner was the oval image of a lady in a loosely draped satin gown of the 1660s, her golden ringlets looped up to tumble down on her bare shoulders. She looked out from the image with wide, sad dark eyes, a ghost of a smile on her painted lips.

"And this is one of our ancestors--Mary St. Claire," Katherine said softly. "Perhaps you have heard of her?"

"Yes," Sophia answered. She stared into Mary's eyes, and it felt as if she was seeing a lost friend for the first time. The woman whose words had been her only friend for a long time looked back at her. "I have heard of her."

Katherine gave her a shrewd glance. "Then you know her sad tale. It was such a turbulent time in history, was it not? I suppose we must be grateful to live now, when things are so peaceful and prosperous. And this painting over here is my mother. She was also an actress, quite well-known in her day, though I fear she died rather young..."

After being shown the rest of the family images and having another cup of tea, Sophia realized it had grown rather late and Dominic hadn't yet appeared. Katherine seemed to notice it, too, for she laughed and said, "I'm afraid when my husband and sons start talking about the theater they never stop! They will be quite late to dinner. Isabel, my dear, perhaps you could summon them?"

"Of course, Mama," Isabel said, half-rising from her chair.

"Oh, no, you'd best not," Katherine said. "You also get caught up in the theater talk, and then I shall lose you all. I will go."

"Let me go, Mrs. St. Claire--Katherine," Sophia said. "I must find the ladies' withdrawing room anyway, and I would love to see more of your house. I promise I will not get caught up in any theater talk."

Katherine laughed. "Of course, my dear, if you are sure." She gave Sophia directions to the library, and as Sophia left the drawing room, Isabel's laughter faded away behind her.

The rest of the St. Claire house was as lovely and tasteful as the drawing room, filled with porcelain objets d'art and intriguing-looking books and theatrical artifacts. Sophia paused to examine a few of the paintings, but she didn't find any more images of Mary. All in all, she felt rather happy about this first meeting. What could have been uncomfortable, or even angry, had been smoothed by Katherine's kindness and Isabel's good spirits.

She turned down the short corridor Katherine had said led to the library. It was darker there, the heavy curtains drawn over the windows. She could hear the muffled sound of voices as she drew nearer, and as they became louder she realized the door was half-open. Unlike in the drawing room, this conversation seemed more an argument than a polite exchange. She raised her hand to knock, but when she heard her name, her hand fell back to her side, and she took a step back.

"...and what is Sophia's last name?" a man said.

"It is St. Claire now," Dominic said, and she recognized that stubborn note in his voice.

"But it *was* Huntington! Don't think I don't know that. Isabel told me all about your wedding. Is this why Brendan stayed in France? Because he knew you were making a terrible mistake and he couldn't bear to see it?"

"I don't know why Brendan stayed in France, Father. He did not confide in me. But I assure you it was not because of my wife."

"Your wife! A Huntington. You have brought a Huntington into our midst, just as your sister did. At least Aidan has his uses. What use is this woman? I don't understand you at all..."

Sophia felt her cheeks burn hot and then turn icy cold. She didn't wait to hear what Dominic had to say. She had heard enough. She backed away from the door and rushed away, holding her skirts so they wouldn't rustle as she ran down the corridor.

Good God. What had she done?

* * *

"You don't need to understand me, Papa," Dominic said as he watched his father pace the length of the library floor. "All you have to do is accept that Sophia is my wife now. She's not a Huntington any longer. She's a St. Claire."

"But why? You have always been impulsive, Dominic, but why marry this woman?"

Dominic shrugged. In truth, he could no longer remember why he had married Sophia. It had seemed so obvious in France. She needed protection from Lord Hammond, a man Dominic loathed. They had fun together, especially in bed. If he couldn't marry a woman like Jane, it might as well be Sophia. And, above all, it was one more blow against the Huntingtons.

All that made a strange, wild kind of sense in Paris. But some-how, on their journey home, it had all been turned upside-down in his head. Sophia didn't seem like a Huntington, some faceless enemy. She only seemed to be--Sophia. A beautiful woman who bore the marks and scars of her own past and fears.

He couldn't make sense of that imperceptible shift yet. But he did know that he didn't like his father's anger toward his new wife.

"Sophia is my wife now," Dominic said. "We have to make her a part of this family, Papa. When you come to know her, you will see that she is different. And you know how much the Hunting-tons will hate the gossip."

"Different!" his father snorted. But he did quit his pacing. He leaned his fists against the edge of his desk and closed his eyes. "I will be civil to her. Your mother wouldn't stand for anything else. You know how she is always going on about manners. And you're quite right about the gossip, I suppose."

Dominic grinned. He knew his father would understand the part about spiting the Huntingtons, if nothing else. "Mama does temper the barbarian in all of us. That's all I ask. Give her a chance."

His father slowly nodded. "Very well. Shall we go in to tea then? I have to greet your wife."

They made their way to the drawing room where the ladies were waiting. Isabel played a Mozart concerto at the pianoforte as their mother rearranged the tea tray.

Sophia sat across from her, staring out the window with a

faraway look in her eyes. When he had left her, she seemed a bit nervous but happy. Now when she turned to look at him, she hardly seemed to see him.

Mystified, Dominic went to take her hand. Surely he would never understand the mercurial moods of his new wife. But he did look forward to trying.

Twenty-Two

LE SCANDALE! *Are the SCs at it again? After a period of quiet respectability, London's favorite family of the theater seems to be coming to life again. First D SC marries--to London's famous eloper Lady S, who we are told was seen in the company of that dashing Lord H many times on the Continent. Sources tell us there was a great romance going on there that went very wrong. Surely there is much to that tale we have not yet heard? And now word has arrived that perhaps the youngest SC pup ran afoul of the French at the Parisian card tables. Must we poor writers--and the rest of London--be wary of their purses when they face him over whist?*

We are all agog to see what happens next. Perhaps the beautiful Miss I SC will run off with the Turkish ambassador...

Sophia shoved the newspaper away from her untouched breakfast plate as anger flared up inside her. She had always hated the tittle-tattle of the Town Talk column, the anonymous bits of gossip, rumors, and party chatter that appeared twice a week. But her mother had followed them avidly, living in dire fear that the Huntingtons might appear there, and Sophia had gotten into the habit of reading them.

Before she married Jack, she'd found herself mentioned there a few times. Descriptions of her gowns and her dance partners, mostly. Surely they had a gleeful time documenting her elopement, but she hadn't been there to read it. She'd never cared what they said about her.

But it was different now. She cared very much what they said about Dominic and his family. She had to prove herself to them now, and trailing fresh scandal in her wake didn't seem like a good way to do that.

This seemed to be Lord Hammond's doing. Why else would they have mentioned him in their scurrilous column? She'd been foolish to think he could be left behind in Paris. His influence in London was too great.

She glanced across the table at Dominic. He was calmly--too calmly--drinking his coffee. He watched her with no expression on his face.

"You read the papers already, didn't you?" she said.

Dominic shrugged. "I always read the papers first thing in the morning. It's useful to keep up with the theater reviews."

"But you saw today's *Town Talk*?" Sophia persisted. His very calmness seemed to drive her anger higher. She crumpled the paper into a ball and tossed it on the floor.

Dominic watched it roll across the carpet before he looked back at her, his brow arched. "I did see it. They often mention the St. Claires. Surely you're accustomed to being gossiped about, Sophia."

"I've been gossiped about all my life, I hardly notice it anymore," Sophia answered. "But your siblings are the subject of today's tittle-tattle! James and poor Isabel. And it's all my fault."

"I agree that it's unfortunate Issy's name got dragged into the matter. She's a young lady, and even for an actress these days, it's important to be thought respectable," Dominic said coolly. "But James has to learn to be more careful, or he'll have to get used to being thought a rake."

"They are doing more than calling him a rake!" Sophia burst

out. She couldn't sit still any longer. She shoved her chair back from the table and paced the length of their small dining room, the hem of her dressing gown whipping behind her. "They are calling him a cheater."

"Only in the most obscure way possible."

"Everyone will know very well what they're saying. And there is only one way they could have gotten that particular piece of gossip--through Lord Hammond." Sophia paused next to the window to peer outside. It was a warm, bright day, and the blue morning sky seemed to mock her dark mood.

She felt like such a fool for thinking even for a moment that her marriage would make a man like Hammond go away. It had only made him angrier at losing something he wanted.

"I should not have done this," she murmured.

She heard Dominic rise from the table. He came to stand behind her, and she glimpsed his reflection in the window glass, his hair tousled, his dressing gown loosely wrapped around his lean body, as he rested his hands on her shoulders.

"There will be some new rumor tomorrow," he said. "Some earl's daughter will run off with her music teacher, or a duke will marry a rich, vulgar American. James, and even Issy, will get over it."

"But if it was Lord Hammond's doing, you know this is only the beginning. And they would never have mentioned a man like him without his complicity," Sophia said. "He has much influence in Society. I have hurt you by bringing him into your life."

"Sophia." Dominic gently turned her in his arms and held her by the shoulders as he looked down into her eyes. The calmness that had made her mad earlier now made her feel a little steadier. She was no longer alone.

Even if a part might wish she was. She wasn't accustomed to her choices affecting anyone else, especially not someone she feared she was coming to care for far too much.

"Sophia," he said. "It doesn't matter. Many people have tried to hurt my family over the years, but they have never succeeded.

We have thick armor, and so do you. Hammond might try, but he will find he is just like the rest--he can't touch us. Gossip is nothing."

Sophia wasn't completely reassured. Gossip wasn't always nothing. Sometimes it was like a slow-eating poison, seeping into everything that was good in life and turning it twisted and dark. "We can't let such rumors spread," she said. "They have a tendency to grow and grow until they're no longer recognizable at all."

"Then surely the best way to stop it is by showing everyone we don't care," Dominic said. "By going about our business."

Sophia nodded, and she felt Dominic's hand slide under her chin to tilt her face up to his. His eyes were narrowed, his jaw set in that hard line she had come to mistrust.

"Unless you are worried about what *your* family will think about your name appearing in the papers," he said. "About them seeing your name paired with the St. Claires."

Sophia broke away from him and turned to pick up the papers she had scattered on the floor. In moments like that, she wondered what her husband was thinking, what he was trying to tell her.

She wondered if she knew him at all.

"If I cared about that, I would never have married you," she said. "Surely they can no longer care what I do."

"Of course they must care what you do," he said. "You will always be a Huntington."

Sophia slowly rose to her feet, the papers clutched in her hands. A shiver tickled up her spine. A Huntington. Was that what he thought of her? Was that all she was in his mind?

"I'm a St. Claire now," she said quietly.

He was silent for a long moment, leaning back on the window ledge to watch her as she straightened the breakfast things. There was no point to moving around plates and cups the maid would just clear away, but Sophia had the sudden urge to be busy.

"Are you done eating?" Dominic said. "You hardly touched your food."

"I'm not very hungry this morning," she answered.

"Then shall we get dressed and go for a walk in the park? It's a warm day, and I'm not due at rehearsal until this afternoon. You've been too kind to run lines with me every evening, and I think we should have a little treat."

Sophia looked back at him. Was he offering a small peace token? A morning spent together, just the two of them? "I would like that."

"Good. We can get started on that 'let everyone see we're happy and we don't care about gossip' business." Dominic smiled and reached out to squeeze her hand.

We're happy and we don't care. Sophia only wished that were true.

"You're very right," Sophia said as they strolled along one of the graveled footpaths of Hyde Park. "It does feel good to get out of doors for a while."

Dominic smiled and took her hand. "I told you it would be. Do you feel like an old domesticated couple yet, with nothing better to do than go walking hand in hand in the middle of the day?"

Sophia laughed. Some of her misgivings that morning seemed to have vanished, or at least gone into hiding for a while, burned away by the sunny day. "Not quite old yet. And domesticated-- never. Not with you."

"No? Shall we not spend all our evenings in front of the fire, me with my dressing gown and pipe and you with your knitting? We might need to get a puppy to gambol about on the hearthrug..."

Sophia laughed even harder, trying to imagine the cozy little scene. "It sounds like a sketch of the queen and Prince Albert, not something real. Besides, I don't know how to knit and dog fur makes me sneeze."

"Ah, well. We'll just have to stay with gambling clubs and theaters then."

"That definitely sounds like more fun." Sophia surveyed the

park from under her lace-edged parasol and smiled at the picture-pretty scene. It seemed they were not the only ones with time for strolling in the sun. Couples walked along arm in arm, whispering together quietly, while children rolled their hoops along the path with shouts of laughter. Babies peered out of prams pushed by nannies in their starched caps, while an elderly man was led along by his resolutely cheerful daughter, as she told him what a grand day it was.

"I forgot how pretty the park is," Sophia said. "When I used to come here, I had no time to look around and see all this life. I was too busy trying to not listen to my mother's lectures."

"I haven't been here in a long time, either," said Dominic.

"Because there are always rehearsals and meetings during the day? Or because you are too tired to go out?" she said with a laugh.

"Rehearsals, usually. But now I can see its time to slow down a bit, learn to enjoy life."

Sophia smiled up at him, thinking how very handsome he looked in the sunshine, all burnished gold. "How shall we do that, then?"

"Well, I would say finding a proper house is the first step," he said. "And my mother wants to give a party for us, to prove to all her friends that I really did get married."

"A party?" Sophia said, surprised. She hadn't been sure Dominic's mother really liked her; she knew his father did not. Would they really want to "show off" the fact that their son had married Lady Sophia Huntington?

"I thought you liked parties," Dominic said with a small smile.

"Of course I do. I'm just surprised your mother would want to give *us* a party."

"My mother will seize any excuse to entertain. Unless you really prefer to live quietly for a while?"

Sophia studied his face. He watched her closely, as if he waited for something from her. She hated not knowing what it was or what she should do.

"No," she answered. "That sounds most enjoyable."

Dominic nodded, and he tucked her hand in the crook of his arm as they continued on their stroll.

Ahead of them on the winding path, Sophia glimpsed two ladies. They were no different from any other well-dressed pedestrians enjoying the day, an older woman in a conservative dark green walking dress with graying black hair peeking from beneath the frilled edge of her green-and-black bonnet, and a young lady in pink holding on to her arm. But Sophia knew with one glance that this was not just any older, rigidly dignified lady.

This was her mother, a woman she hadn't seen in many months. The last time they met, her mother had been weeping as Sophia's father slammed the door between them, and she hadn't heard a word from her since. Only that indirect message sent through Elizabeth, that Sophia should look for a respectable husband who could reconcile her to her family.

Something that would never happen now that she was Mrs. St. Claire.

Sophia had known she would have to face her family one day, but not now, so unexpectedly, on such a nice day. Her steps faltered, and for one wild second, she considered lifting up her hem and running away through the park like a hoyden. As if that would solve anything.

"Sophia, what is it?" she heard Dominic ask, just as her mother glanced up and saw them there.

Allison Huntington froze, as if she was as shocked as Sophia. But her surprise was concealed in an instant, as a lifetime of social training took hold and she concealed every emotion with a polite mask.

"That is my mother," Sophia said quietly. "I haven't seen her for some time."

"Well, I suppose we can't escape the meeting now," Dominic said. "Shall we go say hello?"

Sophia glanced up at him from under her parasol. For the merest glimmer of an instant she saw a tiny smile on his lips, as if he looked forward to the confrontation. Then it vanished, and he squeezed her hand.

"Yes, I suppose so," she said. "At least my father is not here. My mother, much like yours, is always scrupulously polite."

Sophia hardened her resolve as she watched her mother come closer. The gossip in that morning's papers had shown her the futility of trying to be respectable. Whenever she tried, it never worked out well. And now she had a husband to match her. It was either let the pain overwhelm her or use it as she always had, to act out. Sophia pasted on her brightest smile and drew Dominic with her as she went to meet her mother.

"Sophia," her mother said. Her tone betrayed no hint that they had been apart so long or so acrimoniously. "Such a surprise to see you here today, my dear."

"Mother," Sophia said. Her mother leaned toward her for the merest brush of lips against cheek, a whiff of the lemon verbena perfume that brought her childhood back to her so vividly. The loneliness and longing of it. "Didn't Elizabeth tell you I was back in England?"

"Your cousin has already dashed off on her travels again. She cannot stay still since her husband died," Allison said with a sigh. "You young people, I don't understand you. In my day, we were content to stay at home, where we were meant to be." Her gaze flickered to Dominic.

"Mother, this is my new husband..."

"Mr. St. Claire. Of course," Allison said with her most painfully polite smile. "I have certainly heard of you."

Dominic gave her a short bow, a tight smile. "And I of you, Lady Huntington."

"And this is my new daughter-in-law, Edward's wife," Allison said. Her smile grew warmer as she drew the young lady in pink forward. The girl gave a shy smile. "She has been a most welcome addition to the family. We are all so very fond of her."

After a few innocuous comments on the weather, Sophia's mother sent her daughter-in-law back to the carriage to fetch a shawl. Once she was gone, Allison stepped closer to Sophia and said through her unfaltering smile, "I am glad to see you are well, Sophia. But I hope that you and your husband have no thoughts of calling at Huntington House."

Sophia fought to hold on to her own smile. That was more direct than she would have expected. She felt Dominic stiffen beside her. "Why should we wish to go there, Mother?"

"Because you always did enjoy causing a scene, even when you were a child," Allison said in an exasperated tone. "Your uncle was most displeased to learn you were back in London. We had thought you were settled abroad."

"I supposed he would be, with Aidan safely disposed of in Edinburgh with his St. Claire spouse," Sophia said. "But none of you have anything to fear from me. I am just trying to live my life and be happy in my own way."

Allison shook her head sadly. "I never did understand you, Sophia. You throw away all your advantages until we can no longer help you."

"I haven't asked for your help, have I?"

"I must go now." Allison gave her one more cool kiss and backed away. "I hope that you will be happy, Sophia."

"And I you." Sophia watched her mother slowly walk away, never looking back. During all her time away from her family, she'd sometimes imagined what might happen when she met with them again. And even though that brief meeting had gone as well and peacefully as could be expected, Sophia couldn't help but feel wistful.

She felt Dominic's hand on her arm, and she turned away from her mother's retreating figure to smile up at him.

"Is that how your family has always treated you?" he asked.

His voice was so gentle that Sophia was sure her momentary pang of sadness showed on her face. She smiled harder and turned around to walk away. "No, indeed. That was my mother being kind. We're fortunate she talked to us. She wouldn't have if my father was there."

"Sophia," he said, holding tightly to her arm. "What was it like for you before you married Westman?"

"I don't want to talk about 'before.' It's much too pretty a day to waste on my family," she answered. "Let's go have an Italian ice before you have to leave for rehearsal."

Dominic nodded, and they walked on in silence toward their carriage waiting at the park gates. As she climbed up the step, she noticed a couple who had been at the Devil's Fancy. She gave them a smile and a wave, but they turned away. It saddened her even as she expected it.

Don't be ridiculous, she told herself sternly. She was worrying about things that weren't even there. Her mother and the hovering threat of Lord Hammond were making her fearful when she should be thinking about forging ahead in her new life.

When she should be thinking only about her new, handsome husband.

* * *

That sanctimonious witch, Dominic thought furiously as he led Sophia back to their carriage. She smiled, as she always did, but he could see the bright sheen of her eyes, the fierce way she set her lips. Sophia's laughter, that spontaneous, infectious gaiety he loved so much about her, was gone. And all because of her mother.

Any outsider who happened to witness that little exchange would surely have thought it was the height of refined politeness. But Dominic saw it for what it was. A forced encounter, tinged with ice and ringed around with the barbs of years of rigid expectations.

He thought of his own parents, of how his family all fought and bickered and disagreed, but at the end of the day they were all there for each other. They would fight for each other to the last drop of blood.

And he remembered that when he and Lily and Brendan and

the twins were children, their parents would always tuck them into bed before they left for the theater. There were hugs and cuddles, stories, laughter, and no matter what, there was love.

Once, in his bitterness toward the Huntingtons, he had imagined their children growing up amid lavish splendor, like little princes and princesses, reveling in all they had stolen. But today, as he saw the coldness in Lady Huntington's eyes as she looked at her own daughter, he knew that he'd grown up as the fortunate one.

And Sophia's pain hit him like a burning bolt of lightning to his own heart. She had hinted that all had never been well in her family, but today he saw the full extent of what she must have gone through, growing up in a family that could never see her true beauty. Her true worth.

His lovely, laughing Sophia, so full of life that she almost burst with the light of it all--her own family had tried to extinguish all of that. They had forced her to run away, to make her own way through the world alone, and yet she never let them break her. She'd been too stubborn to ever give in.

They were two of a kind. He could see that very clearly now. Neither of them could fight their natures. "She was wrong, Sophia," he said as he helped her into the carriage.

She gave him a puzzled little frown. "Wrong about what?"

"About everything," Dominic answered. He climbed in after her and took her into his arms. For an instant she stiffened, as if seeing her mother had drawn her back into the cold Huntington world. But then she melted against him and hid her face in his shoulder.

"You are an amazing woman, Sophia," he said. "And a strong one, to have stayed true to yourself for all these years."

"I don't feel so very strong," she answered, her voice muffled and thick as if she held back tears. It made him even angrier at anyone who would hurt her. "Once I only wanted them to see me, to know me, but all they could see was how they wanted me to be. And I could never be that."

"*I* see you, Sophia," he said fiercely, holding her against him. "I know you, because we are alike in so many ways."

Sophia shook her head. She pulled herself out of his arms and turned her head away to swipe her hand over her cheeks. "Perhaps we are. But I fear you will only see me as a Huntington, just as they will always see me as not good enough."

"Sophia..." Dominic began, reaching for her again. Somehow it felt as if she was slipping away from him, like a ghost or a dream through the mist, and he wanted to hold on to her.

But she turned away from him. She stared out the carriage window as the streets of London rolled past, her back held rigidly straight. "I was such a fool. I thought we could make something of our marriage, that we were as you said--two of a kind. But Isabel told me that your family has hated mine for a very long time."

"But you are not your family," he protested. "You are only Sophia. The way your mother behaved toward you today was not right."

"Did you not want that to happen?" Sophia suddenly swung around to stare at him. Tears shimmered in her eyes, but they were blazing with anger. "Did you not want us to cause gossip that would embarrass them?"

For once in his life, Dominic had no easy words. He had nothing at all, for he couldn't deny what she'd said. He *had* wanted to embarrass the Huntingtons with their daughter's scandalous marriage.

Somehow, without his even noticing what was happening, the game had changed on him. The hand he'd been dealt was completely different from the one he expected. He had stolen away a Huntington--but she had stolen his heart. Sophia, with her bright laughter and her vivid, spontaneous heart, had burst into his life and completely changed it. What he had thought was one thing was something else entirely, something infinitely more rare and precious.

Something he hadn't even known he was missing, and now it was all he wanted. *Sophia* was all he wanted.

But she stared at him with such anger and hurt in her eyes, and he couldn't find the words to tell her of his sudden confused realization. He, who made a living with language and the counterfeit emotion of the stage, was struck down by the most real moment of his life.

He reached again for Sophia, but she turned away. Her arms crossed tightly across her stomach, holding herself apart from him.

"You got what you wanted," she said. "You have embarrassed my family. But now you are trapped with me as your wife."

"Sophia, it is not like that at all," he said firmly. "If you would only listen to me..."

"No!" she cried. "Please, Dominic, please don't lie to me now. Not on top of everything else. I can't bear it. I need to think."

The carriage drew up outside their lodgings, and as soon as the footman opened the door, Sophia leaped down and ran up the steps.

Dominic's first instinct was to follow her, to catch her in his arms and make her listen. Make her see how things had changed. But he sensed that she wasn't ready to hear him yet, that she would just push him away. And he had to have time to find just the right words. To try to build a new life.

He climbed out of the carriage, too, but he didn't follow her into the house. She said she needed time to think and so did he. And he did that best in the theater. He sent the carriage away and started walking toward the Majestic.

It was a walk he had made dozens of times in his life. Yet today everything around him looked completely different.

From the Diary of Mary St. Claire Huntington

John has returned to Court with the duke, leaving me here alone again. But he took bags of coin and jewels with him, I pray all goes well and that he returns soon, happy once more. I do not think I am with child yet.

Twenty-Three

SOPHIA KNEW something was amiss the moment she stepped into the Majestic Theater.

For the last few days, ever since the uncomfortable meeting with her mother, she'd tried to settle into her new life as Mrs. St. Claire, seeking to find her way. She went to the Devil's Fancy club at night to learn how it was run, and during the day, she left their lodgings to bring Dominic his lunch so he would remember to eat during the long rehearsals. It was one of the few times she saw him, as the new production of *Two Gentlemen of Verona* was due to open tomorrow night and he was always at the theater.

Except for at night, when he climbed into their bed and took her in his arms. Then they were truly together. Then she was sure she'd done the right thing in marrying him. Until she woke in the morning and he was gone.

She tried to find useful ways to fill her days. She called on her new mother-in-law, ran lines from the play with Isabel, did some shopping for things to make Dominic's lodgings more like a home. She tried to help at the club, but James and the manager had things well in hand.

She thought about calling on some of her old friends or even her family, but then she remembered her mother's frosty reception and couldn't work up the courage to try it. She knew her marriage had moved her even further from them all, despite her old, futile hope to return to them. Dominic urged her to write to them, but she wasn't sure why. He'd seen what happened in the park, and she remembered too well what Isabel said about their two families.

So she brought Dominic his lunch and then sat quietly in the stalls to watch the rehearsals. It was enthralling, and for a few hours she was carried out of herself and her worries. She even forgot that Dominic was Dominic, her husband, he disappeared so thoroughly into his role. Sophia had come to find the theater a magical place where everything was transformed.

But not today. Today, when she stepped through the doors from the gilded lobby, the enchanted haven was chaos.

One of the stagehands ran past her, and beyond him she could see the other actors pacing the aisles or slumped in the seats. Onstage, the scenery that was almost finished for Act One was pushed askew. In the half-light, Sophia could see Isabel sitting on a prop throne with her father and Dominic huddled around her. Even from that distance, Sophia could see that her sister-in-law's pretty face was wet with tears.

Sophia saw one of the actors she knew striding out of the nearest rows of seats. She put down her lunch basket and took his arm as he rushed past her.

"Patrick, what is going on?" she demanded.

For a second, he looked at her as if he didn't know her, but then he gave her a quick smile. "Ah, Mrs. St. Claire. I'm afraid the Majestic has had a bit of bad luck this morning."

"What sort of bad luck?" Sophia cried. Her gaze flew to the stage, but she couldn't see much.

"Miss Isabel fell off the stage steps and twisted her ankle," Patrick said with a sad shake of his head. "She can't even take a step now, and the play opens tomorrow."

"Is it broken?" Sophia asked. Even as she spoke, the lobby

doors opened again and a man with a bushy white beard hurried in. He carried a black leather case, and

rushed up the aisle.

"Ah, Dr. Martin! You're here at last," William St. Claire called as he rushed to the edge of the stage. "My daughter is quite crippled, such a tragic accident."

"Papa, that you are an actor doesn't mean you must be so dramatic. I'm sure it is just a twist and I will be up in a moment," Isabel protested. But Sophia could hear the taut pain in Isabel's voice, and her concern grew.

"I will be the judge of that," the doctor said as he climbed the stage steps.

Sophia hurried after him. Dominic gave her a distracted smile, and she went to him to whisper in his ear. "Is Isabel very hurt?"

He shrugged, his attention still on his sister as the doctor knelt in front of her. "It all happened so fast. She tripped and went down the steps before anyone could see what was happening. When Papa picked her up, she was crying and her ankle was already swollen. Poor Issy. She's sure she has ruined the play's opening."

"Oh, stop fussing!" Isabel cried. "You all act as if I am on my deathbed. It was merely a tumble down the stairs. I am perfectly fine."

Before anyone could stop her, she pushed away the doctor and surged to her feet, only to crumple to the stage with a cry of pain. William scooped her up in his arms and carefully set her on the throne again.

"You have wrenched the muscle very badly, Miss St. Claire," the doctor said sternly. "You must stay off the ankle for at least a week if you don't want to cause further damage."

"A week!" Isabel sobbed. "How can I? The show opens tomorrow. I have no understudy since that wretched Elise ran off in Paris. I must walk right now!"

"No, Issy," William said firmly, but Sophia could see how worried he was. He ran his hands through his dark hair, leaving it standing on end. "I won't allow you to hurt yourself any more. We can put on a revival of last year's *Twelfth Night*. You had no role in that one."

"But everyone is expecting a new play," Isabel said. "We have never done *Two Gentlemen* before. And then *The Tempest* is next! I've always wanted to do that one."

Sophia watched the scene helplessly. This was meant to be her family now, and yet she felt so distant from the scene, so powerless. Then she felt a gentle touch on her hand. She looked up to find Dominic watching her with a small smile on his lips. His eyes narrowed as if he examined her for the first time.

"Father," Dominic said. "I think I may have the solution." He drew Sophia closer to his side. "Sophia can take the part until Issy is better. She's been running the lines with both me and Issy, and she knows it perfectly."

Sophia gasped at his words. It was as if the whole scene on the stage froze. Everyone swung around to stare at her.

"It's an excellent solution," Dominic said. "We won't have to comb London for an actress who knows the part, and she would fit into the costume."

Sophia wasn't sure how she felt at his words. Scared, certainly. Unsure. Excited? Her father-in-law was gaping at her as if she was some alien creature who had just wandered into his theater and he had no idea what to do with her.

"A Huntington? At the Majestic?" he muttered. "Perhaps she knows the lines. But knowing the words doesn't mean she can act. You know that, Dominic."

"She can act," Dominic insisted. "And besides, she is so beautiful that, even if she forgets a line or two, no one will care. It would be a sensation."

William's startled stare became speculative. "That is certainly true. But remember what happened when your sister Lily tried to act."

"That won't happen now." Dominic gently tugged on

Sophia's hand and gave her an encouraging smile. "Show him, Sophia. I know you have learned the part."

For a moment, she felt just as frozen as anyone else. The whole situation didn't seem real. All she could sense was everyone staring at her, waiting, judging. She was a Huntington among St. Claires, and surely they expected her to fail.

But Isabel was clapping her hands happily, her tears drying, and Dominic gave Sophia a smile that made her want to try her very hardest. Made her want so much to finally do well at something and please him. Please herself.

That old feeling of rebellion and yearning for freedom, the feeling that had been inside her for as long as she could remember, soared through her again. Being an actress, publicly treading the boards, would mean the disapproval of her own family forever, but she'd never been able to gain their approval anyway. She saw now that, for all her longing, she never could have. She had to make her own life now.

She held her head high and said, with far more confidence than she felt. "Very well. I will do it."

* * *

The confidence was still not fully there the next night, when Sophia stood in the wings waiting for her cue. She was running on sheer nerves, having had very little rest since she agreed to go on for Isabel. Dominic and his father had gone over and over her part with her, dragging her around the stage until she was dizzy with it. Then she had gone back to the St. Claire house and listened to Isabel's lessons on the role as she sat with her injured foot propped on pillows.

William had still looked despairing despite all Sophia's efforts, but luckily tonight he'd vanished somewhere while she was in her dressing room, and she didn't have to watch him pace and tear at his hair.

"You will be fine," Isabel insisted as she pushed Sophia out of the dressing room with the tip of her new walking stick. "Better than fine. Stupendous! They will love you."

Right now, Sophia would happily settle for much less than "love." She would settle for not having rotten vegetables thrown at her.

As the seamstress fluttered around her making last-minute adjustments to her costume, Sophia stared out onto the stage. It was a whole new world, seeing it from back there instead of up in a box. Less mysterious but more intriguing. Her husband hardly looked like himself at all as he moved around the stage, amid the scenery that looked like an exotic city in the flickering lights. And she was supposed to be a part of it.

Don't let me ruin it, she silently pleaded.

She glanced up and caught a glimpse of James on the walkway above. He nodded and gave her an encouraging smile, and she smiled back.

"That is your cue, Mrs. Dominic," the seamstress whispered.

Sophia thought she might faint she suddenly felt so dizzy. But her new family was depending on her. She took a deep breath and pretended this was just another Society ball. She'd playacted her way through plenty of those. She stepped out onto the stage.

At first, she was blinded by the bright gaslights and by the knowledge that dozens of eyes were out there, watching her. Dominic moved toward her, his velvet and cloth of gold costume dazzling, and held out his hand to her.

"Have patience, gentle Julia," he said, in a voice that was her husband's and yet not. Deeper, richer.

And something truly magical happened. It was as if the theater vanished, and she was truly in another world, with the sun beating down on her. She was not herself. She felt such different emotions. She *was* Julia.

She took Dominic's hand and said, "I must, where is no remedy..."

* * *

Dominic had never felt more proud of anyone in his life. And it was for a *Huntington*. Surely at any moment pigs would go flying over London Bridge.

He watched his wife as she stood at the center of a bright, chattering group. After the opening night of a play, his father always hosted a small party for important patrons and friends in the Majestic's sumptuous lobby. It was always a popular soiree, where champagne flowed and everyone tried to hear news about the rest of the Season. And tonight Sophia was the star of it all.

She took a glass of wine that James offered her and smiled up at his brother in thanks as she listened to something Lord Maltravers was saying to her. She'd changed from her costume to a new gown of green satin beaded in sparkling jet, and emerald combs sparkled in her black hair. She seemed to sparkle, too, as well she should after what she had achieved tonight.

His wife was a natural actress. She'd claimed the stage as if she had always owned it, and she'd shown a perfect intuition when it came to working with the other actors, listening to them and drawing out the emotions of a scene. She had blossomed there, and the quiet, worried-looking Sophia he'd seen since that encounter with her cold mother was mercifully gone.

"She did well enough, I suppose," he heard his father say in a comically grudging tone.

Dominic turned to see his parents standing behind him. His mother had her usual serene smile on her face, and she held tight to his father's arm. Dominic had to grin when he saw the disgruntled look on William's face. His father would never have wanted a Majestic production to fail, but neither did he yet want to admit that a Huntington had saved it tonight.

Even if the Huntington in question was now a St. Claire.

"Now, William dear, you know you are being unfair," Katherine admonished gently. "Sophia was wonderful. I haven't seen an actress take so naturally to the stage since our Isabel had her first role. And with only a day's training!"

"Hmph," William said. "If you say so, Katherine."

"I *do* say so, and you know I am right." Katherine reached for Dominic's arm with her free hand and drew him to her side as they watched Sophia charm the patrons. "You must be very proud, Dominic."

"I am," he admitted. The evening, which could have gone so wrong, had been a triumph. He never would have imagined it of Sophia Huntington when he first met her in Paris. He'd sorely underestimated his wife.

Sophia glanced across the lobby and caught him watching her. He feared he must have looked rather fierce, because a flicker of doubt dimmed her radiant expression. He quickly smiled at her, and she smiled in return. She raised her hand as if to wave him toward her.

Then she suddenly froze. Her stare was aimed beyond him and his parents, and her hand fell to her side. James took her arm, his brother's face suddenly dark as a thundercloud.

Dominic turned and saw that the lobby doors had opened. A couple stood there, the petite blonde he'd seen with Sophia's mother in the park and a tall, black-haired man who was the mirror image of Sophia herself. And just behind them was Lord Hammond, watching the party with his usual cold, superior sneer on his face.

"Dominic, what is it?" his mother said. She looked toward the doors, too. "Who are those people?"

"Surely that is Lord Edward Huntington," William said. His father was not easily surprised, yet he sounded astounded that yet another Huntington was at his party.

"Mrs. Dominic's brother. And I do think the other man is the Duke of Carston's cousin. I've never met him, but he has quite the reputation around London. He did not attend the play. What is he doing here now?"

Dominic was already turning toward his wife. He was afraid he knew all too well what Hammond was doing there.

From the Diary of Mary St. Claire Huntington

We are ruined. I can hardly believe it even as I write these words. John rode in today, looking gray and haggard, and I have never seen anyone so angry. He has locked me in my room, raving about my family and how they led him into the loss of so much money. But how can that be? Nick and my father were as deceived as anyone! I cannot cease crying, but he will not come to me. He will not listen.

What will become of me now?

Twenty-Four

"WHAT IS THAT BASTARD DOING HERE?" James said tightly. His hands curled into tight fists.

"I'm not sure," Sophia answered, staring at Lord Hammond in cold shock. The glow from her moments on the stage was fading fast. She looped her fingers around her brother-in-law's arm to keep him at her side, in hopes he wouldn't dash off and do something rash and hotheaded. Not here, in the St. Claires' own theater, with everyone watching. She wanted to try to do right by her new family, not cause them even more trouble.

But what was Hammond doing here again? And with her brother Edward and his new wife, too. What game did he play? She'd hoped her marriage would send him off after other prey, but now she feared that had been a mistake. Maybe it had only strengthened his resolve.

"Come with me now, James," she said, as quietly and calmly as she could. "No matter what he's doing here, we don't need to engage him."

"I didn't cheat in that card game in Paris, no matter what anyone says," James said fiercely. He looked down at her, and his eyes glowed with a hot fire. "I've done some stupid things, I admit, but never that"

"I know," Sophia said, and truly she did know. James would never do such a thing. He was young and quick-tempered, but he had the same personal code of honor his brother did. It was all just part of Hammond's game.

"Come with me," she said. "I need to find Dominic, and I don't want to walk across this room alone."

James gave a reluctant nod, as she knew he would. He wouldn't leave her alone in the crowd when Lord Hammond was somewhere near. She held on to his arm as they made their way across the crowded lobby. She smiled and exchanged a few words with the people who stopped her as they passed, and she held on to James the whole time. She felt how tense he was and saw the way he scanned the crowd, but he stayed with her.

And they didn't encounter Lord Hammond. But they did meet Sophia's brother.

"Sophia," he said casually, giving her a quick peck on the cheek, as if he'd seen her only last week. "You're looking grand. It was quite amazing to see my little sister up on the stage tonight. You did an admirable enough job, I daresay."

Sophia had to laugh. Her brother had never been much of a theatergoer, so she was sure he wouldn't know an "admirable" performance if it slapped him on the face. Even now his gaze was drifting away from her to study the other women in the room.

But his wife was beaming with pleasure, her cheeks as pink as her ruffled gown. "It really was such an enjoyable play, Mrs. St. Claire," she said shyly. "Will we see you often at the Majestic?"

"I'm not sure," Sophia answered. "I am just playing understudy for my sister-in-law, who was, sadly, injured. But I am glad you enjoyed the play."

She chatted with Edward's wife about some of the latest London news, the new style of hats, and Court happenings with the queen and her family, as James and Edward pretended they were somewhere else. Sophia surreptitiously kept her eye on the crowd around them until, just as she had feared, Lord Hammond made his appearance. As always, he had a lady on his arm, a beautiful young redhead dressed in widow's black but dripping with diamonds.

Suddenly she felt an arm slide gently around her shoulders, and she half-turned to find that Dominic had come to her side. He gave her a small, reassuring smile, and she felt calmer in an instant, even as Hammond came closer to them.

"Ah, the happy newlywed couple," Hammond said with an affable smile. His eyes were cold as he looked at Sophia, and she was even more glad to have Dominic close to her, holding her up. Edward and his wife made their excuses and moved away to find some wine. "Allow me to be among the first to offer my best wishes. I'm so glad your dear brother and his wife invited me here tonight, Mrs. St. Claire, so I could congratulate you in person."

"That is very kind of you," Dominic said smoothly. "Considering our last meeting at Madame Brancusi's was not so cordial."

Sophia sensed how stiff James was on her other side, as if he held himself on a tight rein. She only hoped his control lasted.

Hammond waved his hand in a dismissive gesture. "Bygones should be bygones, sould they not? Young Mr. St. Claire here was in his cups, and I'm sure he has learned his lesson now. Unlike others." He glanced around the crowded lobby. "Your father has such a success here with his theater. The Majestic is always the talk of London. Why, they even say the queen has talked of taking a permanent box. I'm sure the new Mrs. St. Claire will be a great asset here."

"She already is," Dominic said.

"Of course. I only hope the two of you, and your family, will be very happy. And that you will never come to regret your marriage. That can be so easy to do in hastily contracted unions." As if he'd said what he intended to say, Hammond gave them a short nod and turned to walk away, the black-clad lady's arm linked in his. They vanished together into the crowd.

"Well, that was short and simple," Dominic said.

"The bastard," James growled. "What did he mean by all that?"

Sophia nodded, but the bright evening was dimmed like the footlights at the end of a play, and she knew she had to find a way to keep Hammond away from her new family and this theater that they loved so much.

From the Diary of Mary St. Claire Huntington

John is sending me away. I am ill and fevered, my heart cracked apart, yet still he will not listen to my pleas. Dear Lord, what am I to do now? I still love him so very much!

Twenty-Five

THE DEVIL'S Fancy was practically empty. For the third night in a row.

Sophia tapped her fan against her palm as she walked through the rooms that were so very quiet, when they should be crowded and filled with laughter.

Dominic had said he wasn't worried on the first night things were empty, the night after Lord Hammond appeared at theater and rumors were flying about the gossipy tidbits in the newspapers. Dominic was caught up in the work of the theater, though, and didn't see what she saw tonight as she tried to oversee the club for him. Isabel had recovered and returned to work, and Sophia didn't have a new role yet, though William had promised her one. But there was little to oversee at the club, even though the manager had suddenly quit. A few rakish old stalwarts playing cards; no one dancing. Surely it was only a matter of time before the receipts fell off at the theater, too. And she realized that, despite all her hopes in marrying Dominic, she'd overplayed her hand. She had underestimated the determination--and the power--of an opponent like Lord Hammond.

Being deprived of what he wanted—her--had only made him want it all the more. It made the game more exciting for him, the opposite of what she had wanted. And now she'd given him new pawns in her husband and his family.

Sophia turned to survey the room again. She didn't *know* that this sudden fall-off in business was Hammond's fault, of course, but some instinct told her that it had to be. And now she needed her own battle plan, a way to fight back.

"Mrs. St. Claire," one of the footmen said. He came up to her holding out a silver tray. Resting on it was a single note, a heavy folded sheet of expensive stationery sealed with red wax. "This just arrived for you."

Sophia's hands turned cold. She reached for the letter as she would for a snake, taking it carefully between her gloved fingertips. "Thank you," she said. She broke the seal and scanned the short missive for a signature.

Hammond. Of course.

My dear Mrs. St. Claire--I would imagine you are having a rather quiet evening. Such a shame at a lovely establishment like your husband's, but such lulls can easily be remedied, along with so much else. If you would like my advice on how to proceed, please call on me at the Hotel Carlyle. Enclosed is my card with the direction and room number.

As ever, I so much look forward to seeing your beautiful face. Remember, I can be a good friend, my dear. Lord Hammond.

A calling card fell out of the letter's folds. Room 414 was neatly printed on the back.

Sophia violently crumpled the letter in her hand and tossed it into the nearest fireplace. But she kept the card.

After the last of the customers left. Sophia made sure the night's meager earnings were accounted for, and she locked up the club to leave for their lodgings. It would surely be a while yet before Dominic left the theater, and she needed the time to be alone and think.

She'd brought Lord Hammond into the St. Claires' lives. She had to root him out again.

On the way home, she watched out the carriage window as

the other vehicles clattered past on the street outside. She remembered how hopeful she'd felt only a few days before, at the theater. She had dared to hope that things were going well for them. That they could truly be married. Then her mother appeared, and Sophia was shown very clearly that the past couldn't be escaped so easily. The barriers between her and Dominic were still there, so high she could hardly see over them. Her family, the reckless mistakes of her past that had brought Hammond into their lives-- it was all there. It wasn't going away.

Sophia closed her eyes tightly. Dominic had tried to be kind after they left her mother, tried to be understanding. She saw the pity in his eyes, and that only seemed to make things harder. She could feel all her armor, her defenses, crumbling in the face of his passion. But now she could tell he was preoccupied with something he kept hidden inside, just as she did. Ever since Hammond appeared at the theater.

And the terrible thing was, she knew now that she loved Dominic. It had crept up on her and wouldn't be banished. So it was better to have that distance between them now, so she could make things right for him however she could. Sophia turned away from the window and dug through her reticule. In the bottom, she found what she was looking for. The small pistol Camille had given her lay there, deceptively pretty with its inlaid handle.

She put Lord Hammond's card next to the gun. Yes, she would do whatever she had to now to repay Dominic's kindnesses to her. Surely she had nothing now to lose?

Dominic was already back at their lodgings when she returned. He lay sprawled across their bed dressed only in his trousers and his unfastened, rumpled linen shirt. The lamplight gilded his bared skin and turned his tousled hair to pure molten gold. Her handsome husband. Her heart ached as she studied him.

He looked up from the script he was reading and smiled at her. "How was the club tonight?"

Sophia returned his smile, but it felt brittle and strained, as if her face would crack with the strain of it. How very tired she was. How very much she wished everything could be different. That she could go back and be with Dominic after that first night she met him and start all over again.

"Slow," she said. She sat down at her dressing table and stripped off her gloves and earrings. She slowly started to pull the pins from her hair as her headache grew stronger. "How was the theater?"

"Issy was in good form, though moving a bit slower than usual. Father kept hinting to know when you might take another role. Everyone was asking about you."

"Was your father really? How kind of him." Sophia remembered the magic of their nights onstage, how rare and wonderful it was. She only hoped Dominic would remember, too. Afterwards.

As she reached for her hairbrush, she saw the worn leather cover of Mary's diary sitting on the edge of the table. She'd finished the last page only that morning. Mary's tale had ended with shocking suddenness, trailing off in smudged ink and tear stains as her husband sent her away. All her hopes had crumbled to nothing.

What had been the real end of her story? Perhaps it was better Sophia would never know.

She heard a rustle as Dominic left the bed. He crossed the room on his bare feet, and as she watched in the mirror he came up behind her and started to unfasten her gown.

"Is that Mary Huntington's diary?" he asked quietly.

"Yes. I just read the last entry this morning." As Sophia studied her husband's half-shadowed reflection, she came to a decision. She reached for the book and took his hand to press it against his palm. "You should read it too, Dominic."

He looked back at her, his expression unreadable. "Should I look at it now?"

"If you like. I think I'll try to sleep." Sophia rose from the chair and let her loosened gown fall away. She kissed Dominic softly on his cheek as he stared down at the book in his hand.

She went to their bed and slipped between the covers. She wasn't sure she really could sleep, but she was so very tired she could feel darkness stealing over her even as she closed her eyes.

She fell asleep to the soft sound of old pages slowly turning.

* * *

The sun was beginning to peek through the window when Dominic finished Mary's diary. As he set the book down carefully on Sophia's dressing table, he was astonished to find the night was gone and he was still in his own room, not on a country estate.

Mary's sadness, even as long ago as it had been, seemed to pervade everything. He could hardly fathom her tale. It was as if the hardened walls of bitterness that had always encased his life, the old hatred of the Huntingtons, had dissipated around him. He hated the raw vulnerability of their loss, but surely to know the truth was always better.

He'd always been told that John Huntington ruined the St. Claire family after he coldly cast Mary aside when she couldn't give him an heir. That he'd used his Court connections to destroy his wife's family. But now it seemed they had both been destroyed, Mary's husband and brother, through a royal duke's ill-fated financial scheme. It was neither family's fault--and yet it was both. And innocent Mary, who only wanted to love her husband, was the one truly destroyed. By that very love.

Dominic went and knelt by the bed where his wife slept. The pale pink sunrise light fell over her face, and he saw she was shockingly pale. Dark purple shadows lurked under her eyes, and her brow was furrowed as if she had disturbing dreams.

And Dominic felt a pang of something he seldom experienced--remorse. Remorse for not being what she needed, what she deserved. For assuming the worst, just as John had with Mary.

He didn't know the ending of Mary's tale, but he did know he could make Sophia's story a happier one. If she would just give him the chance. He just had to figure out how.

He gently drew the blankets closer around her and kissed her forehead. "Sleep well now, Sophia," he whispered. "I'm sorry for not intending to be the husband you need. I'm here now."

He could only hope that somehow she heard him.

Twenty-Six

SOPHIA HURRIED DOWN THE STREET, not looking to either side of her, not paying attention to any of the noise and jostle. It was almost as if London, the real, working life of the city, no longer existed. She could only think of one thing.

Finding Lord Hammond.

She wasn't sure what she would do when she found him. She only knew she had to put a stop to his threats, to the danger he posed to Dominic and his family.

She'd never felt so deeply, achingly angry before in her life. Yet she also felt freezing cold, frighteningly calm, and rational. How dare this man, a man she barely knew, think he had any right to her? That he owned her just because he wanted her, that he could ruin her life because she didn't want him in return?

She wasn't going to take it any longer. Now she had more than herself to protect. She had Dominic, her husband.

The husband she loved. She wasn't going to let her own problems ruin his life. She could never live with that if he suffered from being allied with her. So she would take care of this now. However she had to. She'd left Dominic a note explaining what she was doing, a note he would find only after he got back from the theater and this was all long over. It was the least she could do for him now.

Sophia turned a corner and found herself facing the hotel where Lord Hammond said he was staying. She tugged her hooded cloak closer around her and stared up at the grand building. It looked quiet and genteel, with its heavily-draped windows and liveried doormen. Not a place for dramatic confrontations. But she had no choice.

She drew a deep breath and pasted on the haughtiest smile she had learned from her mother. If she looked as if she belonged there, no one would stop her. She swept past the doorman and into the marble-and-velvet hush of the foyer.

She pulled his card out of her reticule and checked the room--414. As she tucked it back amid the satin folds, she felt the reassuring weight of her small pistol at the bottom. It looked deceptively dainty, all ivory scrolls and curves inlaid in the smooth wood, but she knew it could get the job done if needed.

As she climbed the carpeted staircase, cold distance heightened her perceptions. The dark, rich colors of the hotel seemed to sharpen. She could smell the heavy earthiness of the lilies in the tall, blue and white Chinese vases blended with the scent of beeswax polish and expensive perfumes. And suddenly she felt strong and resolute. This was ending now. Dominic would be free.

On the fourth floor, the stairs opened onto a grand landing, an octagonal space carpeted in plush red and blue and hung with lavish tapestries that muffled the loud laughter of the well-dressed crowd gathered there. A table was laid out with champagne and hors d'oeuvres, and a footman passed out glasses to the people lounging on the satin sofas and along the gilded railings that looked down to the lobby so far below.

And in their midst was Lord Hammond. He sat on a settee beside one of the expensive courtesans he'd been with at the Devil's Fancy. She leaned against his arm, laughing tipsily, while Lord Hammond watched the gathering with a small smile.

Sophia hadn't expected a party, but she had as good a sense of drama as anyone. Perhaps it would be better to have witnesses. Then Dominic could be done with an obviously mad wife.

Sophia swept back the hood of her cloak and stepped forward with a smile.

* * *

Sophia was gone.

Dominic stared down at the scrawled note in his hand, still not quite believing what he had read. He'd hurried back from rehearsal, eager to take her to dinner and start to rebuild something between them. Tell her what he was feeling. But she had gone to find Lord Hammond, had vowed that he and his family would be safe now because she was going to make it so.

He wasn't sure what she meant by that, but he remembered her pale, strained face from last night. He only knew he had to find her now, before it was too late.

Twenty-Seven

"MY DEAR MRS. ST. Claire! I am so happy you could join my little party today. I've been looking forward to seeing you again." Lord Hammond rose from his settee and came toward Sophia with a smile. He ignored the pouts of the woman he left behind, and the curious stares everyone else turned toward her. He only watched her.

He took her arm and bent his head to brush his cool lips over her cheek. Sophia felt a shudder move up her spine, but she forced herself to remain still. This was for all the mistakes she'd made in her life; she had to make them right now.

"I knew you would come to me eventually," he said.

"Yes," Sophia murmured. "I see where my advantages in life lie now."

"You are a very smart girl, Sophia. It's just too bad we've wasted so much time."

Sophia smiled sweetly up at him. "Shall we make up for it now?"

"Of course." Lord Hammond took her arm and turned her toward the corridor that led away from the party. "We should go someplace quieter to talk."

Sophia glanced over at the gathering. They'd all gone back to their conversations, but she could see their sidelong looks at her and Lord Hammond. "I don't want to keep you from your guests. I had no idea you were entertaining today or I would have waited to come here."

"You are the most important guest of all, my dear," he said, running his fingers lightly over the back of her hand. "And soon everyone will know that."

Sophia looked down at the floor in what she hoped seemed a demure, shy fashion. In reality, she was trying to gauge how long it would take to open her reticule. "I-I'm still a married woman, Lord Hammond. Even if it was a mistake."

"A mistake that will soon be rectified." He leaned close to whisper in her ear, his breath warm on her skin. "I can give you so much more than a man like St. Claire could. And now that you have seen that and come to me, the Devil's Fancy can remain open and he and his family can go about their disreputable business without you. My friends will be pleased not to lose one of their favorite places to gamble."

"I hope so," Sophia said. "He can't give me the place in Society I need, but I wouldn't want to lose such an amusing establishment."

"Whatever you want, my dear, it's yours." He turned down the corridor and led her toward the looming doorway of room 414. "Now, let me get you a glass of champagne and we will have a nice, quiet talk about the future." Sophia clutched her reticule tighter in her hand and followed him. Her heart was pounding, and her whole body felt as cold as ice. But her mind was strangely sharp and clear.

"Perhaps you would like to go abroad again?" he said as he pushed open the door and ushered her inside with a possessive hand on her back. "You seemed in your element in Baden-Baden and Paris. London is entirely unworthy of you."

Sophia looked around her. To her relief, they were in a sitting room and not a bedchamber, a small, opulent space that echoed the luxury of the hotel's foyer. The air felt heavy and hot, oppressively scented with large arrangements of full-blown roses.

"Perhaps," she said, watching him as he crossed the room to a table laid out with an array of wine bottles. Now that he had her, Sophia was sure he wouldn't stay interested long enough to take her abroad. She'd met men like him many times. He would be on to the next challenge, leaving her life, and those of her husband and his family, in ruins. Another Huntington destroying a St. Claire.

Hammond poured out two glasses of champagne. She opened her reticule and drew out the pistol. When he turned back around, she held it leveled on him.

And his smile grew even more delighted. "Now, my dear, you had just come to your senses. Don't ruin it now with sad melodrama. As amusing as it all is."

Sophia shook her head. "Yes, I did come to my senses. I love my husband, and I won't let anyone hurt him." Including herself.

"I mean him absolutely no harm," Hammond said. He slowly put the glasses down on the table. "I have nothing against him, except that you were momentarily foolish enough to marry him. But that is over now that you have come to me."

"I haven't come to you," she said, still feeling that strange, cold curtain of calm that held her apart from the whole terrible scene. "I know men like you. I have been subjected to them my whole life. You want to own people, control them. I won't be controlled any longer."

That infuriating smile of his flickered a bit, and she saw a shadow of doubt in his eyes.

"Perhaps you see now that you are dealing with a madwoman," she said.

Suddenly he lunged toward her. His fist closed on the edge of her cloak. She kicked out at him and raised her pistol. In the sudden, panicked violence of the moment, she had no time to aim. She fired blindly.

She heard Hammond's shouted curse, and the shattering of

glass. He grabbed her hard around the waist and shoved her to the floor. The gun was knocked out of her hand and went skittering across the floor. She tried to scramble after it, but Hammond slammed her back down. Her head bit the floor, and for an instant, the room whirled around her in a painful, nauseous haze.

"You insane bitch," he cried hoarsely, and she felt him ripping open her cloak, tearing at her bodice. "I offer you everything, and this is what you do? Try to kill me?"

Sophia opened her mouth to scream, and his hand came down to smother the noise. She couldn't breathe. She tried to free her hand and hit him, to kick out at him from the imprisoning tangle of her skirts, but she was trapped beneath him.

The room was turning dark at the edges. Just as she was sure she would faint, she heard the crash of the door flying open. One of Hammond's hands fell away from her as she sat up, and she rolled onto her side beneath him.

It was Dominic at the door, Dominic with his green eyes blazing with a raw, primitive fury.

"Get off her, you filthy piece of shit," he roared, and he threw himself forward to toss Hammond away from her.

Sophia barely managed to pull herself out of the way before Dominic landed a blow to Hammond's face and sent him reeling back. Dominic followed in relentless pursuit.

Sophia climbed to her feet and scooped her lost pistol off the floor. She pressed close to the wall, out of their way, and tried to get a straight shot at Hammond. But it was impossible. They were flying around the room in a blur of fists, a mist of sweat and blood.

She remembered the night in Paris when Dominic was dumped on her doorstep, covered in cuts and bruises. She'd known even then that all the wounds were not from his street attackers, that he was a dangerous man. She could see that now in the methodical, precise way he went after Hammond, landing blow after blow for the maximum effect. Despite the fury on his face, he never fought wild.

Hammond was no match for Dominic. He obviously had never been forced to resort to physically going after what he wanted. Not when blackmail and powerful relatives did the trick. But he was no weakling either. A right uppercut sent Dominic reeling back, and Sophia screamed. But he leaped back up, as lithe and powerful as before.

Suddenly, Hammond swung around and grabbed Sophia by the arm in a bruising, iron grip. She screamed as he pulled her closer, and one hand came up in a choking hold around her neck. The room started to swim around her again as her air was cut off.

"Let her go," Dominic demanded. "This fight is between you and me now, not her."

"On the contrary," Hammond panted. "I *only* wanted her. You were the one who got in the way. If you leave now, leave her with me, I'll keep my bargain with her, even though she tried to cheat me."

"I will never leave her," Dominic said, horribly calm.

"Then you can die with her. It makes no difference to me. In fact, I rather like this ending--the cheap player and the cheating harlot, done in by getting above themselves."

Hammond's grip tightened around Sophia's throat, and she felt herself falling down into blackness. As if from under a roaring ocean wave, she heard Dominic shout her name.

Dominic. No, no, she couldn't leave him. He'd come after her; she loved him. She reached deep down inside herself for one last burst of energy and managed to throw the gun she still clutched in her hand toward him.

As she started to sink to the floor, she heard a woman scream. Hammond, who still held on to her, suddenly dropped her as if he was startled by the sound. There was a loud explosion, a strong whiff of gunpowder, more hysterical screams and shrieks.

Then everything just seemed to--stop. Sophia could feel the roughness of the carpet under her cheek, but her whole body felt numb. It was almost as if she floated outside herself, in a nightmare.

"Sophia!" Dominic's voice broke through that haze. He sounded frantic, frightened. But how could that be? Dominic was always cool, remote, even in the midst of passionate moments and fights, always hiding his emotions behind his handsome face. "Sophia, talk to me. Look at me. Curse at me, anything! Just be alive!"

Sophia summoned up all her resolve and rolled onto her back. She opened her eyes and saw her husband's green eyes above her. A cut across his cheek oozed blood. "I-I am alive," she whispered. She tried to reach up to touch him, but her arm felt too weak to lift.

"Thank God. You beautiful, wonderful, foolish woman. What would I do without you?" Dominic's arms came around her, and he lifted her up as he stood.

Sophia saw Lord Hammond's body on the carpet, face-down in a slowly spreading pool of blood. The woman whose screams had distracted him stood in the doorway, her face buried in her hands as two men held her up. A gawking crowd was gathering behind them, and a man who said he was the owner of the hotel was shouting for order.

But for Sophia all that seemed very distant, all muffled and hazy. The only thing that seemed real was Dominic, his arms around her, his body next to hers. Real and alive.

And she let herself give in to the darkness, knowing finally, once and for all, that he would keep her safe.

Twenty-Eight

SOPHIA GROANED as she felt her body coming awake. The light seemed to press hard against her eyelids, forcing her out of the warm darkness of her dreams. She rolled over onto her side, but her whole body ached. Her throat hurt when she tried to swallow, and for a moment she was confused. What had happened to her?

Then she remembered. Lord Hammond, her idea to confront him, Dominic--how it had all gone horribly wrong.

She sat up, and her head felt as if it would split at the sudden movement.

"Lie back down, Sophia," a gentle voice said. Cool, soft hands gently pressed her back to the bed. "You have had a terrible shock. You must rest."

Sophia frantically turned her head at the sound and found Dominic's mother sitting on the edge of the bed. She smiled, but Sophia could see the strain on her pretty face, the tense lines of worry. Sophia glanced around the room, a sunny, pale bedchamber, but there was no one else there.

"Dominic?" she said. Her voice was hoarse, and she could hardly force the one word through her aching throat.

"Don't worry, he will be back soon. He and his father went to talk to the magistrate. He wouldn't leave until he saw you settled here, but it couldn't be put off any longer."

"The magistrate? No," Sophia gasped, cold panic roaring through her. "He will be sent to prison, and it's all my fault."

"He won't be sent to prison." Katherine pressed Sophia back to the bed. She was gentle but surprisingly strong. "There were no constables, no manacles."

Sophia lay down on the pillows, but she couldn't rest. She twisted the lacy hem of the sheets between her hands, and she felt the weight of her wedding band on her finger. "But the man Dominic killed--he was a relative of the Duke of Pendrake."

"And there were witnesses who saw what happened, that this Lord Hammond tried to kill you and that Dominic was only defending his wife," Katherine said, her voice soothing and steady. "And one of those men was a cousin to the queen. Even Pendrake wouldn't want to make trouble with the royal family. Dominic will have everything straightened out and return here soon. In the meantime, you must rest."

Sophia nodded and let some of her mother-in-law's quiet assurance soothe her. "I'm sure you are quite right I just--well, I have become accustomed to fighting my own battles."

"You aren't alone any longer, Sophia," Katherine said, gently squeezing Sophia's hand. "Dominic told us about how you broke with your family. But we are your family now. You can be as eccentric as you like, but you will always be one of us now. And we defend our own."

"Dominic should not have to defend me," Sophia protested. "I made so many mistakes..."

"What is past is past. Everything will be well now." Katherine gave her a teasing wink. "And it was good that Dominic could come to your rescue. The St. Claire men like to behave as if they were heroes in a medieval poem sometimes. It makes them feel useful."

Sophia gave a choked laugh. "Surely there must be an easier way for him to feel useful?"

"I do hope so. This family has seen quite enough perilous dramas for the time being." Katherine reached for a glass on the bedside table. "Here, drink some of this. It has honey and chamomile to soothe your throat."

Sophia took the glass from her and drew in a sip. "Thank you. It does seem to help."

"The doctor says you must take extra care of yourself now, with the baby and everything."

Sophia nearly dropped the glass. "Baby?"

Katherine smiled at her. "Yes. Did you not know? You were in a faint when the doctor came, but I thought you must already know."

"No, I--no." Sophia pressed one hand gently over her stomach. She could feel nothing, but was there really a little life there? Dominic's baby? "Is he sure?"

"As sure as a doctor can be, I suppose," Katherine said with a laugh.

"I never would have gone to see Hammond if I knew." She felt sick when she thought about what might have happened to her child.

"Of course not. But I am so terribly happy, Sophia; my second grandchild. First Lily and Aidan, now you."

Even if it was a half-Huntington baby? There was still that tiny, cold doubt deep inside Sophia, but she couldn't say the words. She couldn't say anything at all. She was overwhelmed by emotion.

"Just rest now," Katherine said. "Dominic will be back soon. I'll be just outside the door if you need anything."

Katherine tucked the blankets closer around Sophia and quietly left the room. Sophia closed her eyes and imagined the baby nestled within her, the baby that had already survived so much.

"I will never do anything to endanger you ever again," she whispered. "You will always come first with me, no matter what. I promise."

And your father will be home soon, she added. He had to be. She had to tell him how sorry she was. How much she wanted a new beginning for all of them.

She drifted into sleep again, until she woke to a gentle touch on her hand. She opened her eyes to find that the room was shadowed in evening, and Dominic sat beside her. He looked tired, his hair tousled and his eyes shaded with purple, but he smiled tenderly at her.

"Are you feeling better?" he said quietly.

"Dominic!" Sophia cried. She sat up and threw her arms around his neck, holding him close. She only wanted to know that he was real, that he was there. "You came back."

"Of course I did," he said, laughing. "Where else would I go?"

"Prison? I was so afraid when I woke and you weren't here..."

He shook his head. "There is little chance of that. I will have to testify at the inquiry, but the queen's cousin and the other witnesses have signed statements that it was self-defense."

"But there will be a great scandal," Sophia said. She knew the furor that would erupt over such a lurid scene as the one at the hotel.

"Very, very great," he agreed. "Yet that's nothing now for either of us. I doubt we can ever aspire to dull respectability."

Sophia had to laugh. "No, never. But the baby..."

"Poor baby, with such ne'er-do-well parents." Dominic slid down next to her on the bed to lay his hand gently over the spot where their child nestled. "We will do our very best for him or her, though. It will always know that it's loved--no matter what trouble it gets into."

Sophia softly ran her fingers through Dominic's hair, smoothing back the strands. "Dominic, you must believe I didn't know about the baby before I went to confront Hammond. I never would have put our child in any danger. I only wanted..."

He looked up at her. His green eyes glowed in the shadows. "Wanted what?"

"To protect you. You married me to help me escape

Hammond, and he would have used that to destroy you. I couldn't let that happen."

"So you put your own life at risk? Why would you do that?"

Sophia looked deeply into his eyes, those beautiful eyes she loved so much, and she took the greatest leap of her life. Even confronting Hammond had not demanded greater courage.

"Because," she said, "I love you. I love you, and I would do anything to protect you. You were right when you said we were two of a kind. We rush out into life without thinking sometimes because we crave it so much. But if we watch each other's backs..."

"Then we were made for each other. No one else could ever do for either of us." Dominic sat up beside her and gently took her face in his hands. "I love you, too, Sophia. And I could never do without you. I would do anything for you, anything to make up for the way I treated you."

Sophia laughed, even though she feared she would burst into tears. Surely there had never been a more perfect moment than this one. "I would say rushing in to save me from a murderous madman makes up for a great deal." Dominic laughed, too, and kissed her on her cheek, her brow, and the tip of her nose. "Any time you need saving, I will always be there. Just as I know you will, too."

"I will." Sophia wound her arms tightly around his shoulders and held him close. "Promise me there will be no more secrets. That we will never leave each other."

"I promise. I am yours, forever," Dominic said. "You and me and this child. I will do whatever it takes to make us a real family."

"An unconventional family though."

"Of course. We're the Huntington-St. Claires. Surely there has never been a stranger match."

Sophia kissed her husband and gave him a smile full of every joy in her heart. "No, there has never been a more perfect match than that one."

Epilogue

EDINBURGH, ONE YEAR LATER

"NOW, darling, we must be very, very quiet. Papa is rehearsing." Sophia smiled down at her tiny daughter as she pushed the pram down the theater corridor. Little Mary St. Claire smiled up at her, green eyes shining from beneath her lacy cap.

"But of course you will be," Sophia cooed. "For you are the best baby in the world."

She steered the pram through the open doorway of one of the boxes, and the theater suddenly opened up before them. A vast, darkened space of empty velvet-and gilt chairs, except for the well-lit stage below, where a rehearsal of *As You Like It* was going on. Sophia's scenes were not being rehearsed today, so she had hours to spend with Mary and introduce her daughter to the theater.

Dominic sprang across the stage, laughing as he swung a stage rapier in his hand. All the light seemed to gather only on him, and Sophia could see he was in his true element there. No villains any longer, only heroes to thrill an audience's heart. Just as he thrilled hers every time she looked at him. Just as she knew her true place every time they took the stage together.

Sophia smiled as she settled in one of the plush chairs and took Mary in her arms. Ever since they'd come to Edinburgh so that Dominic could appear at his sister Lily's theater and escape the scandal of London, all seemed like a golden idyll. The troubles of London and Hammond's death seemed far behind them now. Here, in this old city of hills and cobbled streets, of new theaters, they'd made a fresh start.

"Your papa will take Edinburgh by storm in this role," Sophia said, and Mary gurgled happily before grabbing a ribbon of Sophia's bonnet to chew on.

"Indeed he will--and so will Mary's mama," Sophia's cousin Aidan said as he stepped into the box. "We're going to have a great success here at the Northern Majestic. Everyone wants to see the famous Mr. and Mrs. St. Claire. And how are you two beautiful ladies today?"

"We are very well indeed," Sophia answered with a laugh. Mary smiled and held out one chubby little hand to her favorite uncle.

Another of the advantages to getting away from the troubles of London was that she got to see Aidan again, and come to know his wife, Lily, and their new twin sons. No one knew better the trials of trying to build a Huntington-St. Claire marriage--or the rare joys. They were happier than any other couple Sophia had ever seen.

Except for herself and Dominic.

"How is Lily today?" she said as she watched Aidan play with Mary.

"Deep in her account books, so ridiculously happy. I will never understand that woman's passion for numbers," Aidan answered. He smiled at her and Mary as the rehearsal went on below them. "It's so wonderful to see you so happy, Soph. I used to worry about you."

Sophia laughed. "You worried about *me*? You were in trouble far more often than I was."

"But you always seemed so discontented where you were, always wanting more, always fighting against everything."

Sophia looked down at the stage. Dominic was explaining a stage move to another actor, his arm sweeping in a wide gesture as he laughed. Her handsome, dashing, wonderful husband. "I *was* unhappy then, and it made me behave in foolishly wild ways because I could see no way out. I couldn't see another way to be. But now"

"Now you have everything you want. A family, an acting career."

"Yes." Sophia held Mary's tiny hand in hers and watched Dominic as he reached for his coat, still laughing with the other actors. "I do have everything I could have wanted. And so do you."

"I do." Aidan gave her one of his rakish grins. "Who would ever have thought it of us?"

"The two black sheep haven't done so badly."

Aidan looked at the stage. "It looks like they've finished for the morning. Should we go join Lily for luncheon?"

"Of course." They made their way down the theater's back stairs, Aidan carrying the pram for her. Mary stared around her at the scenery flats, her eyes wide and enthralled as they always were when she was in the theater. A tiny actress in the making.

"There are my favorite girls!" Dominic said when they emerged onto the stage. "How does the scene seem to be coming along?"

"Very well, of course," Sophia answered as he took her in his arms. Mary gave a happy coo and stretched her little arms out of her blankets. "Mary was completely engrossed. Whenever she fusses, we only need to bring her to the theater and she calms down right away."

"My little darling." Dominic took Mary against his shoulder and leaned down to kiss Sophia warmly, lingeringly. "Have I told you I love you today?"

Sophia laughed and kissed him back. "Not since this morning. But I can never, ever hear it enough..."

Also by Amanda McCabe

Kate Haywood Elizabethan Mysteries

Murder at the Princess' Palace

Murder at Westminster Abbey

Murder in the Queen's Garden

Murder at the Queen's Masquerade

Murder at Whitehall

Murder at the Royal Chateau

Daughters of Erin

Countess of Scandal

Duchess of Sin

Lady of Seduction

Scandalous St. Claires

One Naughty Night

Two Sinful Secrets

Flora Flowerdew Victorian Mysteries

Flora Flowerdew & the Mystery of the Duke's Diamonds

Regency Rebels

Because of Miss Everdean

The Earl's Misplaced Bride

Delighting the Duke

The Earl's Second Chance

About the Author

Amanda McCabe wrote her first romance at the age of sixteen--a vast historical epic starring all her friends as the characters, written secretly during algebra class (and her parents wondered why math was not her strongest subject...)

She's never since used algebra, but her books (set in a variety of time periods--Regency, Victorian, Tudor, Renaissance, and 1920s) have been nominated for many awards, including the RITA Award, the Romantic Times BOOKReviews Reviewers' Choice Award, the Booksellers Best, the National Readers Choice Award, and the Holt Medallion. She lives in New Mexico with her lovely husband, along with far too many books and a spoiled rescue dog.

When not writing or reading, she loves yoga, collecting cheesy travel souvenirs, and watching the Food Network--even though she doesn't cook. She also writes as Laurel McKee. historical Elizabethan mysteries as Amanda Carmack., and Eliza Casey...

Please visit her at http://ammandamccabe.com